THE RED DRESS

Dave Asthouart

ISBN: 978-1-915576-02-6

Dedication

For everyone who keeps on trying.

Acknowledgements and Preface

This book -*The Red Dress* - came about after I had written the initial draft of my first novel – *The Unnatural Woman*. One of my dedicated manuscript readers (MaBog), having read to the end of that draft asked me: 'what happened then?' I didn't have an answer. I had written *The Unnatural Woman* as a one-off novel. In order to find out what happened next, I felt that I needed to get to know the people and the society in which they lived in more detail. I thought the best way to do this was to write about what had taken place before. The present book is therefore an attempt to chronicle events in the years leading up to, and, to an extent, including those of, *The Unnatural Woman*. I have tried to write it as a stand-alone novel so hopefully it will make sense to anyone who hasn't read my first book.

The Unnatural Woman was published in July 2022. I hope that a third book - *The Eternals* - will be published in the not too distant future and will finally answer the question: 'what happened then?'

My thanks, once again to everyone who has supported me in writing this book.

Dave Asthouart, November 2022

Contents

Part 1: Nineteen Days

(A) Station, Parliament and Convent

(B) Pilgrimage

Part 2: Twelve Years

(C) Early Years

(D) Middle Years

(E) Final Years

Part 1: Nineteen Days

(A) Station, Parliament and Convent

Chapter 1: The Shot of Stephanie Huntington

Steph looked down at the body at her feet. There was no doubt that this was the body of a Marginal –a female. There was no doubt that she was dead and there was no doubt that Steph had killed her. The body was slumped against a bush as if it had sat down rather than fallen. She could have simply been asleep if it wasn't for the blood seeping from the bullet wound and turning her white dress red.

With her gun still trained on the semi-recumbent figure Steph glanced nervously around. The other three members of her patrol would have heard the shot and would be homing in on her now – but were there more Marginals here too - and were they armed? The hand holding the gun was shaking. She grabbed it with her other hand to steady it. "Should have used a two hand grip; training – two hands! Two hands!" she said to herself as she started to back away from the dead female. "Come on guys, where are you?" She wanted to call out; let them know she was OK; where she was … but what if there *were* more Marginals? What was the right thing to do? Even with both hands gripping the hilt of the revolver it was jerking about. Her arms; her whole body was shuddering uncontrollably. Then, to Steph's horror the Marginal moved – she *wasn't* dead!

Steph's inner turmoil stopped. Her hands and pistol became rock steady – but she did not squeeze the trigger. The female was looking straight at her.

Steph's parents, her teachers in school, the priests at her temple all through her childhood had drilled into her the evil of The Marginals. Was this part of it? Was she being hypnotised into paralysis? The eyes were big, gentle, imploring and then, the pallid lips moved. A word, repeated that sent a shiver down Steph's spine. The voice was barely audible … but Steph felt sure that what she heard was, "Steph … Steph".

In shock Steph tried to say, "Who are you?" but all that came from her dry mouth was a comical, owlish, "hoo...hoo." The Marginal remained still, her eyes unblinking looking at Steph – or through her. Maybe she had died – like that, her eyes open, but then her arm moved – reached out towards Steph.

Again the whisper of a voice, "You … Steph …tell … topsy… Our Med," or something like that, to which Steph could attach no meaning. The arm fell but the eyes remained open. How long? Five seconds, ten? Steph was about to speak but a sudden noise from behind and Steph swung round to see her best friend, Chung emerge from the bushes his handgun blasting repeatedly. When she turned back the hypnotic eyes were gone as was the mouth and most of the Marginal's face.

Karl and Lina were close behind Chung. At some point one of them must have called the drilling station because it wasn't long before Steph heard an unfamiliar sound, and looking up, saw a helicopter coming to take them back. All the time she waited Steph sat with her back to the body. Only when she got up to go did she look again and see a couple of the helicopter crew, clad in green suits and masks, unceremoniously bundling the corpse into a body bag as if it was refuse.

Chapter 2: The Shock of Stephanie Huntington

Steph flopped down on her bed. She and the other members of the patrol had been given time off for visits to, or from, family. Steph had no family – at least none that she could contact or would want to contact. Unlike Chung and the other patrol members she was only here, at Drilling Station 60, on secondment from the convent of The Good Sisters that she was attending as part of her preparation for marriage. In accordance with a secret, internal childhood promise that she had given to her dead mother, Steph was pursuing a Trueway Enhanced Marriage with permission to have two children. She was not sure whether this incident would have any impact on her marriage plans. That would be something for the convent to decide. She didn't think that it would have an adverse effect – just the opposite maybe – but there was no point in thinking about that right now. Now, was *her* time.

It was good to be showered. It was good to be alone – and it was good to be naked again. She didn't object to patrol duty but she hated the gear that she had to wear for it – even though she recognised its necessity when in The Margin. Steph had been born in Trueway – and Trueway was a naked society. It had become such generations before, following The Terror Wars. That was when the planet was divided between the comfortably inhabitable area called Trueway – protected where necessary by its eco-shield - and the inhospitable *Outlands*. The latter was roughly divided into *The Margin* where life of some sort could be sustained – though with difficulty – and *The Beyond* where life was pretty much impossible. If you were born in Trueway then you were a Citizen. If you were born in the Outlands then you were a Marginal since it was assumed that The Margin was the only part of The Outlands where people could survive.

Steph lay on her bed – a slender, attractive woman of twenty-seven years. Her long, auburn hair (which she often wore in a plait held with a ribbon or two) was now loose and pulled round onto her chest where, still wet from the shower, it clung to her pale skin – a skin that displayed a growing number of tattoos testifying to her achievements as a Citizen. She lay in silence, her hazel eyes staring at the ceiling of the small bed-sitting room in which she lived here 'on Station'. She liked the solitude of her room. She liked silence. Many of her friends hated silence and would always have a radio or TV or music playing – but she liked it. She closed her eyes, and despite all that had happened, it wasn't visual images that filled her inner world but the sound of the helicopter. She had seen helicopters in films and old newsreels but they were hardly ever used in Trueway these days. She had certainly never flown in one – or flown at all. She didn't want the sound of the helicopter in her head – but she didn't want sound in her room either. She took in a deep, deep breath – filled herself with clean air. The air in The Margin had a thickness to it. You could taste it but here, in the ecodome of the drilling station it was pure. She held her breath a moment. She held in the purity. She could hear her heart beat; feel it pumping. She slowly let the air out of her lungs; let it go with a hiss between her teeth. She counted to ten as she gradually expelled all the air before taking another deep breath. She continued this steady, rhythmic breathing until she felt fully relaxed.

She thought of the debriefing she had just completed. She and her colleagues had been patrolling an area of The Margin a few miles from the drilling station. While in The Margin they had seen nothing untoward. She was heading back to Trueway. Mentally she had felt that the mission was over and she was about to holster her pistol when the Marginal woman

11

appeared. During the debriefing Steph had been candid about freezing when she realised that her first shot had not killed the Marginal. She knew that she should have fired again – finished her off – but she had frozen. She was asked to confirm that she had taken the revised prescription of DAMP (Desire and Aggression Modification Pills) while on patrol duty. She confirmed that she had. Every Citizen took DAMP to reduce sexual desire and aggressive tendencies in order to help maintain the smooth running of Trueway, but a revised prescription was issued to patrol members so as not to suppress aggression in an emergency.

Her superiors were very sympathetic. Even with modified DAMP she was still just an auxiliary – not a regular soldier - and this had been a traumatic incident. The fact that she had 'frozen' was a completely understandable shock reaction.

The doctor recommended that a nurse or councellor stay with her for the rest of the day and into the evening but she said she was fine. They told her not to hesitate if she wanted to speak to someone - at any time. She thanked them but repeated that she was fine. With the debriefing over, and the compulsory health and toxin scans for anyone returning from the Margins completed, she was allowed back to her quarters. She had said nothing about the Marginal speaking. All she had heard were the barely audible groans of someone dying. She was sure of that now. A Marginal could not possibly have known her name. Just thinking about it, let alone telling her superiors, made her feel stupid and embarrassed. None of the rest of the patrol had been there to hear anything, so it was best forgotten.

Steph allowed the silence of her room to embrace her and the clean air to fill her. She had done well. She had killed a Marginal – or at least *contributed* to its death. This female had almost certainly been on a terrorist mission of some kind. There would be no other reason for her being where she was. Regular military personnel would now scour the area for any clues as to the nature of this mission. Steph had not seen what the Marginal had been doing. She was only aware of her when she suddenly appeared from some bushes and it was in that split second that Steph had opened fire. It was still all so clear behind her closed eyelids. The Marginal went down from that one shot- slumped in the bush like a rag doll. Steph had never shot anyone before. In fact she had never shot anything except practice targets. Yet, lying here on her bed, she felt calm and totally at peace with herself. It was almost as if it had never happened – or if it was just another training simulation.

Incursions by Marginals were periodically reported in the media – but less frequently now than when Steph's parents were young. Most of the incursions that did occur were close to The Margin itself – either in towns on the border or outposts like the drilling station on which she was working. The raids often involved thefts and sometimes the laying of explosives. These resulted in damage to property and occasional injury to people, but Steph could not recall the last time she had heard of a Trueway Citizen dying in a Marginal raid. In her parents' generation however – and certainly that of her grandparents and great grandparents, many Citizens had perished – especially in The Terror Wars.

Steph had never met her great grandparents or even her grandparents but, as a child, she had loved looking through her parents' photo albums from those times. Lying calmly on her bed now, with her eyes closed, the thought brought a smile to her lips. The pictures of her great grandparents in particular were the ones she loved to look at. They had been born in the earliest days of Trueway – in the clothed times! She understood why Trueway was a naked society – and she wouldn't want it any other way – but she couldn't help feeling something had been lost. Steph hated the protective clothing that she had to wear outside of the Station's ecodome, but that stuff was nothing like the clothing of her great grandparents.

The albums showed her forbears in smart suits, casual clothes, shirts, ties, blouses, hats! One great grandfather looked dashing in a military uniform and one of her great grandmothers looked so romantic in her long white wedding dress – but it was one picture in particular that fascinated her and to which, as a little girl, she had returned again and again. It was of a young woman – her maternal great grandmother wearing a red dress. The image flashed crystal clear behind her closed eyes and suddenly, unexpectedly the image of the woman she had shot filled her inner vision – the limp form, the mess where her face had been and the white dress turning red with blood.

Steph sat up abruptly. She was shaking uncontrollably, her heart pounding. With legs giving way she managed to make it to the bathroom where she fell to her knees throwing up, partly on the floor and partly into the bath.

Chapter 3: The Relief of Councillor Montgomery-Jones

Councillor Stella Montgomery-Jones paced her spacious, wood panelled office in The Capital. She was Territorial Councillor (Civil) with responsibility (among other things) for engineering and development. She was in her thirties and had progressed well in her political career. She was a tall and handsome woman of mixed race. She did not have any tattoos. To her it was important to do what was right because it was *right*. She had no interest in, as she saw it, *advertising* how good a Citizen she was. Although her skin was unadorned she did indulge in hair decoration and this could sometimes be bright – garish almost – which some saw as being curiously at odds with her otherwise serious and measured nature. Even her shoes (when she wore them) were plain – other than on special occasions when she indulged in brightly coloured laces!

She glanced anxiously at the clock. She was waiting for her Secretary – Sahid Cummings. His knock was a pointless convention as he burst into the room, closed the door and leaned back against it panting. He had clearly run the length of the private corridor.

"Well?"

"We've got her Ma'am."

There was a brief relaxation of Montgomery-Jones' shoulders. They had at least taken back some control of the situation.

"Is she alive?"

"No, Ma'am," gasped Cummings shaking his head sadly.

"Here, sit down … get your breath, man." Montgomery-Jones motioned him to a chair, and without asking, poured him a glass of water from a jug on the table. She drew a chair out for herself and sat sideways-on to him while he composed himself.

"The staff at the drilling station medical centre confirmed, 'Dead On Arrival'."

"And …?" Montgomery-Jones looked straight at Cummings.

"Nothing Ma'am. Nobody gave any indication of anything untoward - of any suspicion."

Montgomery-Jones said nothing but maintained her steady gaze. He knew she wanted more – wanted convincing.

"Our people had gone on red alert as soon as they had heard about the shooting. They had taken her into the mortuary as soon as she got there – though apparently they went in through the main entrance of the Station's medical centre. There will be full written reports of course but we – *I* - have checked and double checked and she only passed through one scanner – the one at the entrance to the medical centre. I've looked at the security video and it was pretty chaotic as they brought her in – people all over the place, bustling in and out through the scanner. There was certainly no effort to scan her individually. We've removed the recording for customary security review so there is no chance of anyone else reviewing it." As he said this, Cummings took the recording pellet from his bag and put it on the table.

"And this is the only record from the scanner? Nothing left there at all?" asked Montgomery-Jones.

"Nothing Ma'am. It was a Sedcourt B unit. They only record to pellets."

"And there is no other way anyone could have realised? She had no ID on her?"

"No Ma'am. If nothing was spotted at the instant she was taken through into the building … and there is no indication of that … then there would be nothing else to alert anyone."

"And you are sure that nobody has reviewed the pellet images?"

"Nobody Ma'am. Local security are the only people with access for review and they only do that if the need arises. We checked and no review had taken place. You now have the only record. I think we're in the clear."

"I hope you are right." Montgomery-Jones let out a long breath. "OK – so tell me more about this bunch of trigger-happy heroes. How the hell did this happen?"

"The exploration rigs and stations working in The Margin have always had their own armed militia. It was a regular patrol."

"But why the fuck are they doing patrols? There haven't been any armed Marginal attacks for years in that area. What are the press doing?" Montgomery-Jones was back on her feet.

"Trying their damndest to get in and get a story! So far they are just reporting that a suspected Marginal incursion has been foiled."

"So what story are *we* going to give them?"

" 'Hero kids stop Marginal raid' Ma'am. It's got to be 'heroes' ".

"What, and encourage more trigger happy half wits?"

"What's the alternative Ma'am ... tell them she was a tourist?" Cummings heard the sarcasm in his own voice and averted his eyes. He hurried on in a more even tone. "If we say that she was anything other than a Marginal then we are into investigations and the possibility of putting the patrol members on trial for murder or manslaughter or something."

"No, you're right. I know." Montgomery-Jones sat back down. There was a look of defeat about her but Cummings knew that behind her vacant gaze her brain, like that of a chess player, was visualising the permutations of what could follow from any given press release.

"I take it that Safia wasn't armed?"

"No Ma'am."

"So, how do we make it 'heroes' rather than, 'trigger happy numb-skulls'?"

"She didn't have to be armed Ma'am. An incursion by any Marginal – armed or unarmed - has to be repelled. The patrol was doing its duty. It's as simple as that. The vast majority will be excited by the reminder that Marginals are still out there – still a threat but a threat that can be averted."

"And the people who aren't what you call 'the majority'?"

"Members of the senior network of Trueway know which side their bread is buttered Ma'am – apart from the 'dinosaurs' of course. Membership of *The Trueway-Marginal Alliance* may be officially quite small ... but we both know that there are senior people in Trueway who are fully aware of our activity – our *illegal* activity – and yet not a word about *The Alliance* has been leaked to the media and nobody ever gives so much as a knowing wink. There will be a few liberal types, do-gooder organisations and conspiracy theorists that will make a bit of vague, directionless noise about cover-ups and about the death needing further investigation but they won't be able to keep shouting for long. It will be a flash in the pan. The World Games are coming up too – so there will be loads of distractions."

Montgomery-Jones considered this. "OK, let's nip it in the bud - a short statement, a very, *very* brief moment in the spotlight for the 'heroic' patrol members and then distraction stories to keep the press busy. I want this group of patrol heroes totally forgotten about ... and I also want something done to restrict these militias. It's absurd that we still have armed patrols of untrained people out there capable of creating cock-ups like this. I suppose they were all on reduced DAMP to make them even more likely to do something stupid – And don't look at me thinking that my anger means I should be on a higher DAMP prescription." She shot Cummings a warning glance – though there was the hint of a smile. "Anyway, see what you can do about them."

"I'll get Homeland Security, onto it."

"See? ... We still have terms like that - 'Homeland Security'! Even our institutions have titles that suggest we are still in the immediate post-Terror War period. When are we going to start looking forward for pity's sake?" Montgomery-Jones was back on her feet.

"Yes, Ma'am," said Cummings hurriedly standing up and peeling the disposable sitting cloth from his chair.

"Where is she – Safia - now?"

"Here In our medical wing Ma'am. I brought her in myself with scanners turned off. An Alliance doctor will do the post-mortem. There's no further risk."

Montgomery-Jones paused.

"What is she like – her body, the injuries?"

"Bad, Ma'am ... bad."

Montgomery-Jones nodded thoughtfully.

"Thank you Sahid," and then as he opened her office door "... and ... Sahid"

"Yes, Ma'am?"

"Get out of the habit of calling The Supreme Triumvirate of The World Council, 'dinosaurs'. I know it is a term everyone uses but if you slip into that habit then it might slip out at an inappropriate time or place."

"Yes Ma'am. I'm sorry." He turned to go again.

"And one more thing Sahid,"

"Yes, Ma'am?"

"Well done."

Chapter 4: Puzzlement

"We thank thee Great Spirit of the One True Way for our protection." The priest spoke in a solemn chant, eyes closed and hands held aloft. "We thank thee Great Spirit of the One True Way for the strength and courage you gave to your faithful children here present. We thank thee Great Spirit of the One True Way for keeping us safe through the bravery you gave them. We thank thee Great Spirit for the One True Way for showing us yet again, that through faith, Evil and its henchmen will not prevail. Amen."

"Amen," came the echo from the congregation – almost the entire population of the survey and drilling outpost.

"Sounds like The Great Spirit killed that Marginal not us!" came the cynical whisper into Steph's ear from Chung.

"Shhh!" came the reproach from a solemn Steph.

Steph quite liked Chung. She didn't regard him as a close friend. She had only known him since being on placement here at Drilling Station 60 but almost as soon as they met she had felt some kind of bond. Like Steph he came from quite a poor background and also like her he had a strong internal drive. He had studied hard and gained qualifications that had enabled him to obtain a post at the station as a support researcher. He wasn't satisfied with that however. He wanted to progress further. He worked hard. He did extra. He studied. He aimed to impress his superiors. She had told him early on about her goal of qualifying for an Enhanced Marriage with Two children.

"That's good," he had said. "You have purpose. I don't understand people who just drift. I may have come from poor beginnings but I will be head of research on a station like this someday. That is my purpose."

*

As the congregation dispersed there were many handshakes, pats on the back and thanks offered directly to Steph and her colleagues. Following the initial press releases by senior staff at the drilling station the four patrol members had been interviewed jointly by the media. Steph didn't enjoy the attention and liked even less some of what she read and heard in the media afterwards. Much was made of the heroism of the young guards – auxiliaries, not regulars – and although Steph found this embarrassing she didn't mind it too much. What dismayed her were reports that were clearly factually incorrect – using words like "gun battle" and "armed attackers" when neither Steph or anyone at the Station had made any mention of such things.

"I shouldn't worry about it," said Chung as they walked away from the ceremony back towards the dormitory quarter. "Everyone knows the media likes a bit of drama – and I'm happy to make the most of it. I certainly don't think it will hurt my career prospects. Anyway, the main bit is true - there was a Marginal incursion and we foiled it. After that the details don't really matter."

"The truth matters!" said Steph indignantly.

"Oh, come on - don't beat yourself up. The media is the media. We will be yesterday's news all too soon and nobody will think any more about it."

"*I* will."

"Well don't!" He gave Steph a hug but she shrugged him off, stopped walking and looked straight at her friend.

"You want to know something?"

"What?" he asked feeling somewhat hurt.

"I threw up on the bathroom floor in my room."

"How do you mean?"

"Threw up. Puked."

"Yes, I mean why – something you ate?"

"No, just thinking about it – about her – the Marginal. I shot her."

"*You* shot her? *I* shot her too remember? … And I'm proud of the fact. My part in this headline making incident will be written in large letters on my future CV. What we shot was a Marginal; an evil terrorist that would have done who knows what to you, me and others. One report said that our Regulars have now found a stash of weapons and explosives not far from where we shot the bastard. The place is staked out now with Regulars in case others try coming across. Hey, and even though we're not Regulars, we qualify for 'service hero' tattoos now you know. We should get them done."

Steph didn't respond and they walked on in silence until they came to what was colloquially known as 'celibacy junction' or 'chastity corner'. In one direction lay the male dormitories and in the other the female dormitories – a physical arrangement to show that the Station was playing its part in upholding the strict moral norms and corresponding sexual laws of Trueway. A completely separate area was reserved for married couples. Chung suggested that they meet up later but Steph, quite genuinely said that she was tired and wanted an evening in by herself.

Back in her room and alone she thought about the Marginal. All of the media focus had been on the heroism of the patrol members. She didn't recall reading anything about the woman they had shot; *she* had shot. Maybe it wasn't surprising. Her identity, beyond being a Marginal, was irrelevant. Giving her a name would make no difference. From the point of view of Trueway society she had no history, no family. She was simply a female Marginal. She was an enemy of Trueway – a Marginal combatant. Nevertheless Steph was annoyed with herself for not having checked the woman's body for ID of some kind. Steph then reminded herself that the Marginal may have been a suicide bomber and that to have got close and checked for ID might have resulted in the death of both of them.

Steph sat down at her computer. "MyBook," said Steph authoritatively.

"Hello Steph," came the response from the blank screen in the androgynous voice of MyBook.

"Search today's news for, 'Marginal shot'."

The screen came to life. Again and again pictures of Steph, Chung, Karl and Lina appeared and many of the articles seemed to be repetitions of the same report – the same words and sentences being used. The references to the dead woman however never seemed to say anything more than, "a female Marginal". Steph tried different wording in her searches and followed links to see if she could find any further information –but could find nothing.

*

Having searched without success Steph sat silent for a while.

"MyBook – Diary please."

Almost instantly the androgynous voice of MyBook responded. "Hello Steph, I have the diary open. Today you have been granted rest an…"

"Yes! I know!" cut in Steph tetchily. The MyBook algorithm recognised this as unusual behaviour for Steph.

"Is something wrong Steph? It is not like you to interrupt."

"I was sick last night. I threw up on the bathroom floor."

"Oh dear, Steph. I am sorry. Was it something you ate?"

"No, it was the woman, the blood, her face her …." Steph's voice trailed off. MyBook remained silent.

"You don't understand do you, MyBook?"

"There is a lot I don't understand Steph."

"The thing is, MyBook, I am not sure I understand either."

"Do you wish me to make that a diary entry, Steph?"

"No – just listen. You don't have to understand … but I do. I was sick. I pictured the woman I'd killed … or helped to kill … and I was sick. I started … after the shooting … after I got back home … by feeling really good. I had killed a Marginal. I had proved that I was capable. That's what it's all been about MyBook - me proving myself - but maybe they were right all along. I was being too big for my boots … I was being fanciful coming out to the convent thinking I was different … better than everyone else when really I should simply have done like everyone else and got a local job and been happy with a Level 1 marriage. After all, I've got a few Citizenship tattoos to be proud of." Steph fell silent. MyBook said nothing.

"Fuck."

MyBook said nothing.

"Fuck, fuck, fuck."

MyBook said nothing.

"MyBook?"

"Yes, Steph?"

"Why was I sick?"

"I don't know Steph. Was it something you ate?"

Steph almost laughed out loud at the absurdity of this one way conversation.

"No, MyBook, it wasn't something that I had eaten."

Silence from Steph. Silence from the computer.

"It was a Marginal, MyBook. I had killed a Marginal and that was a good thing to have done yet somehow it got to me – made me feel sick; made me puke up. I'm a sinner, MyBook. Caring about a Marginal makes me a sinner doesn't it? What do I do MyBook?"

"If you feel that you have sinned then you should speak to the priest," said MyBook confidently.

"Ah yes," said Steph with a smile. "And will the priest help me accept that I am not as strong as I thought I was? Will the priest tell me to go back home and be content? Will he tell me to be a 'house keeper', a 'run-of-the-mill', a 'fit in with where you come from little girl', a good, Trueway, Level 1 at best? --- Well? Well? Clever, clever MyBook? Well? Fuck you! Fuck you! "

Steph grabbed a cushion and flung it across the room at the wall where it 'plopped' and fell ineffectually.

MyBook said nothing.

Steph stared at the wall and at the cushion. Steph rarely experienced anger, or any extreme of emotion for that matter, and was a little taken aback by her own outburst. She wanted to cry … but tears did not come … just a pathetic feeling of deflation like a balloon going down. She felt certain that she loved her fiancé, Paul – but she was glad that the protocol

21

of their marriage preparation prevented him from coming to see her or contacting her in any way. She hoped that he was all right, and that when he heard about what had happened – as he most certainly would – that it would not 'knock him off course' and make him do something – no matter if it stemmed from his concern for her – that would affect their marriage plans. "Great Spirit," she said aloud, "your ways are mysterious."

She went and lay down on her bed. Tomorrow she would go to work. She didn't have to. Her manager had said that she and the other three could take time off, but she didn't see the point. It was better for her that she kept busy. She wouldn't be on guarding duty. It would just be her regular work. She also felt that returning to work would be looked on favourably at the convent. Right now she wasn't sure what to do with the rest of her day. Maybe she should have agreed to meet Chung after all. She thought about texting him but something – a kind of lethargy - stopped her. All she really wanted to do was go to sleep but whenever she closed her eyes she saw something of "the incident". Sometimes it was the woman lying at her feet. Sometimes it was of the helicopter journey – with her sat talking to her colleagues while the black body bag 'looked' at her. Sometimes it was the moment after landing when she and her patrol team *dashed* behind the paramedics hurriedly pushing the body bagged corpse on a trolley from the helipad directly into the medical centre.

It seemed absurd, this rush. The woman was dead. Then again, it was what paramedics – all medics – were trained to do – act quickly, save lives … even when there was no life to save; even when the body was that of a Marginal. She and her patrol didn't really have a role after the helicopter had landed – but they rushed along with the trolley, caught up in the moment, the activity of 'the now'. What else should they have done? Training hadn't covered that – but training hadn't really foreseen a killing … not *really*.

When they had reached the medical centre entrance she and the other members of her patrol hadn't followed the trolleys inside. The entrance seemed to act as some kind of professional barrier. Her work and that of her colleagues was outside. This was the edge of their territory. Maybe that was why she couldn't visualise the entrance to the medical centre as clearly as everything else; why everything about it seemed foggy. Maybe.

She found herself feeling nauseous again. She sat up and took slow deep breaths until the prickly sensation in her scalp started to subside and the churning in her stomach calmed. She couldn't stay in. She couldn't allow herself to keep thinking about it. She had to go out – be in the open. She wasn't sure where she would go … and it didn't matter.

Chapter 5: Introducing Major David Bloombridge

"With respect Councillor, protocol – let alone common sense – dictates that I should have been consulted and *my* officers deployed in response to the Marginal raid. As it is…"

"As it is Major," interrupted Montgomery-Jones, "I am the one who would have carried the can if things had gone wrong and so I made the decision on the basis of what I felt I *needed* to do and not on the basis of what 'protocol' told me I *should* do."

Major David Bloombridge, District Head of Homeland Security was a squat, balding, rotund man in his late 40's – though he looked older. There was no love lost between him and Montgomery-Jones. He saw her as a liberal upstart. Her dislike for him stemmed from the moment they were first introduced at a meeting of District Councillors. Very politely she had said, "Pleased to meet you Councillor" only to be haughtily corrected in front of everyone present with, "'Major', young lady, I'm 'Major Bloombridge'," he had said, pointing to his discrete tattoos of service that she had failed to notice. Montgomery-Jones was a newly appointed District Councillor at the time and Bloombridge quite long serving. She had been very embarrassed and had felt foolish, blaming herself for not having known that he was the one District Councillor that was addressed as 'Major' and not as 'Councillor' because of his former military service. As the months and years passed however she had witnessed his overbearing manner towards others with growing contempt; a contempt that deepened as he came to embody one of the things she hated most – a person with inherited authority rather than authority earned through ability; power without merit.

They were both councillors at District Level when they first met, but to his chagrin and her satisfaction, she had now progressed to the next and higher level - the Territorial Parliament - while he had failed to make any further progress in his political career; a lack of progress that probably stemmed as much from his traditionalist views as his personal manner both of which the present electorate found unappealing. The shooting had occurred in the District where Bloombridge was responsible for security and so he was answerable to her.

"But with respect Councillor …"

"Please stop saying 'with respect' Major. If you have respect, then simply accept my decision. Now, has Mr Cummings spoken to you about these armed militia? If additional security is needed in association with drilling rigs and the like then surely it should be professional people – *your* people, Major. Wouldn't you agree?"

Montgomery-Jones knew the response that she would get to this.

"With respect the budget doesn't allow for it Councillor. Funding for Homeland Security has been cut year after year. I don't have sufficient personnel for everything."

"Then you have to prioritise Major."

She could see the hackles rise on Bloombridge. She knew he was a man used to having his own way and this was a red rag to a bull.

"Prioritise?" he blurted with indignant incredulity. "Do you really think that every prioritisation possible hasn't already been made; every corner that could be cut, cut? All of my staff are deployed in essential duties." He was almost shouting.

"Then you should be grateful," said Montgomery-Jones calmly, "that I didn't request that you and your personnel rush off to this Marginal incident at a moment's notice, since clearly I would have been pulling people away from *essential duties*." She felt a little guilt at this stab since she wasn't sure how much it stemmed from necessity and how much from her desire to 'get one over' on him so she didn't give him chance to interject. "So now I imagine that you are going to tell me that you need more funding and more staff. And you know that I will tell you that that will be an argument that you will have to put alongside those of other departments for the chancellor's consideration. So let's not continue the pantomime further. I acknowledge your concerns regarding protocol and Cummings will provide you with a report on the Marginal incident and the concern over private militia which will assist you in your arguments to the chancellor."

Bloombridge, teeth clenched, made no response.

There had been no niceties when Bloombridge had entered her office and both of them had remained standing. Now, Montgomery-Jones stepped forward her hand just perceptibly moving to a handshake when Bloombridge gave a curt nod, turned and left.

Montgomery-Jones slumped down in a leather armchair in the corner of the room as soon as the door closed. She had not been looking forward to the encounter that had just taken place but had known that it would come from the moment she had sent Cummings on his mission. She was grateful that Bloombridge was the self-important, arrogant man that he was. That egocentricity, she felt sure, would not allow room for broader questions to develop in his thinking. She felt that the incident at the drilling station would resolve itself without serious ramifications or damage but the incident had been unforeseen and there was a dead woman – an Alliance woman, one of her women. She needed to know what went wrong.

Chapter 6: Pray, Says the Reverend Majumder

Steph walked without any specific destination in mind. It was a pleasant sunny morning. Most mornings – most days – were pleasant and sunny. Climate control wasn't absolute but here, inside the Station's ecodome, the temperature was always comfortable even when the sun wasn't shining. Steph walked along familiar streets, past familiar buildings. Drilling Station 60 was similar to a number of other stations across the globe constantly searching for and then extracting mineral deposits. It was about the size of a large village or small town. It had shops and amenities as well as the drilling site itself. It was situated a few miles within The Margin and an elongated extension connected it with Trueway itself.

Steph found herself at The Temple. She stopped. It was as if her feet had carried her here of their own accord. She hadn't planned on coming to see the priest – just the opposite in fact, given that it was 'clever' MyBook that had suggested speaking to the priest, but maybe, deep inside, her inner self - her soul - had directed her. She believed that such things happened; that people were guided by forces that they didn't understand.

"Stephanie!" The Reverend Majumder's smile and tone in that one word was like a soothing balm and Steph instantly relaxed as he ushered her into The Priesthouse. "Thank you for coming to see me Stephanie. Can I get you tea or lemonade or something? Please have a seat." He indicated a large sofa. "I was just about to make some tea for myself if …?"

"Yes, thank you. Yes, that would be lovely," said Steph taking her sitting towel from her shoulder bag and draping it over the seat. She liked The Reverend Majumder. She didn't know him well but whenever she had had occasion to talk to him it was as if he was a family member she had known all her life. He was tall and in his late sixties – maybe even early seventies. He was slender and looked as though he may have been an athlete in his youth – even a boxer – though his face bore no scars and his manner now was one of peace, calm and gentleness.

"I hope you liked the service this morning Stephanie," came his voice from the kitchen as he prepared the tea.

"Yes, thank you Reverend. It was a bit embarrassing to be honest," she called back and then hurriedly added, "… nothing *you* said … I don't mean that … just being the centre of attention."

The reverend came back in with a laden tray – biscuits as well as the tea things – and set it down on a low table in front of Steph.

"Yes, the whole Station is so grateful to you and the others – and more than just the Station, Trueway itself. All of Trueway - but you don't need me to tell you that. I guess that is what you meant about being the centre of attention."

"Yes, but I'm not sure I deserve it Reverend. That's the trouble. I guess that's why I'm here. Steph felt her face starting to flush. I didn't plan to come. I didn't plan to disturb you. I'm sorry I just …"

"Slowly, slowly, slowly Stephanie," entreated the priest gently as he squatted down in front of her and took her hands in his. They were cool, smooth and reassuring. He didn't speak at first, just knelt there holding her hands and Steph felt as though his stillness was enveloping her.

"Now, Stephanie," he said as he stood up and pulled over a chair. "Tell me what is troubling you. You have been through so much these past couple of days. Milk…?" he added as he reached for the teapot.

"Yes, thank you." Steph felt calmer now.

"Is it the shooting?"

"Yes … well, yes and no … I'm not sure, Reverend. I just find that I keep thinking about the Marginal; about the fact that she is dead and that I helped kill her. I keep wondering who she was. I know that's wrong. I know that she was a Marginal and that she had to be stopped. Maybe it's because she looked so ordinary – so much like everybody else. I'm sorry Reverend." Steph looked to him for reassurance. "All these people are praising us – praising me - and yet I am questioning whether I have done the right thing … and that feels so wrong and I feel so guilty. I shouldn't want to know about this woman should I Reverend?"

"You have been through a sudden and violent experience Stephanie. If I had been out there on patrol I don't know whether I would have acted as swiftly and as decisively as you managed to do … and not just because I am getting old and slow witted!" he smiled and she smiled too. "We all react differently, and I don't think that you should be blaming yourself for having these thoughts."

"But they seem so wrong – sinful – to be wondering about a Marginal as if she were a believer rather than the evil creature that she is … *was*."

"Yes, it may have been easier for you if you had seen her smashing a Trueway baby's head against a wall … but it is because you did what you did that such a thing has been prevented."

"I was sick yesterday Reverend," said Steph, ignoring his words. "I pictured her soaked in blood and I was sick. I can tell myself that what I did was right but inside I am churned up … and now I am churned up with guilt about being churned up about her! How do I get away from this Reverend? How do I cleanse my mind, my soul? How do I rid myself of these sinful thoughts of caring, of concern, of inquisitiveness about this evil woman?"

"I don't think The Great Spirit sees you as sinful Stephanie. It is natural to care for others - even Marginals. They are people – but they are people who, long ago, chose the wrong path, the path of evil. Like I said, if you had seen with your own eyes the evil of The Marginals then it would be easier for you, but The Great Spirit has seen fit to test you without such reassuring and helpful experiences. That is a true test of faith – and you have proved yourself strong in your faith." Then, after an almost imperceptible pause he added, "And I assume that your DAMP had been adjusted?"

"Yes Reverend, it had – but that's just it – with an adjusted level of DAMP I was strong in the heat of the moment – but now I am faltering, aren't I?" she suggested pleadingly. "Then I was acting on instinct but now I am questioning … and that is a sin – isn't it? The Book of Truth says that we must not give succour to the deniers of truth doesn't it? Then there's the passage that says something like, 'Blessed are they who defend truth and smite the non believers' or something like that."

"Yes, indeed Stephanie – or listen to the evil of the non-believer." The Reverend then quoted The Book of Truth, " '… for the words of the non-believer will entice and beguile, and like a worm will corrupt'." He then looked with concern at Steph and asked, "This creature – it did not attempt to 'entice' or 'beguile' you with its words did it Stephanie?"

"No, oh no," said Steph with some urgency.

The Reverend Majumder poured the tea.

"Drink some tea, Stephanie." She did as she was told though she didn't now feel much like having tea – and certainly not any biscuits. They sipped tea in silence for a while. The silence was not awkward. It seemed natural. She had said what she had to say. He had been reassuring. Maybe that was it.

"Do I just have to live with it Reverend?" she asked eventually "All this praise on the outside from everyone around when, on the inside, I feel I should be punished – because although I have *done* the right thing I am *thinking* the wrong things."

The Reverend Majumder looked kindly at Steph. He spoke slowly and with genuine care – a care in his eyes as well as his words.

"I think that you should be kind to yourself Stephanie. I think what you are experiencing is natural. I don't think you are some terrible sinner. I think, as time passes, that you will forget these thoughts and be less troubled." He leaned forward, and again took her hands in his. "You are young – and life, *your* life, will take over." He paused. "I know what you are thinking Stephanie. You are thinking 'that's all very well nice Mr Reverend, telling me it will all be better in *time* ... but what about *now*, what about how I am feeling now?' Am I right?" He asked with an almost cheeky grin on his face.

His smile was infectious and she smiled back – even though she wasn't sure that he had read her thoughts correctly.

"And do you know my answer to your question, Stephanie?" He paused to give his next words gravitas. "Prayer. Pray to The Great Spirit. It is The Great Spirit who has given you your strength in carrying out your duty. It is The Great Spirit that has tested you ... *is* testing you ... in this way, so seek help through prayer. Let us pray now." As he spoke he slid off his chair and onto his knees in front of Steph, his head bowed and his hands still enclosing hers. Steph felt awkward, not sure if she should slide off the sofa and kneel too – but there wasn't really space, so after the slightest hesitant shift of position she remained where she was, looking at the top of the holy man's head as he beseeched The Great Spirit to support her and bring her comfort.

Steph left The Priesthouse with mixed feelings. On the one hand she felt a little relief at having shared her concerns with the Reverend. He was so kindly and reassuring. His advice to pray – such an obvious suggestion – she also felt would help her. It was something she could *do;* a strategy to try! But, as she walked away from The Priesthouse, she was uneasy with a new concern. Had she lied? She had instantly and emphatically denied being enticed and beguiled. Why hadn't she, at least, told the kindly Reverend that the woman had spoken – even if all she had heard were the meaningless groans of someone dying? Maybe she would pray about that question too.

Chapter 7: What went wrong?

"Do we know why she was there?" asked Montgomery-Jones as she thoughtfully rotated the pen in her fingers.

"No Ma'am." Cummings knew not to elaborate when it wasn't necessary – especially when Montgomery-Jones was sitting pensively like this.

"Last recorded location?"

"Within Trueway proper - buying a chocolate bar and sandwiches in a Calthorpe's store four days before the incident. Then she disappears for a while."

"Anything significant about this Calthorpe's store?"

"She periodically bought a snack of some kind there. It's on the way to a place she used to go quite often to paint – up towards Grand River."

"Well she wasn't going there this time. An effort to put someone off her trail, do you think?"

"Possibly Ma'am."

"OK – carry on. What next after buying chocolate?"

"Well, like I say she disappeared – went off the radar for four days. Then, on the day of the shooting we picked her up entering Pipe 5 – that's a Pipe up towards Northport. Two hours later she has gone the complete length of Pipe 5 and through the exit into The Margin."

"The Margin is narrow there isn't it?" queried Montgomery-Jones looking at Cummings but leaving no time for a response. "In fact she must almost have been in The Beyond at the exit of Pipe 5 mustn't she?

Presumably she was wearing pretty substantial protective gear?" Montgomery-Jones leaned forward. Now she was asking – not thinking.

"We assume so Ma'am – but the exit is not equipped with cameras. I'm even surprised that the scanner was working at all to be honest. Pipe 5 isn't a significant thoroughfare. The Margin is so narrow at that point that Pipe 5 had become virtually redundant. That was part of the reason she was given access to that specific Pipe. Almost nobody used it so it was possible for her to have brief contact with Marginals with minimal risk. She could use the pipe to exchange messages and leave or collect items with little likelihood of detection."

"Mmm." Montgomery-Jones sat back and ran the pen over her lips. "Did she have access to any other Pipes?"

"No Ma'am."

"Could she have learned the location of any other Pipes?"

"There is a remote possibility of that but she would have had no way to unlock them."

"So, her *only* secure route in and out of The Margin was via Pipe 5 which means that her destination may not necessarily have been close to where she emerged from the Pipe."

"True Ma'am but travelling in The Margins isn't all that easy so I don't think she will have been intending going all that far."

"Yet she got from Pipe 5 to the drilling site somehow … and you yourself said that was a surprise, so I am assuming she couldn't have done it on foot?"

"No Ma'am. Transport of some kind."

Montgomery-Jones leaned forward again and placed the pen carefully into the groove of a house-brick that she kept on her office desk.

"OK so let me get the timings clear. What time was it when she left Pipe 5?"

"Just before 10.30am"

"And the shooting was four hours later around 2.30pm. What was she doing? Do we have any idea?"

"No Ma'am. We don't know what she did when she left Pipe 5 and we don't know why or how she made her way to the place where she was shot other than what I have just said about having to have had *some* form of transport."

"And all she was wearing was the white dress?

"She actually had underclothes as well Ma'am – but nothing else. She had no protective gear with her, no equipment; no bags even. Military Regulars have now been stationed up there and have done a thorough search of the immediate area of the shooting and found nothing other than the fake arms stash we planted for maintaining the terrorist story. It's a mystery Ma'am."

"I don't like mysteries. How did we get to her so quickly?"

"Well, obviously we were tracking her as a matter of course. Then, when she disappeared after buying the chocolate, she was 'red flagged' through our entire system. When we got news of the shooting we didn't know for certain that it was her. In fact we were doubtful since it's quite a way from the Pipe 5 exit but, since we knew she was in The Margin it seemed too big a coincidence not to be her."

"And we are certain that it is her?"

"Yes, Ma'am. Her face was badly damaged by the gunfire but biodata confirms it is Safia."

"OK Sahid. Do we have anything between the Pipe 5 exit and the shooting site that she could have been attempting to get to for some reason?"

"There is nothing obvious Ma'am. There are a few above ground ruins. We have no record of subterranean stuff."

"OK, what about the woman herself? Anything flaky? Anything odd?"

"No Ma'am. Obviously, any ordinary Citizen who works for us is, by definition, unusual. Over the past two or three years she has provided a steady stream of information that has proved reliable and helpful. She has got in and out of one or two places that would have been difficult without osteodata combined with a really clear life history."

"And her present work? Was she doing anything for us?"

"We didn't have her doing anything major. She was a self-employed artist and we had got her a temporary job working on preparations for The Games. It would top up her income while she just kept an eye on things for us – but we weren't really expecting anything from her and she hadn't flagged up anything suspicious."

"Do you think she *could* have found something?"

"Maybe Ma'am … but on previous jobs whenever she had had something to report she had got it back up the chain of command quickly and through the expected channels. If she had found something then we would have expected her to have done the same again. Like I said – we didn't really expect anything from her. The Games is a big event and we always station an agent or two simply for that reason … but we had no intelligence to say there might be any issue related to The Games."

Montgomery-Jones pondered. Sahid Cummings waited – but he could see how perplexed she was and he felt she was 'clutching at straws' when she eventually said,

"OK, run a check on her tax returns and stuff to see how well her art business was doing," swiftly followed by, "How was she recruited?"

"She was identified through a textilist club - the *Northport TILE*. It's a TILE group we have recruited through before. The recruiting officer was Yusef Murphy."

"Murphy?"

"Yes Ma'am – Abdul Murphy's son."

Montgomery-Jones nodded. She had never met Abdul Murphy but knew him by reputation. He was a biologist. He was highly respected for work he had done on skin grafting. He was a Marginal and remained in The Margin. He did his work there and both Marginals and Citizens had benefited from it. As far as she knew only she and The Alliance knew that some of the techniques in use in Trueway hospitals had their origin in The Margin. She knew nothing of his family but was not surprised to learn that he had a son, and that his son had been actively involved in recruitment through TILE.

"I think I might want to speak to this Yusef Murphy – see if he can shed any light on what Safia might have been up to. Was Safia still an active textilist? Was she still attending TILE meetings?"

"I'll look into it Ma'am."

"OK let's look at the shooting itself. It says in the incident summary that there were two phases to the shooting. A single member of the patrol – the woman Stephanie Huntington - encountered Safia first and shot her but didn't kill her - yes?" She looked at Cummings for confirmation.

"Yes, Ma'am."

"The other three patrol members then arrived – led by one Chung Wallace and he *immediately* shot Safia again several times because this woman – Stephanie Huntington – appeared to have frozen. Yes?"

"Yes, Ma'am"

"So, are we sure that Safia was still alive when this Chung Wallace arrived?"

"We can't be certain Ma'am but Stephanie Huntington was very clear that she only fired one shot and that this had not killed Safia."

"Could Safia have said anything to this Stephanie Huntington before the others arrived on the scene?"

"It's possible Ma'am, though Stephanie Huntington says nothing in her debriefing about Safia having spoken."

"Was she asked explicitly?"

"Yes Ma'am. It seems that Safia was conscious. The girl Stephanie says that Safia opened her eyes. It was that which made her freeze, she says. She said nothing about Safia speaking – only that she groaned."

"So how long was Safia conscious and alone with this Stephanie woman?"

"All the patrol members were interviewed independently for their debriefings. Accounts vary a little but it seems they arrived and carried out the second shooting between 20 and 40 seconds after the first shot from Stephanie Huntington."

Montgomery-Jones pondered the word 'groaned'.

"Did the de-briefing interviewers press her about this 'groaning' that Safia did?"

"No Ma'am, but Stephanie Huntington appears to be quite religious. She went to visit the Station priest – a Reverend Majumder – and he reported the interview to his Bishop. Majumder asked her whether Safia had '…enticed or beguiled her by words' – that's a quote…"

"Yes! I do know The Book of Truth!" cut in Montgomery-Jones.

"Sorry, Ma'am. Anyway, she was (and here I quote The Bishop quoting Majumder reporting the conversation) … she was 'quick and emphatic' in her denial."

"OK, let's leave it at that - for now at least." She paused briefly before speaking again. "OK – so where was she going Sahid – and why? Did she achieve whatever it was she went to do? And why try crossing back into Trueway illegally, rather than coming back through Pipe 5?" Montgomery-Jones made no eye contact with Sahid Cummings despite the question being directed to him by name. Cummings remained silent. He knew when she was thinking out loud.

"From the regular work she has done for us, how sensitive is the information she has in her head?" This was unambiguously seeking an answer from Cummings.

"Embarrassment level stuff Ma'am – nothing critical. I don't have exact dates to hand but it has been quite a while since she fed us any information, and whatever she did feed us has been acted on by now. Maybe it had nothing to do with the work for us ... maybe it was something personal."

*

A few days later Cummings was again in the wood panelled room – but this time he and Montgomery-Jones had been joined by the pathologist. He had almost finished giving a verbal summary of his post-mortem findings on Safia.

"And one more thing Ma'am," he began to say.

"She was pregnant," interjected Montgomery-Jones as she contemplated the pen with which she was fiddling.

"Y- yes ... Ma'am," faltered the doctor unable to conceal the disappointment of his stolen thunder.

"How many weeks?"

"Only about a week to ten days, Ma'am. Standard practice to check on the blood tests."

"Would she have been aware do you think?"

"Possibly Ma'am. If she knew she might be then there may have been some early signs. A urine test might also have shown it up – but this early on they can be a little unreliable."

"Thank you, doctor. If that is all then you are free to return to the many pressing things I know you must have to do. I am very grateful."

Once the doctor had gone she placed the pen on the brick. She didn't need to express her thoughts to Cummings.

"Nothing Ma'am," he said. "No indication in the records of a boyfriend. In fact she doesn't seem to have had much of a social life at all. I did as you asked and checked for TILE membership and she hasn't been active for well over a year. There is no record of other club attendances – gym or anything like that. She seemed to have become quite a loner in the past eighteen months to two years. She goes on painting trips and has some of her pictures for sale in a local gallery – but that's about it. Given the pregnancy thing I will get them to re-check her movements and 'MyBook' entries but nothing leapt out during the first trawl so I doubt that we will find anything. She was also a good agent, Ma'am and knew how to cover her tracks well – even from us if she felt it necessary."

"Well, do your re-check. You never know. We don't have much in the way of leads. How are things going with arranging a meeting with Yusef Murphy?"

"Proving more difficult than expected Ma'am. He rarely comes into Trueway. He tends to remain somewhere in the Margin most of the time. Apparently he tends not to move about much when he does come over. He is something of a 'purist' for want of a better term. He will carry a chip card but he has refused implant and there is even talk that he used to risk coming across with nothing."

"And yet he recruited Safia … and she proved a good recruit? Did he recruit anyone else?"

"No Ma'am, only Safia. He attempted a second recruitment but messed it up and stopped working for us after that – not refused – but just withdrew himself."

"Well, keep working on it. I feel like I am clutching at straws, and this Yusef Murphy is the only straw I can see, so get it arranged as soon as possible – and of course I won't be able to do it personally. This will be a job for you – and just the two of you alone."

"Yes, Ma'am," said Cummings heading for the door, but then pausing. "Ma'am, forgive me for asking … but the pregnancy. How did you know?"

"I didn't know did I Sahid? How could I? But you said that she might have been there for personal reasons … and abortion would fit with a clandestine trip to The Margin."

"Yes, Ma'am. Thank you," said Cummings as he left – feeling that, for once, he had failed to recognise one of Montgomery-Jones' verbalised musings.

Chapter 8: Revelation

"MyBook!"

"Hello Steph."

"MyBook, read last diary entry."

"OK Steph. '*Tuesday, 7.30pm. Last day of patrol duty tomorrow. Last day of clothes Yip! Yip! I might go out wi…*'"

"I didn't know what was going to happen did I MyBook?"

The computer remained silent. It was programmed to recognise the interjection and stop its oral output but did not have a response to such a rhetorical comment.

"Do you want me to continue the diary entry Steph?"

"No," said Steph with resignation. "No, MyBook, no. I shot someone. On that last patrol, I shot a person." From Steph's earlier searches the computer knew about the incident, about Steph's involvement and about some of what Steph had been trying to find out. Since Steph had now put it into conversation mode it therefore collated the information so as to be able to continue the conversation should Steph choose to pursue the issue further.

"Yes, Steph," said MyBook. To an outsider the tone of the voice would probably have been neutral but to Steph it sounded concerned, caring even. Steph remained silent. Over the course of many conversations Steph's 'MyBook' had learned the high percentage likelihood of this silence being an invitation to say something further so, after only little pause added, "You shot a Marginal, Steph. You are a hero."

"I think about her – the Marginal. Who was she?"

"She was a Marginal terrorist, Steph. You stopped her. That is all that matters. Well done."

"I still can't help thinking about her though. I know that is sinful. I spoke to Reverend Majumder. He told me to pray."

"Reverend Majumder is wise. Have you prayed and asked guidance from The Great Spirit?"

Steph thought for a second. She realised that she hadn't prayed. She had just kept dwelling on the same thoughts, and had just kept going round in circles in her head.

"No, MyBook. No, I haven't. Thank you. Maybe you are as wise as all of us."

"Thank you, Steph."

"No, 'thank you' MyBook. One last thing, MyBook. Just have a look at the headlines to see if there is anything more about the shooting or the woman."

"There is nothing new Steph."

"Have you checked, 'True Reflections'?" Steph liked the 'True Reflections' web-feed. It often covered stuff ignored by the main media.

"I have now Steph. There is only information on, The World Games."

"MyBook. Sleep."

Pray, thought Steph. "Pray," she said aloud as she wandered across to the window. It was dark outside. It was past midnight. She could see lights at the all-night store on the corner of the street. "Pray," she repeated. "I need fresh air … and maybe a beer." She wasn't a great drinker but she had been too long indoors. Getting a beer would give her a purpose for going out.

It was quiet. The street was smooth and cool under her bare feet. There was a fragrance to the night air that was absent during the day. Some flower she guessed … though her knowledge of such things wasn't sufficient to tell her what flower exactly. She had heard the words 'Night Scented Stock' and wondered whether that was what she could smell. She was musing idly on this and how she might find out, when she reached the shop.

She went in. The entrance scanner light gave a brief flash as it registered who had entered. There was no shop keeper and there were no customers. She wasn't surprised, given the time. She went to the cooler and selected a bottle. The scanner light flashed again as she left, recording both her and the beer. The cost of the beer would be deducted from her account. Steph, like all Citizens of Trueway, had had her personal information coded into her bones at birth. This 'osteodata' was known colloquially as 'biodata'. Citizens could opt for different levels of biodata activation but most people had at least the minimum to allow for everyday shopping and travel.

Back home Steph set the bottle down on the table. *A woman has died and it is already yesterday's news*, she thought. *Everything now will be about The World Games.* But to Steph it was not yesterday's news and something forgotten. It was still there in her head – swimming round. Steph fell to her knees. She screwed her eyes shut and said aloud:

"Oh Great Spirit, Great Spirit how can I escape this?"

She took a deep breath, flipped open the quick release top on the beer and took a big mouthful. She wiped her mouth with the back of her hand. She flopped down onto the couch and drank the rest. She was soon asleep, drifting through a landscape that she didn't recognise. She knew she was looking for something or someone. The ground was rough and stony but she couldn't feel the stones under her feet. She seemed to be floating above the ground – gliding effortlessly from place to place searching for whoever or whatever it was. Then she was in front of a building. It was dark and imposing. It was the medical centre – she knew this even though it looked more like a medieval castle. She floated round the walls. She seemed unable to float any higher. She just glided a few inches above the ground looking up at the imposing stones.

Now she was in front of the main entrance to the castle. She couldn't see the entrance. There was a moat and a fog was rising from the water. A drawbridge came down – cutting through the fog. There on the drawbridge was the trolley with the Marginal woman on it, though she wasn't lying down. She was standing in her blood soaked dress. Her face was no longer shot to pieces. She was looking at Steph with her arm outstretched, her lips moving trying to say something but no words coming out. Slowly the trolley moved away from Steph into the entrance of the castle – the medical centre - and as the woman passed through the scanner the light flashed.

Steph's eyes snapped open and the beer bottle slipped from her fingers. Her heart pounded furiously. The scanner light had flashed. It had flashed when the woman went through. And now Steph remembered. This was not just in her dream! In reality the scanner light had flashed when Steph watched the woman being pushed into the medical centre. It had flashed twice – once for the paramedic pushing the trolley and once for the woman. The woman had triggered the scanner. She had biodata. Only Trueway Citizens had biodata. She was not a Marginal!

Chapter 9: Yusef and Cummings

Cummings had been waiting at 'the safe house' all afternoon. He had been assured repeatedly that Yusef Murphy was 'on his way' – but nobody seemed able to say quite how close he was to arriving. It had been difficult communicating with Murphy but, once he had been contacted it had been his choice to meet here at this 'safe house' and so Cummings did not see why the man was late – even if he was having to travel from The Margin into Trueway. Cummings had been kept supplied with refreshments and treated very cordially by the house occupants. Earlier he had even been for a stroll in the well-tended garden, but now it was dark outside and now he was irritated. He went to the window through which he had previously been able to see a verdant lawn but could now only see his own reflection. He reached up to draw the curtain across, and as he did so he saw a figure on the far side of the room behind him reflected in the pane. He tried to conceal his nervous start, and with exaggerated care drew the curtain across before turning to look directly at the figure.

Were it not for the fact that the man stood silent and impassive looking directly at him he would have thought it was a member of the household come to offer yet another cup of tea, but he had no doubt that this was Yusef Murphy. Nevertheless he made his gambit a query:

"Mr Murphy?" He advanced with outstretched hand.

What Cummings could not know was that Yusef Murphy's silence was the result of distrust and fear. The distrust arose primarily from the fact that he had never heard of, let alone met, Sahid Cummings. The fear stemmed from what had happened the last time that he had left The Margin and travelled into Trueway. That had been only a few weeks earlier. On that occasion he had made a foolish mistake that had resulted in him being pursued by Trueway security forces. He had escaped but only with the assistance of somebody else. That person had died as a consequence. That person had been his mother. Wracked with guilt and grief he had retreated to The Margin where he intended to remain. He had certainly not expected to be back in Trueway so soon – but if Montgomery-Jones wanted to talk to him then it had to be something important and since he did not have anywhere in The Margin to which he would have felt comfortable inviting her or her envoy, here he was, reluctantly back in Trueway – distrustful and nervous.

Unbeknown to Cummings, Yusef Murphy had been at the 'safe house' for some time, and in the vicinity even longer. With the house security cameras he had watched Cummings arrive and had watched him while he was waiting for the meeting, including his perambulation of the garden. Murphy had seen nothing untoward. People from the house, who Murphy trusted, had patrolled the lanes and area around, along with camera bearing drones. He had wanted to make sure there was no possible ambush. All indications were that Cummings had come alone as requested.

Yusef Murphy gave a polite handshake which Cummings took to confirm the man's identity. Cummings was a little unnerved by the lack of any verbal acknowledgement. He was also surprised at how young the man looked. Had he not known better he would have estimated a youth in his late teens or early twenties. He was tall and slim with black hair. His dark skin and handsome face with aquiline nose spoke of Arab heritage - but out of that brown face gazed two startling, ice blue eyes.

"Was it a difficult journey, Mr Murphy?" ventured Cummings.

Murphy had not been told the purpose of the meeting. This was not unusual for Alliance meetings– but it heightened his anxiety. Nevertheless, the meeting had been requested in an appropriate way and with all the security procedures of The Alliance. This, with his own additional surveillance, left him reasonably sure that Cummings was not an immediate threat. He would not however, relax his guard, though he did feel he needed to behave in a more welcoming fashion.

"Of course!" said Murphy his face suddenly lighting up with a broad smile. "Journeys from The Margin to Trueway are always difficult – but that is no excuse. I am sorry if I have kept you waiting. I hope that you have been looked after well. Shall we sit?" Murphy gestured towards two easy chairs. "Can I get you a drink or something to eat maybe?"

It was as if a switch had been tripped. The silent brooding youth had suddenly become a charming host. The voice was confident and the manner easy. The self-assured maturity from someone who looked so youthful seemed as incongruous to Cummings as the blue eyes in the brown face.

"I have been plied with more than sufficient," Cummings smiled back as he went to an easy chair on which he had already been sitting and where he had left his sitting towel. Yusef Murphy took a colourful piece of cloth from his shoulder bag and draped it over the other armchair.

"You are an elusive man, Mr Murphy," said Cummings with a smile in the hope of encouraging more of the social affability, but although the smile did not fade, the response was brief.

"I like to keep myself to myself," was all that Murphy said.

"Yet you have been active in TILE?"

"Yes, but that was a bit back now. I don't get over much anymore. But, you must know all that, I am sure."

Cummings wanted to say 'You credit me with too much' but held his counsel. In response to his silence Murphy continued.

"Anyway, Mr Cummings, you have come a long way and I have kept you waiting. How am I able to help you – or more correctly, how am I able to help Cllr Montgomery-Jones?"

"Please, don't concern yourself. As I said, I have been well looked after. You're aware of the shooting at Drilling Station 60?" Cummings had intended his question as rhetorical but the shake of Murphy's head and look of indifference made him pause. Murphy seemed genuinely unaware of the shooting. "It's been headline news," added Cummings as if that might somehow jog Murphy's memory.

"I don't watch regular news or read papers or use social media; too much establishment and not enough fact."

"You make yourself sound like a recluse Mr Murphy," said Cummings to maintain the exchange while his brain came to terms with the fact that he was about to tell this young man potentially upsetting news.

"I like to keep myself to myself," he repeated.

"Well, I'm not sure quite how to put this. I had assumed that you would be aware of the shooting." He paused. "I'm sorry Mr Murphy but I may be the bringer of sad – and possibly painful news. A girl was shot by a patrol at Drilling Station 60. It's a station right on The Margin. She was clothed and appeared to be trying to cross into Trueway. The patrol assumed she was a terrorist but she was an Alliance agent – a girl you recruited." Cummings said no more, but did not take his eyes from Yusef Murphy. Murphy met his gaze unblinking – emotionless. The silence lasted only a couple of seconds, but to Cummings it seemed an age.

"When?" asked Murphy eventually.

"Three days ago." Yusef looked away. Was it to hide his shock? wondered Cummings; prevent those blue eyes giving something away? After a moment Murphy spoke:

"I only recruited one girl – Safia Philips."

Chapter 10: Revelation ...But What then?

Chung sat quietly beside Steph on the settee as she told him of her dream and her belief that the woman she had shot was not a Marginal but a Citizen.

"I think my brain somehow buried the fact that I had seen the scanner go off. It was as if my eyes had seen it but the thinking bit of my brain did not want to believe it - maybe because it was too absurd, maybe because it didn't fit in with what I was expecting and wanted to believe. I don't know. Anyway, my eyes had seen it and sent the picture to the seeing bit of my brain and that bit of my brain had been battling with the thinking and believing bit ever since until finally they compromised to show the truth to me in a dream. I can understand my concern for the woman now

– understand why everyone else had no care but why I had feelings of concern. I was the only one who knew she wasn't a Marginal. "

Chung had no doubt in *his* mind that the woman that Steph had shot *was* a Marginal. He had not seen the scanner light register the body and nobody else had said anything to that effect. What Steph was now telling him sounded like a desperate attempt on her part to come to terms with the incident and with her confusing feelings of concern for the woman she had shot. To him, the dream – assisted with some alcohol – was not the uncovering of a hidden memory but a cathartic creation. He therefore remained silent, staring down at the carpet when Steph had finished, struggling to find a response that would be supportive – yet honest.

"It makes sense, doesn't it Chung? It all makes sense now."

"Yes, I can see that Steph but …" faltered Chung.

"But?"

"But … but what do you intend to do with this …" he struggled for the right words, "… this discovery … this insight, Steph?"

"Well, I don't know. I hadn't thought about *doing* I just wanted to tell you, share it with you." Chung looked at his friend but couldn't read the look in her eyes. Was she sensing his scepticism?

"You believe me, don't you?"

"Yes, yes, of course I believe you – come here," he said, swivelling round on the settee and putting his arm around her. He drew her gently in towards him and kissed the top of her head. "Will you tell anyone else is all I mean? To have shot a Marginal is one thing. To have shot a Citizen is something else."

"But I thought I was shooting a Marginal," she said pulling away and looking at him, "and everyone thinks that is exactly what I have done so it's obvious that I haven't intentionally gone out to harm anyone."

"I know," he said with genuine care, "but if I am the only person you have told so far then I think it might be best to keep it that way for now – take time to think things through. In the mean time," he then added with a beaming smile, "I've booked us a slot at the tattooist!"

Chapter 11: Who is Questioning Who?

Yusef Murphy listened impassively as Cummings gave him the details of the shooting. He declined the opportunity to ask Cummings any questions.

"In that case would you mind if I asked *you* one or two things?" ventured Cummings. Yusef shrugged almost imperceptibly. He made no verbal response. He wasn't really interested in any questions Cummings might have. His thoughts were elsewhere. He stared into space. He had fled Trueway leaving his mother dead and now he had returned to Trueway to be told about the death of a friend. Cummings couldn't understand this silence or the demeanour but interpreted the slight shrug as permission to ask his questions.

"When did you last see Safia?"

Again silence from Murphy. Cummings wondered whether Safia was more to Murphy than just a person he had recruited to The Alliance. Was his silence an indication of upset or did his silence stem from a brain rapidly thinking through the ramifications of any response he might make? Cummings was about to speak again when Yusef Murphy simply said,

"A couple of months ago."

"Were you and she close?" he asked somewhat hesitantly.

"We were friends," answered Murphy calmly turning a steady gaze at last towards Cummings.

"Then I am sorry to be the bringer of such sad news. Were you very close? – I don't mean to pry but …" He deliberately left his sentence unfinished.

" 'But' what, you will pry anyway? I know the world in which you live and work. Safia's death was unexpected wasn't it? Not only that, she died before you could talk to her about what happened – what was going on – so now you are investigating." It was clear to Cummings that leading questions – subtlety of any sort – was not going to elicit anything from Yusef Murphy. He wanted to be sensitive – but maybe he simply had to be blunt.

"I mean what I say about not wanting to pry. It's just that Safia was pregnant – about a week to ten days." This information was again met by silence from Murphy. Cummings could detect no reaction. "If you and Safia were lovers then that is your business and I will pursue it no further, but if you were, then you sincerely have my sympathy and that of Mrs

Montgomery-Jones. She asked that I pass that on to you as an expression of personal sympathy. The public, official Montgomery-Jones however needs me to try and establish what happened … or more correctly what was happening. Safia crossed into the Margin via Pipe 5 last Wednesday. Did she meet you? Was that why she came across?"

"No, she didn't meet me. I didn't know she was coming across. I was not expecting her. She had made no contact to say she was coming, and as I have already said, it is two months since I last saw her." This string of information from Murphy took Cummings a little by surprise.

"If she had been coming to see you, do you anticipate that it would have been for personal reasons, or had she been working on something that I – that is that Cllr Montgomery-Jones - should have been aware of?"

"As I said, I don't know why she was coming across. When we met it was usually in Northport. I don't think she has been across to the Margin for quite some time – well not as far as I know. You may know different." He gave Cummings a brief questioning glance before continuing. "Safia and I met socially. We would talk about art and everyday things. I don't recall her saying anything startling or memorable or even vaguely secretive. Is that enough information?"

"Thank you, Mr Murphy. It is certainly helpful information. I'm sorry to press you – but had you asked her to find anything out; bring you information on anything?"

"No, nothing."

"If she had wanted an abortion is there a clinic in the Margin that she could have accessed?"

"Yes, of course – and you know that." There was undisguised contempt in Yusef Murphy's response. Abortion clinics existed in The Margin for many reasons – from those necessitated by malformed foetuses consequent upon Trueway's use of biological weapons following The Terror Wars to clinics of convenience for wealthy, elite Citizens who could not easily obtain abortions within Trueway, where such practices were illegal.

"Well, she may have been thinking of that, or if you are the father, she may have been coming to tell you. I don't have any more questions for you Mr Murphy, but Mrs Montgomery-Jones requested that I ask you to pass on her thanks to your father for all the work he has done. Is he well?"

"Yes, he is fine." This was an assumption on Yusef Murphy's part since he hadn't spoken with his father, Ahmed for some while.

"Well, that is all that Mrs Montgomery-Jones wanted me to ask or pass on," concluded Cummings standing up. Yusef Murphy did not respond to this non-verbal signal that the meeting had ended and remained sitting. Without looking at Cummings he simply asked:

"Who killed her?"

"She was shot by Drilling Station employees on regular patrol duty. Their names are in …"

"I can find out who *shot* her from the computer," interrupted Murphy, standing abruptly.

"Yes, but I thought…,"began Cummings.

"Goodbye, Mr Cummings," said Yusef Murphy curtly, and left the room.

Chapter 12: The Reverend Majumder Passes the Buck

In keeping with Chung's suggestion he and Steph obtained official 'hero' tattoos. Chung had his drawn large on his shoulder but Steph, feeling awkward because of her belief she had killed a Citizen, insisted that hers was only small and completed under her hair. For several days after that Steph did not see Chung and he did not contact her to suggest a way forward regarding her dream. She therefore went to him and said that she needed to tell someone else of her revelation – her discovery. As well as Chung's tardiness there was the fact that she was scheduled to return to the convent in just two days time and she needed to do something before then. She would tell the Reverend Majumder. It was he who had advised her to pray and it was after prayer that she had had her dream - her revelation. Chung knew that without an alternative course of action to propose the best he could do would be to accompany her. So it was that Steph and Chung found themselves side by side on the Reverend's settee while he busied himself making tea for the three of them.

Steph felt a little awkward with Chung there and wondered whether she should have simply come to speak to the Reverend by herself and said nothing to Chung – but it was too late for that now. Chung too felt awkward and sat stiff and upright. Like everyone else he was a member of The Church of Trueway but he would freely admit that he was not the most religious of people. His attendance at temple was almost exclusively confined to the prescribed 'devotional days'.

The Reverend entered bearing a tray and a broad smile. Chung shuffled forward until he was perched on the edge of the settee where he looked, and was, even more uncomfortable.

"It's quite all right Chung– sit back, I can manage," said The Reverend setting the tray of tea things down on the low table to the side of the settee. "To what do I owe this lovely surprise visit … and so soon after your last Stephanie?"

"I did as you said, Father." Steph liked the term 'Father'. It was not often used when addressing a Trueway religious officiate but she spontaneously used it now.

"How do you mean, Stephanie?"

"I prayed, Father. I prayed and it well … 'worked'."

"Good, good. Let's leave that to brew a moment," he said nodding at the tea and sitting down in the chair opposite his guests.

"I prayed, just as you said," continued Steph, "and then, in a dream, I found out what it was; what it was that had been troubling me."

"Go on Stephanie," encouraged the Reverend Majumder, possibly pleased on the one hand that his advice had been so effective – but simultaneously a little apprehensive as to what Steph was going to say next.

"You remember that I felt sinful – felt that there must be something wrong with me because I had concerns about the woman I had shot?"

"Yes, Stephanie, I do remember. I don't recall now whether I said as much at the time, but I think it reflects the depth of your humanity and the natural goodness that is within you. You find her a good person don't you Chung?"

"Yes, of course Reverend," blurted Chung, startled at suddenly being spoken to directly. He gave an awkward smile.

"But go on Stephanie. I have interrupted," smiled the Reverend.

"Well, I prayed to The Great Spirit. I asked for help and then, in a dream, I remembered something that I had seen when the medical people pushed the woman that I had shot into the medical centre." Steph paused, almost frightened to continue in case she sensed the same questioning in The Reverend that she had sensed in Chung, but The Reverend Majumder's eyes were kind and so Steph told him how the dream had shown her that the woman was a Citizen. As soon as she had finished the

Reverend Majumder, in a similar manner to before, fell to his knees in front of her. He took the hands of both her and Chung and this time Steph, unhesitatingly, fell to her knees as well dragging Chung with her as she did so.

"We thank thee Great Spirit for this revelation to Stephanie. She has prayed and you have answered. You have revealed your truth in her. You have revealed *her* truth."

Steph's heart beat faster as the Reverend continued his prayer of thanks. His hand tightened round hers and she felt herself enveloped in warmth - the warmth of acceptance and belief. Chung was puzzled by the words, '*her* truth'. The Reverend finished his prayer but remained kneeling, head bowed, in silence. Steph felt ecstatic. Chung felt uncomfortable. After a few moments silence the Reverend raised his head, eyes closed, and took a deep inhalation of breath before standing slowly and gently raising his visitors with him.

Without further word he went and poured tea.

*

The Reverend Majumder drew two nesting tables from under the one on which he had placed the tea things and Steph and Chung resumed their seated positions as he placed the two small tables between his chair and the settee.

"What should I do Father?" asked Steph earnestly.

"I think it is more a question of what *we* should do." He looked towards Chung for approval of this view.

"Yes, I certainly felt that some thought needed to be given to how to proceed. I said that didn't I Steph?" prompted Chung.

"Yes. It was me that felt we should come to you, Father."

"Well, I am glad that you did. Please … don't let your tea get cold." He gestured towards the cups before continuing. "A revelation such as this … and I am certain that it is a revelation, given to you in response to prayer … requires consideration. It may require further prayer as well. It requires time. Now, Stephanie, you are a novice at The Convent of The Pear Orchard are you not?

"Yes, Father."

"When do you return?"

"The day after tomorrow, Father."

"In that case my advice is that you discuss this with Mother Beneficence."

Steph's heart sank. She had hoped that the Reverend Majumder would have taken some action himself or suggested some appropriate route of investigation. Did he too not really believe her – not really want to address this issue? Had the prayer and the tea just been thinking time? *No, that is a wicked thought*, she told herself in silent chastisement.

"You don't think we should tell the police … or report it to my superiors at the drilling station?" ventured Steph.

"I am a humble priest, Stephanie. The authorities have already confirmed the woman to be a Marginal. Both you and I would be ignored in such a situation … but the Good Mother Superior? She would not be ignored."

Steph could see the sense in what the Reverend was saying but … but the truth was she feared The Good Mother Superior – Mother Beneficence.

Chapter 13: Family History… And Duplicity

Yusef Murphy had been born in The Margin. His father, Ahmed Murphy, had been born in The Margin but Yusef's mother, Miriam O'Donnell, had been born in Trueway. Yusef Murphy by place of birth and lack of biodata was unequivocally a Marginal and yet, because of his mother, he always felt himself to be 'different'. He felt himself to be a half-breed – even if such a thing had no official standing in either Trueway or The Margin.

Whether The Alliance knew of his half-breed nature and watched as he grew up, or whether by happenstance he came to their attention as someone who might be sympathetic and useful in their aim of bringing together the two elements of the planet, was unclear. Whatever the truth of the matter, he was receptive when the call came. He began attending TILE meetings in the Trueway town of Northport and became a scout/recruiting officer of Trueway Citizens.

After an upbringing within the limitations of The Margin it was a great adventure – but it was more than just an adventure. He had a deep desire to see unification, and when he met Safia – a rebellious, middle class Citizen, he quite rightly sensed a soul similar to his own – a person wanting adventure and who enjoyed being 'different' but who also had a fundamental desire to see wrongs made right. She was his first recruit and she proved herself a good recruit. Praise for both of them came down the 'chain of command'.

If Yusef's first recruit was a shining success then his second was the direct opposite. It was a man at the TILE group, and having been so successful with his first endeavour, Yusef thought that he 'had the gift' and was far too quick and eager. Nothing extremely serious happened but the man threatened to report Yusef to the authorities and this caused Yusef to retreat to The Margin. He still wanted to see Trueway-Margin unification but felt that he was not cut out for being a recruiting officer. He had a deep interest in science. It was his passion and was fundamentally what he wanted to pursue. He therefore determined to remain in The Margin and simply get on with his research and development work. He felt sure that this would play a better and more important part in peoples' lives than anything he could do as a recruitment officer. He maintained his friendship with Safia however.

Safia was an artist. Yusef's mother was an artist. Yusef's father was a scientist. Yusef was a scientist. It should have been a balanced grouping … but it wasn't. Ahmed was driven – driven by science and his work. Montgomery-Jones had not simply been extending a courtesy when she asked Cummings to pass on her thanks to Ahmed Murphy. The work that he had done in The Margin on skin grafting and on skin cell re-growth had benefited countless people in Trueway over the years. Ahmed Murphy was the perfect example, in her mind, of why the divide between Trueway and the Margin; between Marginal and Citizen had to be removed, and why The Alliance mattered so much. To her knowledge Ahmed Murphy had never worked inside Trueway – had certainly not held any post within Trueway – yet his discoveries had migrated (via The Good Sisters), without charge and without demand or conditions, to Trueway for the benefit of Citizens. In her eyes Ahmed Murphy was a scientific saint. To Ahmed Murphy's wife and son he was something different.

Was the union of Ahmed Murphy and Miriam O'Donnell a pre-arranged marriage engineered by The Good Sisters? There was little doubt that they had facilitated the relationship. Ahmed Murphy, although not an orphan, had been brought up by The Good Sisters at one of their convents in The Margin while Miriam – also an orphan - had been brought up by Good Sisters at a convent within Trueway. Whatever the precursors, the marriage occurred and Miriam went to live in The Margin with Ahmed. They had a son – Yusef. Ahmed gave little attention to his wife. He was more wedded to his work. Initially he also gave little attention to Yusef, but as the lad grew and became more independent of his mother, Ahmed's interest increased. There would be times when young Yusef was away from his mother and the family home for days on end staying with his father at his father's laboratory in the convent where Ahmed had been brought up – The Convent of The Burning Legs. It was during these visits that Ahmed, limited in his work by lack of experimental subjects, conducted experiments on his son.

In pursuing his work on skin grafting Ahmed had become increasingly interested in cells – the way they regenerate, age and deteriorate. Increasingly, his work focussed on longevity. He didn't, at first, discuss it with The Good Sisters who had brought him up, educated him and supported him. He certainly did not discuss it with his wife. His first experimental subject was himself. His experiments showed promise and he saw no ill effects so unhesitatingly he began to conduct experiments on his son. The impact of what he was doing was not immediately obvious to an outside observer, but over time, it became clear that Ahmed was ageing more slowly than other people and that Yusef was maturing more slowly than other children. With Ahmed people put it down to 'ageing well'. With Yusef – a slight 'developmental delay'. It would be some time before the truth became known – and then only to a limited few.

It wasn't the experiments on her son that drove Miriam Murphy away from her husband. She didn't realise the experiments were happening. There was a build up of other factors leading to the separation. Central was unhappiness. She loved her son and time with him as he grew gave her solace, but other than that she felt alone and isolated. Even when Ahmed was at home he spent most of his time by himself in his study. He would have sex with his wife – but it was simple copulation rather than love making. This functional activity resulted in a second child – a girl, but she died shortly after birth. This broke Miriam's heart. It clearly affected Ahmed too, but instead of this loss drawing Ahmed and Miriam closer together in mutual support it seemed to widen the gap between them.

Miriam could see no way to escape and so resigned herself to loneliness as her lot in life. She devoted herself to bringing up Yusef whenever he was not with Ahmed. When left alone she put as much energy as she could muster into making her paintings and sculptures; artworks that almost nobody ever saw. Eventually, as was only natural,

Yusef reached the age when he left home and she was left with nothing but the art and his infrequent visits.

It was on one of these visits that he brought with him a girl called Safia. Like Miriam she was a Citizen. Like Miriam she was an artist. She was young, lively and energetic. Miriam had been excited by the girl's enthusiasm but she had also been jealous of her youth and freedom. Safia had looked at Miriam's paintings and sculptures. She had praised them and said that Miriam would do well as an artist in Trueway. Miriam felt simultaneously flattered and frustrated. It threw into stark contrast the dullness of her life and the feeling of worthlessness consequent upon the way her husband treated her. It was after this visit that Miriam did something that she had never dared do before. She went to her husband's laboratory at the convent. Since making her initial journey to The Margin for marriage, she had not visited the convent but after the visit from Yusef and Safia she felt compelled to confront Ahmed. Heated words were exchanged between them:

Why was she here at the convent?
    Why did he give more time to work than to her?
    And why was the convent more important than their home?
What home had she provided – one son and a dead daughter?
    How had he been any kind of father beyond the act of insemination?
What had she given to the world?
    She had tried to give it art – but only Yusef's friend Safia seemed to appreciate that
What had she given to him?
    She had given him a son. She had left Trueway to do that.
Then maybe she should go back to Trueway.
    Was that his advice?
Maybe it was. The nuns sacrificed more for him than she did.
    How could he say that?

It was then that he took her to see the Room of The Tables. She had always assumed that the name of the convent – The Convent of The Burning Legs – was a reference to some historical event. She left the convent in horror at what she saw in The Room of Tables. Ahmed felt he had proved the sacrifices of others to support his work and shown how they dwarfed her petty self-pity. She felt that all he had proved was that he was a deluded, selfish, madman prepared to allow – even coerce through the appropriation and manipulation of religious belief - devout nuns to deliberately burn their own flesh in order for him to have subjects for developing his skin grafting methods.

Safia's words of praise may only have been the trigger to Miriam's action after years of suppressed frustration, but after seeing the horror of The Room of The Tables (a horror about which she never spoke but which remained with her until she died) it was certainly Safia's admiration that gave direction to Miriam's flight. When her husband next returned home she was no longer there. There was just the briefest note: "I am an artist. I will be an artist. I am a Citizen. I will do as you say."

First she went to Yusef at his house and from there utilised his Pipe connection to travel to Trueway. Once there she went and stayed briefly with the nuns at her old convent. With their assistance she obtained her own, independent accommodation and began exhibiting at a local gallery under her maiden name - Mrs O'Donnell.

By the time that Yusef's mother left The Margin Yusef had learned that his 'developmental delay' was due to experimentation by his father. He didn't know the details but since he felt healthy he hadn't been overly concerned and although he maintained links with both parents he rarely visited his father whereas he had made periodic visits to his mother – and to Safia. Now, with both Safia and his mother dead, he felt very alone.

*

Following his brief flirtation with The Alliance and his decision to return to The Margin and devote himself to work Yusef rarely gave any attention to the world at large. In Cummings' words he had become a hermit – or at least a recluse. Sometimes weeks – even months – would go by and Yusef would never watch a television programme or read a newspaper or an on-line article. With Safia's death that changed. While Cummings was returning to Montgomery-Jones Yusef was already at the computer in the safe house scouring the net – both surface and sub-surface - for all he could find about Drilling Station 60, about the shooting and about the patrol members involved. Despite his apparent calm while with Cummings, Yusef had been severely shaken. It wasn't just the news that Safia was dead – but the fact that he had not known. For selfish reasons, he had buried himself away in The Margin and largely ignored Trueway. He should have known that Trueway could not be ignored, would not be ignored and that one day Trueway would come for him and would force him to engage – whether or not he wanted to.

Now, as he trawled through article after article all he really wanted to do was punish himself. His stupidity had led to the death of his mother, and now he felt that his ignorance may have played a part in the death of Safia. If he had been more alert to what was happening in Trueway maybe he could have prevented her death. He glanced across at a pad of drawings on a shelf. She had brought them with her the last time they had met and left them for him to look at. She was a good artist – but he knew that she still, on occasion, continued to do work for The Alliance - the work for which he had recruited her. He should have asked her about that – but he hadn't and she hadn't volunteered anything. Now, as he battled with guilt, grief and anger he tried to focus his mind on how to find answers to the questions he should have asked when he last saw her and establish what led her to be in The Margin and to her death.

After hours of reading he felt he had learned little more than he had gleaned from Cummings. It didn't amount to much. A woman – described as 'a female Marginal terrorist' - had been intercepted and shot by a guard patrol from Drilling Station 60 while attempting to cross into Trueway. The auxiliary patrol had four members. One of them – a Stephanie Huntington - had been by herself when she first encountered the Marginal and had opened fire. A second patrol member - Chung Wallace then arrived on the scene and also opened fire. Two other patrol members arrived with Wallace and also seem to have discharged their weapons. A stash of arms and bomb making material had been found shortly afterwards and it was assumed that it was to this that the terrorist had been heading.

The drilling station appeared to be an unremarkable enterprise mainly extracting lithium. The auxiliary officers – Stephanie Huntington and Chung Wallace - also appeared to be unremarkable workers from the station. Yusef did not believe that there had been an arms stash and bomb making materials. *If these things existed at all,* he thought, *they must have been planted by Trueway after the event.* He was so out of touch however that he couldn't be sure. If there had been an arms stash then it might suggest some level of renewed military activity in the Margins. Even with his self imposed isolation however he felt he would have been aware of that. All the media that he was able to access was fundamentally that of Trueway. He needed information from The Margin. He would go to his father.

*

Yusef sat across the other side of the slate table from his father. They were at Ahmed's house – the underground dwelling, deep in The Margin that had been the family home and where Yusef had grown up. Now only Ahmed lived there. They were in his study. It was a room that Yusef had hardly ever entered as he grew up. To his knowledge his mother had hardly ever entered either. The books and few essential furnishings struggled to combat the subterranean gloom.

"It is good to see you," said Ahmed. Yusef felt there was genuine tenderness in his voice. "It would be nice to see you more often – as a fellow scientist as well as my son."

"Thank you … on both counts," said Yusef with a smile before adding more sombrely, "I am sorry that I did not come to see you when mum died."

"I didn't come to see you either son, so don't feel guilty. Is that why you have come now – to apologise?"

"Maybe it should be – but it isn't. No, I have come about the death of Safia Philips."

"Safia?" queried Ahmed somewhat startled. "The young girl you got involved with when you were playing go-between for The Alliance?"

"Yes. I had a visit from someone called Cummings – claimed he had been sent by Montgomery-Jones. I didn't really trust him … but all the code words and things were right so I have no reason to think he wasn't sent by her. Anyway, he said that Safia had been mistaken for a Marginal terrorist. She had been shot by an auxiliary patrol attached to a drilling station – Station 60. She was clothed and appeared to be attempting to enter Trueway from The Margin."

"I knew nothing of this. Then again, I don't pay much attention to Trueway news. I'm so sorry, Yusef. Were you and she still close?"

"I don't know that we were ever – as you put it - 'close'. We were friends. I would see her every once in a while. She liked to show me her paintings or drawings and talk about them. We never talked about The Alliance or the work she may or may not have still been doing for them."

"Well, even if you were only friends, I am still sorry."

"Thank you. I was shocked and I will miss her. I can't help feeling that if I had not buried myself in my work but had kept abreast of things then she might still be alive. I keep thinking that by going to Trueway I caused the death of mum … and now by staying away I have caused the death of Safia. After all, it was me who recruited her."

"You mustn't think like that, son. Whatever led Safia to her death it was not you. You were not responsible. You are certain … or should I say 'they' are certain that this person shot by the patrol is Safia?"

"It would seem so. This Cummings person certainly did not leave me thinking there was any doubt."

"So, why have you come to talk to me about it, son? I am happy to help in any way … though I don't know how."

"I don't know how much contact you have with The Alliance these days. I trawled through article after article about the shooting … but they were all saying the same thing. Even, 'True Reflections' and the sub-web produced no additional information. They all just said that a nameless terrorist had been shot trying to infiltrate Trueway. Apparently an arms stash has now been 'found' close to the point where she was killed. I guess guilt has been pushing me to try and establish what really happened; why Safia was where she was when she was shot. If she was not doing something for The Alliance then why would she be in The Margin? I even wondered whether the story of her being involved with some form of Margin based terror group could be true. I am not the most trusting of people, and so I wanted to see whether there was any information from the Marginal side – and who better to trust than my father?"

"I am like you, Yusef. I too have busied myself with my work and ignored pretty much everything else. Maybe that is what people like you and me do. Maybe that is our calling, our vocation. Maybe we should do – and do do – our research and follow our interests for our own selfish reasons and maybe it is only through this focused selfishness that we make progress for ourselves and have anything meaningful to 'give to the world' – if that is not too arrogant a thing to want to do … or think we are capable of doing."

"So, there is nothing that you are aware of that could shed light on why Safia may have been where she was when she was?"

"No, I am sorry. I can make some careful enquiries … but at the moment this is the first I have heard. Maybe she had some personal reason for going into The Margin." Ahmed's intonation did not imply a question – simply speculation – but Yusef controlled his urge to shoot a questioning glance at his father. Yusef had intentionally withheld the information that Safia was pregnant to avoid giving his father a simple, default explanation.

"And do you know this Cummings person? Do you trust him ... and Montgomery-Jones for that matter?"

"I have heard of Cummings. I know nothing about him. I think Montgomery-Jones is as straight as an arrow. If Safia had been assigned a job then Montgomery-Jones would have known about it. If Safia had stumbled across something inadvertently that The Alliance needed to know about then I don't see why she wouldn't have simply passed the message on in the usual way. Like I said, maybe she had something personal that was driving her – something only she knew about." He looked up at his son. "I guess we will never know." This time Yusef felt more strongly that the words were spoken in the tone of a statement but the glance was a question. His response was to pose a question of his own.

"I expect that The Alliance will have been through her things pretty thoroughly – papers, movements, 'MyBook' records - to see if there were any clues?"

"Yes, and I am sure that Montgomery-Jones would not have come to you – albeit through her envoy - if there had been anything that gave a more straight forward explanation."

Yusef stood up. "You are right, dad. Despite what you say about me not being to blame I can't help thinking Safia might still be alive if I had been alert to what was going on maybe asked her questions. There may have been things troubling her or she may have been involved in something ... but I didn't ask. I was content to be in my cocoon."

"We don't know that, Son. Safia was more than capable of telling you stuff if she felt she needed to. She was probably just glad to spend time with you and talk about her paintings. Maybe your self-imposed isolation, your separation from Trueway, was what she liked ... maybe what she felt she needed for doing that."

"You may be right," said Yusef with resignation in his voice. He turned to leave.

"You must not blame yourself for whatever it was that brought Safia to that fatal encounter ... and whatever it was probably died with her."

At these words Yusef could not prevent the questioning glance at his father, who after just slightly too long a pause, then added,

"If Montgomery-Jones has found nothing then Safia will have told nobody what it was that sent her on her fateful journey."

Yusef left with his father's words still playing in his head - *Safia will have told nobody* - and he realised that his father could be wrong.

*

Following the conversation with Ahmed, Yusef could think of no way to go forward. He reflected on his father's words about the two of them being scientists and that their role in life was to simply plough on with their own egocentric interests, and that this very selfishness might be what led them to their destiny. Was that his father's view of life and progress – that it was all just a by-product of selfish individuals – a spinoff of the pursuit of self-interest?

Yusef mulled over what he perceived to have been his father's persistent, oblique interrogation regarding personal reasons for Safia travelling to The Margin. Maybe his father had concluded that she was pregnant and had gone to The Margin to seek an abortion. If that was the case, then Ahmed would probably make no strenuous efforts to establish whether there could be any other reason for her having been there. Yusef could do nothing about that, but sadly, he could see no way of doing anything about the one possible remaining line of enquiry to pursue.

When his father said, "Safia will have told nobody" it had crystallised a thought in Yusef's head regarding the only remaining avenue open to him to try and establish why Safia had died ... and who had been genuinely responsible for her death. He knew from the media reports that Safia had spent her last few seconds of life alone with someone else – a woman called Stephanie Huntington – the woman who had shot her. There was the slimmest of possibilities that she had said something to this woman - to her killer. Yusef, however resigned himself to the fact that he had no way to contact this patrol woman. He therefore resolved to bury himself in his work.

Chapter 14: Fear of Good Mother Beneficence

Steph lay on her bed. Tomorrow she would return to the convent. She had so wanted the Reverend Majumder to do something; to take action on her behalf yet here she was alone with the prospect of having to recount her dream to Mother Beneficence. On a day-to-day basis Steph had little contact with The Good Mother Superior other than in group prayer. Only once had she spent time alone with her. That was the day that she had entered the convent. Steph respected the elderly nun – but she feared her more. As she lay in the silence of her room, the memory of that one and only individual encounter made her doubt whether she could divulge her revelation to the head of the convent … but worse still whether she could withhold it. In her mind's eye, she relived that meeting.

*

"Why do you want to come and join us Stephanie?" was the innocuous question with which Mother Beneficence opened that interview all those months before. Steph stood as erect as a soldier. She was twenty-five years of age, but with her small frame and waist length auburn hair she looked younger. Her hands were clasped behind her back and she rubbed her thumbs together nervously. She looked straight ahead to a point on the wall above and beyond the wimpled head of the diminutive nun seated behind the leather topped desk.

"I seek the truth, Sister," answered Steph respectfully. She thought it more appropriate than, 'I want a marriage with two children' – and she knew that only after six months as a novice would she have to formally declare her longer term hopes.

Mother Beneficence smiled inwardly at Steph's use of the word 'Sister' and did not correct her. She could see the nervousness in Steph's eyes and stance. She had watched those eyes scan the wood panelled room when Steph first entered. Mother Beneficence knew how awkward and out of place Steph was feeling.

"Have you read The Book of Truth, Stephanie?"

"Oh yes, Sister – well not every word – but at school and at worship."

"And what is the first part of the book that comes to mind when you think of it?"

Steph went blank. She knew the Book of Truth but everything was crowding into her head- *what bit? What bit? What's right? Any bit? Think! Think! Stop talking to yourself!*

Mother Beneficence smiled. "Have I put you on the spot Stephanie? I think if you had asked me that question I would go quiet as well. The book of truth says so much, and different parts will be more important to us at different times won't they?"

"Yes, I think so."

58

"Have you ever been upset Stephanie – maybe as a child – when something made you cry – a real hurt, not falling and grazing your knee but something that made you sad or hurt inside?"

The image of 'Tar' her pet dog flashed before Steph's mind's eye.

"My dog, Sister. The day my dog died. I thought I would never get over that. I cried for … well I don't know how long."

"How old were you, Stephanie?"

"Ten."

"Tell me about Tar."

Steph had not expected to be talking about her old pet – but his cheeky face and big brown eyes looking up at her was as clear as if he was in the room and she smiled as she spoke. "He was small – some kind of mongrel. He was black – hence the name. He was a lot of fun – always looking for scraps to eat, always going where he shouldn't go." Steph fell silent. She could feel his warm ears as she fussed him in her thoughts.

"And what happened?"

"He had wandered off – probably followed the scent of something." Steph paused. Why was she being asked to remember this? Why not just stop with the happy memory? But she continued. "He was hit by a glide train. I don't remember who it was that found him or how they had got him back to us but someone had wrapped him in a towel. I could only see his head. His tongue was hanging out. The towel was blue but it had gone a dark purple where blood had soaked into it." Steph fell silent.

"That must have been very hard for you Stephanie. You were only a child. How did you cope?"

"The grownups kept telling me they would get another dog for me … but I didn't want another dog. They seemed to think I was crying because Tar was gone and I would miss him and be lonely without him – and that was true – but that wasn't the reason. I was crying because he had suffered and because this terrible thing had happened to him."

Mother Beneficence wondered to herself whether a ten-year-old would have such thoughts or whether these were the thoughts that an older Stephanie had imposed on her younger self as, over the years, she had periodically revisited that sad event.

"So, when the grownups failed to understand and thought your grief could be overcome with a new pet what did you do?"

"All sorts of things. I prayed. I asked 'why?' Why would The Great Spirit allow this to happen to Tar? I got angry. I smashed things – broke my young cousin's toys. I did it deliberately as if he was to blame. Another girl had once done that to me. We had been playing chase and she had fallen over and blamed me even though I was miles away from her and she had simply fallen. She went home and told her Mum that it was my fault. Anyway, I know I did all sorts of stuff. I stayed by myself a lot too. I kept thinking of Tar."

"And do you think of Tar much these days?"

"No, it was a long time ago. Other things have happened. I think of him occasionally."

"And do you cry and get angry?"

"No, my thoughts are generally fleeting – and when they do come they are usually of something fun that he did – some of the stories that used to get retold in the family that usually started with, 'Do you remember when Tar …?' Steph looked at Mother Beneficence and smiled. She didn't know why she had been asked to recall this painful event but she felt calm.

"Looking back now Stephanie, is there anything in The Book of Truth that would have helped you at the time?"

"'And time will heal their suffering like balm on a wound'." The quote came to Steph very readily. "I don't know if I was told that by grownups at the time. I don't remember. If they did say it, then I don't think it helped – well, not then, at any rate."

"But now, looking back, would you not say that it was true?"

"Yes, I suppose."

"So, Stephanie, if you seek the truth you need look no further than The Book of Truth. Just as you, when you were a child, would have probably derived little comfort from those words and probably even not believed them to be true, time has shown you that they are. If you come to us seeking truth Stephanie, then time and again, we will take you back to The Book of Truth and slowly, but surely you will come to *discover* what you are told by that great book … because that is what seeking truth is all about - it is discovering for ourselves, within our hearts, what the book has told us in its words." She paused and looked at Steph before adding. "Did you get another dog?"

"Yes."

"Did you grow to love it?"

"Yes."

"Do you still wish to come to join us in your search for truth Stephanie?"

"Yes."

"Then welcome."

Mother Beneficence smiled. She looked steadily at Steph without moving or saying anything further. Steph looked away, unable to meet the unblinking gaze of the older woman. She looked down – rubbed her thumb nail nervously. Was the interview over? What was happening? Why this silent staring?

"Stephanie."

"Yes, Sister?"

"I am *Mother* Beneficence – not Sister."

"Oh, yes, Mother. . .Oh, I … I'm sorry," stammered Steph looking at Mother Beneficence and blushing in embarrassment.

"It is of no consequence." Again the silence fell but somehow Steph felt compelled to keep looking at the elderly nun. "Why do you wish to come and join us, Stephanie?"

Steph was confused to be asked again the question with which the interview had started. "I … I seek the truth …*Mother*," repeated Steph, correcting her earlier address and wondering whether it was for this reason that the question had been repeated – but it was not. Mother Beneficence smiled at Steph's confusion and at the emphasis on 'Mother'.

"What you *call* me is of no consequence Stephanie. But, what you *tell* me is. You say you seek truth … so look into your heart and tell me what it is that you *truly* seek from us. I ask you again, why do you wish to come and join us?"

Now, Steph stood silent before looking down and quietly repeating, "I seek the truth, Mother." She looked up with tears in her eyes, "I do mother. I seek it … but …"

Mother Beneficence sat passively. She was going to offer no help. Steph looked down.

"I want to move up, Mother," her voice almost a whisper. "I want to better myself."

"And…?" prompted Mother Beneficence. Steph again looked the Good Mother in the face as tears now rolled down her cheeks.

"A husband … and children … I'm sorry, Mother … I know it's selfish …I …"

"We are all selfish, in our own ways, Stephanie," interrupted Mother Beneficence. "Stand up straight!"

Steph did as ordered.

"There is nothing wrong in wanting marriage or in wanting children, Stephanie." Mother Beneficence, slowly stood up as she spoke and began to walk round from behind her desk "... and it is good, very good, that you want to seek those things - and are prepared to seek them - through devotion to The Great Spirit." She was now behind Steph who stared ahead. "What is not good is that you have tried to hide these wishes from me. There was the briefest of pauses before she continued, "... But I have lived a long time Stephanie and I know why young women come to me – to The Good Sisters. Never, never try to hide anything from me." There was now a longer, more ominous silence. "Do you understand me Stephanie?"

"Yes, Mothe…"but before she could finish her breath was taken in a gasp as the hand of Mother Beneficence struck Steph's left buttock with such force that she lurched forward and only stopped herself falling by grabbing The Good Mother's desk. As she did so another stinging blow hit her right buttock. Steph gasped. She had never been hit before.

"Stand up," ordered The Good Mother as she circled back towards her chair.

She tinkled a small brass bell that had been sitting on her desk. "This is Sister Adolorardah," she explained when a nun, as elderly as The Good Mother herself, entered the office from a side door where Steph assumed she must have been waiting all this time for the tinkling call. Sister Adolorardah was small – no more than 5' tall if that. She was lightly built – like a sparrow and her tanned skin increased the resemblance. "Sister Adolorardah will look after you while you are with us. There will be a formal 'Giving Ceremony' this afternoon but for now, Sister Adolorardah will show you to your room where you can contemplate all that I have explained to you."

The lined brown face of the 'sparrow' smiled out kindly at Steph from its white wrapping. She took Steph by the hand and led her to the door through which she had just entered. When they reached it Sister Adolorardah turned and bowed to Mother Beneficence. She turned Steph to indicate that she should do the same. Steph, still trembling, awkwardly dipped her head. Sister Adolorardah turned and went through the door. Steph half turned to follow but was halted by The Good Mother's voice.

"Stephanie."

Steph looked back. The Good Mother, still holding the bell, looked straight at her.

"Welcome."

*

With this memory of Mother Beneficence still so vivid in her mind after almost two years Steph was not sure that she had the courage to tell The Good Mother of the revelation given to her in her dream – and yet The Good Mother's warning, "never try to hide anything from me" made Steph wonder whether she could avoid it. Steph felt sure Chung had not believed the revelation. She even now questioned the extent to which the Reverend Majumder believed her, despite his prayers. If she was to face Mother Beneficence with her dream then she had to have something more in her armoury.

"MyBook!"

"Yes Steph, how can I help?"

"Are there any people with biodata living in The Margin?"

"I can tell you about the people of The Margin," began MyBook and Steph wondered whether it would have been better to do the search herself if all she was going to get was a standard history book entry, but she was comfortable lying down and decided to just listen for now. MyBook continued. "These people are known as Marginals. The term was first used at the end of The Terror Wars. At that time the straggling bands of defeated terrorists fled to the lands just beyond the border of Trueway. This area was inhospitable but it was possible to survive there, and for many years the terrorists – The Marginals - used this area as a base from which to launch terror attacks on Trueway."

"MyBook, stop."

"Yes, Steph."

"So, MyBook would the terrorists who became the first Marginals have had biodata?"

"No Steph. Biodata cards were not introduced 'til after The Terror Wars."

"So they wouldn't even have had biodata cards, let alone implanted chips or osteodata encoding their personal information?"

"That is correct, Steph."

"OK MyBook, continue."

"Certainly Steph. The Marginals were fragmented – geographically, ideologically and organisationally - so were incapable of creating a coordinated offensive against Trueway. The terror attacks by individual groups however were often devastating to the Citizens of Trueway in the locations targeted. Buildings were destroyed by bombing, homes and shops were looted, Citizens were tortured, raped and murdered. Sometimes Citizens were kidnapped and taken back to The Margins with the raiding band of Marginals."

"MyBook, stop!"

"Yes Steph."

"MyBook, tell me more about the people who were kidnapped. What happened to them?"

"That depended upon the needs of the specific Marginal group. Some captives were used as slave labour, especially in areas where the Marginals needed buildings to be constructed. Some were used as bargaining tools – maybe for the release of Marginals held in Trueway prisons. Some were ransomed in exchange for equipment or even food for groups on the edge of survival. The larger, better organised Marginal groups quite often kidnapped children. Young children especially could be indoctrinated and used to swell fighting numbers as they got older."

"MyBook ,stop."

"Yes Steph."

"MyBook, have Trueway Citizens been kidnapped and taken into the Margin – possibly as children – since the introduction of implanted biodata – whether chip or osteo?"

"Yes, Steph there are reports of this having happened."

"MyBook."

"Yes Steph?"

"Have there been any reports of Trueway Citizens being kidnapped and taken into the Margin in the past thirty years?"

"No, Steph. There are no reports of Trueway citizens being kidnapped and taken into the Margin in the pa.."

"MyBook, stop!"

"Yes, Steph."

"MyBook, is there any other way that a Trueway Citizen might end up in The Margin?"

"Yes Steph. Citizens often go into the Margin to work. You have done this yourself."

"MyBook."

"Yes, Steph?"

"Are there ways in which Trueway Citizens could be in The Margins unofficially?"

"Yes, Steph. Occasionally people get lost in border areas and inadvertently go into The Margin. There are also people who go there intentionally. These people are usually referred to as 'walkers'."

"MyBook."

"Yes, Steph?"

"Are there any reports of people called 'walkers' or of people thought to have got lost accidentally in the Margin in the past year … no past five years?"

"Yes Steph, there are eighteen."

"MyBook."

"Yes, Steph?"

"Give me a printout of the eighteen people. Give me the name of the person, gender, ethnicity, age at disappearance and where they disappeared … oh and whether they were thought to be 'walkers' or accidentally lost – oh and whether they came back or were found."

"Yes, Steph. Printing now." Steph heard the printer start up.

"MyBook, sleep."

Chapter 15: The Official Truth

"Is it all wrapped up?" asked Montgomery-Jones calmly.

"We have seen to it that Safia Philips appears to have made several purchases with her biodata after the shooting incident and that there are records of her being places – even having been seen - after the incident as well. It would take a very determined sleuth to link her with the Marginal shot at the drilling station," confirmed Cummings.

"And what is the official explanation for her disappearance?"

"A boating accident Ma'am. She went drawing up on The Grand River – wanted the isolation for her artwork – not unusual for her – but was swept away. The currents would mean it unlikely that her body would be found."

"OK, I guess that is as much as we can do," said Montgomery-Jones in resignation. "The essentials are covered but I still feel uneasy. She was in The Margin for some reason, Sahid. She had got there through Pipe 5 so why not come back that way?"

"Our people have gone back over her movements, her internet searches, her 'MyBook' – everything for the past six months with a fine toothed comb. We have pulled her flat apart and talked to known friend and colleagues – discretely of course as part of the investigation into her disappearance on her painting trip. There is nothing. She was just doing what she always did – painting, taking stuff to the gallery, giving some tuition and generally getting on with life. Needless to say, Homeland Security have stumbled around in their usual way via the Peoples' Enforcement of Truth Service and found nothing."

"But somebody made her pregnant. Did your searching bring up her visit to Yusef?"

"No Ma'am, but as I said before, she was a good agent and knew how to cover her steps."

"Then short of her making an amateur error all the 'fine-toothed comb' work may have been a waste of time. Still, I guess it has been done and so we know she hasn't made any obvious errors. It looks like we have done all we can do – for now at least," sighed Montgomery-Jones clearly still uncomfortable. "But," she announced in a more resolute tone, "we have made progress in the elections and need to consolidate that – despite the terrible news on the economic front."

"Indeed Ma'am – and we have had downturns before – depressions even - so I am sure we will climb back out of this slump … and don't forget," added Cummings with a broad smile, "The World Games, Ma'am."

"Yes, of course." Montgomery-Jones sounded less than enthusiastic. "So how are things with, The Games?"

"All going as expected Ma'am. I'm sure 'Rubber' will get it all off to a good start."

"Oh preserve us! I had forgotten that prattling idiot would be doing the opening speech – or should I call it 'performance'? He's bound to try and outdo everyone and everything. He gets his nose in everywhere – and he's got nothing to do with sport! What do people see in him?"

"He's all right Ma'am. At least he keeps everyone happy."

"Yes, I'm sure … and I am sure he will do a very entertaining opening speech." Then adding with mock alarm, "It is *just* the opening speech he's doing isn't it? Great Spirit preserve us if he was consulted on the *organisation* of anything."

Chapter 16: Introducing Richard 'Rubber' Ronson

'Rubber' Ronson – real name Richard Ronson was a man with ambition but a muddled sort of ambition. He wanted to do well – but at what he wasn't sure. He had tried various 'careers' and was now in his late forties. Seen in a photograph he would not stand out as especially good looking – and yet in real life he was somehow appealing and strangely attractive. There was something absurdly compelling about him from things that he sometimes said that did not quite make sense to his shock of red hair that equally did not quite make sense! He came across well. He left an impression. People liked him, and he liked being liked. Despite all his contradictions – and maybe because of them – he had actually been quite successful and was a well-known personality throughout Trueway. To many people he was like beer or ice cream - hard to resist even when they knew better.

Some say he had gained the nickname 'rubber' when he was at school because he used the eraser so much to rub out his mistakes. In adult life those who disliked him said nothing had changed, claiming that he still covered his tracks and distorted the truth to his own advantage. Those who liked him however said the name reflected his bouncy personality – always jolly, always everyone's friend, always a laugh – and those who liked him were definitely in the majority. This included the media, and that in turn, meant organisers of media hungry events like The World Games. It should have been of no surprise therefore to Montgomery-Jones that Richard 'Rubber' Ronson had been selected to give the opening speech.

The Games happened every four years and brought together the very best athletes and sportspeople to compete in a programme that lasted for several weeks. Events took place at numerous venues across Trueway and the media coverage was intense. Ronson had worked tirelessly in preparing for them. He planned to use them as his next step towards personal glory. Being keenly aware that the mass of Trueway loved The Games he knew that to associate himself with a successful 'Games' would boost his popularity – for what he wasn't sure – but being popular was what Rubber liked. Maybe it was an end in itself – and at an emotional level he didn't mind if his popularity was with a high ranking member of the elite or a factory worker on the shop floor – and his appeal did seem to transcend social boundaries. As a result, he was good for The Games and The Games were good for him. It was pure symbiosis.

He had been working on his speech and wanted to run a couple of ideas past someone not directly related to The Games, so who better than Mrs Christina at the art gallery?

Chapter 17: Mrs Christina and Private Viewings

Mrs Christina was the proprietor of an art gallery – 'Mrs Christina's Gallery'.

Art – especially traditional painting and sculpture – was highly prized in Trueway. Despite the reliance of Trueway on technology such as the eco-shield for climate control and osteodata for identification, science was fundamentally distrusted. The accepted wisdom was that science had been at the root of the planet's ills, and despite the fact that science had also been at the heart of innovation to rescue the planet, the predominant view was that science should be kept in check and not be allowed to explore new and possibly dangerous avenues. Art, on the other hand, was to be admired as the highest of human achievements.

Institutions, places of work, public spaces and individual homes all proudly displayed original works of art. Very few of these creations however became permanent fixtures. Everyone was encouraged to change the art they displayed on a regular basis. In this way the many artists of Trueway and the galleries displaying their work, were kept busy. 'Mrs Christina's Gallery' was no exception.

Mrs Christina may have had a first name but nobody knew it. She was just Mrs Christina. She had not been running her art gallery all that long, but it had gained quite a reputation and was very successful. It represented some leading artists, and was sought out by new talent as well. This was a good mix, enabling her to have a price range and variety to suit middle income Citizens, a few celebrities and several of the Trueway elite. Richard Ronson was a regular customer – and so was the politician, Major David Bloombridge. Sometimes special exhibitions would occur - maybe the launch of a new artist or a group show of recent works by established artists. On such occasions a lot of polite, inconsequential chit-chat would occur between guests – "oh his work has such depth" …"Isn't it wonderful … a riot of colour" and so on. But whether something is inconsequential depends on who hears it.

Bloombridge overheard a young councillor talking to Richard Ronson about an abstract looking painting. The councillor (a boorish fellow) said he didn't like the painting and wouldn't waste his money on it – but would pay handsomely for the young lady who had painted it. Bloombridge saw an entrepreneurial opportunity. From this snatch of conversation grew the business of 'private viewings' – though the boorish councillor was never to reap the benefit of his casual remark.

Managing the size of the world population was a central concern in Trueway. The laws in relation to reproduction and to sexual activity were strict, diligently policed and rigorously enforced. A couple wishing to have children would need to meet very high standards of Citizenship and even then permission would only be granted if it was considered unlikely to compromise the birth-death balance. Sexual activity was only permitted between registered couples and prostitution was illegal. To help control natural inclinations Citizens took their Desire & Aggression Modification Pills (generally without any need for coercion) and the pills were individually prescribed to match the biology and metabolism of the user. Periodically people were allowed to refrain from taking the pills and enjoy sex – as long as offspring did not result. These brief periods of sexual activity were termed 'DAMP Holidays'. Sexual activity outside these DAMP Holidays was forbidden. Punishment for anyone found guilty of flouting the sexual and reproduction laws could be harsh – especially if the breach was a serious and obvious one. To be 'found guilty' however necessitated being caught – and avoiding being caught was easier for some than for others.

Bloombridge was a man with connections. He was fully aware of the wish for some elite colleagues in government and elsewhere – almost exclusively male colleagues – to have a safe and secure sexual outlet. With the overheard snatch of conversation in the context of Mrs Christina's Gallery and Richard 'Rubber' Ronson everything clicked into place. Although Mrs Christina's business had been doing well Bloombridge was aware that the world economy was in a fragile position. He could foresee that there would be fewer paintings being sold in coming months and young, needy artists looking for other ways to make a living. If he could bring together those poor, financially needy artists with his wealthy but sexually needy contacts in a totally safe way then money could be made.

The key was Ronson – because Ronson's house was between where Bloombridge lived and Mrs Christina's Gallery – and Ronson's house was in one of Trueway's surveillance blind spots – a place where biodata did not register on any monitors; a place where Citizens could not be seen. Bloombridge, because of his role in Homeland Security, was very much aware of this.

Bloombridge discussed his proposal with Ronson. Although Ronson was anxious, due to the illegality of the proposal, his fears were easily allayed by the authoritative reassurances of Bloombridge in his capacity as Head of Homeland Security. Ronson therefore floated the idea with Mrs Christina. She cautiously tested the water with a couple of likely artists and the 'private viewings' were born. A room was set aside at Ronson's house to act as a 'gallery'. The artist and client were brought together for the purpose of an in-depth private viewing and purchasing of artwork. Whatever else happened while they were together (possibly in the bedroom adjoining the viewing gallery) was entirely their concern.

The 'private viewings' had been taking place for quite some while by the time that Richard Ronson felt he needed someone on whom to try out his speech ideas for The Games. He therefore knew Mrs Christina well and knew that he could trust her not to 'leak' any of his wonderful ideas to the media and so reduce the impact of what he intended saying at the opening ceremony. She was the perfect confidant.

Chapter 18: Good Sister Adolorardah and Unburdening

Steph went through each of the eighteen names. Not one of them could have been the woman that she had shot. For all eighteen there was something that eliminated them. She even did searches on the individual names manually to cross check and verify the facts as printed off by MyBook without finding a potential match.

There was no more she could do. Why had this terrible shooting happened? It would all have been so perfect if she hadn't been on that patrol.

Following the lesson she had learned from Good Mother Beneficence on that first day at the convent she had always been totally candid with Sister Adolorardah. Although seeking truth and betterment was all part of what she wished to achieve she had been honest that her central goal was to obtain the right for an enhanced marriage. Specifically, she wanted to be permitted an enhanced marriage with two children, often referred to as 'Enhanced Marriage 2' which, in turn, was often abbreviated to 'EM2'. Population control in Trueway was so strict that prospective parents had to prove their worthiness as Citizens in order to be granted the right to have children. A couple wishing to marry could do so quite easily if they could guarantee that they would not bring any more people into the world. Same sex marriages were the most straightforward – and were encouraged, especially if the couple wanted to adopt an orphan child. Heterosexual marriage, where one partner at least was certified sterile, was also quite easily arranged. A couple who wanted a child however had to meet quite high standards, and if the couple wanted two children the standards were higher still. Steph and her fiancé, Paul had agreed that they wanted two children and were prepared to go through the preparation process.

This process required them to spend time in separate convents where The Good Sisters would evaluate their suitability for parenthood. Healthy living, religious devotion, environmental awareness, care for the planet, readiness to work hard and make a productive contribution to society were all part of what needed to be displayed and proved prior to being granted the right to enhanced marriage. If potential parents were not able to meet standards in areas such as these for themselves, then clearly they would not be able to inculcate such standards in their offspring, and so the suitability and value of such offspring to the world would be questionable. Steph's period at the drilling station had been part of the preparation relating to skills for useful, personal contribution, and if it was completed successfully, then apart from the final ritual of her 'devotional pilgrimage', her preparation for marriage would be complete.

She knew from Sister Adolorardah that she had done well in her time at the convent. She knew in herself too that she had gained a great deal. She had matured. She had become more confident in herself. She had done much to confirm her religious beliefs and prove her worthiness as a Citizen. She was on the verge of fulfilling all demands that would qualify her for marriage and motherhood – but now there had been this shooting and with it her doubts and sin – and maybe, worst of all, her belief that she had received divine help in revealing to her that she had killed a Citizen and not a Marginal. She felt trapped. If she had to speak to The Mother Superior then she would do so – but first she would share all this with the one person at the convent with whom she shared everything and who had guided her since the day she arrived – Sister Adolorardah.

*

"Sit, Steph," invited Sister Adolorardah kindly. "You have been through so much."

Steph looked into the kindly eyes of the time-worn face of her spiritual mother, her guide – her confidant. When Steph first came to the convent Sister Adolorardah had been 'given' to her as her mentor. The Order of The Good Sisters adopted the unusual practice of 'reverse authority'. This was based on the philosophy of seeing the convent as a family and the newcomer as a newborn baby. Although a newborn is the weakest and the most vulnerable member of a family it is paradoxically the most powerful – able to control its parents with a single cry. The baby demands and the parents acquiesce. Why do the parents acquiesce? What power does this squirming, inconsequential newcomer have? Love. It controls its parents through love. The Order of The Good Sisters was based on this fundamental principal. So it was that when Steph entered the convent she was not told that Sister Adolorardah would be her mentor or her tutor but rather that Sister Adolorardah – this venerable and kindly lady – now *belonged* to her. She was given to Steph, and Sister Adolorardah just like a good parent, embraced her subservient role of acquiescence to the young Steph out of love.

Steph was not the most demanding 'baby' and an even less demanding 'child'. A loving, trusting relationship quickly developed between the two women.

Although Sister Adolorardah was singled out to be 'given' to Steph and to have this special relationship with her the other nuns acted towards Steph with tolerance and understanding in much the same way as other adults would respond to someone else's baby or child. If, however one of the nuns saw Steph behaving in a way that she did not think was appropriate it would be to Sister Adolorardah that she would report her concern and it would be for Sister Adolorardah to address the issue. This principal even extended to the most senior member of the convent, Good Mother Beneficence - The Mother Superior.

Babyhood does not last forever however, and just as a child grows and is expected to take greater personal responsibility, so too with the new entrant to the convent. Steph, through counselling with Sister Adolorardah, had grown from baby through childhood into adolescence, and agreement had been reached that she was approaching the point of returning to the 'outside' and to the marriage she desired. Although she and Paul had been kept apart, supervised communication through letters had been permitted (up until the weeks immediately before marriage) and was considered necessary marriage preparation. She and Paul were well matched and there was no contrivance in the fact that they were coming to readiness at the same time. Neither would have to 'tread water' waiting for the other to reach the required level for the marriage they desired. Steph's time at the drilling station had been part of her preparation for departure and Paul had been having a similar experience in a facility elsewhere outside of his convent. These final preparations and then the devotional pilgrimages should have been little more than formalities to complete the plan – but then came the shooting. The shooting had not been part of the plan. It had shaken Steph, and like any child, she was now coming back to her parent for reassurance and guidance.

"I was sick 'Ardah." (From early on Steph had abbreviated the Good Sister's name). "After the shooting I was all right. Even by myself in the evening … but then all of a sudden I was sick. It was awful, Sister."

"My poor child. My poor, poor child." The elderly nun crouched in front of Steph and stroked her hands. "My heart goes out to you."

"Why did this have to happen Ardah? Why?"

"It was a test Steph; a terrible test but I am sure that it is part of the plan of The Great Spirit. There is no doubt that The Great Spirit has given you this challenge and has chosen to do so at this point in time. As you go forward to marriage and to new life – both a new life for you with Paul and hopefully new life in children – The Great Spirit has seen fit that you confront death – the possibility of your own at the hand of the Marginal and the certainty of that of the Marginal who died at your hand."

Steph looked into the calm, kind eyes of the Good Sister. She wanted to believe her. "How do you know Ardah? How can you be certain?"

"I prayed Steph – how else? Surely after all our time together you know that is the way…"

Steph's heart leapt at these words. Yes, she should have known – and maybe she did know but had needed to hear it from the venerable nun's lips before she dared to unburden herself.

"Oh Ardah, Ardah. I must sound such a foolish child to you. The answer is in prayer. I knew that. Why can I not hold on to these things? Why do I lose grip as soon as something goes wrong? I spoke to Reverend Majumder on Station after I had been sick. I told him how troubled I was and what did he tell me to do? Pray, of course! Why must I still be reliant on others to tell me what I should already know?"

"It is natural Steph," said Sister Adolorardah with a smile. "And did you pray? And did it help?"

"Yes, of course I did and yes, it *did* help. The Great Spirit gave me a revelation. It was a shocking revelation … but it made sense of all my mixed-up feelings. I had shot a Marginal and I was proud and happy at the good that I had done and then I was sick and feeling guilty and then I prayed and The Great Spirit revealed to me what the problem was!" Steph was talking very quickly, almost ecstatically, and a darkness entered the eyes of Sister Adolorardah. It was the darkness of the clouds that are portents of the storm.

"That is good, Steph. That is very good. You prayed and your prayers were answered." Sister Adolorardah was talking in an urgent attempt to stop Steph saying more. Prayer bringing comfort was a balm and she welcomed it – but prayer that brought revelation was something to be feared. Steph, however, could not be halted. She was with her trusted convent 'mother' and incapable of seeing the anxiety in her eyes.

"The Great Spirit showed me in a dream that the woman I had shot was not a Marginal. She was a Citizen. That was why I felt upset – I had shot a Citizen. I didn't know the poor woman was there by some mistake … but The Great Spirit showed me!" Steph was almost panting and her eyes were glassy.

Sister Adolorardah desperately tried to think of a response that would accept Steph's revelation while preventing the need to pursue it further. She gambled.

"And did you tell The Reverend Majumder of your revelation?"

"Yes."

"And what did he say?"

"He advised me to talk to Good Mother Beneficence." Steph paused, unsure whether to say more or wait. Sister Adolorardah paused trying to think through the implications. Steph spoke again. "I felt I needed to talk to you first Ardah. To be honest, Good Mother Beneficence frightens me. I know I shouldn't be frightened – but I am."

"Is it the fear of how this might affect your marriage?"

"Yes, there is that … and that's a big worry. I've come so far … and Paul as well … but she just frightens me. What should I do Ardah?"

"I think that The Great Spirit revealed this to you to bring you *comfort* not pain. You did what was right. If the woman that you shot was not a Marginal then I am sure that The Great Spirit revealed this to you so that you could understand your confused feelings. The Great Spirit would not do something in order to lead you into further conflict … and since the authorities have said that the woman was a Marginal, then for you to assert that she was not, would be to say that you are right and they are wrong. Be humble, Steph. Allow The Great Spirit to give comfort."

Adolorardah stopped short of advising Steph not to talk to the Good Mother. She hoped that Steph would make this decision for herself. Steph felt reassured by Sister Adolorardah's words of counsel but she also felt uneasy at accepting what she believed to be a falsehood – accepting as true that a Marginal had been killed, when in fact, the person was a Citizen.

"So, are you saying that I should accept that The Great Spirit gave this revelation to me only for my comfort and expects no further action from me?"

"Not necessarily Steph. The Great Spirit revealed this to you and you have taken further action – quite appropriate action – in seeking guidance and counsel from The Reverend Majumder, and from me. All I am saying now is that I believe you should do what remains to be done – and that is to humbly accept the comfort given to you by The Great Spirit."

"And The Reverend Majumder's advice to speak to Good Mother Beneficence?" queried Steph.

"I have known you longer than Reverend Majumder. His words were wise, but knowing you as I do, I think that you have taken all the action that was demanded by your revelation and now is the time to accept the comfort of it – the comfort of knowing why you felt conflict and the comfort of knowing that you have taken the action that was appropriate in the circumstances."

Sister Adolorardah did not want to say, outright that Steph should not follow Reverend Majumder's advice, but hoped that Steph would understand that she was obliquely saying, "Let it rest, Steph."

Steph silently nodded as she pondered Sister Adolorardah's words. She fully understood the message being given by the older woman. She still felt uncomfortable but Sister Adolorardah knew her well, knew The Book of Truth and had guided her faultlessly to this point. What right or reason had she to ignore her counsel now – especially when her future and that of Paul hung in the balance?

"Thank you, Ardah. I will be satisfied. I will be humble and will pursue this no further." Steph could see the relief in Sister Adolorardah's eyes at hearing these words. She assumed the relief to be solely for the on-going upset that Steph might now be avoiding. She therefore felt no concern in saying:

"There's more Ardah. I have told no-one this … but I will tell you. Before the woman died she …"

"No, Steph!"

The urgency in Sister Adolorardah's voice brought Steph to an abrupt halt. Sister Adolorardah had never cut across her before.

"No Steph," she said more calmly. You mustn't tell me what you are about to tell me … please."

"But Ardah…"

"No Steph..."

"But you don't know what I'm going to say and …"

"I know … believe me I know – and you mustn't."

"Well, if you know what I'm going to say … and you can't possibly … but if you do then what difference does it make if I do or don't say it?

"*Every* difference. You don't understand, Steph"

"She spoke! She spoke!"

"No! Stop! You idiot! Idiot!" Sister Adolorardah was on her feet – almost shouting.

Steph stopped – utterly shocked. Sister Adolorardah had never spoken like this before; never raised her voice. The elderly nun was trembling. Her eyes were wide – but she was not angry. She was terrified.

Chapter 19: Ronson Knocked off Course

"Hello Chrissie," beamed Richard Ronson as he sauntered across towards her desk. There was nobody else in the gallery.

"Hello Rick," responded Mrs Christina looking up from the book she was reading. Mrs Christina was one of the few people who called him Rick. He liked that. He found it refreshing – not as formal as, 'Richard' but more respectful than, 'Rubber'.

"I wasn't expecting you," she said cautiously, "I thought you would be far too busy sorting your plans for The Games. You sorted your speech yet – theme and all that?"

"Yeah – been working on it," he said veering off to look at a painting.

She put down the book and stood up. "Drink?" she enquired.

"Mmm – OK," came the distracted response as he peered closely at a picture.

"Beer?"

"Mmm --- ta."

Mrs Christina went out the back to get a beer from the fridge leaving Ronson to his musings. She needed a moment to order her thoughts. Earlier that day she had received a visit from two officers of the Peoples' Enforcement of Truth Service (PETS). They informed her that one of the artists that she represented – a Safia Philips - had gone missing in a boating accident up at Grand River and was presumed dead. They asked a few questions about her, gave their condolences and left. Despite her calm appearance when Richard Ronson had arrived she had been shaken by this visit and had been thinking things through. Her concern stemmed from the fact that Safia had been involved in the private viewings and she didn't want the investigation of Safia's disappearance to result in the authorities inadvertently uncovering this illegal sideline to her business. The likelihood of an in-depth investigation that might do that was increased by the fact that only a short while before another of the artists that she represented had died tragically – a Mrs O'Donnell.

Two deaths with links to her gallery could, indeed *should*, raise concerns, if not suspicions, with the authorities. Mrs Christina was able to take comfort however from the fact that one of the three people involved in organising the 'private viewings' – in fact the instigator of them - was David Bloombridge. As District Councillor in charge of Homeland Security she knew he would do everything in his power (quite considerable power) to minimise any attention given to her or to the gallery that formed such a central role in his illicit project. She felt sure had already taken steps in that direction. It would certainly explain why the visit from the PETS had been so short. It was a 'tick-box' exercise she was sure. Should anyone raise a concern about two deaths with the common link of Mrs Christina's Gallery, then Bloombridge could say that the gallery owner had been interviewed and that there was nothing suspicious requiring further investigation. The fact that there had been two deaths would be seen as nothing more than a coincidence. This was more or less the point that her cogitations had reached when Richard Ronson arrived. She was feeling calmer because of having thought things through in this way whereas Ronson's nonchalant manner did not suggest to her a person who had been through a similar process but rather one who simply didn't know of Safia's disappearance.

"This is quite nice," he said looking at a seascape as she returned.

"Yes, he's not an artist I have shown here before; quite an old chap … so probably not of interest to you." She handed him the bottle. She knew he didn't like it in a glass.

"That's a bit harsh Chrissie. You know I'm interested in paintings as much as the painters … and this is nice no matter who painted it." He took a swig of the beer as he wandered over to her desk.

Mrs Christina secretly had to acknowledge that Richard Ronson displayed a genuine sensitivity to paintings but she also knew that his interest became even more focussed if he knew that the artist was a young woman suitable for the private viewings.

"Have you come about Saffie?" she asked, using the familiar diminutive to sound as matter of fact as possible. His blank expression indicated that she was right - he hadn't heard. "She's gone missing – and worse still, presumed dead." She saw the instant panic in his eyes. She continued speaking as she turned and walked back towards her desk. "The PETS were here earlier asking questions." She turned to look at him. He was ashen. "Anyway, if it isn't Saffie then what is it that brings you through my door, Rick?"

"Oh - just wanted a look at what you had. Take my mind off things. I was going to run some of my ideas past you – you know, for the opening speech at The Games – but Safia. Did they say anything more? What they think has happened?"

"No, they were not here long."

"Then she might still be alive – they only said 'presumed dead'?"

"Yes, Rick. Let's hope, hey? So do you want to tell me about this speech?"

"Can't say I feel like it now. I must say, Chrissie, you seem very calm."

"Well, David has a vested interest. He won't let investigations dig too deep."

"But what has happened to her?"

"I don't know – but the PETS said it was probably an unfortunate boating accident up at Grand River – so that's probably what it was. Those waters can be treacherous … and I did tell her *that* - more than once as it happens."

"OK Chrissie. Anyway, I don't think I can concentrate on the speech right now." He turned to go. "Let me know if you hear anything more."

"Will do Rick," she called as he went out the door. She sat back down with her book – and the beer that he had left.

Chapter 20: The Die is Cast

Good Mother Beneficence knew her Sisters well and each of the Good Sisters knew this. It was as if she could see into their very souls. When Sister Adolorardah entered the wood panelled office of The Good Mother she felt she was a rat entering an experimental maze.

"How is she?" asked The Good Mother, her tone one of 'efficient kindliness' thought Sister Adolorardah.

"She has had a shock, Good Mother. It has set her back a little – 'knocked her confidence' you might say."

"Yes, a shocking thing. We could not have predicted … but that is part of returning is it not? Meeting the unpredictable? This 'knock back' – how serious do you think it is? Is she hopeful of continuing to marriage as planned? Do you think she is capable of pilgrimage?"

"Oh yes, Good Mother. I have no doubt that Stephanie wishes to continue along the path that she has been travelling."

"I have no doubt of her *wishes*, Good Sister, but I do not know exactly what you mean when you say the incident has 'knocked her confidence'. Has it affected her faith? Has it affected her readiness and suitability for marriage and motherhood within the embrace of The Great Spirit? Has it affected her ability to uphold and inculcate in her children the values of Trueway?"

"I am confident that Stephanie has a deep faith and that she will make a worthy mother of children of Trueway," came Sister Adolorardah's, almost formulaic, response – and to Mother Beneficence that is exactly how it sounded - rehearsed. Sister Adolorardah had prepared herself. Mother Beneficence had expected as much.

"What makes you so sure?"

The same 'efficient kindliness', thought Sister Adolorardah … but she sensed that the preamble had moved a step closer to the true purpose of the meeting.

"I have spent many hours with Stephanie since she joined us and it is my feeling that all will be well with her." As soon as the word 'feeling' was out of her mouth Sister Adolorardah knew she had made a mistake. Mother Beneficence had a low tolerance of 'feelings'. She liked 'evidence'.

"Is that a strong feeling Sister – a weak feeling or something in between? No, don't answer that – I am merely thinking out loud – but you knew that. We have known each other a long time." She smiled but remained silent just a little longer than was necessary before continuing. "What has Stephanie *said* to you that leads you to your feeling that all will be well?"

"Well, we talked about what had happened. She was candid and said that it had upset her and even that she had been to talk to the priest on the drilling station." Sister Adolorardah had no doubt that Mother Beneficence would be aware of Steph's meeting with the Reverend Majumder but was unsure of how much detail she would have obtained of what Steph had divulged to him. Did she know about the revelation dream and the Reverend's advice that this should be discussed with Mother Beneficence herself? "Stephanie said nothing to me that led me to think she was any less committed to Paul, to marriage or to her faith and Trueway."

"As things stand, Good Sister, Stephanie and Paul should both be embarking on their pilgrimages of devotion shortly and simultaneously so that they can marry here, in this the bride's convent, on their return. Do you think Stephanie is ready for her pilgrimage? Does she need more time to recover from this unfortunate incident?"

"I would bow to your wisdom in such things Good Mother but I think that to defer the marriage would damage Stephanie. It would leave her feeling that her effort and everything she had done was being questioned. To go forward as planned, on the other hand would be a confirmation of the love for her of The Great Spirit."

Mother Beneficence sat silent – seemingly studying the little brass bell on her desk before speaking.

"Good. Thank you Sister. I am glad that Stephanie is in your hands." Mother Beneficence stood up to signal the end of the meeting and Sister Adolorardah did likewise with a feeling of relief. She gave the customary nod of respect before turning to leave.

"Oh, Sister!" The words halted Sister Adolorardah as surely as a heavy hand on her shoulder. She turned to face Mother Beneficence and tried to look as calm and unsuspecting as possible while her heart beat furiously.

"Yes, Good Mother?"

"Your sitting towel," smiled Mother Beneficence looking down at the chair where the Good Sister had been sitting.

"Oh," said Sister Adolorardah coming back and reaching down to gather it up.

"No Sister, please sit down again. The Great Spirit has seen fit to make you forget what you have probably not forgotten in decades – or maybe your haste to escape is to blame. There is more isn't there? What else has Stephanie told you?" Sister Adolorardah sat down. She had failed to find the route out of the maze and back to freedom.

(B) Pilgrimage

Chapter 21: Going

Steph was high on a nervous mix of anticipation and apprehension. 'Anticipation' because Sister Adolorardah would be here in a matter of minutes (she was never late) and then they would start their journey – Steph's 'devotional pilgrimage' – the final ritual before her marriage on the day she returned. Her apprehension stemmed from not knowing how arduous the pilgrimage would be or where indeed, the journey would take her.

Steph had said no more to Sister Adolorardah – or anyone else - about the woman she had shot having spoken. She didn't understand what had caused Sister Adolorardah to behave as she had but it had frightened Steph to see her elderly friend so upset. During their time together in the convent she and her mentor had spoken freely about some of the most intimate things. Steph felt that she could talk to 'Ardah' about anything – so what had happened was unprecedented and incomprehensible, but the look of terror in the old woman's face left Steph in no doubt that she must speak of this no more.

Steph looked out onto the cloister where her wedding would take place in exactly nine days time. Her rucksack was packed and on the chair beside her. She hadn't yet put on her boots, and they sat beside the chair. She had plaited her hair. As a novice she was not required – not allowed – to wear a wimple. She turned from the window - and there was Sister Adolorardah.

"Oh! Sister, I didn't hear you." It was unusual for Steph to use this formal address. True, she had been a little startled by the Good Sister's silent entrance – but Steph *had* been expecting her so it was something more than surprise that had evoked the use of this formal title. Maybe it was a gravity in the Good Sisters face – in her eyes – or maybe the impassive, silent stance. It was fleeting, whatever it was, and as Steph smiled and went over to her and the older woman stretched out her arms for embrace she was again, 'Ardah'.

"Put on your boots Steph. I thought you would be ready!" scolded the Good Sister playfully.

"I am ready – well as ready as I can be! I was just waiting… and I hate boots!"

"Well, you're going to need them … and I hope you have packed your rucksack properly and not forgotten anything."

"Well, I have ticked everything on the list … and we have talked about *that* enough … so I am blaming you if there is anything missing!" teased Steph as she finished tying her boot laces and stood up.

"Well, it sounds as though we are ready … at least in the practical sense." Sister Adolorardah looked at her charge – the charge to whom she paradoxically belonged. They were both bound by ritual and custom. There was no option but to perform this pilgrimage yet the Good Sister so wanted Steph to rebel and refuse to go – but Steph was not a rebel and even if she was, she would not be rebelling at this. She wanted this journey, this time away to prepare her for the marriage. Sister Adolorardah reached out and placed one hand over Steph's eyes and the other over her mouth in a curious way. For the second time in minutes Steph was startled by the older woman. Apart from a slight intake of breath however she remained passive. Was this some part of the pilgrimage ceremony about which she was unaware.

"Great Spirit," began Sister Adolorardah, "Great Spirit …" she repeated but said no more. In a single movement she let her hands fall and had turned to the door. Steph snatched up her backpack and followed as the Good Sister left the room.

*

All of their pilgrimage was to be on foot, but since the pilgrimage was traditionally a thing of contemplation and challenge, it usually took place in a remote area. Consequently, it was not unusual to see a Good Sister with a bride to be on a glide train heading off to one of the more remote terminals in order to reach a starting point from which to begin walking. Steph had fully expected that she and Sister Adolorardah would begin their journey in this way. She was therefore surprised and perplexed when the Good Sister led her through the corridors, then out across the quadrangle and into the garden before traversing the lawn and going down into the orchard. As soon as they were among the trees Sister Adolorardah stopped.

"We begin here," she announced, taking off her rucksack and delving inside. She withdrew a collar and lead and proceeded to put the collar round her own neck. This was not as much of a surprise to Steph as the fact that the Good Sister was doing this here, in the orchard. Tradition required that for part of the pilgrimage the bride to be walked blindfold, led by the Sister that she owned. Like a blind person with a guide dog it was the embodiment of trust and mutual support and therefore symbolic of the mutual trust and support of marriage. Steph, recognising that this element of the pilgrimage was about to commence said nothing but set down her own bag and took from it her blindfold. She put her rucksack back on, tied the blindfold round her own eyes and waited to be given the leather loop of the lead, but instead, felt something cold, hard and cylindrical being placed in her hand.

"Drink this Steph," said Adolorardah. Steph did not know what she was being asked to drink or why, but although a little surprised, felt no reason to question the request and lifted the vessel to her lips. It contained only a small amount of liquid and she had to tilt her head right back before it found her lips. It was not unpleasant to taste, though she could not say it was anything recognisable like apple juice or tea. She swallowed it and the Good Sister took the vessel from her. Steph, now without sight because of her blindfold, listened more intently. She could hear birds, a slight rustle of breeze through the leaves. There was the sound of Adolorardah presumably putting the cup or whatever it was back in her bag. Then the lead was put into Steph's hand and Sister Adolorardah silently led her away. Now that they were walking it was customary for neither to speak unless emergency demanded it. This was called, 'the silence of the walk'. The silence gave the bride-to-be the time to contemplate. When Steph had asked Adolorardah what it was that she should contemplate the Good Sister had simply said, 'your breath, your foot fall. The rest will come'.

The elderly nun did not walk quickly and Steph knew that the grass around the trees was always well mown, so she walked with confidence in the darkness. Steph found the silence peaceful. Without the overpowering dominance of vision she sensed things that she might otherwise have missed – the faintest smell of soap from Sister Adolorardah, the soft sound of their steady footfall, little changes in temperature as they went in and out of shadows and the movement of her plait.

They walked like this for a little while – maybe 5 minutes before Sister Adolorardah broke the silence.

"We are going to stop now." The lead went slack and Steph stood still uncertain as to where she was but thinking that she must be close to the far wall of the orchard given the length of time they had been walking.

She would not remove the blindfold however until told to do so by Sister Adolorardah or until the Good Sister removed it for her. Steph felt Adolorardah's dry, smooth hands come to rest gently on her shoulders.

"Everything is a combination Steph – everything." Adolorardah spoke softly. Steph felt that she sounded sad. "Nothing is clear and nothing works without something else. Everything is locked until the combination to unlock it is discovered - and combination will often discover itself. You and I are combination now. What the combination will be in the future I do not know. I will not be here to know. Give me your hand Steph," She did not wait for Steph to do anything but simply took Steph's left hand – the one not holding the lead. Steph did not resist as her hand was placed palm down on what felt like a stone wall. Maybe they were at the orchard boundary as she suspected.   There was a brief silence. She sensed Adolorardah was doing something but she did not know what. Then she heard the elderly nun say words that she didn't understand.

"Pipe 17. Boundary. Culpa."

Something happened but Steph, in her darkness could not tell what though there was a very perceptible change to the air around her. It was cooler and it was still and the smell of Sister Adolorardah's soap was stronger now. It was as if they had suddenly entered a confined space.

Steph blinked as the Good Sister removed the blindfold.

"Where are we?"

"At the boundary, Steph."

"The boundary?" queried Steph still blinking and peering round into the gloom to try and make something of her surroundings. Both she and Sister Adolorardah were bathed in a feint greenish light. The Good Sister was standing immediately in front of Steph. Beyond her was darkness but to left and right the sickly light revealed claustrophobically close stone walls hemming them in.

"Yes, Steph. We are at the boundary. This is the boundary to the final stage of the pilgrimage."

"I'm sorry Sister bu…"

"Don't worry Steph," interjected Sister Adolorardah. "I know that you don't understand. I know … I know." The Good Sister's voice began to break. "Please don't ask me questions … please. Unlike The Great Spirit I can't give you answers or guarantees. Unlike The Great Spirit – or those that speak for The Great Spirit – I can't offer salvation … other than … other than maybe, in the end, the salvation of death." The old woman hung her head. "Now, as we stand here in a place you can't possibly comprehend all I can offer you is a choice." She turned, what was now a tear-stained face – cadaverous in the green light, to look at Steph, "… and it is a choice that you must make blindly because I cannot explain. The choice is that you go on with me … in combination on this, your pilgrimage … or that you go back alone. This, I know is a stark choice and … if I am absolutely honest … I do not know what the right decision is for you." Again she hung her head and Steph thought how small she looked - small and defeated … and her heart and her arms reached out and embraced the old woman.

As she held her she strained her eyes to peer into the inky black but could see nothing. She gazed back over her own shoulder as best she could but there too she could see nothing but the walls either side disappearing rapidly into blackness. What was this place? How had she got here? Was it the drink Sister Adolorardah had given her? Was this some kind of hallucination? Suddenly Sister Adolorardah pulled away.

"You must choose Steph." Her voice was resolute. The tears had stopped. "Forward with me in combination or back alone?"

"Go back? But Paul - our wedding …? I have to do the pilgrimage. Where are we Sister? What is this place? What's happening?"

The Good Sister reached up and took Steph's face in her hands. Her hold was firm. Her voice gentle, calm and steady.

"I'm sorry Steph. You must choose to either go forward with me on this, your pilgrimage, or go back alone."

Steph could make no sense of where she was or of these options. This was a dream, a nightmare, an unreality. She heard a voice – it was her voice

"I will not leave you Ardah. I will not leave you. I believe you love me and I love you." The Good Sister took the blindfold from Steph's hand.

"Kneel down Steph."

Steph did as requested and the blindfold was again wrapped round her head and eyes.

"Give me your hand." She did so and felt it placed on the wall to her left. Again she heard the old woman doing something before she spoke and then the single word, "Culpa".

The blindfold was removed.

"Stand up." She did so.

She blinked as her eyes again adjusted. Where were the walls? Where was the green light? She and Adolorardah were in some kind of passage that stretched away as far as Steph could see in a pale white light that seemed to emanate from the walls themselves.

*

"You will not need this again," said Sister Adolorardah handing the blindfold back to Steph. The Good Sister then unfastened the collar from her own neck and proceeded to put it, along with the lead, into her bag. Unsure what she should do with the blindfold Steph took her bag from her shoulders and knelt down to put it away in similar fashion to Sister Adolorardah with her collar and lead - but stopped. There, on the ground was a blindfold almost identical to the one she held in her hand. She glanced back at Sister Adolorardah who appeared busy with her own bag and not to have seen the blindfold on the ground or noticed that Steph had seen it. Steph put her rucksack on top of it while she put her own blindfold inside. For some unfathomable reason she felt guilty at seeing the blindfold on the ground and didn't want Sister Adolorardah to be aware of it. Steph stood up but left the bag where it was concealing her discovery. She watched Sister Adolorardah finish her packing, put the bag on her back, and without a word to Steph, start walking down the passageway. Only then did Steph pick up her bag and sling it on her shoulders. She took a final glance at the blindfold on the ground and then followed Sister Adolorardah.

Now that they were walking neither of the women spoke and Steph, without distraction of conversation, gave her attention to the passageway. Although she and Adolorardah were walking in single file it would have been just wide enough and high enough for them to walk side by side without scuffing their shoulders on the walls or banging their heads on the roof. The floor appeared to be earth – dry and compacted. The walls and overarching roof were grey rock, streaked here and there with rust brown. Steph could make out what she took to be scars in the rock left by drilling. Was this some kind of mine shaft? The illumination she now could see came from lights recessed into the walls and the roof. The passage, as far as she was able to see, continued in a perfectly straight line.

Although Steph was mystified by her circumstances her questions about where she was and how all this was possible – even whether it was real or some kind of hallucination – slipped from consciousness. The rhythm of the walking was soothing. She was here, wherever 'here' was and she was on pilgrimage – *her* pilgrimage at the end of which she would stand in the quadrangle of the convent and be married to Paul. What was he doing now? She wondered if he was on as mysterious a pilgrimage as this. Was he thinking of her? Was he wondering about her pilgrimage?

Steph looked ahead at the diminutive figure of Adolorardah and remembered the blindfold on the ground. She assumed that a bride to be had walked this tunnel before – maybe many brides. How many? Did Adolorardah know? Had she accompanied them? She had definitely been on pilgrimage before – Steph had asked her – but the Good Sister had politely told Steph that she was not at liberty to divulge any more than that. When evening came the 'contemplative silence' of the walk would end and she and Adolorardah would eat and talk. Steph was hungry – but neither she nor the Good Sister was allowed food between breakfast and the evening meal. Steph felt strangely enthusiastic about her own fasting. It seemed right and an important part of the ritual of the pilgrimage, but she felt sorry for Adolorardah. She was old and to walk without food all day seemed an unnecessarily harsh requirement.

They continued their silent walk for quite some time, but then, as Steph looked past Adolorardah, she thought that she could make out a speck of light ahead that was more intense than the general light of the passage. As they walked it grew in size confirming to Steph that they might be approaching the end of the tunnel. Steph also became aware that the air was getting warmer. It had been cool – chilly even – while they walked but now, as Steph began to make out something of the outside world appearing in the patch of light, each step seemed to be into ever increasing warmth.

Sister Adolorardah stopped and Steph came and stood beside her. Steph was not sure whether this pause was sufficient to allow her to speak but she was dumbfounded anyway. They were still just within the tunnel but Steph could see a world in front of her that she did not recognise. The sunlight was very bright and even here, in the shade of the rock, the temperature was far higher than anything she had experienced before. The landscape was rocky and grey-brown. It stretched away in a slightly undulating plane to a distant line of blue hills that seemed constantly to be moving - reshaping themselves in shimmering heat. The only vegetation she could make out was the occasional spindly bush.

*

Sister Adolorardah did not look out at the grey-brown landscape.

"Take off your rucksack," she instructed as she removed her own and rummaged within it. Steph silently did as requested, and when she turned again to Sister Adolorardah found her standing holding a jar.

"Stand still Steph, with your feet slightly apart." Steph did as she was asked and the old lady knelt down in front of her and began a sonorous and repeated chant: "With this ointment I beseech the protection of The Great Spirit." She dipped her fingers into the jar and began to spread the creamy ointment onto Steph's feet, then her lower legs, thighs and eventually her stomach. Not raising herself from her knees and not ceasing her chanting, she shuffled round behind Steph and worked up the back of her legs and over her buttocks. She then stood up and smoothed the ointment into Steph's back, shoulders and arms before moving round to do the same to her breasts and eventually her face so that Steph's entire body now glistened.

Steph had not been aware that she would be anointed in this way, but was not especially surprised at such a ritual being performed, though she felt it would have made more sense to beseech The Great Spirit's protection at the very start of the journey rather than part way through. What happened next however *did* surprise her. Sister Adolorardah, having returned the jar of balm to the rucksack turned and held out to Steph a hat. Hair *decoration* was common in Trueway but actual headwear was reserved exclusively as a mark of office or as protective ware for recognised trades and situations where it was deemed necessary. Seeing Steph's puzzlement Sister Adolorardah simply said:

"The sun."

Steph took the hat – a soft cloth thing, creased from having been squashed into Sister Adolorardah's bag. She had worn a helmet while on patrol duty so was not entirely unfamiliar with headwear, but it felt odd nonetheless to be donning this floppy bit of cloth - especially as protection against sunlight! The UV filters and climate control arrangements of Trueway meant that excessive heat and exposure to dangerous rays was not something that ever troubled Citizens.

"Sister…" began Steph but was cut short.

"No, Steph!" and then, less urgently, "later, tonight … ask your questions tonight."

Steph looked at the rocky landscape and understood why Sister Adolorardah had insisted on the boots. She too was wearing boots though she didn't have a floppy hat. She had her wimple.

*

With a hat on her head, boots on her feet, a bag on her back and a body glistening Steph followed her sparrow-like guide into the rocky, sun scorched wilderness. The route picked out by the nun avoided obvious large boulders and promontories of rock, but other than that Steph could discern no obvious path or track. She silently, trustingly followed the Good Sister. The sun, even though well past its zenith, was scorching and Steph was grateful for the little shade provided by the hat and its floppy brim. Steph wondered whether Ardah's wimple was helpful against the heat or whether it exacerbated it. Her pace definitely slowed as the day wore on. It was clear that the heat and the walking were increasingly hard for the old woman. Steph wanted to do something to help – maybe transfer some of the things from Adolorardah's rucksack to her own but she knew that to speak or try to do anything other than follow in silence would provoke rebuke and achieve nothing. Tonight, when they reached their resting place and she was no longer bound by the silence of the walk, she would suggest this.

They trudged on. Periodically Sister Adolorardah would stop and look round seemingly checking her directions. She would take a drink too from her water bottle – a signal that Steph was permitted to do the same. The rules of the pilgrimage, although prohibiting food and conversation did not restrict drinking water. The sun became lower in the sky and the light began to fade and Steph started to look round as best she could for some sign of habitation. Where, in this monotony of rocks was their night's lodging? Late afternoon gave way to twilight but Steph could see no tell-tale lights to indicate a settlement or even a single house. As twilight began to give way to darkness they stumbled on and Steph became increasingly anxious that one of them might miss their footing and be injured. As the dark shadows between the rocks began to coalesce Steph was on the point of speaking when Sister Adolorardah stopped, and in an exhausted whisper announced, "Here!" The barely discernible figure of the Good Sister then seemed to be swallowed by the dark.

*

Steph edged forward straining to see where Ardah had gone.

"Wait Steph, wait," came the disembodied voice. Then the sound of a match being struck and a pupil shrinking pinpoint of light revealed Sister Adolorardah's face as she lit a candle, and then from that, another. Steph could now see that the Good Sister was standing inside a small building almost entirely hidden amongst the rocks. Steph was beckoned inside and she found herself in a room with two beds and some rudimentary furniture. Sister Adolorardah slumped down on one of the beds. She looked very small. The black shadows cast by the candle seemed almost to swallow her.

"I thought I had missed it – got lost." Her voice was thin and distant, as if she was simply thinking aloud rather than telling this to Steph. The nun's rucksack was still on her back so Steph assumed that the candles and matches were already here. She eased her own bag off her shoulders. It was painful doing so. She had never experienced sunburn before. She placed the bag on the floor at the foot of the other bed.

"Let me help you with your bag, Sister," suggested Steph seeing that her companion seemed to have sunk into silent immobility from exhaustion. The nun looked up, her small face smiling and trusting like a child. She co-operated with Steph in getting the straps off her shoulders. Even in the poor candlelight Steph could see how red the old woman's shoulders were and how the straps had rubbed them raw.

"Is there no-one here Sister? No keeper of this pilgrim's rest?" queried Steph glancing about her into the pools of darkness. At first Adolorardah made no response and Steph was about to repeat herself when the Good Sister said:

"There is water – through there," and pointed to the far corner of the room." Steph could see a doorway. "Take a candle. There are plenty on that shelf. And take the bottles and fill them, please. Thank you, Steph. Thank you."

"I need to wash your shoulders Sister, they are red raw," advised Steph as she collected both their water bottles and lit another candle from one of those already alight. Evidently they were alone. There was no 'keeper' at this pilgrim's rest – if indeed this place had such a designation. The doorway led into a small kitchenette. There was a sink and two taps. She tried both. Only one worked.

"Let it run," called Sister Adolorardah from the adjacent room. Steph put her hand under the stream of water. It was tepid at first but then became cool. She assumed she had let it run enough so filled the water flasks. She gulped a few mouthfuls before returning and handing one of the bottles to her companion.

"Thank you." Sister Adolorardah held the vessel in both hands and took her customary small sips.

"I will see if I can find a bowl for some water, Ardah. I must bathe your shoulders."

"We are lucky," called Adolorardah as Steph rummaged in the kitchenette for a bowl. "I thought I was lost. This is the only shelter - and the only place with water. It rises under its own pressure from underground you know."

"I couldn't find any cotton wool or towels or in there," announced Steph returning and setting a bowl of water down beside the bed. "I will have to use this." She drew the blindfold from her rucksack, and having soaked it in the water, gently dabbed Sister Adolorardah's shoulders.

"Thank you, Steph. You are kind." Steph used her sitting towel to pat the old lady's shoulders dry.

"Would it be wrong Sister to use some of the anointing cream on your shoulders?" queried Steph with concern. "Even then I don't see how you can continue tomorrow with your backpack."

"You are kind, Steph," repeated Adolorardah "but we must continue. Tomorrow we will go to Yawa. My good, good sisters await us at Yawa. There is no choice but for me to carry on tomorrow – and I will need my pack – but it will be lighter. There is food in it. You should eat that Steph. Find it in the main compartment of my pack and eat it now. You will make my burden lighter for tomorrow."

"I have never heard of Yawa. Why have I never heard of it, Ardah?"

"There are many places in The Margin that you and most Citizens have not heard of," said Sister Adolorardah as Steph went to get food from the bag.

"Is that where we are – in The Margin?" asked Steph as she took things from the bag.

"Where in Trueway would the sun burn like this, child?" responded Adolorardah almost in a whisper.

Steph had guessed where they were and was really only seeking confirmation.

"So, I assume there is a convent at Yawa if there are Good Sisters there," said Steph returning with the food - but Sister Adolorardah was already asleep. Steph covered her with a blanket before eating the food as she had been instructed. When she had finished she found the 'anointing cream'. Sister Adolorardah had given her no answer about its use so Steph gently applied some to the sore shoulders of her sleeping friend.

*

It was only just getting light when Sister Adolorardah said it was time to leave. Even huddled in the thick blanket Steph had been cold and had slept only fitfully. There was no functioning toilet so they both found themselves a space outside. They washed – primarily just their faces – more to freshen themselves than get clean. Breakfast was just a little bread and water. To Steph's surprise Sister Adolorardah again initiated an anointing ceremony. Steph complied, but once it was finished, took the jar before the Good Sister could return it to her pack.

"Now you, Sister."

"But I am not the bride to be…"

"No, and this is not simply a holy tincture. My back and shoulders are sore – but not as bad as yours." Steph was surprised at the almost strident authority in her own voice and added more gently, "The tincture protects, good, Good Sister. You must have it too …Please."

The old nun neither gave or withheld her permission but simply stood in silence and allowed Steph to apply the creamy ointment. Steph applied it to her shoulders, as she had done while Adolorardah had slept, before going on to make the rest of her body glisten like her own. Thus prepared they set off in the still chilly morning on the second day of pilgrimage.

As the sun rose Steph was fearful that the roasting of the previous day would be repeated and that it would be even worse because now, they would have to walk the entire day including the hottest hours. The terrain however began to change. It was subtle at first and did not appear significant but the boulders became larger and the path more prescribed until they were walking between the high cliffs of a gorge. It was still hot, but the shadows gave protection from the sun's rays. As they walked Steph became aware that they were gradually going downhill. At first it was a gentle incline but steadily it became steeper until they were actually picking their way down a slope, and Steph could see what looked like steam rising towards them. Contrary to anything she had experienced before they seemed to be descending into clouds.

The cooling effect was immediate as the fog enveloped them but now Steph's anxiety about the heat was replaced with anxiety of losing sight of her guid. Most of the time she could keep up with the nun but occasionally a steep section of descent was followed by a more level section and Adolorardah walked off into the whiteness while Steph was still carefully picking her way down. On one such occasion Steph became so panic stricken that she almost broke the silence of the walk by crying out, but just at that moment she discerned the little silhouette, and then moments later, they were out of the fog and in the grey-green world beneath it.

This took the form of a narrow valley. Steph could not work out whether it was part of the same structure along which they had been walking when they were above the cloud, or something completely different. There was water here - a gurgling stream - but otherwise the place was silent. Steph could hear no birds or see any sign of animal life. There was grass and other foliage and a path was clearly visible following the line of the stream but the place was eerie. Now, however Steph was able to keep an even distance behind the Good Sister as she led the way.

The pace was purposeful but unhurried, and despite the weight of her pack and the soreness of her shoulders, Steph felt relaxed. The morning wore on, and she imagined what the heat would be like above the cloud layer. Periodically Sister Adolorardah would stop for them to drink water, but it was no longer the desperate quenching of thirst like it had been in the scorching sun. It must have been about mid-day when they stopped for one such break. Steph was hungry but knew that they had no food, even if it were allowed. She assumed that the pilgrims rest for this evening would be more substantial than that of the previous night, and would provide victuals. Sister Adolorardah had eaten nothing before falling asleep the night before, and it was only through Steph's insistence that she had agreed to eat some of the bread that morning.

They took off their back-packs and stood silently on the path drinking. When they had finished and safely put the bottles away Sister Adolorardah did not immediately pick up her pack. Instead she looked back up the valley in the direction from which they had come before looking at Steph with distant eyes. Without a word she then turned, went to one side of the track and hurriedly began to gather twigs, dry grass, green foliage and bits of wood into a pile. She pointed to leaves, indicating that Steph should gather them and add them to the heap that she was creating. Together they worked feverishly for about ten minutes with Steph having no idea why. The Good Sister then stopped as abruptly as she had started. She went over to her pack and returned with matches. She expertly lit the pile they had created and soon a plume of smoke was rising from it. Only then did she put on her rucksack and gesture that Steph should do the same.

Sister Adolorardah recommenced the walk along the path and Steph began to follow her, but again the nun stopped abruptly. Steph, still behind her stopped also. The nun's arms suddenly spread wide as if yanked by ropes round her wrists. Her head jerked backwards and a single word was screamed by the diminutive being – a scream so visceral that it seemed to have been wrenched from her very soul.

"Yawa!"

The sound penetrated Steph like a dagger.

"Yawa!" rang out a second time from the cruciform figure and then a third time before she lowered her arms.

She turned, came forward reached up and took Steph's face in her hands. She pulled Steph towards her and kissed her on the cheek – pushing her face into Steph with the fervour of a final kiss before turning and resuming the pilgrimage. Bewildered, Steph silently followed, leaving the billowing smoke behind them.

After about five minutes Steph became aware that there were two paths. The one following the stream was below them now and they were on one that gently sloped upwards. She had missed the point at which they diverged.

Chapter 22: Meeting

(i) "Where Am I?"

Steph began to gain some form of consciousness, a consciousness on the edge of dreaming. It was a consciousness without memory – a kind of floating, disembodied awareness. Gradually, sound and smell seeped in but there were no images behind her closed eyes. An involuntary twitch and her arm slid against the sheet. She didn't know that it was her arm but the sensation informed her that she was something greater than unanchored sentience. Her left eyelid quivered and opened a slit. There was light. Her right eye remained buried in the pillow, still in the dark. That was how she was, half in and half out of something - of somewhere.

"Hello?" The voice came from above her. She lay, unmoving. The voice was in her head – but whether *from* her head or from the world beyond her she did not know. She was not startled by the voice. It was a calm voice. It was as if it was supposed to be there, as if she had expected it – but she couldn't have.

"Hello, can you hear me?" Steph's left eye saw a movement. Gradually something came into focus – some white cloth, moving white cloth. Slowly it sank down in front of her until a face came into view above it.

"Hello," said the face, and smiled. Even sideways on and despite being barely conscious she liked this face.

The face receded until it remained atop a person sitting in a chair by the bed in which she lay.

"How do you feel?"asked the face.

Steph said nothing. She silently looked – that was all, just looked; a room, a man, a sweet smell, a gentle light, a feint, mechanical background hum. Her brain, unconsciously, started to incorporate the information. She came back to the man. He sat silent, his head, slightly to one side. She watched him – and he watched her. There was something familiar about him – a vague image recalled from her childhood – an image of times gone by that she had seen in picture books. Was this Sinbad? She felt no fear and she felt no urgency. She closed her eye. She would work out who *he* was and where *she* was in due course. Right now she just wanted to sleep a bit, but as she drifted back into nature's temporary, oblivion her brain kept asking why the brown face had blue eyes and why the body was covered in clothes.

*

She was in a garden. It was sunny. She could smell the flowers but then there was a fish floating in the air and blowing bubbles at her. It was blue. "You shouldn't be here," she said and the fish fell down onto the grass. She tried to pick it up. She knew there was a pond – just there behind her but she couldn't pick up the fish. It flipped and struggled. "I want to help you, stupid fish," she said but still it flipped and squirmed. It started to rain and Steph felt that maybe the fish would be OK if it rained enough but she herself then started to sink into the mud and soon it was over her head. She struggled and suddenly there was light and she had pushed the duvet away from her face. She could still see the blue fish in her head.

She lay still a little while the dream decayed and then, with some effort, she shuffled painfully up the bed into a sitting position. She remembered Sister Adolorardah and the sun. She looked around. There was no sign of the Good Sister but the room was familiar. She had woken up here before. There was a brown man – or was he part of a dream like the fish? There was a sweet smell. Was that the flowers? No, they were in a dream. There was a chair. That was where the brown man had sat. He had a kind voice

96

and blue eyes – blue like the fish. As sleep and dream gave way to the world around Steph became aware of how much her head was hurting. It was as if someone was tightening a vice behind her eyes. She felt slightly sick too. She went to lie down again but saw that there was a jug of water, a glass and some pills on a cabinet next to her bed. There was also a piece of paper, a note:

You will probably have a headache when you wake up. Take a couple of the pills and rest a little longer. Come out when you're ready or if you need me just shout. I will be around. Yusef.

Was 'Yusef' the brown man? If so, then he was not part of a dream – but who was he and how had she come to be here in this bed – wherever 'here' was? She looked at the blister pack of pills. It bore the name of a brand of common aspirin. The water smelled like water and a little sip did not suggest otherwise. She realised the absurdity of her caution. She had been unconscious and at this man's mercy for … well for how long? She released two pills from the foil and noticed as she did so that her thumb nail appeared bluish. Was it something about the light in the room? She didn't care. Her head hurt and her mouth felt thick and dry. In fact she had to gulp down two whole glasses of water before she could even take the tablets. With the pills taken and her thirst at least partly quenched she lay down again.

*

When she next woke she could not recall any dreams. Her headache was gone. She lay for a minute, eyes open looking at the ceiling. She was in a room, but beyond that, had no idea where she was. She remembered setting off on her journey and some of the terrain she passed through with Sister Adolorardah. Where was Sister Adolorardah? She remembered the two of them walking and that breathing was beginning to get increasingly difficult. There were some walls, ruined buildings. Sister Adolorardah in particular needed to stop and rest for longer and longer periods of time - but then it went blank. Had she fallen asleep – out there in the Margin? Had she collapsed? She didn't know. Anyway, she was here now … wherever this was.

She sat up, swung her legs out from under the duvet and sat on the edge of the bed to take a better look at her surroundings. The water was still on the bedside cabinet – in fact the jug had been refilled and the sight of it made her realise how thirsty she still felt. She filled a glass and looked round the room as she drank. As well as the bed and bedside cabinet there was a small chest of drawers, a table with a stand-up mirror and a couple of upright chairs. Her backpack was on one of them. The boots she had been wearing were underneath. There was no sign of Sister Adolorardah or *her* things. All the furniture appeared to be unpainted, pale brown wood. Lamps set into the pale grey walls gave out a uniform, soft light. The floor seemed to be made of slate but with one or two colourful rugs here and there. There appeared to be no windows. Was she in some kind of basement room? There were two doors. One was half open and she could see it was an en suite bathroom. The other was shut and presumably led into the rest of the building. She remembered the note and looked at it again:

Come out when you're ready or if you need me just shout. I will be around. Yusef.

She was still thirsty. She filled the glass again and gulped it down. She stood up. She was a bit wobbly but she steadied herself. She was no longer nauseous, and after making use of the en suite toilet and shower, felt considerably better. Her skin was still red from the sun and her shoulders sore and chafed (though probably not as bad as Sister Adolorardah's had looked at the end of that first day). She towel dried her hair but left it loose to allow the air to finish the job.

She looked round the room again. There were no clocks or screens. She checked her bag. It appeared to have everything in it that it should have. She tried her phone. The battery was flat. She had her charger but could see no electrical sockets. There was some cologne in her bag. Surely some glamorous, cardboard film star some time must have said, 'What girl needs a phone when she has cologne?' She gave herself a squirt. She felt ready to face the day … or was it night? It didn't matter, she was ready – but she hesitated. She felt too ready, too confident. She didn't know this Yusef and she didn't know what had happened to her out there in The Margin. She didn't know where Sister Adolorardah was. She didn't even know where she was herself or how she had got here. Could she still be in The Margin? Could this man Yusef be a Marginal? All the fears of Marginals that had been so deeply implanted in her from infancy came flooding back. Had she been kept alive in order to be abused, tortured, executed? She looked at the door and remained frozen to the spot as she felt her breath become shallow and her heart start to race. Her legs began trembling. She felt faint and sank down onto the bed. She sat gripping the side of the mattress until her knuckles were white.

"Slow breaths Stephanie, slow breaths." She said the words out loud. Hearing her own voice seemed to help. She breathed in deeply and held the breath a moment before letting it hiss out through her lips. A few more slow breaths and she could feel the panic starting to subside. After a couple of minutes she was breathing more regularly and her heart had stopped racing. She looked round the room – the bed, the soft lighting, the en suite, the aspirin and the note. No, she wasn't going to be tortured – well, at least it didn't seem likely given the consideration that had been shown to her so far.

"Wherever you are Steph and whoever he is you are going to have to deal with it as best you can. Keep alert. Listen and watch. Think before you speak." Again Steph had spoken out loud to herself. Speaking the words and hearing her voice somehow made her internal conversation more real – more achievable.

She stood again. She steadied herself. She was OK. She tied her boot laces together and placed the boots carefully round her neck even though it was sore. Bare feet were silent feet. She put her bag over one shoulder but the soreness made her flinch. She carried it by a strap instead. She faced the door - the door that lead out of the room - and she went forward to meet whatever was beyond.

*

She opened the door a cautious crack. She was looking down a short corridor – maybe ten metres long - with the same slate floor and the same soft lights set in grey walls like those of the room. She opened the door fully. There was another door set in the right-hand wall about a third of the way down and another set in the left-hand wall about two thirds of the way. At the end of the corridor she could see what appeared to be a balustrade overlooking what she guessed was a room – though from where she stood, all she could see of it were some lamps that appeared to be hanging from a ceiling that was out of sight.

She left the door open and slowly but steadily walked towards the balustrade. Her bare feet made no sound on the slate. She stopped when she reached the door in the right-hand wall. She pushed it gently. It didn't open and she did not try the handle. She stopped and did the same at the second door with the same outcome. She was glad they were shut. If someone were to come out behind her there was a greater chance she would hear the door opening if the person had to turn a handle.

She slowed right down as she neared the end of the corridor. She was still unable to see down into the room but she was able to look up. There was no ceiling as such and the lights, she discovered, were suspended from two thick ropes that stretched from side to side across the room. Above the ropes there just seemed to be blackness. Looking right and left she was able to see that the balustrade formed the edge of a gallery. It appeared to fully encircle the room below. She gingerly crossed the gallery until her hands were able to rest on the balustrade itself and she could look down.

Her initial impression was one of warm red and gold – such a contrast to the grey. Richly patterned carpets, a small table and several comfortable looking chairs with cushions, as sumptuously patterned as the carpets, occupied the space and there, in one of the easy chairs, reading a book was the brown faced man. He looked up and smiled.

"Hello Stephanie. How do you feel?" he said rising to his feet.

Steph was startled to hear her name being spoken by this stranger – but he had had access to her bag and so it was not really surprising. He may even have had a scanner and read her biodata.

"There's a staircase in the corner," he said pointing, "if you want to come down."

Steph walked along the gallery to her left, found a spiral staircase and cautiously went down to join her host – or was he her gaoler?

"How are you feeling?" he asked again as he came forward, his hand outstretched to greet her. "I'm Yusef."

"I'm not feeling too bad," she said shaking his hand quite formally. "The pills you left seem to have done the job. Thank you."

"My pleasure; just so long as you feel OK now. I expect that you may have lots of questions – but first, are you hungry?"

"I don't know. I wasn't until you asked. Where is Sister Adolorardah?"

The man called Yusef paused. The smile faded.

"Please, have a seat Stephanie," he said indicating an armchair just to her left and that faced the chair in which he had been sitting. She took the boots from her shoulders, bent down and placed them to the side of the chair. She tossed her hair out of her face as she stood up. She was aware of him watching her. She was aware of his gaze but carried on as casually as possible. She could see no dispenser for sitting towels so she took hers from her bag before setting her bag down by her boots. She sat down and Yusef returned to his chair. Now it was her turn to watch. He leaned forward, his forearms resting on his thighs. He looked at the floor a second before speaking as if reading in the carpet the best words to use.

"Your companion was old Stephanie," he said gravely. "The place where you were walking did not have a healthy atmosphere. You were unconscious when I found you but I'm afraid that your companion was already dead." Steph said nothing. The news was more confirmation of what she had feared than a shock. "I have her bag," said Yusef and he reached behind his chair and brought out the unmistakable bag of Sister Adolorardah. He placed it on the small table.

"And Sister Adolorardah?" asked Steph. "Where is she – her body?"

"I was alone when I found the two of you. I had to get *you* away from where you were or eventually you would have died too. I had no time, or means to bury your companion or to move her body."

"You left her?"

"Yes, Stephanie. I had no choice."

"Then we must go and retrieve her body. She has to finish the pilgrimage. I have to finish it. She must be buried …"

"Stephanie, Stephanie, slowly … slowly." Yusef slid forward off his chair so that he was kneeling in front of Steph. He moved as if to take her hands in his but she moved them back and after a barely perceptible hesitation he continued. "Maybe we can do that … maybe but now Stephanie you have to think of yourself. If I hadn't found you the chances are that you would be dead as well as your companion, the Good Sister … and there would be nobody to bury either of you or finish whatever pilgrimage it was that you were on."

Steph looked into the brown face. It was calming and reassuring. The blue eyes were like two calm pools of water. She was still thirsty.

"Could I have a glass of water, please? I drank what you left in the room. Thank you for that. I'm just very thirsty."

"Yes, of course. You are probably still dehydrated." He stood up and went over to a cabinet on one side of the room where there were glasses and a jug similar to the one that had been next to the bed. She watched him briefly before scanning the room again – now from her vantage point within it. No windows – just like the room in which she had woken up. No screens and no clocks either. There was no clue as to whether it was day or night. She let her eyes rest on Yusef as he came back with two glasses of water. He placed one on the table in front of her next to Sister Adolorardah's bag. She ignored it.

101

"Why are you wearing a …dress?" The question was out of her mouth before she could wonder whether it was a rude enquiry – or even why she was asking it.

Yusef stood in speechless surprise.

"I'm sorry," said Steph. "I didn't mean to be rude."

"There is no need to apologise," said Yusef sitting down. "I was just a bit taken aback. It seems such an odd question – and now who's the one being rude?" he smiled, "– but a person wakes up after two days in a place she …"

"Two days?" Steph cut him short; startled.

"Yes, two days – give or take a few hours. I am not certain *exactly* how long you had been unconscious before I found you."

Steph remained silent, assimilating what she was being told. She looked at the brown man. The blue eyes looked back.

"Where am I?" she eventually asked.

"At my house."

"Which is where?"

"There is no street address, no house number, no town or city as such so it is difficult to tell you simply other than to say you are within a mountain on the edge of The Margin."

"On the 'edge'? So are we just inside The Margin or just inside Trueway?"

"No, Stephanie – you misunderstand. You are just inside the *far* edge of The Margin. We are just short of The Beyond."

More silence for assimilation. Should she believe this? She glanced about her. Could this be in The Margin? Could the evil, murdering terrorists – now relatively few in number – live in anything other than makeshift squalor?

"If that is true then how come you are here? How come all this is here?" She said looking around.

"I am here because I was born here. This is here because we - my family; parents, grandparents, great grandparents and their friends - created it." He smiled, and after a couple of seconds more silence from Steph added: "While you digest that, why don't we both give our stomachs something to digest too? Your body was screaming for water when you woke up – but you have been two days without food as well. After we have eaten I can show you around a bit – if you would like that?"

"Did you get a doctor … for me I mean?"

102

"No. A doctor would have done no more than I have done. Once I had got you away from the place where you collapsed it was just a matter of giving your body time to sort itself out. I could see that you had taken a prophylactic against the worst toxin."

"A what?" asked Steph.

"A prophylactic. It's a drug to prevent infection or susceptibility to toxins. Your toenails and fingernails were blue so I knew that you had taken the prophylactic specific to the main toxin found in that area. The blue nails are a side effect of the drug once it has been triggered by the toxin." Steph looked bewildered so Yusef added, "You would have taken it twenty-four to forty-eight hours before - an injection or pill maybe?" He looked at her quizzically.

"Oh – OK … sorry carry on," said Steph as she recalled the mysterious little cylinder from which she had been told to drink by Sister Adolorardah in the pear orchard.

"You seem not to know about taking or being given any preventative medicine?"

"Sister Adolorardah did give me a tiny drink when we started out. I didn't ask what it was."

"Well, if you are not aware of a pill or injection then that was probably it. Anyway shall we have some food and then a look round?"

Steph gave an uncertain nod of agreement. She needed time to think. Two days without food. If that was true she needed to eat … even if she still wasn't sure if she was hungry. Yusef stood up and offered his hand to assist her.

"I'm fine – thank you," she said, in what she hoped was not too unkind a tone. As she stood to follow him her hair again fell forward and he noticed her shake it back off her face with a toss of her head. He fleetingly wondered why she didn't use her hand. He thought it would be easier. She picked up her sitting towel and before she could ask he said, "You can leave your bag if you want. It will be fine. There is nobody else here." She left the bag and her boots but wondered whether they really were the only people here.

"We'll go and eat in the kitchen," he said turning round and leading the way towards the right-hand corner of the room. "I have what I call a 'dining room' – He pointed to the left-hand corner of the room as they walked "…but I don't use it much. I tend to live between this room – which I call 'the atrium'," he gave an almost imperceptible pause and smile, "...my office," he indicated a door just to his left, "... my bedroom and living quarters," he pointed up to the gallery, "...and the downstairs kitchen – which is where we are now."

They entered a small square room with a wooden table in the centre. The walls were a happy yellow. A delicious smell of coffee had grown in intensity as they had walked and now she could see the filter jug from which it was emanating. A quick glance round revealed the basic kitchen necessities – sink, cooker, fridge, cupboards – and Steph even noticed a couple of cereal packets that she recognised as leading brands in Trueway.

"What do you fancy? I can offer most of what you would expect – cereal, toast, eggs?"

"Some cereal and toast would be lovely," she said and then, "So, is it breakfast time?"

"Oh yes ... Oh, please forgive me, you have no idea! Yes ...," he said glancing at his wristwatch, "... well probably 'brunch' would be more accurate. It's 10:30. I found you on Sunday evening."

Steph was invited to sit and she pulled out a heavy wooden chair from under the table. She watched as Yusef cut the bread and put it into a toaster. The toaster looked like any regular toaster that one would find in Trueway. She scanned the other fixtures and fittings. Was there anything to suggest or prove that she was in The Margin and not in Trueway? Most people in Trueway used ready sliced loaves – but unsliced loaves were available. She recognised the manufacturer name on the coffee machine. There had been one in the kitchen at home when she was a child. The cooker too was a name she recognised. If it were not for the subterranean feel this could be any kitchen in Trueway.

They remained silent while he busied himself and while she tried to think through her situation and what she should do – or even could do - other than sit and watch and wait. Having decided that she could learn no more from the kitchen's fixtures and fittings she watched her gaoler-host.

He was a slim man of average height. His bearing and broad shoulders suggesting an athletic body beneath the full length, white robe. A good-looking face with only a few lines was topped with curly black hair. She was uncertain of his age. His manner was mature but he looked quite young. She was not used to guessing a person's age from little more than their head. Fine yet strong looking hands; *a piano players hands* she thought, placed utensils, crockery and other breakfast things carefully and quietly

104

on the wooden surface. His actions were unhurried and she found herself almost hypnotised by the flow of the robe as it followed his movements. She liked watching this Sinbad. He took a jug of milk from the fridge and this broke the spell since it struck Steph as unusual to have a jug rather than a bottle of milk – but it proved nothing.

"Help yourself," he said as he placed the jug of coffee on the table.

"Thank you, it smells delicious."

"Let's hope it tastes as good. I do tend to make it rather strong!" he said jovially as the toast popped up with a 'ping' and he turned to get it. He brought the toast and sat down – then immediately got up saying "spread" – as he went to the fridge and came back with a tub. He poured coffee for both of them since Steph had not yet helped herself as he had invited. They busied themselves in silence with cereal, toast and preserves.

"So, you were here, in The Margin on a pilgrimage?" he suddenly asked - as casually as if he were addressing an old friend that he had unexpectedly encountered in town. Steph was taken aback.

"Yes, but I'd rather not ..."

"No, of course. I am sorry to have reminded you," he said assuming he had reminded her of Sister Adolorardah's death whereas in fact Steph wasn't sure what she was going to go on and say. All she knew was that she didn't want to talk about herself until she knew more about this man and about this place. His mistaken assumption had helped her.

"Thank you," she said meekly – and sipped her coffee. She wanted to ask how it was that he had come upon Sister Adolorardah and herself but again she held back. Most people, she felt sure, would have volunteered that information straight away. Why hadn't he? She would follow the advice she had given herself - to watch and listen rather than talk.

*

"If you would prefer to go back to the bedroom and have a little more rest rather than a look round then you can do," said Yusef over his shoulder as he stood washing the breakfast things. Despite Steph's remonstrations and offers to help he had insisted that she remain seated. He said she was his 'guest' – that was the word he had used – and so Steph sat watching, slightly amused at this domestic scene.

"No, a look round would be good. Thank you." She scanned the room again. There was no dishwasher. Maybe he really did live here alone and the small amount of dishwashing that needed to be done did not require one.

"You are my guest," he repeated "and I only suggested a look round to help you feel more comfortable – give you a clearer idea of where you are and help you orientate. If you are sure…?"

"Yes, really. I don't need any more rest after two days of sleeping!"

"Then, we can start with the dining room," he said coming back over to her and drying his hands on a tea towel.

Typical man, thought Steph and could hear her mother's voice saying those words.

Steph stood to follow him and picked up her sitting towel, though she would either have to nip back and put it in her bag or carry it. She paused only briefly in a moment of indecision.

"Leave that there if you want," said Yusef, "- and I'll tell you what… wait just a sec." Yusef walked off across 'the atrium' so quickly he was almost running. She went to the kitchen door in time to see him nipping up the spiral staircase. He ascended two steps at a time despite the 'dress' he was wearing and the sight reminded her that she had not yet got the answer to her question about why he was wearing it. He disappeared from view somewhere along the gallery but was quickly back and trotting down the steps carrying something.

"Here," he said, and held out a bundle of red cloth towards her. She took it, uncertain of what it was or what she was supposed to do. Was he giving her some cloth of his own to sit on instead of her sitting towel? She held the scrunched-up bundle of cloth and looked at him mystified. He chuckled.

"Here," he said, taking it back from her. "What I am wearing is called a 'thawb' – traditional Arabian clothing, not a dress as you called it – *this* is a dress" – and he held out the red bundle by one edge letting the rest fall away. Steph's heart leapt at the sight and began beating inexplicably fast. Whether one regarded this as improper clothing or an historical artefact it was beautiful – a deep red velvet that rippled and shimmered as Yusef turned it this way and that, but the beauty confused her because in it she could see the dress of her great grandmother, and at the same time, the blood of the woman she had shot. All she could do was stand and look – attracted and repulsed simultaneously.

Having shown her what it was he again proffered it. "Think of it as an 'always with you' sitting towel," he said, smiling - either blind to her confusion or misinterpreting it as incomprehension. She took it from him, hesitant and uncertain.

"Well, put it on … or is it the 'wrong' colour?" He joked – but her continued, immobility and bewilderment brought home to him just how lost Steph must be. "Here," he said and he slowly reached out and took back the dress. "Lift up your arms." Unsure what he meant she made a vague sideways movement with her hands. He smiled and draped the dress round his shoulders before cautiously reaching forward saying, "Like this." He put his open palms under her wrists. His hands were warm. He slowly raised her arms until they were above her head and she looked as if she were about to dive into a pool. He took the dress from around his shoulders, gathered it expertly and lowered it over her up stretched arms. He held the shoulder straps and let the rest of the dress fall and encircle her before lowering his hands, still holding the straps, until they met Steph's shoulders and she was standing – silent in the red dress.

*

"It suits you," he said, stepping back to look at her admiringly. Steph looked down at herself. "I wasn't sure it would fit – but it seems spot on!" He smiled broadly. "It was my great grandmother's. She must have been the same size as you. So, shall we go and have a look round?" Steph gave an uncertain nod. She felt that she should be saying something – but 'thank you' would imply that she was pleased with being dressed when in fact she wasn't sure what she felt. The dress was very lovely and reminded her of the pictures of her forbears in the old photo albums – and to that extent she liked it – even felt, unexpectedly that it gave her a kind of connection to them that she had not experienced before. On the other hand the impulse came over her in waves to simply pull it off and throw it on the floor shouting in anger at his impertinent assumption that she would be happy at being dressed up as if she were some kind of doll or shop mannequin out of a history book. Torn in both directions she remained silent and warily followed him as they began the tour.

*

"I mentioned the dining room and since it doesn't get used much we can start there and move on swiftly." She followed him out of the kitchen and then down to the right. Above her was the underside of the gallery. A little way over to her left she could see her bag and boots where she had left them. They passed the door on the right that he had said led to his office and came to the door in the corner which he pushed open. It was dark inside, but as they entered lights automatically came on to reveal a wood panelled room, not unlike the office of Mother Beneficence, though

107

instead of a desk there was a table in the centre with four chairs round it. The room immediately struck Steph as being 'cold'. The soft light and rugs on the floor seemed to be a failed attempt to give it warmth. She was not surprised that Yusef made little use of it.

"I guess you would only make use of somewhere like this if you had guests," she ventured – her tone leaving it to him to decide whether or not this was a question.

"Yes, or sometimes a meeting – though I must admit that has been pretty rare," he said in a quite matter of fact way. *So, even if there is nobody else here at the moment, he isn't a complete, 'Yusef Cruso'* she thought as they turned to head back to the office door. He did not push this one open but instead put his hand on a small glass panel that she had not noticed and said something like 'Mick'. The door opened as lights, brighter than those she had encountered so far, simultaneously came on inside.

"My office," he announced, standing to one side in order to allow her to go in first. There was no question of this room being 'warm' or 'cold', it was simply 'busy' – or was that the generous part of her nature not wanting to say that it was an 'utter mess'?

"I can see that you make use of this place," she said surveying the table strewn with papers, the chair on one side of the room unusable as such because of box files piled on it and the waste basket in the corner overflowing with screwed up bits of paper, orange peel and blackened banana skins. On the wall behind the 'box file chair' were shelves filled with books. On the other walls there were pictures in frames. They were all sizes and several were hanging at odd angles. Amidst the desk clutter however was a keyboard and a screen. She wondered whether it was stand alone or connected to the outside world.

"I could do with a cleaner," he said apologetically, "or more truthfully, not let it get in such a mess in the first place." He shrugged his shoulders as if to say, "well there you go, I've heard myself say that before!"

"Well, as long as you are happy working in it …" She left the sentence hanging and simply smiled before adding, as casually as she could, "seeing your computer there reminded me that my phone needs charging. Can I do that somewhere?"

"Yes, of course. The power supply and sockets here are compatible with Trueway."

"Oh good – I'll just go and get it … from my bag," and she turned to go back into the atrium.

"By all means … though you won't be able to make any calls. Trueway operates a transmission/reception shield for all communication devices."

"So your computer there," she pointed to the screen and keyboard, "that is not connected to the internet?"

"No, not the live internet that you know from Trueway. This machine here connects to servers that have some key content … but not the full internet and not anything live – in real time. If I want the internet, I have to go into Trueway."

"And that is something you can do?"

"Yes, if I have to … but generally I don't have any wish or need. I prefer to be here. Anyway, if you want your phone charged, then by all means get it and we can leave it here." He moved some papers on his desk to reveal a sliding cover which he pushed back exposing a standard electrical socket, before adding, "…or you can wait 'til later and we can continue the tour."

Not wishing to appear anxious or distrusting Steph agreed to charge her phone later and continue the tour.

"This way," he said, pointing to one of two doors in the far wall. She had seen them when they entered his office, but for some reason, had assumed one to be a cupboard and the other a toilet. Maybe it was because unconsciously she had assumed that the building did not extend beyond a suite of rooms encircling what Yusef had called, 'the atrium'. The door on the far side of his office was leading away from there but to where; to what? He was already walking across to it and she found herself following. What else could she do? The door opened and a corridor some twenty meters long became visible. It was narrow and the ceiling was only just above head height. Just the sight of it made her feel claustrophobic, and as she followed him she took one backward glance to the screen and keyboard and wondered if she should have put her phone on charge despite what he had said.

*

"Where are we going now?" She hoped her tone sounded inquisitive rather than apprehensive but felt no more at ease when he responded with:

"You'll see, soon enough."

There were doors all down the corridor on either side at regular intervals. She noted that they all had glass panels like the door into Yusef's office. When they reached the end of the corridor she saw that it too was a door with a glass panel. Again Yusef put his hand on the glass. She listened carefully:

"Meck."

She felt certain she had heard correctly this time. He had said, "meck" not "mick". She was sure. The door opened. The lights went on. There before her was what looked like a workshop of some kind. It was not big – about the size of a school classroom. It was longer than it was wide and she was looking down the length of the room. Three workbenches ran almost the full length from where she stood. On each bench there were items of equipment – tools, electronic gadget of some sort. She noted that there was a door in the far wall. She could see no other exits, and in keeping with everywhere else, there were no windows.

"This is my office too ... well an extension of it," he announced and she felt she detected a certain pride in his voice. "A bit neater than the other one?" He looked at her. He was beaming like a child who was showing his mother how good he could be. He looked absurdly endearing! She could not suppress a grin. "What? What are you smiling at?"

"Nothing," she said as her grin grew wider. "I guess it's just that the contrast is pretty striking." As she spoke she could feel her shoulders relaxing and she realised how tense she had been.

"The other office is my thinking office. This is my doing office."

"And the doors off the corridor?" she asked boldly.

He hesitated and looked at her thoughtfully before responding, "Done offices."

She didn't understand his answer but there was something unsettling in the pause and the word 'done' and she felt the tension returning. *Why are you showing me all these things? What is in the 'done' rooms?* was what her head was asking but her mouth maintained casual chat.

"How come your 'doing office' is so much tidier than your 'thinking office'?"

"Goodness – how many of us have 'tidy' thoughts or think in a 'tidy' way?"

"So 'doing' is a tidy process then?" she asked just to keep the conversation going and not intending that it should lead him on to anything more, but in response he quite candidly said:

"When you are making precision electrical equipment it has to be. You have to keep things tidy and clean – especially clean."

110

"And that is what you use this room for – making electrical equipment?"

"Yes, and the 'done offices' are where the stuff goes after it has been made."

"Ahh – right." Steph nodded.

"Shall we continue? There's not a lot more," and without waiting for her response he began to lead the way towards the door on the far side of the room. Beyond the door there was a spiral staircase similar to the one she had used to get down into the atrium. They ascended and she found herself on a landing that opened onto a corridor. At the far end she could see the gallery balustrade. There was only one door on one side of this corridor about halfway down and Yusef went ahead of her and pushed it open.

"And finally my living quarters," he announced, inviting her to go in ahead of him with a sweep of his hand.

The room she entered was a gently lit living space. Richly patterned rugs in russet hues covered the floor. A deep sofa and a couple of armchairs all in different styles and colours – deep blue, mauve and bottle green – scattered with bright cushions in yellow, lilac, red and white invited comfy repose. The rest of the furniture and fittings were an equal mix of unmatched styles that appeared to have been selected at random from second-hand shops – curves here, square corners there – and the whole area embraced by walls of wood-ash grey on which hung paintings in diverse frames. It was a chaos – yet, unlike Yusef's 'thinking office' it was not untidy. She liked this room. It was oddly welcoming in its quirkiness.

"Did you design all this?" She was puzzling out the contrasts between the untidy, the scrupulously ordered and this happy chaos, that on the face of it, all emanated from this one man. Whether or not he was a Marginal she found him fascinating.

"Mmmm – I suppose you could say there is some sort of 'design' – but it's really just what I managed to acquire." He followed her in. "There's a little kitchenette over here," he said leading her across the room towards a door in one corner and pushing it open so she could see. "It's handy to have somewhere up here to make coffee and stuff rather than going downstairs. The bedroom is over here," and he led the way to a door in the other corner of the same wall. "It's – en suite of course. One wouldn't want to go downstairs for that either!" A broad smile spread across his face as he pushed open the door.

She felt like a prospective house buyer, being shown round by an estate agent as she went into the bedroom – then it hit her! That was exactly what was happening. She was being shown her new home. He was not going to let her go. She was being shown everything because she wasn't leaving. He was going to keep her here.

"Why are you showing me all this?" she said taking a step backwards and making no effort to disguise the anxiety in her voice.

"Well, you are my guest. I thought you might like to see it," a look of apparent bewilderment on his face.

"Fine – and then what?"

"Well, I don't know. What would you like? It's a bit too soon for lunch."

She had no time for flippancy. "No – I'd like to go." The urgency was clear in her voice.

"Go where?" he asked calmly.

"Home – Trueway." She backed away from him but he was between her and the door. There was a table to her left with some ornaments – mostly small ceramic figures but one – a ballet dancer looked to be bronze. It was only about as tall as a beer bottle but it looked heavy. It was the best 'weapon' she could grab if she had to.

"Stephanie, please…" he said.

"Don't come any nearer," she warned, as he took a step towards her and she, trembling, edged towards the table and the figurine.

He stood still. He had seen her glance towards the little sculpture. "I don't know what I have said or what has suddenly happened but I mean you no harm Stephanie. If you want to go back to Trueway then I am happy to arrange that. I just thought you might want a bit of recovery time - and to learn a little."

He fell silent but held her gaze. She was not near enough to the little statue to get it without him intercepting her.

"Well, I think I have recovered and learnt enough," she said shakily, "so I want to go."

He took a deep breath – his eyes and the inclination of his head questioning before he spoke:

"Of course. Do you want to go now or a bit later? I would personally suggest tomorrow … but it is really up to you. I'm just sorry for whatever it is that has unsettled you all of a sudden." His tone was even. Was this a trick, she wondered - an attempt to make her relax, only to be taken off guard? "You are not in any danger from me Stephanie but if you are thinking of clubbing me with that statue when I turn my back and then making a run for it well … then you *would* be in danger … not from me but from the world up there." He pointed to the ceiling. "And, of course, that is assuming that you could find your way out."

They stood looking at each other – a silent stand-off. If they were deep in the Margin as he had said then she knew that her chance of getting back to Trueway was almost nil without his help – but it might be a chance she would have to take – better to fight and lose than simply give in … and he may be lying. They might not be in The Margin at all and he might not be a Marginal. She had no proof of either. The world 'up there' as he put it might actually be Trueway.

"Show me the outside."

"Of course," he said turning to go before adding. "You can bring the little statue if you want."

She picked it up, and almost threw it in the air with the excessive force she had used in her expectation of it being made of heavy bronze – when in fact it was made of papier-mâché! Her uncontrolled movement knocked a smaller ceramic figure of a woman to the floor. An arm broke off when it landed. Yusef didn't reappear at the door and so she left the broken ornament and went to catch up. He was almost marching away.

*

She followed him along the corridor and gallery before descending the stairs after him into the atrium. He walked towards the corner of the room diagonally opposite the kitchen.

"Wait! … Please," called Steph. She went across to where she had been sitting. She took off the red dress and put it on the table. She sat down and put on her boots then picked up her bag before returning to follow him. In the corner of the room was another door and she heard the word "Meck" as she approached. He held the door open.

"You first," she said, unwilling to let him get behind her. He went through and held the door. She entered and found herself in a small, rectangular chamber with another door in the opposite wall. The door behind her closed with a click. Yusef then opened the other door, walked through and held it for her. They were now at the bottom of another spiral staircase – but she could see that this one went up considerably further than a single floor - though how far she could not tell. From where she stood it seemed to disappear into blackness. Immediately around them was panelling similar to the walls of the rooms from which they had just come but above that the stairs ascended through the bare, grey slate. Without speaking, Yusef started the ascent. She followed.

Round and round. Up and up. Once away from the lights of the panelled area at the base, she could see that the staircase was lit at regular intervals by lamps fixed in the slate walls, but they were only sufficient to illuminate the few steps either side of them. If she looked down she could see the more brightly lit panelled base but looking up all she could see was the pale figure of Yusef in his thawb. Yusef was not going quickly but he maintained a steady pace. Gradually Steph saw that the gap between the two of them was growing. She had been carrying her rucksack by the strap but despite the soreness of her shoulders she now put it on her back. It helped a little and she tried to speed up but the stairs continued to wind upward. Soon her legs were aching and her lungs were burning.

Round and round. Up and up. Minutes passed and the gap between them grew. Yusef did not look back. Steph clutched the handrail and increasingly found herself pulling with her arm to help her legs. She wanted to call out to him to slow down. Wanted to ask how much further, but stubbornness or fear or exhaustion … or something … prevented her.

Round and round. Up and up. Every step was becoming a challenge. And she had to keep stopping which meant Yusef became ever more distant. She looked down. The lights of the base were visible as a distant dot. She looked up. She could no longer see him. She peered into the gloom. Was that him passing one of the wall lights? She wasn't sure. Maybe if she just stayed where she was he would come back – but no, there was no point in that. She would still have to continue climbing even if he did. She had to go on. Rested a little she started again, though even more slowly than before.

Round and Round. Up and up – aching, hurting. She stopped again. Her legs were trembling with the effort. Again she started upward but no longer looking either up or down - just at the steps in front of her until, all of a sudden, there were two feet and the hem of Yusef's thawb. She stopped and looked up at his impassive face. He was sitting on some kind of platform, his feet resting a couple of steps down the staircase.

"Come up and sit Stephanie," he said and shifted across to give her space. "You should have kept the dress on," said Yusef. "This platform

114

will be cold." Pathetically she fumbled in her bag for her sitting towel – and then realised it was still on the chair in the kitchen. She struggled onto the platform beside him. They sat like that in silence while Steph recovered as best she could. She dreaded the thought that she would have to go all the way back down. Maybe he had some kind of vehicle outside. Maybe he could drive her back to Trueway now so that going back down would not be necessary.

She was cold and shivery. Her legs ached and she felt nauseous again. Whatever happened she was here to see 'the outside' and despite how she felt she resolutely grabbed the hand rail and pulled herself to standing.

"Right, show me." Despite how she felt her tone was resolute. Yusef stood up.

"We're not there yet Stephanie," he said gently. "This is just a platform where we have to move across to another shaft. We're only about halfway."

She remained silent. Halfway? The same again? It was too much. She knew she couldn't do it.

She clenched her teeth determined not to cry as she sank back down shaking with exhaustion and humiliation. He sat down beside her.

"I shouldn't have allowed you to do this," he said. "You are a long way from full recovery. I knew that. You didn't. I am sorry. I obviously said something that frightened you."

(ii) "Who am I and What do I believe?"

For the third time Steph woke up in the bed in the room with grey walls. The climb back down the staircase had been slow with many stops. Yusef had taken her backpack and had needed to support her most of the way. To add to her humiliation she had had to pee as well.

She looked at the ceiling. She could do with a pee now. With effort she managed to turn onto her side – and there he was, sitting in the chair!

"Here let me help," he said coming over to her.

"I need the loo," she said slipping her legs out from under the covers and sitting on the edge of the bed. He helped her stand and walked holding her arm to the bathroom.

"I'll be OK. Thanks," she said when they got to the door. She held on to the door frame briefly after he had let go before she slowly, walked in.

115

She turned to close the door and looked at him. "How many days this time?"

"Just a few hours." He glanced at his watch, "Well, fourteen to be precise. It's now 5:00 am on Thursday." She nodded and closed the door.

*

Steph spent the remainder of that day, and a good part of the next, in bed. Yusef brought food and drink. He encouraged her to eat, but she had no appetite. What little she did consume was mainly to placate him. It was a relief when he took away the food things and left her to sleep. Her body required food and drink – she knew that – but her mind required dark and silence. Repeatedly he came with the former and repeatedly she slid back into the latter. The sleep was deep and dreamless. Three times he came to intrude on her dark silence, and three times she returned to it. At some point in this third darkness however her brain began to face the struggle that her mind wanted to avoid. She began to dream.

The darkness of a cave enveloped her but a little way off she could see light and she went towards it. The light was from the other side of a waterfall that fell like a curtain hiding what was beyond the cave mouth. She walked through the tearful screen and out into the light but there was no vista to behold – only a white fog. In vain she tried to see into or through the mist. She could see nothing. Then, as if the sun were setting behind it, the fog began to turn red and from it came a voice:

"Steph, Steph, Stephanie."

"Who?" escaped from Steph's lips as she startled into consciousness.

"It's only me, Stephanie," reassured Yusef, who had again taken up his seat by her bed. "I think you were dreaming."

"Yes," muttered a disorientated Steph.

"I'm sorry," he said. "I didn't mean to startle you. I don't know which you need more – sleep or food ... but I can only provide the latter. Do you feel like eating?" He indicated a tray that he had brought. "It is only a little porridge – but with sugar I thought it might not be too much to eat, and would help give you a little energy."

To her surprise the thought of the porridge actually appealed. She was hungry. She smiled, shuffled up into a sitting position, and for the first time, consumed his offering with pleasure. He remained silent until she had finished.

"Do you want more – either porridge or something different?"

"No, but I enjoyed that. Thank you."

116

"That's good. Maybe the sleep is doing its job and now your body will welcome more food soon," he ventured as he took the tray and empty bowl from her. "Is there anything else you want - something to read perhaps?"

"No, I will be fine, but thank you."

"In that case I will leave you to rest and maybe sleep a little more." With a smile and a nod Yusef left and she watched the white clad figure as he went. After he had closed the door she stared at it, as if trying to see through to what he was doing. She stared for a long time before whispering to herself, "It takes more than clothes to make you a Marginal." She had started to think again.

*

As always there was a jug of water and a glass on the bedside cabinet. Steph filled the glass and sat contemplatively in bed, taking little sips. She had enjoyed the porridge, and although she did not feel like reading or getting up, neither did she feel like sleeping. In fact she wanted to avoid sleep and the dreams that might come with it. The voice from the fog had reminded her of the shooting and of death, but more than that, the red mist filled her with foreboding. Beyond the mist were words – not just the ones she had heard – but other words and with words came thoughts. Already a song had started to play in her head. It was one that had been popular in Trueway and which she had heard many times during her period working at the drilling station:

An endless quest for fairy castles,
Like little clouds they fill the air,
Down on the ground the path you wander,
Doesn't lead you anywhere.
With no more thoughts of where you're going,
Or of who you used to be,
There's no-one there so you tell yourself,
With sentimental dignity:
'I have been the bird on the wire.
I've sung the drunkard's midnight song.
I've reached to take my heart's desire.
Time too short and now it's gone.
Heart ache. Heart ache. Heart ache now it's all gone wrong

– but the singer will still sing one last song'.

Was her pursuit of enhanced marriage with two children just a quest for a fairy castle? Had the reality down on the ground simply come to this – a pilgrimage that had led nowhere and which would end in heartache?

She stared at the door as she sipped her water. Who was he – this Yusef?

He was a good looking man and she found him attractive, especially when he was kind and attentive to her. She didn't want to admit that to herself. It confused her. This was a man that she doubted and who professed to be a Marginal. Despite her confusion – revulsion at herself even – her fundamental honesty would not allow her to deny the attraction she felt. In the awful circumstance of Good Sister Adolorardah's death and of being on pilgrimage in preparation for her marriage to Paul Lepton – a marriage for which she had sacrificed so much – she was here with a man that she did not trust ... and yet a man to whom she felt attracted both emotionally and sexually ... if such a distinction can be made.

Was he really a Marginal? He did not conform to everything that she had been brought up to believe about Marginals. Maybe he wasn't a Marginal at all. Maybe he was a Citizen. Maybe he was part of the pilgrimage – part of the test of her worthiness to be a wife with enhanced marriage rights.

Maybe that was what this was all about. Maybe she was being tested to see whether she could resist temptation. Maybe Sister Adolorardah wasn't dead at all but was waiting somewhere to see how Steph behaved when cut off from all her usual support.

The more Steph thought about it the more this made sense. As was customary for a bride-to-be she had stopped taking DAMP at the start of pilgrimage. So, for the first time since the onset of puberty when, like other Trueway girls, she began taking DAMP, her body was full of unsuppressed sexual hormones. Yes, this all made sense. What was happening here in this cut-off grey place was all part of pilgrimage. She was supposed to find Yusef attractive in order to prove that she could resist him and be worthy of marriage to Paul. Yes, this grey room was not in The Margin at all, it was in Trueway and Good Sister Adolorardah was not dead.

When Yusef had said that Adolorardah was dead Steph's thoughts had been instantly to retrieving her body and of arranging burial. Her thoughts
118

had even been about completing the pilgrimage. She should have been racked with grief but that had not been the case. Why? Because deep inside herself she did not believe that her aged friend was truly gone. It was all starting to make sense.

Before she knew it she was on her knees by the bedside. "I thank thee Great Spirit. I trust in thee. I will pass your test. I will. I will. I believe Great Spirit. I believe." She spoke the prayer quietly but aloud just as she had on the night of her revelation at the drilling station. On that occasion The Great Spirit had answered her prayer through her dream. The Great Spirit had been with her then and The Great Spirit was with her now. The Great Spirit was guiding her as always.

Feeling at peace she got back into bed and lay down. She no longer feared sleep. She closed her eyes and soon drifted into a silent contented nothingness - until the face of Good Sister Adolorardah pierced it from within.

The expression on the face of her revered confidante began as kindly and as comforting as ever but then the eyes widened in terror as they had when Steph had told her that the Marginal that she shot had spoken. Now the Good Sister's eyes changed again and became red rimmed as tears spilled from them to course down the creases of the time worn face. Tears fell and fell, more and more until they were running hot and wet down Steph's own cheeks and she was thrust violently into half wakefulness with the nun's anguished face still visible behind her closed eyes.

When Steph broke through the shell of dream that surrounded her she was sitting upright with her body convulsing with tears of a devastating sadness the like of which she had never felt before. Had she been anywhere else such tears would have brought forth wails of anguish but here, in this grey room, cries were choked off. Here only a low, barely audible, guttural rasp accompanied each gulped intake of breath.

Eventually the nun's face disappeared and Steph sat in still, bewildered silence. Prior to falling asleep she felt certain that she had worked everything out. Before sleep she had felt sure that she was not in The Margin, that Yusef was not a Marginal and that Good Sister Adolorardah was still alive – but now, the vision of her weeping friend's face, had wrenched tears from the depth of Steph's being. She did not know whether that meant the tears emanated from her soul or from The Great Spirit. Maybe the two things were one and the same. Of one thing she now felt certain, this dream and these tears were showing her the truth, just as her dream on station had revealed the truth that had been buried within her.

Her spiritual mother – her Ardah – would not leave her suffering in this uncertainty if she were here somewhere in league with this Yusef. She would not push this test to these lengths and make her spiritual daughter suffer this confusing uncertainty. Steph could draw only one conclusion. Good Sister Adolorardah *was* dead.

She sat a moment longer before going to the bathroom and washing her face.

*

When she returned she sat for a long time, not in bed but on the chair where Yusef would usually sit and over the back of which he had draped the red dress. If Good Sister Adolorardah was dead then did that mean that everything she thought she had worked out was wrong? Did it mean that this grey room really was in The Margin and that this man, Yusef, really was a Marginal? It all seemed so preposterous. Maybe it was possible that this was still part of the pilgrimage and that she was in Trueway and that Yusef was a Citizen and that she was still being tested … but how was she to know? All her touchstones for reality – the 'accepted' reality of Trueway on which she had grown up – were gone.

She was here, in this grey room. There was a man – Yusef. Beyond that she knew nothing. She didn't know if she was in The Margin or somewhere in Trueway. She didn't know if Yusef was a Marginal or a Citizen. She didn't really and truly know whether Sister Adolorardah was dead or alive. She didn't know whether what was happening to her was part of pilgrimage and part of her test or not. She did not know whether The Great Spirit was guiding her, punishing her or even whether The Great Spirit existed.

What was she to do? She felt she was going in circles. What was real? What was true? She felt the cold slate under her feet. That was real. She touched the chair and the red dress. They were real. She touched her leg. That was real. She pinched her skin. It hurt. That was real. At that moment she had the profound realisation that this was all that she could rely on – the here and now. This was the only reality, and in this reality her only touchstone was herself. Her truth was *the* truth.

She would stop trying to think it all through. Thinking took her in circles. She would simply 'be' and simply 'do'. Reality now is this grey room, this red dress, this man Yusef and herself. Her old self and her old world did not exist. This was the only reality. This was the only truth. She would face it head on and make decisions as and when she needed to and in line with the truth of the moment – *her* truth.

"What will be, will be," she said aloud. This would be her mantra.

(iii) "Who is He and What does he Want?"

Yusef was in the atrium. He was about to go up and see if Steph needed anything when she appeared at the gallery balustrade. She was wearing the red dress.

"Hello!" he said in a tone of pleasant surprise. "I was just about to come and see if you wanted anything. It's Friday evening and I was about to cook up something for myself."

"I *am* a bit hungry," she said as she made her way to the spiral staircase, "and more than glad I only have one floor to go down." He watched as she carefully made the descent. She took her time but her progress did not appear too effortful. The dress shimmered with each step and it was Yusef's turn to be hypnotised.

"And how are you feeling?" he asked as she came over.

"I'm feeling OK." She smiled and then, after the briefest pause, "Thank you."

"Well, I should never have allowed you to try. I knew how far it was. You didn't. I should have explained what seeing the outside would involve."

"I don't think I would have listened to any explanation – not at that moment anyway. Did you carry me down all those stairs after you found me out there?"

"No, there is a chute from my vehicle parking bay. You would probably like that. It's a bit like a helter-skelter! Sadly they don't work against gravity!" He smiled. "Something to eat then?" She nodded her assent and they repaired to the kitchen.

*

Steph picked up the papier-mâché ballet dancer. "This is very convincing!" she said smiling over to Yusef who was getting them both a drink from a cabinet in the corner of his lounge.

"Yes, the lady that made it was very skilled."

121

Steph realised that this was the first reference she had heard him make to anyone else other than the oblique reference to meetings. She wondered, in some surprise, at her own lack of curiosity about other people here, in his life. She was even more surprised by a distinct feeling of jealousy at the confirmation that she was not the centre of his world.

"Thank you," she said, taking the glass of orange juice and sitting down in the green easy chair with red cushions. "By the way," she added glancing over at the ballet dancer, "I knocked another figure onto the floor by accident. I think it broke. I'm sorry."

"Yes, don't worry. I found it. Only the arm was broken. How's the orange? Would you like some ice?"

"No, it's fine."

"Maybe, when you are fully recovered, we could indulge in a glass of wine, but 'til then ...cheers!" He lifted his own glass of orange in salute as he took a seat in the mauve chair with lilac cushions.

"That was a lovely meal. Thank you."

"Just roasted vegetables," he said dismissively.

"Yes, but not too much and not too little. I'm feeling much better but I couldn't have eaten a lot, and well, you got it just right."

"Thank you. Am I safe from attack then – in the short term, at least?" he teased.

"I'm sorry."

"No, I'm the one who should be sorry."

"As you have told me several times!" she said mockingly in jest.

"I'm sorr…"

"Stop!" she interjected. "Let's agree no more apologies either way – yes?"

He smiled and nodded. She looked at her drink and they fell silent a moment. The silence wasn't awkward. She looked at him. He wasn't going to speak. She knew he was waiting for her. She thought about how to phrase it – of a preamble - but what came out was simply:

"Who are you? And don't just say 'Yusef' and force me to drag it out of you!" She smiled. "You know what I mean."

"Yes," he nodded "and maybe showing you around was a step towards that. I don't know how much you want." He paused briefly but continued without giving her time to respond. "If I am going on about stuff you don't want to know then stop me and if there are things that you *do* want to know but that I haven't mentioned, then ask. Yes?" She nodded.

"OK, my full name is Yusef Murphy. I am an Outlander – what you would call a Marginal. My father is a biologist. His home and laboratory are some little way from here. My mother was an artist, but sadly, she is dead. She made the ballet dancer. She also painted some of the pictures you see here on the wall. That one, for example." Yusef pointed at a painting of a girl sitting on a chair. "And that one." A face in profile.

"They are very good," said Steph with honesty even though she was distracted by the uncomfortable sense of relief she had felt at realising the 'lady' who had made the ballet dancer had been Yusef's mother.

"I am a technical scientist – electronics and robotics," continued Yusef.

"Is that your job – the way that you make a living?"

"Yes, pretty much."

"So you are here in The Margin and you make stuff and sell it … where?"

"Most of it goes to Trueway and some to other places in The Margin."

"I've never seen a shop called 'Yusef's Robots' in my town or an advert for one."

"No, I use a middle-man … or more correctly a middle woman. You probably think in terms of Trueway and The Margin; of Citizens and Marginals … but there is a third group." He paused to see if she would show any sign of realising the group to which he was referring, but all she said was:

"Go on."

"The Good Sisters."

"The Good Sisters act as go-betweens for selling what you make?" She made no attempt to disguise her incredulity.

"They show no favour to Marginal or Citizen. The biodomes around the convents here in The Outlands form hubs for interaction and communication. It is where I get my groceries and such like. It is easier than travelling into Trueway proper."

"Well, it sounds a bit farfetched to me … but carry on. I think you were saying about your mother and family before I interrupted." He had guessed that she would find a lot of what he was saying difficult to believe and understand. He knew how limited and how Trueway-biased her upbringing would have been – but he continued.

"My mother was born in Trueway but she was an orphan and was brought up by The Good Sisters. They arranged the marriage between her

123

and my father. I was born here in the Outlands just as he had been and just as his parents and grandparents had been. My great-great-grandparents were born in the pre-Trueway era. They were driven out of the newly formed Trueway during the Great Expulsion. From what I understand life for those people driven into The Outlands at the time of the Great Expulsion ..."

"Sorry," interjected Steph.

"No more 'sorrys'!" said Yusef with a grin.

"No... I mean ... 'wait a sec'," said Steph only half smiling at his joke.

"Yes, I know ... please ...," and he gestured for her to ask her question.

"What's this 'Great Expulsion'? It sounds like some kind of deportation of people from Trueway."

"That's pretty much what it was. The official history of Trueway paints a picture of terrorists fleeing to the Outlands at the end of The Terror Wars as the only way to escape the victorious Trueway forces. There is some truth in that – but the official history ignores – or at best makes passing reference to thousands of people who were not terrorists but who were displaced and sent into the Outlands for any number of reasons – whether valid or bogus – to say nothing of people who lived in what became The Margin and simply didn't want to abandon their homes to move within the Trueway borders. Then there were other people with deep religious beliefs who didn't want to convert to Trueway so left of their own accord. There were even a few more 'emigrants' from Trueway when biodata started to be rolled out and legislation restricting scientific study was brought in."

Yusef fell silent. Steph sipped her orange juice, not looking at him but aware of his eyes on her. Was he looking to see whether she was believing him? She wasn't. It was preposterous - but then so much seemed preposterous.

She looked at him and calmly invited him to, "Go on."

"Well, life in The Outlands, even in the most hospitable marginal area, was extremely harsh. It wasn't just the natural conditions outside of the readily habitable and climate-controlled areas of Trueway. As you have said there were terrorist groups in the marginal areas. Those groups only had allegiance to their own members and many civilians found themselves caught between the Trueway military on one side and the terrorist militia on the other. Many completely innocent people perished in this way." He

124

looked at her and pointedly added, "– including aunts, uncles, cousins, brothers and sisters of my forbears."

Steph remained impassive.

"Anyway," he continued, diffidently "over time those who survived organised themselves into viable, interlinked communities. These, in turn, began to make links with people inside Trueway and an increasingly complex symbiotic relationship evolved – and here I am today."

"Are you a terrorist?"

"Do I look like a terrorist?"

"Are you a terrorist, Yusef?" she asked more insistently.

"No, Stephanie. I am not a terrorist. I am a scientist – electronics and robotics."

"So, what do you make? What is in those locked rooms? Weapons? Bombs?"

"No, just gadgets. Stuff that is similar to what you use on a daily basis in Trueway. In fact there are probably some things that you use or benefit from that my father or I have been involved in developing."

"So, when did your family stop being terrorists?"

"Nobody in my family has ever been a terrorist."

"Of course they have! The Margin was where terrorists fled at the end of The Terror Wars. Nobody went into The Margin unless they had to. Only the terrorists fled. Why would your ancestors run off to the Margin if they weren't terrorists? It doesn't make sense!"

"My great-great-grandparents didn't go to the Outlands because they wanted to! Have you not heard anything I've said? I know it is contrary to what you have been taught – but look around you," he gestured at the room. "This is all in what you call, 'The Margin'. Does this look like some terrorist encampment - even if such a thing would exist three or four generations on from the end of The Terror Wars! Look at me." He stretched his arms wide. "I am a Marginal. I don't have any guns or bombs or camouflage outfit! ... and neither did my forebears. They were forced out – forced out by the Trueway military under the instruction of the Trueway Government. Yes, you are right, bands of fighters – quite possibly terrorists – fled to the areas outside the Trueway border but Trueway forces evicted lots of other people – anyone they considered might be a terrorist or might have sympathies with any one of a number of disparate groups that Trueway considered might pose a threat. Nobody in my family has ever planted a bomb or killed anyone!" His voice was more shrill and loud than he intended. He tried telling himself that this was all new for her but she seemed so blinkered. He was angry.

"You know that for a fact do you?" Steph was getting angry too. "You were there all those generations ago to see?" she said getting to her feet. She was a Trueway Citizen as were her parents and forebears. She knew the facts of history.

"I wasn't – and neither were you …. so what makes you so sure you're right?"

"Because I know Trueway and I know the truth!"

"Truth? What truth? - whose truth?" They were both standing and near shouting now.

"The truth of The Great Spirit … the ultimate truth!"

"Is that the same truth that told you that you're a hero for shooting a Marginal?"

The words stilled them both – Yusef because he had not intended to utter them; Steph because she wasn't certain she had heard them.

"What did you say?"

"I'm sorry." He averted his gaze.

"You know about the shooting? All this time - and you haven't said anything."

"There seemed no need. I know your name. I can search it on the net. I can read the news. Did you really think anyone in my position wouldn't have tried checking you out?"

"Was that your restricted Marginal net or the full internet? One minute I'm believing you and the next you are keeping stuff from me and freaking me out. What is all this? What's going on? You sounded surprised when I mentioned the pilgrimage … as if you didn't know. Was that a sham as well?"

"No, that was not a 'sham'," he said turning away and going to the drinks cabinet. She watched him in silence; waited. He poured a drink – whisky maybe – into the remnants of the orange juice in his glass before continuing. "I didn't know about the pilgrimage. I had no idea that you and a Good Sister would suddenly appear here, in the Margin and when you did appear, I had no idea why you had come."

"Appeared? Appeared where? How did you know we were here? How did you find Adolorardah and me? How did you know where we were? It wasn't some lucky chance was it? How did you know? How?"

"I have robotic detectors above ground. They are programmed to alert me if anyone from Trueway comes close. They don't get a lot of use – but I keep them running. I always like to be on the safe side. It was only when you triggered them that I knew you were here and within a day's walk. The detectors triangulate and so I sat here and watched where you went…"

She felt as if he had been stalking her. It made her recoil. As if reading her thoughts he added, "…not 'watched' with a camera … just a pin point on a map where the detectors placed you."

"So what made you come out on your white charger?"

"Well, I thought I had worked out where you were going – then you went a different way … and then the pin point stopped moving." He looked at her and added with sinister implication, "And I knew where you had stopped and that you were unlikely to survive very long unless you had the right equipment."

"If you couldn't see us how would you know what equipment we had?"

"It was a guess. Like I said, people from Trueway very rarely trigger my detectors but it has happened once or twice – walkers, lost souls, Good Sisters. They rarely have equipment."

"And do you ride out and save them all?"

"I have helped one or two – but not all are lost. Some know where they are going and I leave them to it."

"So, you guessed we were in trouble and came to save us?"

"Yes."

"Pure altruism? Or were you lonely and wanting some company?"

"If you saw someone drowning, and you had a lifebelt, you would throw it to them wouldn't you? Or do you think that because I'm a – 'Marginal' - I couldn't possibly have concerns for other human beings – particularly ones from Trueway?" He paused briefly. "You needn't answer that. What you think doesn't matter. I would have thrown you the lifebelt whoever you were – and your companion, the Good Sister. But – at the risk of confirming your prejudice - it was more than altruism. My detectors can read biodata. I knew it was you and I needed to get to you while you were still alive."

She was taken aback … and had to let this sink in a second.

"So, you're telling me that you knew exactly who it was that had triggered your detectors? Did you know it was Sister Adolorardah as well?"

"No, I didn't know it was the woman you tell me was Sister Adolorardah. In fact I didn't know for certain that there was anyone with you." He paused. He could see that Steph had no idea what he was about to tell her – and almost certainly would not believe him. "Your friend, Sister Adolorardah of The Good Sisters had no biodata and it is the biodata that tells me something other than a stray dog has entered the area of my detectors. Good Sister Adolorardah was a Marginal."

Steph looked at him in silence. What he was saying was as preposterous as everything else he had said – but she could see no reason why he would make up such an absurd tale.

"I don't believe you. How could Sister Adolorardah be a Marginal? Don't try and answer. Sister Adolorardah was a Good Sister – a good woman and a good Citizen. I don't know why you want to make up such strange things." She paused to calm herself. She *needed* to keep calm; to keep in control as best she could. "So, assuming I believe you about these tracker things and that you had read my biodata - what makes me so important to you?"

Yusef had hoped that when this question had to be addressed Steph would be more receptive – more understanding, but circumstances were what they were so he said it plainly. "Because I think you were the last person to be with Safia when she was alive." He looked straight at her. She returned his gaze – motionless, impassive, uncertain. "Safia was the woman that you shot."

A name. A real name? A false name? Steph didn't know, but for the first time someone was talking about a person. She remained silent. This could be a trick.

"Can we sit down?" suggested Yusef indicating the green and mauve chairs where they had been sitting. "Would you like another drink?"

"No," was her curt response but she returned to the green chair.

"Safia was a friend of mine," he said as he sat down. "The last time I saw her was a couple of months ago. She was an artist. She brought me some pictures. We used to talk about what she had been doing. Here," he said standing up and crossing to the wall. He took down a small painting and handed it to Steph before sitting down again. "That was painted by Safia."

Steph glanced cursorily at the small, fairly abstract image of what she thought might have been a landscape with trees and a river. A part of her wanted to make the woman real … wanted to make her 'Safia' … but she did not want to be 'beguiled'. A shiver of fear also ran down her spine.

Fighting to keep her voice steady as her heart pumped furiously, she asked,

"So, its revenge – revenge you're after." She wanted to run but there was nowhere to run to. She glanced furtively about for a weapon but could see nothing – only the papier-mâché statuette.

"No, I am not seeking revenge," said Yusef calmly – apparently oblivious to her rising anxiety, "… and anyway, your shot was not the one that killed Safia was it?" He paused, seemingly seeking confirmation. She remained silent – only half hearing his question as her mind raced to think of what to do. Having not received the confirmation for which he was hoping, he continued.

"I don't know why Safia was near the drilling station where you were on patrol. I don't know anything about her movements within The Margin that day. She certainly didn't come anywhere near my detectors. I don't know why she was here or what she was doing. I wanted to speak to you because you were the last person to see her alive." Again he paused, seeming to want her to confirm that Safia had been alive, to take up the story and explain what happened, but again Steph remained silent. Yusef sat back in his chair – frustrated, uncomprehending. "I don't know what else to say. I have tried to be honest about myself – share all this with you," He gestured around. "Can you at least tell me whether she was still alive after you shot her? The reports imply that she may have been – but there is nothing explicit." He leaned forward, "Please," he implored.

"No … No," was all that Steph could say as she abruptly stood up and edged away in an effort to put distance between herself and Yusef.

Steph's denial had been due more to confusion and a wish to end the muddle of thoughts that this man was creating, than an intention to lie. He looked at her a moment after this response before slowly standing himself.

"Then, it is up to you what you do now," he sighed. "You can stay here a little longer or I can take you back to Trueway - or there is still this pilgrimage that you were taking. Again, I am willing to help if I can."

"Can I go to my room?"

Yusef shrugged – a mix of diffidence and bewilderment. "Of course," and then, as she left, "…thank you."

*

Steph's emphatic, "No", echoed round and round in Yusef's head. He felt suddenly empty. When Cummings had told him of Safia's death he had been shocked. After that he had been 'busy'. He had had questions. He had had to do research. He had had to find answers. How had Safia died? Why was she in The Margin? Why was she trying to cross by the drilling station? Why wasn't she crossing using a Pipe? All his lines of enquiry had met with the brick wall of Trueway bureaucracy and vacuous media. Even his father – a man with connections – had been able to shed no light on these questions. Only one ember of hope had remained alive. Safia had been shot twice. The girl who fired the first shot had been alone with Safia for a short period. If Safia had been alive and spoken to that girl … but no, that girl said that Safia had said nothing because she was dead. It seemed the last avenue ended in another brick wall.

*

In 'her room' Steph immediately searched for a socket cover like the one she had seen in Yusef's office and there, sure enough in the wall, she found one with a power point behind. She plugged her phone in to charge, cursing herself for not having done so sooner. She pulled off the red dress with a shudder before dropping down to sit on the floor with her back against the bed.

Gradually she regained her composure and her thinking became clearer. Had Yusef rescued her and treated her well just so that he could find out if the woman she had shot had said something before she died? If so, then what now? Now that he believed she had no information for him was there any reason for him to continue to treat her well … or even keep her alive? She crawled across to her phone. As Yusef had said, there was no signal but she made a guess at the time and set the date. She left it continuing to charge in the hope that at some point she would get somewhere where she was able to use it to text or ring someone.

What should she do now? He had offered to help her do whatever she wanted. Was that a sincere offer or just an attempt to keep her calm? Maybe she should tell him the truth – tell him that the woman he called Safia had mumbled something. Would he believe her – or think that she was just trying to buy time?

Again questions and anxiety started to crowd back in and she couldn't think. When she tried she went in circles. She was trapped. Even if Yusef dropped down dead then she was still trapped. She felt certain that putting her hand on the door panel and saying "meck" would have no effect.

Then, quite suddenly and quite paradoxically, she felt calm. She realised, *fully* realised, that every avenue she considered led her back to, 'trapped' and if there is no escape then there is no point in struggling. She stood up.

"Once the inevitable is accepted then fear disappears," she said aloud as if her voice was some wise mystic instructing her brain. Whether this was the revelation of a deep and fundamental truth or simply a means of coping didn't matter. It brought her peace.

She went and had a shower.

*

"Is there enough for two?"

Yusef turned, startled by the unexpected voice and even more startled to see Steph standing at the kitchen door. Her feet were bare, and her approach had been silent. She was wearing the red dress.

"The coffee?" she prompted.

"Yes... yes, of course. I didn't expect ... didn't hear. Yes," he stammered in mild confusion before gesturing towards a chair, "please ... anything to eat?"

"Whatever you're having ... if that's OK?" she smiled sitting down.

Steph was hungry. After showering she had stayed in 'her room', messed about with some standalone games on her phone, looked through photographs that were on it, thought about her situation, gone round in circles a few more times and come back to 'trapped' and then had eventually fallen asleep. Possibly because she was resigned to her situation, possibly because Yusef had not acted unkindly towards her, possibly because she was still not fully recovered, she had slept very soundly. When she woke she had instinctively looked to the chair. He had not been there. She had looked at her phone. It seemed that she had been left undisturbed all night. From everything she had been taught about Marginals, then to have been kept alive would only have been to meet his carnal needs, and if he had no use for her in that regard then she should now be dead - yet neither was the case. Was it possible for him to be both a Marginal and a decent person?

"Have you thought about what you want to do?" he asked as he set a mug of coffee down in front of her on the wooden table before turning to cut and put bread in the toaster.

"Does your offer still stand ... to help me?"

"Yes, of course," as he placed the cereal and preserves on the table.

131

"Then I think I will have to return to Trueway. It's Saturday now and I don't have much time."

"Time for what? I don't understand."

"The pilgrimage. It is meant to last nine days. I have to be back on the ninth day for the marriage ceremony."

"Right," he said thoughtfully sitting down – and then standing almost immediately to get milk but continuing to speak. "So, you're getting married … and this pilgrimage is something to do with that?"

"Yes. Have you never heard of the arrangements for enhanced marriage and birthing rights?"

"No, not something that interests me. Anyway, I get the idea. You had to do a pilgrimage as part of getting married. What's your fiancé's name?"

"Paul – Paul Lepkowski. We have decided to combine our names to become Mr and Mrs Lepton," she said smiling.

"That's nice," he said with some affection, "And is he doing a pilgrimage somewhere too?"

"Yes, though I don't know where." As Steph spoke she realised how little she had thought of Paul since arriving in this place.

"OK." The toaster pinged and Yusef attended to it. "So, where were you going on this pilgrimage of yours?"

"I don't know. Sister Adolorardah was charged with guiding me. I would only have known the destination when we arrived. She did say something about a place called Yawa. She said we would be going there that day and that there were some Good Sisters there. I guessed it was one of the mission convents that they have in The Margin, and that we would be staying there on our second night."

"Yawa?" said Yusef endeavouring to cover his surprise.

"Yes, do you know it?"

"Not really," he said cautiously. "Are you sure she said Yawa? Because Yawa was destroyed many, many years ago in a raid by Trueway forces. Most of the inhabitants were killed. A few children survived and were taken to orphanage convents. After that Yawa was covered in toxins by Trueway soldiers – supposedly to stop it being resettled and used as a terrorist base."

"Well, I thought that was the name. In fact I'm pretty certain," said Steph as she remembered the screams from the nun after they had made the bonfire. "It was certainly somewhere I hadn't heard of before."

"So, Yawa – or whatever place she was aiming for - was that to be the end of your pilgrimage?" asked Yusef thoughtfully.

"Oh no – like I say, I didn't know where that was and since the total pilgrimage takes nine days I would expect the outward journey to be at least four."

"And what do you think you might find out here in the Outlands if you travelled four days?" queried Yusef as he sat down once again.

"I don't know … maybe there *was* no end destination as such. Maybe it is the trust of the guide and endurance of the journey that makes the pilgrimage."

"Well you certainly trusted your guide, and followed her to her death … and almost to your own." Then, after the briefest pause and with a smile, "Does spending all this time with me qualify as the endurance element do you think?" Steph smiled too, interpreting his hesitant comment as an effort to avoid the conversation becoming too sombre, rather than flippancy. She felt quite relaxed – content almost. It seemed absurd given the tension of less than twenty-four hours before. "So, what time is your marriage due to take place … and where exactly?"

"It will be at The Convent of the Pear Orchard tomorrow at mid-day."

"Well, it sounds like your pilgrimage is nearly over then." Steph nodded and thoughtfully took a sip of her coffee before speaking.

"When you were explaining about where you found Sister Adolorardah and me, you said that you thought you knew where we were going. Where was that?"

"The only place that is out that way … but it doesn't matter."

"No, I guess it doesn't."

"Please, help yourself to cereal," he said in an attempt to deflect the conversation.

"I don't suppose I could get there now and get back to the convent in time, could I?" She looked at him for confirmation. He was spreading jam on his toast and made no response, so she continued. "If Sister Adolorardah got lost on the way to this place then there may be someone there that was expecting us. Is there a way you – I – can contact them? They need to know what has happened."

He looked up from his toast.

"I like you Stephanie," he said trying to suppress his irritation at her persistence, "but you are so locked into the Trueway fantasy that the fantasy remains more real to you than the wooden table that you are touching right now." His tone of disdain hurt her more than the words – the relevance of which she didn't understand.

"I only wanted to know whether there was someone we could contact in case they were expecting Adolorardah and me. They could have been out looking for us – and maybe putting themselves in danger." A sudden panic gripped Steph. "Oh Great Spirit, is this all part of the pilgrimage? Am I being tested? Should I have put Adolorardah and the pilgrimage before all else?" She stood up her eyes wild with panic. "We must contact the people ... tell them what's happened. Help me! Please, help me," she implored reaching across the table and grabbing his hand.

"Oh, shut up!" he exclaimed standing so abruptly that the chair fell over. "We don't need to contact anyone. Your Sister Adolorardah was taking you to your death!"

"How dare you!" retorted Steph, startled and outraged in equal measure. "Sister Adolorardah was the kindest woman. You didn't know her. How dare you! She would never have hurt me."

"Oh sit down!" he ordered. "I don't know if you are stupid or just conceited. Then again, maybe most of Trueway is conceited ... and stupid ... locked inside its bio-bubble of cosseted comfort." He turned and righted his chair. "Sit down," he said again ... and then more calmly, "Sit down Stephanie, please. Why do we always start off so well and end up like this?"

Still shaking Steph sat down.

"I think you are right Stephanie. I think Sister Adolorardah cared for you a great deal ...but people can sometimes be placed in situations where there is no way out - when the only option they have is to decide which is the least of two evils. Even though I never met her, I think she loved you - loved you more than her own life...but I think someone placed her in one of those impossible situations ... but that is just my guess. Anyway, I was so preoccupied with trying to please you and to learn from you what I hoped you could tell me of Safia's last moments that I didn't think about you, about your pilgrimage, about Sister Adolorardah ... and the whole world that you were in."

"I don't understand anything you say – or care about it," she said with sullen contempt. He ignored her.

"After Safia's death I knew that I had to try and speak with you – but how? I could get into Trueway ... but to you in a drilling station? I could see no way to do it and then, miraculously, you came to me. I didn't really question the coincidence – it was just fortune smiling – but does fortune smile at random?"

She met his question with silent indifference.

"If I say the words, 'Convent of Correction' does that mean anything to you Stephanie?"

Silence.

"OK – if I say 'prison' wha…"

"Please don't patronise me." she interrupted angrily. "I know what a prison is and yes, I have heard of Convents of Correction."

"And have you ever seen a Convent of Correction or been to one?"

"What's your point Yusef? Have I seen one? Haven't I seen one? … What's the difference? What's your point?"

"My point," he looked at her gravely, "is that I think Sister Adolorardah had been charged with taking you to a Convent of Correction and either got lost, or out of her love for you, decided that death was preferable. I am increasingly more certain that it was the latter. Her fingernails and toenails were not blue like yours. She had not taken the prophylactic. I think she knew she was walking to her death but that you stood a chance of survival if someone found you in time. She would have known it was a slim chance – but a chance." Steph was hearing the words but not taking in their meaning.

"She was taking me on pilgrimage. She was preparing me for my marriage. That's it. I am not a criminal. I was not being taken to a Convent of Correction or a prison, so if you can't help me contact anyone that may have been expecting Sister Adolorardah and myself, then the best thing you can do is help me get back to Trueway. At least then I can explain everything to the Mother Superior…" Steph faltered, "And she …"

Steph left the sentence unfinished. She looked at Yusef. How could he possibly take her back, knowing she could tell people about him – about all this?

"Yes Stephanie? What will the Mother Superior do?"

She felt the fear starting to mount once again in her stomach.

"… well, tell the people who were expecting us … that's all … just explain … maybe get Sister Adolorardah's body and take it back for burial."

"And what about me? Do you think the Mother Superior will come to take me back … or get some regulars to hunt me down? That's what you're thinking now isn't it Stephanie? You're thinking – 'how can he let me go when I know about him and all this?' "

She made no response and the cold blue eyes stared at her in menacing silence from across the table. He slowly rose to his feet, gathered the cups and plates and turned to the sink to wash them.

Her heart was pounding and a sickening fear was mounting. What to do? What to do? She looked at his back as he washed the dishes. There was a kitchen knife on the table. Kill him – but what then? If not kill him then what? Placate him? Surrender to him – accept that whether he killed her or kept her a prisoner her fate was in his hands? Yes, don't try and work out what you can't work out. While her brain had been struggling with this tangle of thoughts her body, seemingly of its own volition, had swivelled on the chair, brought her to her feet and taken her silently to stand behind him.

Surrender, give in and the struggle will stop. The uncertainty will stop. Jump to oblivion rather that teeter on the cliff edge. She looked at his thawb and at his black hair. She wanted to find the will to fight the desire to touch him, but could not. There was a voice in her head. It was her voice, and yet it sounded like someone else: *Once the inevitable is accepted then fear disappears.*

He stilled as her hand touched his back. They stood like that, him with his hands in the water and she with her hand on his back. Slowly he turned to face her and she took a small step backwards. He lifted his thawb and used it to dry his hands … but continued to gather and lift it to reveal the erection that was beginning to rise from a mass of black pubic hair. She was only aware of it in her peripheral vision since she never took her eyes from his, and they, in turn looked unblinkingly at her while he revealed his desire. There was still something of menace in those eyes – but it was not the menace of anger and contempt.

Still not looking down she reached out and placed both her hands on his firm midriff. He released the thawb and her arms continued to hold it up while he lifted the hem of the red dress and guided her backwards towards the kitchen table. He gently pushed her down onto it and parted her legs. The folds of the dress gave some protection to the small of her back where it met the table top. Bearing his weight on his hands he leaned across and kissed her softly on the mouth before separating from her just a little so that he could look at her. She laced her fingers into the hair on the back of his head and drew him back.

Slowly, their bodies moved and responded one to the other. A natural, unhurried quickening and arousal grew, enveloping them both until, at the height of their rhythmic, mutual yearning, he entered her. Despite her wetness, she gasped at the sudden penetration and grabbed him tightly as he began thrusting. Whether it was the shock of being entered or the pain from the pounding of her back on the edge of the table, her eyes suddenly sprang wide with horror as the enormity of what she was doing rushed in. Before she knew it, the knife was in her hand.

The blade sliced through the sleeve of his thawb and across his upper left arm but his right hand was round her wrist before she could deliver a second blow. He slammed her hand down so hard onto the table top that the knife span crazily away onto the floor. He deftly exchanged right hand for left around her wrist and simultaneously managed to fend off an attempted blow to his head from Steph's left fist. He grabbed the wrist of that hand, and in so doing inadvertently grabbed the dress at the same time. He pinned both wrists to the table and the dress covered Steph's face while he continued to thrust relentlessly until he exploded inside her. Her body went limp and she shuddered with sobs. He took the dress away from her tear stained face. His own eyes began to fill with tears and, as they did so she pulled him to her and forced her tongue into his mouth as insistently as he had pushed himself into her while her hips continued to squirm and push down on him. It was only moments until he was again aroused and stabbing mercilessly until he climaxed. A brief moment of his weight lying still upon her and then he was gone.

She lay still. The dress, table, her skin were covered in blood. Hers? His? She didn't know. She didn't care. The blood stained thawb was on the floor and he was at the sink tending to his arm as best he could. She felt between her legs. She was sore – but it was her lower back that hurt the most as she tried to stand. It had been repeatedly banged and rubbed against the edge of the table.

"If you had killed me then you would almost certainly have died here. I have no visitors," he announced in a matter-of-fact way as he fumbled with soap and water in an attempt to wash the cut and stop the bleeding.

"You need a bandage," she advised in an equally matter of fact way. She was aware of the incongruity of her calmness in the face of what had just taken place. Yet, what surprised and confused her more was the seemingly absurd satisfaction she felt in having made him lose control. To this point he had controlled everything – her, the situation and himself.

Maybe she even felt a perverse satisfaction that he was behaving in the way she had been brought up to believe all Marginals behaved and through this display of unbridled animal aggression was confirming her long held beliefs.

"The drawer behind you over there," he nodded, and between them they staunched the flow of blood and bandaged his wound. He then covered the bandage in a bio-plastic wrap and took her to the shower in his room upstairs. He awkwardly attempted to wash her. He was gentle and the warm water was like an embrace to both of them. His injury made his efforts cumbersome but she permitted him this as a kind of penance.

"Your back is raw – the skin …" He left his sentence unfinished.

"Whose fault is that?" she asked calmly.

I'm sorr…"

"No more 'sorrys'," she interjected, and they fell silent. She allowed him to continue his task a little longer before telling him she would do her hair and finish by herself. He got dry while she did so. He apologised that his towels were not as fluffy as they might have been while he patted dry her back. She took the towel from him, finished the process of drying and silently wrapped the towel round herself before saying, "I will go back to my room now, if that's OK?"

"Yes, of course." He stopped himself saying 'sorry'. "If you are hungry then take anything from the kitchen," he said as he followed her across the bedroom. "Or I am here if you need me." He stopped following and watched her cross the living space. As she opened the door onto the balcony he called softly, "Stephanie."

She stopped, half in and half out of the room, her hand on the doorframe, her gaze and mind not focused on anything. She did not answer. She did not look round.

"Your friend, Sister Adolorardah was true to her word. The place where I found you – the ruins - that is Yawa; all that remains of it. Maybe she is with her family, her sisters. I think she will be at peace there."

Now she lifted her head and looked at him silently across the room. They stood like that, looking at each other for how many seconds – three? four? – No more, before she quietly turned and left him alone.

She spent the rest of the day in her room and he did not come near her.

She showered again and did what she could to use the shower head as a douche but with little urgency since she felt that she would never see

138

Trueway or Paul again. She lay in silence on the bed with her eyes closed. She feared that she would be a captive here forever.

What had just happened in the kitchen? Was she responsible? Was he? Had it been mutual attraction? What had been in his head? She wasn't even sure what had been in her own. Was he filled with uncontrollable passion for her? Maybe it was some kind of revenge for Safia. Was it his way of saying, 'Trueway, pilgrimage and The Great Spirit count for nothing when I am stronger than you and can lay claim to you with this single animal act'? Maybe it was her way of accepting that her true nature was a lustful one when released from the constraints of DAMP.

All these questions swam aimlessly around in her head with no hope of finding an answer until she suddenly told herself aloud, "Don't try and think it through. You can't work it out." At the sound of her words she felt an immediate calm – no, more than that, she felt relief. She had tried to kill him. She had failed. She had tried to stop him. She had failed. She had tried to 'better herself' and obtain an enhanced marriage – and maybe now she had failed at that as well. All that struggling and all that trying could now end. Matters had been taken out of her hands and surrendering responsibility was a relief.

"What will be, will be." She spoke her new mantra aloud and opened her eyes to stare at the ceiling.

She thought about what Yusef had said. His belief that Sister Adolorardah had been charged, for some unfathomable reason, with leading the pilgrimage towards a Convent of Correction and that maybe the only way to avoid this duty was death. She thought about stories she had heard of some brides or some bridegrooms not returning from pilgrimage. She had always assumed these to be 'scare stories' but she thought about the blindfold she had seen when she and Sister Adolorardah had first entered the strange tunnel at the start of their journey. Had that belonged to a bride to be who had returned or to one who had not? It was all conjecture – but the image that she could not dislodge or deny, was of the plume of smoke rising like a desperate signal while her spiritual mother screamed the word, "Yawa" as if hoping against hope, that in the silent valley, someone would hear.

She couldn't stop herself thinking and asking unanswerable questions no matter how much she told herself the exercise was pointless, but there was one question the answer to which she *should* have known. Had Sister Adolorardah said that 'Good Sisters' or '*her* sisters' were waiting for them at Yawa? Steph knew that it was useless to keep trying to remember the *exact* words … but if only she had listened more carefully. She chastised herself in a whisper: "Talk less and listen more".

Chapter 23: Returning

"It's morning." She opened her eyes at the sound of his voice. He was there in a fresh thawb sitting once again on the chair by her bed.

"And?" she queried as she somewhat painfully propped herself up on one elbow.

"And it's your wedding day, so unless you want to exercise the bride's prerogative of being late, then we need to think about having breakfast and getting you back to Trueway."

"You have quite a bruise on your cheek," she said without moving.

"You throw quite a punch."

"How is your arm?" She asked.

"Sore … but you bandaged it well. Thank you. And you? How do you feel?" She ignored his question.

"Why would you take me back?"

"Because it is your wedding day." He spoke with a smile. He was clearly trying to keep the exchange light. She simply looked at him in questioning silence. Eventually he spoke.

"You are no danger to me Stephanie. Anyone of any significance in Trueway is already aware of me … or of people like me … out here in The Margin. Walkers and lost souls before you have gone back – often in high dudgeon determined to 'spill the beans' or to 'rectify the wrongs' or to do whatever their inner self had urged. The fact that you didn't know this should tell you everything. I'll leave you to get up while I go and put the coffee on."

*

After breakfast Steph gathered her few things. She left Sister Adolorardah's bag where Yusef had put it. She felt a strange fear of even touching it. When it was time to leave they did not go to the spiral staircase that had so exhausted her. Yusef explained that the staircase would take them to 'the outside' but would not be the best way for returning to Trueway. Instead, they went to a much shorter flight of steps through a door in his living quarters. Despite the fact that it was a much less severe climb Yusef insisted on carrying her bag.

The vehicle to which Yusef led her was in a garage within his subterranean home. The machine was unlike any she had seen before. Yusef explained that it was like an old style funicular. The small carriage in which they would ride down towards Trueway was balanced by another, empty vehicle coming up the other way. He had transport alternatives for moving about within the Margin – but for home to Trueway connection - it was this funicular 'pod'.

"We will still have to walk a bit after we get out of this at the other end," he explained, gesturing towards the pod.

She made no response. Despite all that had happened the sight of this strange vehicle gave her a cautious optimism that she was actually about to be travelling back to Trueway – and that very feeling of confidence triggered the inner voice that told her to be on her guard. *Emotion and reason are not always in harmony*. It was at that very moment – as she was about to get into the vehicle – that she saw the window. It was only a small one in a deep recess in the subterranean wall but through it she could see sky. She glanced about her and there in another wall was a door with the now familiar glass plate.

"What's through there?" she asked accusingly.

He knew there was no point in lying. He went across to the door. "Meck." He pushed it open and a shaft of blinding sunlight entered. She went across and looked out onto a dusty platform from which a trackway curved out of sight behind the rock wall to her right. Beyond that the ground sloped away down a bolder strewn hillside. On the platform itself stood a vehicle – some kind of car with seats for two people. Here, just a few short steps from his living quarters, was the outside world she had previously asked to see. She looked at him with incredulity.

"The spiral staircase … yet this door …?" Her eyes questioned him in bewilderment.

"I didn't want you to go," he said and averted his gaze.

She wanted to ask 'why?' but simply went to the funicular pod and got in.

*

So it was that they set off in a silence filled with incomprehension, distrust and shame. They remained that way, absorbed in their own thoughts and conflicts for ten minutes or more until Steph made a simple enquiry.

"How long will we be travelling?" The question and her tone were matter-of-fact. His answer was equally concise.

"About thirty minutes in the pod – then a bit more walking - about two hours, I'm afraid." He smiled apologetically - hopefully.

They returned to silence. It did not seem that a momentous conversation had started – but even if she followed her own dictum of, 'listen don't talk' there had to be something to listen to and so she asked a second question.

"Will I ever see you again?" It was not a question Yusef had expected.

"Well, no … I don't suppose so. I mean, it seems unlikely – me in The Margin and you about to get married in Trueway."

"You seem to live a very solitary life," she said and instantly followed it with, "Sorry – that was insensitive," as she thought of the death of Safia.

"That's all right – my solitude is largely of my own making."

"I am sorry though – for the loss of your friend … and for my part in that." She paused before adding, "You must hate me."

"No. You did not force her to be where she was. You shot her but you didn't kill her. Whatever – or whoever – forced her to be there was responsible for that. That's where my hate is directed." He glanced across at her and added, "…but, thank you. She didn't deserve to die and I will miss seeing her."

"Was she your lover?" Steph felt no apprehension in the forthright nature of her question.

"No, we were friends though." His tone was even.

"Had you known her a long time?"

"Not that long," he said with a reassuring smile as he felt the conversation becoming more relaxed. "I had known her a few years only. We met in Northport … It's a long story and I am sure you don't really want to know!"

"Northport? That's in Trueway. I've been there," said Steph taken aback. "What were two Marginals doing in Northport – or am I not allowed to know that?"

"Ha! Ms nosey! Safia was not a Marginal. She lived in Northport. I was visiting her and some others there … but it really is too much to go into. Really it is." He smiled to draw the subject to a close, unaware of the significance for Steph of what he had just said. Her brain reeled at the words – *Safia was not a Marginal* – and the battle between emotion and reason raged as never before. Emotion wanted to tell him everything – tell him she knew that Safia was not a Marginal, tell him of her dream, tell him that Safia had been alive and had spoken …. While reason repeated her old dictum to be wary and keep her mouth closed.

She remained silent, thinking things through. She had time. The journey was long enough to think, long enough to work out what to do and say, long enough to be sure – sure that he really was returning her to Trueway.

In the silence she pictured Safia in front of her; relived those last moments – Safia saying 'Steph' and pointing at her. What had she said? 'You tell topsy' … something like that then the gunfire and the faceless mess of blood that had been the Marginal – that had been Safia.

*

The funicular pod came to a halt and they alighted onto a small platform in an underground chamber. They began the walk that he had said would follow. It was along a dimly lit subterranean corridor wide enough for them to walk side-by-side. The whirlwind inside her had calmed. Maybe it was the eye of the storm, but she would try to use what time she had left to learn from this man whatever she could.

"I promise I won't get angry – but why did you think Sister Adolorardah was taking me to a Convent of Correction?"

He shot her a sideways glance. Considered and then said, "Trueway maintains little bubbles of itself in the Outlands. I am not sure how many there are but they are actual, physical bubbles – ecodomes. Many – possibly the majority - house Convents of Correction. Had Sister Adolorardah continued to lead you along the valley then you would have come to one such bubble – and, among other things, it has a Convent of Correction."

"I knew there were missionary convents of the Good Sisters in The Margin, but I have never heard of these 'bubbles' as you call them – but if they exist and if they contain other things besides Convents of Correction what makes you think the convent was the destination of our pilgrimage?"

Another considered glance. "I don't know. Maybe I am just a very suspicious person. Maybe you are right. Maybe there was something else in the bubble – some Trueway thing that I know nothing about - but going to Yawa and giving you a prophylactic, well I find it hard not to make a

143

connection." He stopped. He looked at her in the dim light. "When you get back to the convent for your wedding what exactly will happen?"

"Oh, well…" She had not expected this. "Ummm – well, had I arrived with Sister Adolorardah at the end of the pilgrimage then she would have taken me to the marriage antechamber where I would have put on the head wreath and waited, alone and in silent contemplation, until the appointed time. At the sound of the bell I would have walked out from there direct onto the cloister where Paul, my groom and the marriage guests would have already assembled, and the marriage would take place."

"Then do *exactly* that. Don't report to anyone. Don't do anything other than what you have just told me. I never met your Sister Adolorardah when she was alive but I think she knew the Outlands. I think she knew them very well. I think she sacrificed herself to give you a chance. It was a slim chance … but I think she knew exactly what she was doing." He took Steph by the shoulders. "After you leave me today do everything in your power to avoid being seen 'til you come out into that cloister for your marriage. Only at that point will you be safe – when people from *outside* the convent see that you are back. I know you don't understand and that you don't trust me … but people have died because of my stupidity. Please, please Stephanie, do just exactly as you have said."

He was right she did not understand but the urgency and sincerity in what he said had found its mark. They recommenced their walk along the corridor. He remained silent. She remained silent, not fully comprehending and not fully trusting … but this brown man, without prompting, had said that the woman she had shot was not a Marginal. This man was the only person … the *only* one … to unequivocally and with certainty confirm her own belief. She had to trust him now to deliver her to Trueway. She could do nothing more than walk with him and hope … but if he did deliver her to Trueway, then she would do as he advised.

They continued along the subterranean corridor for about two hours. As they walked, she noticed side branches. She wondered where they went – but she didn't ask. This was almost like the silence of the pilgrimage. They met nobody. Eventually Yusef turned into one of the side shoots. The path they walked sloped gently upward. They came to a dead end in a rocky tunnel.

"This is where we say 'goodbye'," was all that he said as he turned and handed her bag to her. She looked at him. She looked at the stone that surrounded her. Her heart raced – but whether from continuing uncertainty that this 'goodbye' was the prelude to her sudden death or her release to Trueway she didn't know. Either way this was the last time she would see him. She was accepting. It was all she could be. He looked at her and she looked at him. He embraced her and she returned his embrace. A split second when they could have kissed – but didn't.

"I wish you happiness in your marriage Stephanie," he said smiling and then, "Meck".

The solid stone seemed to dissolve, and another tunnel was revealed. He gently guided her across the threshold.

At first she thought that she was just in another part of his subterranean world, but then she saw the blindfold on the ground and she knew exactly where she was. Although stone appeared to surround her she knew that somewhere there was a way out and that this Yusef knew how to open the door.

"Was Safia your lover?" Her question was desperate as she realised that she may never see him again. He smiled.

"You asked me that already. No, you are the only Trueway Citizen with whom ..." He stopped short, maybe out of modesty or embarrassment or guilt or simply because he didn't know quite what to say – but Steph was as oblivious to his awkwardness as he was to the significance for her of the confirmation he was giving that Safia had not been a Marginal. He put his hand on the stone wall. "Meck" and Steph was surrounded by a green light, before he said, "Meck" once again and she felt warm sunlight on her back. She glanced over her shoulder and there was the convent orchard. He ushered her towards the threshold. She shuffled backwards away from his world and into her own. She stood in the orchard looking into a chasm. He stood in a chasm looking into an orchard.

"She was alive! ...She was alive! She said my name – 'Steph' ... she pointed at me and said, 'You, Steph tell topsy'.... Something like that ... and 'our med' she ..." but the chasm and the smiling brown man had disappeared and she was confronted by the impenetrable boundary wall of the orchard. Had he heard her? Made sense of what she said?

*

Mother Beneficence looked out onto the rectangle of cloister. Guests were filing in for the wedding of Paul Lepkowski and Stephanie Huntington; a wedding that only Mother Beneficence knew was not going to take place. Paul did not yet know that his beloved Stephanie had not

145

returned from her pre-marriage pilgrimage. Parents, relatives, friends – all the wedding guests – all equally unaware. It was rare – but not unheard of - that a marriage failed at this final point. The pilgrimage was the last part of the long courtship and betrothal ritual that ensured the suitability of bride and groom; of family and family. There was no way to prepare or forewarn those who had gathered. Only when Stephanie did not emerge from the bride's anteroom with the bridal crown around her head would the terrible truth be known. At first there would be disbelief, then anxious hope that it was just a delay but then, as minutes ticked by and the officiant and helpers started talking in whispers, the truth would be inescapable. Then the grief would be immense. If a betrothed did not return from pilgrimage for her wedding then she would not return at all.

Mother Beneficence left the window. It would be another ten minutes until all the guests were assembled and the bell would ring three times to herald the entrance of the bride – only there would be no bride, just the hollow fading of the bell followed by shocked silence, then anxious mutterings rather than the customary, joyous cheer at the sight of the crowned pilgrim's return. Mother Beneficence knelt and prayed. She gave thanks to The Great Spirit for giving her the strength to follow through this painful duty. For Mother Beneficence it had been genuinely painful. She had liked Stephanie. She prayed that The Great Spirit would provide the strength needed for the painful duty still to come when she would have to meet with Paul – and maybe other family members. Then, having prayed with words, she prayed with silence, her face in her hands. Maybe the silent prayer was for forgiveness. That would have been wrong – she of all people knew that – but she had liked Stephanie and wanted to shut out what she knew had befallen her … or maybe she was trying to shut out guilt. Just as it seemed the silence was unbearable the bell struck and she counted:

"One … Two … Three."

Eyes tight shut she put her hands over her ears in an attempt to block out everything, especially the awful silence that followed – but the cloister below her window erupted with cheers and shouts of joy!

In confusion she stumbled headlong to the window. There, standing in the appointed place, her wreath upon her head, was Stephanie. The guests were jubilant. The noise was deafening. Paul was beaming. Mother Beneficence looked on in disbelief and then, a fraction before she began her proud walk to Paul, Steph fleetingly turned her head to the Mother

Superior's window. It was the briefest glance but it was enough. The old nun's eyes were eloquent. Steph now knew that she had not been expected to return.

Part 2: Twelve Years

(C) Early Years

Chapter 24: Nothing and Nowhere is Perfect

Trueway was a society that had achieved a great deal – world peace and ecosystem protection being high on the list - but it was not Utopia. A little less than a year before Steph's marriage there had been a serious downturn in the world economy. Politicians were grateful that the world elections had taken place before the downturn and that their posts were secure for at least a couple of years. The World Games were coming up as well and they would surely dominate media space and distract the masses from their woes. The economic problems were fundamental however and distraction was not a long term solution.

The economic difficulties stemmed from two things – greed and incompetence. The greed was principally related to creating money that was not there and the incompetence was that of not recognising that such a position was unsustainable.

In the earliest of human days people – just like other animals - obtained what they needed *directly* from the world around them. They progressed to bartering in order to get what was not immediately available – 'you have apples I have bricks let's exchange'. Then came money – and then came credit. Trueway currency gradually became a terminology rather than a cash reality. Payments were made – whether as wages or for goods – in currency *terms* but effectively these were now credits. This notion of credits – electronic numbers - was, in itself, a prime example of money that was not there – let alone real goods such as apples or house bricks.

People with nothing but the ability to manipulate the electronic numbers could accumulate, from a digital world, as many apples and bricks as they wanted in the real world. People with nothing – possibly not even a few apples and a couple of bricks in the real world and limited ability to understand – let alone change - the numbers they were allotted in the digital world could not accumulate much at all.

Inevitably the greedy elite, with knowledge of the digits, targeted those that could be exploited – the poor without such knowledge. The elite promised to provide bricks in exchange for some digits. The poorest citizens were lured into the credit world of loans, especially mortgages, with spiralling borrowing costs that they could not meet until they didn't even have enough digits to buy an apple let alone another brick. A snowball of accumulating failure was starting to run down the economic hillside. When the snowball engulfed the banks Trueway had to use the money it had accumulated from the Citizens over the years to bail them out – taking them in part or entirety into public ownership.

Cllr Montgomery-Jones understood the roots of the financial crisis. She feared the forthcoming social consequences and also recognised the actions that would need to be taken. Richard Ronson was financially secure and reasonably well cushioned against the economic downturn. He had his own bricks and mortar. He wasn't reliant on the ups and downs of the digits. His main focus was The World Games. Yusef Murphy was outside the borders of Trueway. Certainly those, like himself, in The Outlands would be affected by events in the Trueway economy but it was the political fallout that concerned him more. Steph and Paul Lepton however were among those who had a mortgage. The process they had gone through to qualify for enhanced marriage status would help them. It provided good incomes and credit ratings which enabled them to take a fixed rate mortgage. Nevertheless their savings became stagnant as interest rates tumbled and it was their salaries alone that now had to cover repayments as well as buy everyday essentials.

*

The Games were about a week away. Ronson, having learned about Safia's disappearance, had found it increasingly difficult to focus his mind on them. Montgomery-Jones regarded the approach of The Games with a degree of tedium. Yusef considered whether he should risk making a trip to see any events. Paul was anticipating the games with eagerness but Steph barely registered their approach.

Chapter 25: The Picnic Day

Paul and Stephanie Lepton set off for a one week honeymoon by the sea immediately after the wedding ceremony. As was tradition, neither asked questions of the other regarding their experiences on pilgrimage. On the surface both were blissfully happy. They had taken the first step to achieving the family life that they both wanted. It had been a struggle but the sacrifice had been worth it. They had both invested in Trueway and now Trueway was, dutifully, repaying them. On return from honeymoon there would be a nice house in a nice area and guaranteed employment. The biggest and most important achievement however was the right to have two children. Steph felt that she had everything she wanted, everything she had dreamed of, everything she had worked for. She was being rewarded. Her belief in Trueway and The Great Spirit was being confirmed. She was certain that Paul felt the same. It was a significant achievement for both of them.

Young people born into elite families (known colloquially as 'leets') often seemed able to gain enhanced marriage rights with relative ease. For Steph and Paul however it had been a struggle – especially for Steph. Paul was not a member of the elite but he was of higher social standing than anyone in Steph's family or any of her childhood friends and neighbours. His parents had gained Enhanced Marriage 2 status and they had close relatives who were also EH2 or EH1. Paul had a sister and cousins. Steph had no siblings or even people of a similar age to herself in her extended family. Although Steph was still a child when her mother had died, Steph knew that this lack of a larger family had been a great sadness to her. It was now a huge sadness to Steph that her mother had not been able to see her daughter's wedding and be able to anticipate the gift of grandchildren.

Although their honeymoon had been short it had been an exciting week. They had each other, they were free of the constraints of DAMP and they had the prospect of the future for which they had both strived. The days were full of fun and the nights full of passion – but beneath the surface Steph could not escape the continuing dread that it was all about to come crashing down. Locked inside her head was the death of Sister Adolorardah, the eyes of Good Mother Beneficence at the window and thoughts of Yusef. These things haunted her. She had the constant fear that another disaster was round the corner waiting for her – some repercussion of recent events or even divine retribution for multiple sins. She felt completely unable to share this trepidation with her husband and so she existed as two people in one – a largely internal person of fear and a largely external person of happiness.

*

What Steph did not appreciate however was that the routines and rituals from which the fabric of Trueway was woven had gaps. Incompetence occupied those spaces. As a result of the shooting and her subsequent dream of revelation, Stephanie Huntington had gained knowledge that she should not have had, or at the very least, a *belief* that she should not hold since it ran counter to the incontrovertible Trueway version of what had occurred. She had innocently spoken of this knowledge to Chung, to The Rev Majumder and to Sister Adolorardah. Although Steph was unaware of it, The Good Sister, when interrogated by Mother Beneficence, had confessed that Stephanie Huntington believed that the person she had shot was a Citizen rather than a Marginal and that this belief stemmed from a revelation by The Great Spirit.

Mother Beneficence prayed, sought council, determined her duty and knew the way in which to carry it out. Sister Adolorardah, for whom obedience was sacred obligation as well as the route to salvation, would take Stephanie Huntington on her pre-marriage pilgrimage, but Steph would not return. That was how the system worked.

When Steph stood in her wedding crown on the edge of the cloister she was a bride-to-be and there would be a wedding in accordance with the plan for Enhanced Marriage with Two Children. That was how the system worked.

There was nothing in the system that said that this or that action should be taken for a bride-to-be who arrives when she should not. If she was there, then she was meant to be there.

There was nothing in the system to account for Sister Adolorardah. When she guided Steph to Yawa she guided her into one of Trueway's gaps of incompetence. That incompetence was The Good Sister's last thread of blind Hope; that and the possibility that someone of The Outlands – *her* Outlands - was watching or listening.

Steph did not know any of this but the look on the face of Mother Beneficence had convinced her that there was some truth in what Yusef had said - Steph was not meant to have returned from pilgrimage. During her honeymoon therefore she was in a fearful and lonely place. By the end of the week however – maybe in part as a result of her outward display of happiness – she had started to feel a little less apprehensive. She had also repeated to herself the dictum – 'what will be, will be'.

At the week's end she and Paul returned home and settled into the family sized accommodation that had been prepared for them. This crystallised in her, even more than the wedding and honeymoon, that everything associated with an Enhanced Marriage 2 was materialising as it was supposed to. When this combined with her *que sera sera* outlook she began to relax. Fear began to diminish and calm – even inner happiness – started to become dominant. She celebrated. She went to an official tattooist and took advantage of her right to have an "EM2" tattoo proclaiming her reproductive rights.

She determined that she would think less – and indeed she did think less and less - of the shooting, the convent, the death of Sister Adolorardah, Yusef, the pilgrimage and The Margin. She would banish these things from her inner world. It was as if all of them were part of a former life – a former Stephanie – and indeed they were because she was now Stephanie Lepton.

*

"Let's go for a picnic," suggested Steph at breakfast.

"But The Games start today." There was a hint at incredulity in Paul's voice.

"Yes, but nothing really happens 'til the afternoon. Even then the climax of the opening ceremony won't be 'til this evening. Most of the stuff before that is just parades, and celebrities saying how excited they are. C'mon – we can get a glide out to the woods … or the lake."

"Well…," hesitated Paul "…as long as we are back for Rubber's opening speech. He's always hilarious … and he's so, 'on the mark' with some of what he says, even though he doesn't always seem to realise it."

"OK, it's a deal," grinned Steph cheerily standing to clear the breakfast things, "I'll make some sandwiches."

Steph wasn't sure to what extent Rubber Ronson was, 'on the mark'. She found his quips a bit predictable and didn't really understand why Paul was so keen to watch him. She briefly wondered whether Paul liked that predictability and enjoyed – in a slightly condescending way - his capacity to foresee the targets and nature of the man's puns and jokes. To her, Richard Ronson came across as just another example of the people with whom she had grown up. Somehow he had been more successful and so was more affluent. Maybe she saw something of herself in him – someone who strove to emulate the elite but failed because they would never truly be elite. Maybe the thought of that scared her.

*

The picnic was a success. Steph and Paul had taken a long walk in the woods and enjoyed a paddle in the lake before sitting in the sun with the simple packed lunch that Steph had prepared. When they were back home they opened a bottle of wine, and a well pleased Steph snuggled up on the settee with Paul to watch the broadcast of the opening ceremony of The World Games. She felt content and a little sleepy. She could sip her wine and attend to as much, or as little, of the events on TV as she wished. She was happy. Paul too was happy – but, for both of them, it was more than just the happiness of having had a lovely day. The happiness of the day was a happiness that rested on the foundation of their EM2 marriage.

In years to come Steph would think of 'the picnic day' as the day that the wedding ceremony was truly complete. It somehow encapsulated all she had achieved and confirmed in her the validity of herself and her belief in Trueway – both spiritual and temporal. On that day she had not, for one second, thought of the shooting or the events of the pilgrimage. It was as if none of it had happened at all – but it had. A small, one armed ceramic figure and a red dress that she had discovered, packed at the bottom of her bag, were reminders. They were evidence, telling her that the nineteen days from shooting to marriage, with all they had contained, were real, and like it or not, she had been changed by them. She had been made more questioning. Maybe, on that 'picnic day', she should have come home and destroyed these relics – but she had not.

Chapter 26: Yusef The Muddled

Yusef Murphy was a muddle of a person. His mother was a Citizen with mainly Celtic ancestry. His father was a Marginal with substantial Arabic ancestry. His father was a scientist. His mother was an artist. Yusef, like his father, was a scientist and was driven intellectually by his work on micro robotics. He had the understanding and the skills for this. Emotionally however he was more like his mother. He would have liked to have been an artist and to have painted pictures. Unfortunately he did not have the skills for this. He could however derive great pleasure from art and would spend hours looking at paintings and sculptures and become emotionally absorbed in them and in learning about the lives of the people who made them.

Yusef had been born in The Margin and was undoubtedly a Marginal and not a Citizen but he felt he had a kind of dual nationality with rights and duties to both Trueway and The Outlands. He had no qualms in conducting his scientific work at his home laboratory in The Margin with the hope that, like his father's work, it would benefit both Marginal and Citizen alike. He was equally happy to spend time in Trueway which, as the mainstream society, had wonderful art galleries to visit and cultural events to attend.

Since he had not been born in Trueway and was not a Citizen he did not have biodata coded into his skeleton. In order to move freely in Trueway therefore he had to use micro chip based biodata. This he did by carrying a Bronofsky card. A Bronofsky card was not the same as osteodata. This did not matter for most day to day things like going through the scanner in a shop doorway. For high security situations however the checks were more thorough and only a genuine Trueway Citizen with osteodata and a pedigree could function in such a setting. This was why agents such as Safia had been so invaluable to The Alliance in obtaining information from areas that might otherwise be out of reach.

Not every Marginal had a Bronofsky card and the vast majority of people in Trueway were not even aware that such things still existed. For the vast majority of Citizens osteodata was so much a fact of life that it seemed it had always been there even though history lessons in school would have taught them that it had been preceded by chip based technology.

It was in the period immediately after The Terror Wars that this chip based technology was used while biodata was still in its infancy. It was developed at pace through the work of two scientists – Henry Malowics and Petra Bronofsky. Initially Trueway Citizens were issued with identity cards that contained basic bio information. After this came implanted micro chips and then finally the technology was developed to allow fully transmittable biodata to be encoded into a neonate's bones. The implants and the identity cards contained pretty much the same level of information as each other but the osteodata was far more sophisticated and individuals could opt for different levels of activation. Newborn babies were activated at the basic level but could increase the level of functionality when they were older.

Although a pioneer in the development of this technology, Petra Bronofsky became increasingly ill at ease. She was concerned about the move towards osteodata, especially the ethics of implanting babies with code, and so she left Trueway for a life in The Margin. When she departed she took with her a stash of biodata micro chips and cards. This became known as The Bronofsky Legacy since it provided Marginal people – or at least some Marginal people – with false Citizen Identities and the means to function within Trueway. It was the foundation for the covert movement to unite the people of The Outlands with the people of Trueway known as The Trueway-Marginal Alliance – or simply *The Alliance*.

For someone like Yusef, becoming involved with The Alliance seemed a natural thing to do. He was operating in both worlds out of choice anyway, and was fully familiar and confident in both locations. Possibly that familiarity and confidence made him careless and one day, not long after his mother had moved back to Trueway, he had come across to visit Safia. He inadvertently dropped his Bronofsky card in a public place. The card was seen and recognised by a member of Trueway security, forcing Yusef to flee. He sought refuge with his mother, and in assisting him in his escape, she fell and died. After this he became very reluctant to enter Trueway and retreated to The Margin and his work. The death of Safia and his encounter with Steph had now convulsed his peace like an earthquake.

He had heard some of the words that Steph had called as the Pipe closed. Initially he puzzled over them but soon dismissed the idea that Safia could have known Steph's name. He concluded that Steph had misheard, either because of her own stressed state or the difficulty in a dying woman trying to speak. The same may well have been true of the word 'topsy'. It was certainly a word to which he could attach no meaning. The one thing he had derived from Steph's words was some comfort in the knowledge that the bullet from Steph's gun had not been the one that had finally killed his friend.

The rational scientist part of him said that he had done all that he could to establish what had led Safia to her death, but the emotional artist part of him would not allow this without a struggle. In particular he found that his thoughts returned again and again to Steph and the fact that he wanted to see her. Despite the short amount of time she had spent in his subterranean home, and despite the tension between them, the place was empty without her. He thought again and again about taking his Bronofsky card and going in search of her … but he knew that he would not do that. It was a long time before he was able to genuinely settle to working on the development of his 'mini-drones' – sophisticated, programmable miniature drones. He had to perfect these before he could go on to make them smaller and so develop his 'micro-drones'.

Chapter 27: Ronson and the Basis of Fear

Prior to the news of Safia's disappearance Ronson had been very much looking forward to The Games. He had ensured his central role in the opening ceremony and had pretty much worked out how he was going to utilise that to enhance his popularity with both the masses of Trueway and the influential elite. The disappearance of 'Saffie' however had made him wonder whether there was something, or someone, that he had misjudged – and whether he was now being watched with malevolent intent.

From the outset Ronson had not been entirely comfortable with Bloombridge's proposal for 'private viewings'. He trusted Bloombridge but had nevertheless gone over and over the proposal in his mind to make sure that there was nothing that could lead him into trouble. It was only after considerable deliberation that he eventually convinced himself that he was safe and agreed to host them.

The 'private viewings' were not illegal if all that happened was a client looking at art and talking to the artist before making a purchase. But Ronson knew full well that more occurred at a 'private viewing' than that – and that what occurred *was* illegal … and that that illegal activity took place at his house. Even if it couldn't be proved that he knew such activity was occurring he was implicated. It would be a scandal. His ambitions could be dashed. The fact that Chrissie had appeared so calm when she had told him of Safia's disappearance suggested to him that he was overreacting. Nevertheless, he once again, found himself going over and over the arrangement to convince himself that he was not in any danger.

He had been careful, and up to this point, had felt sure that there was nothing illegal to which he could be linked and no scandal to which he could be subjected. Chrissie identified the girls. He could not be directly linked to that. Bloombridge identified clients in the elite who were interested in art and for whom private viewings could be arranged. There was nothing illegal in that. His house was between where Bloombridge lived and Mrs Christina's Gallery – so providing a very plausible explanation as to why he was hosting such viewings. He had not been greedy. He had not received any money. The advantage to him in being a host was that it developed his relationships and links with the elite. He regularly took DAMP and had never sought any favours for himself from the artists so he was not in danger for having personally transgressed any sexual laws. There was no coercion of the girls by Mrs Christina and any money the artist received was for the sale of her art. Everyone was happy and nobody was in any danger – least of all the elite because, in addition to the 'cover story' of purchasing art, their location was generally unknown to anyone else due to the 'blind spot' nature of Ronson's house.

He went over all this again and again in his mind. Again and again he told himself that everything was all right … and yet he couldn't rid himself of his uneasy feeling that Safia's disappearance was more than a tragic boating accident and that he was in the path of danger.

He rotated the whisky glass repeatedly as his brain tried to identify different explanations for Safia's disappearance - and the possible ramifications for himself. Scenario 1: It was just as Chrissie had been told by the PETS. She went on a painting trip, got into difficulties and drowned. If that were the case then there *really* should be no implications for him. Scenario 2: She tried to blackmail an elite client and that client removed the danger by removing her. That could definitely have implications - certainly for Bloombridge and then, by association, himself. He had provided the biodata 'blind spot' for their liaisons. It would not be unreasonable for such a client to assume that Safia and Ronson were in collusion. If such an elite client had seen fit to eliminate Safia there was no reason why he would not arrange elimination of Richard Ronson. At the very least a powerful elite could block any further career development for him. Scenario 3: Was there a scenario 3? He felt sure there must be but scenario 2 was as bad as it could get and so there was no point in thinking any further.

From discussion with Chrissie, Ronson didn't see Safia as the sort of girl who would try blackmail. There was nothing greedy about her but he couldn't think of a scenario 3. So, if he was in danger then all he could think of was something along the lines of scenario 2 and that led him back to the elite clients … and that led him to having to face what really lay at the bottom of his fear. Safia had only had one client – and Ronson didn't know who it was. Ronson's potential nemesis was faceless and nameless. This should not have been the case – but it was, and he was largely to blame for his predicament.

Bloombridge had been responsible for identifying the elite clientele but Bloombridge had always shared who they were with Chrissie and himself. This transparency had been a cornerstone of the arrangement. Everyone had to be comfortable and confident since everyone was reliant on the confidentiality of everything that happened in order to remain safe. The situation was one of co-dependency. Short of there being an 'undercover agent' the arrangement appeared to be foolproof. There were no loopholes. Ronson, however had allowed a loophole to develop – and his present predicament – and possibly even Safia's death – was the result.

Bloombridge had said that there was a client who wanted a private viewing with Safia Philips. Bloombridge claimed that the client would pay well and that he was someone for whom Bloombridge could vouch completely. The client was totally trustworthy – but the client insisted that only he, Bloombridge, be aware of his identity. Ronson knew at the time that it was a risk, but in order to ingratiate himself with Bloombridge and hopefully through him other significant members of the elite, he had agreed to this deviation from the standard protocol. If this client was so concerned about remaining anonymous he was, presumably, someone well known. Could it be that Safia recognised him, and even without any attempted blackmail, the client felt that any risk to himself needed to be eliminated and so arranged her murder?

Was Chrissie calm because she didn't recognise all this? Had Bloombridge not contacted him because he knew from the elite client that Ronson was to be eliminated as well so didn't want to be too closely associated with him? This muddle of confused, irresolvable thoughts swirled in Ronson's head like the ice and whisky in his rotating glass. He could see no action that he could take to allay his fears. He had the opening speech of The Games coming up but he felt so churned up that he considered withdrawing and saying he was ill but he knew that fundamentally this would change nothing. He concluded that his best option was to try to overcome his anxiety and see things through – but even as he told himself this he knew that he would be constantly looking over his shoulder – and not just metaphorically. He therefore decided that he would remain at home. He would not go out and place himself in any situation of danger. He would keep doors and windows locked. He would have groceries delivered and left outside. This would be his strategy – at least until after The Games had started and he had completed his integral part in them.

It may have seemed a good strategy – but The Games were still several weeks away when Mrs Christina had given him the news of Safia's disappearance. It is possible to hide away from what is outside … but not from what is inside. Ronson was guarding himself from what he perceived as the dangers of the world outside his house but opening himself blindly to the demons of the world inside his head. Maybe, if Bloombridge had contacted him with a request for another private viewing, then that would have been a reassuring signal that his fears were ill founded. Maybe that was what he hoped when he hid himself away. He may then have relaxed more, but Bloombridge did not contact him, and with each passing day, his anxiety grew.

Chapter 28: Montgomery-Jones' Brick

"Can I ask you something Ma'am?"

Montgomery-Jones looked quizzically at Cummings.

"The brick Ma'am," he indicated the brick on her desk, "why?"

"Bricks are real." The quizzical look did not fade from her secretary's face so she elaborated. "It reminds me never to lose touch with what is real; what is true. Take the media for example. The mainstream media provided plenty of information which, on the surface, could not be accused of being 'fake' or 'biased'. The topics are real enough and two or more sides of a debate are always given – but the debates covered are always selected – and arguably *selective*. What did you hear about this morning?"

"The Games Ma'am."

"Exactly. Not much about the economy today is there? The coverage is balanced but it's not a true reflection of what is happening in the world. Speaking of *True Reflections* they invented words for this kind of thing. It's not *dis*information exactly so they label the more comical coverage '*entertain*amation' and the more sinister '*Confuse*amation'."

159

Chapter 29: Paul, Steph - and 'Trigger' Ronson

Paul Lepton had never taken any notice of the media outlet called *True Reflections*. Paul was quite happy with the regular Trueway newsfeeds. When he settled down on the settee with Steph to watch the opening ceremony of The World Games he knew he was going to enjoy what he was watching. The only things on which he had to speculate were what new splendours and extravagances would have been thought up to be lavishly proffered to delight the Citizens of Trueway. The fireworks, the music, the dancing, the parades and theatrical drama, so tediously predictable in Steph's mind's eye, were anticipated as bigger, better and more startling in his. As the two of them sat on the settee sipping wine their differing expectations were simultaneously confirmed by the identical images they were watching. All of that changed however when Richard 'Rubber' Ronson took to the stage at the climax of proceedings.

Maybe, if Ronson had been forced to carry on as usual after hearing about Safia's disappearance in the way that Steph had been compelled to go on her honeymoon after the realisation that she had been expected to die on pilgrimage, his anxiety might not have festered. As it was, by the time reclusive Ronson came to give his opening speech, he was in a state of heightened paranoia.

Initially there was silence – a terrified silence from Ronson and an anticipatory silence from both the people present and people watching around the world. Paul and Steph, as was probably the case with many others, assumed that his prolonged quiet was an intentional creation of tension to act as a foil that would enhance the impact of Ronson's first words – but, for too long, the first words didn't come. The silence continued and Ronson looked panic stricken. Eventually he found his voice but by this time anticipation in the audience was turning to discomfort and puzzlement. Ronson stumbled on but was muddled and incoherent. Jokes fell flat. There was absolutely no enthusiasm or conviction either in his words or his demeanour. It looked at one point as if officials were going to intervene and bring him off the stage but they didn't need to – Ronson left of his own accord amidst boos and cries of derision from the crowd. He had not completed his allotted time or delivered any concluding remark. He just left. It seemed that nobody associated with the broadcast or event knew quite what to do.

For a couple of seconds Steph sat agog. One part of her wanted to burst out laughing – with a kind of delirious delight that something startlingly unexpected had occurred – while another part of her, despite her dislike of the man, almost wanted to cry for Richard Ronson. She was about to turn to Paul but suddenly he sprang to his feet screaming furiously at the television:

"What in the fuck! What in the name of fucking fuck?" His wine glass was in his hand and wine splashed over Steph as he gesticulated. She recoiled – more to avoid the splashing than out of any immediate fear of this, never before witnessed, anger. She thought for a moment that Paul was going to hurl the glass at the TV but his outburst stopped as abruptly as it had started and he placed the glass onto the table as he walked from the room saying, "Sorry, Steph, sorry," but not looking at her.

"But …," she began. He stopped at the door and looked at her.

"I'm sorry."

"Ronson was odd … I know." Her voice was shaking, "… but … but … so angry … why?"

"I don't know. I'm sorry." He was calm now. "It's late. I'm going to bed. I think I must be tired. It's been a long day." He came over to her. "I'm sorry – I must have scared the living daylights out of you … and you're dripping with wine!" They giggled and hugged in a release of tension. "Anyway, I think I really do need to go to bed. You coming?"

"I'll follow in a sec. I just want to wipe the rug – lucky it was white wine. You go ahead. I'll be there in just a bit." He smiled, nodded and left her as she took the glasses to the kitchen. She washed the few drops of wine from her skin and dried herself before returning to sponge the rug. She then intended going to bed, but when she reached the bedroom door she could hear Paul snoring. She went back to the kitchen, took her glass, emptied the last of the wine into it and returned to flop down on the settee.

She had never seen Paul lose his temper. That, in itself, was a shock – but the trigger for his outburst seemed absurd. Throughout their courtship they had both been taking DAMP. They had both stopped taking this in readiness for their marriage and honeymoon. This might explain Paul succumbing to an outburst – but the apparent trigger for his loss of control she could not explain – and this disturbed her. Puzzlement, disappointment – even irritation at Ronson would have been proportionate but what she had witnessed was not. She began to question who she had married and who was the 'real' Paul – the one who took DAMP (if indeed it was the drug that had been a control on his pre-marriage behaviour) or the one she had just seen – and which one was she in love with?

His loss of control led her to think of Yusef and the incident in the kitchen. Fury had raged in both herself and in Yusef. Was that rage any more or any less understandable than what she had just witnessed? Although Paul's venom had been directed harmlessly – pathetically – at an image on a TV screen what if the day came when it was directed at her? She had not voluntarily gone into her relationship with Yusef. No blame or guilt could be attached to her for difficulties that occurred in a relationship that she did not instigate – or to which she had even been invited to agree. With Paul, on the other hand she had willingly gone into the relationship – pursued it and the goal of enhanced marriage. What if she had made a huge mistake? It would be her fault. She had chosen this path – or had she? Would she have taken this path if she had not believed that it was what her mother would have wanted? And would she have followed it so doggedly if her mother had not died? She looked at the glass in her hand. It was empty. She told herself she wasn't thinking straight and that it was time to go to bed.

Chapter 30: The Failed Games

"The Rubber's Perished" and "Rubbish Rubber Ronson" were typical of the headlines that followed his opening speech. They seemed to be a portent for The Games themselves which were regarded as lacklustre at best. They had been so keenly anticipated, so eagerly awaited and yet, somehow, this time The Games didn't live up to the hype and expectation. Richard 'Rubber' Ronson instead of being seen as the sparkling, bouncing 'bringer of the best games ever' found himself associated with what the media termed, 'The Failed Games' … and in the eyes of many, possibly because of the lack of enthusiasm, commitment or cohesion in his keynote speech, Richard Ronson was even regarded as the *cause* of the failure. He was seen to have set the tone – a bad tone – and participants (both competitors and spectators) responded accordingly.

Rationally a single person and a single speech cannot be blamed for the failure of a worldwide event but the truth of why The Games failed was anyone's guess and everyone came up with their own explanations. The economic situation was high on the agenda but other, more conspiratorial notions, filtered in such as clandestine interference by Marginals. The truth was probably not known by anyone. Possibly it was simply 'one of those things' … but people always want an explanation – an answer to the question 'why?'. In the absence of consensus on a rational answer Ronson became the scapegoat. Why Ronson's opening speech had been so poor was also hotly debated – for a day or two at least - and that debate came to no conclusion either despite a variety of explanations being postulated. Only one person knew the answer – and that was Richard Ronson. He knew that you can't bounce when you fear there is a gun at your head – and that was how Ronson felt.

As soon as his duties for The Games were over he disappeared from public view. The media tried to pester him for a while but soon turned their attention elsewhere. At first he was very scared. He feared that some hostile creature was lying in wait for him around every corner, but as the days – and then weeks – wore on with no harm having come to him his fear turned to self pity.

Self-pity had been a common feature of his childhood. It stemmed from his failures – particularly his failure to be liked. When he was growing up he always felt there were other children who were liked more than him who were, in some way 'better' than him – in his family, at school, in sports, in his efforts at romance – there was always someone smarter, always someone more popular, always someone better looking, always someone more talented.

He worked hard and he was polite and he did his best but he never seemed to get the reward he thought he deserved. If he couldn't get success and reward then he could at least get attention and at home he became the naughty one and at school the class clown. The clowning had been good. It seemed to be the thing he did best and somehow – for a while at least - it seemed to work. However, he was never able to get accepted by those in the groups to which he aspired. Then, an incident in his early teens changed things.

A party of youths with whom he was loosely associated were baiting another boy in the school playground. The subject of their mockery was a lad who was regarded as a bit 'odd'. He was very much a loner – far more an outsider than Ronson who could at least tag along with the crowd. A few girls were watching and Ronson did much the same. The bullying was not severe and was over quite quickly. The crowd moved off in search of some other distraction, and Ronson set off with them but almost fell on his face as he tripped over a loose lace on his boot. He knelt down to tie it. He stood up with the intention of running to catch up with the gang but, as he did so, saw that 'the loner' was sitting immobile on the playground. He was so still, that at first, Ronson thought that maybe the group had done more than tease the boy and possibly he had been hit and injured.

All round the playground there were children running, walking, standing, chatting, laughing but nobody was coming anywhere near this seated figure or paying him any attention. It was as if he didn't exist. A girl chasing her friend almost fell over him before skirting round and continuing her pursuit. The boy turned his head slightly to watch her go before returning his gaze to the ground. Ronson concluded that he wasn't seriously injured – if in fact he was physically hurt at all – and was about to go, but realised he could no longer see the group that he had been with. He looked back at the solitary sitter, and inexplicably, simply went and sat down next to him.

Ronson didn't know the boy. He didn't even know his name. He had never wanted to know his name. He had never wanted to be associated with him. This lad wasn't anyone to seek out as a friend. Ronson had nothing to say to the boy and had no idea why he had walked across and sat down. He was about to stand up and go when the boy said, "Why were they calling me 'Margie'?"

Ronson looked at him. The boy just continued to look at the ground. Ronson wasn't sure if the question had been directed at him or whether the boy was simply musing aloud. The term 'Margie' – short for 'Marginal' - was a common insult. Ronson wasn't sure if the boy was asking what 'Margie' meant or why it was being directed at him. Ronson hesitated – unsure whether to make any response or just get up and go when the boy spoke again.

"I told them how many bricks there were in that wall and they started calling me 'Margie'. Do you know how many bricks there are in that wall?"

Ronson looked towards the wall of the school gymnasium that flanked the playground. There were no windows in it. It was a high rectangle of uninterrupted brick. Again, Ronson didn't answer so taken aback was he by this seemingly absurd question – but he was starting to see why this boy was regarded as a bit odd and why he came in for taunting.

Before Ronson could either answer or get up and go the boy spoke once more. "There are nine thousand, eight hundred exactly – though in making that calculation I have counted the half bricks at the end as halves and then added the halves together to count them as whole bricks. In fact they are whole bricks because the bricks that look like half bricks are all at the end of the wall and are really whole bricks endways on with their 'whole' sides running down the wall that joins at right angles to the one we are looking at. I thought for quite a while about whether I should count them as whole or half and decided on half since that was the visual impression. Someone else might have done it the other way."

If, at that point, Ronson had said anything it would probably have been something along the lines of, "I don't think most people would have counted the bricks at all" but, before he could speak the boy had stood up. Ronson did likewise. The boy looked at him. "Thank you for listening. Most people don't. My parents say I shouldn't tell people things like this – about the bricks and things. It doesn't hurt anyone does it – telling them things like this? I don't mean to hurt people by telling them. I don't think it possibly can. I'm glad I told you. I'm glad you listened. Thank you," and with that the boy walked off.

Apart from being bemused by the episode young Ronson wasn't aware of giving it any more thought once the boy had walked away. But, when next he was in the company of the group however, he didn't speak. This was unusual for him. In the past he had attempted to impress. If anyone spoke about something he was quick to interject and tell them his experience and knowledge of whatever it was. He thought people would be dazzled by his knowledge and experience of just about anything and everything but they weren't dazzled. More often than not they were irritated.

Now Ronson began to listen. Was it because he had found the monologue of the boy sitting on the playground boring and he didn't want to be the same, or was it because the boy had thanked him for listening? Maybe it was neither of these, but for whatever reason young Ronson started listening rather than talking. He didn't become mute. He didn't behave in what anyone might regard as an odd way – but he listened to others, and when he spoke it was often brief and relevant to what he had

165

heard the person say. He didn't talk about himself or try to boast but found that he either said something supportive or remained silent.

As he watched and listened he started to learn about the people in the group with which he wanted to be associated. He learned of their differences, their individualities. He learned that some of them, like him, were desperate to be accepted while others seemed to lord it over everyone else. He learned it wasn't a 'group' but a collection of individuals. An unfastened bootlace had inadvertently forced him to be an individual and do something he would not have otherwise done. From that chance event he had learned.

Nothing more significant or momentous occurred for a while after the bootlace epiphany but then came another teasing encounter with the brick counting boy – and young Ronson did not stand and watch. He did not join in. He did not keep quiet. He spoke. He stood next to the brick counter. He stood *with* the brick counter and he spoke. Some taunting was directed at him – 'Margie lover'. He waited for it to stop and spoke again. The taunting stopped. The group walked away … but not all the group. Some stayed with young Ronson and the brick boy. A new group had been born.

Young Ronson did not become the most popular boy in school overnight. In truth he probably never became the most popular boy in school – but the incident had given him confidence. He felt more secure in himself and, as the weeks, months and years passed he discovered that he no longer needed to seek attention. People seemed to gravitate towards him of their own accord and when Ronson spoke people listened.   It became almost effortless.

Maybe because he had not analysed what he was doing but had simply internalised this way of interacting he remained vulnerable. His confidence could be knocked when his natural charm (still occasionally bolstered with bluster and clowning) seemed to fail since he was unable to devise a strategy to rectify the situation. To some extent this may have been what lay behind his repeated changes of job. Something went wrong. He didn't have a recovery strategy and so he moved on and let responses to his natural charm guide him into something else. It probably wasn't a conventional career path – but he nevertheless did quite well overall. When between jobs however he would be very down and periods of self pity, like those of his childhood, would surface again. His desperate need to be liked was still there.

So, after The Failed Games, and with the uncertainty around what had happened to Safia playing on his mind, he could think of nothing but to run and hide. Then, as time passed and his fear of imminent demise subsided maybe he should have been brave and ventured out – but that wasn't what he did. Instead he wrapped himself in self pity for comfort and waited - though for what he was waiting he didn't know. He hadn't dared to contact Chrissie or Bloombridge and they had not contacted him so his sense of isolation and rejection increased and that, in turn, fed the self-pity in which he wallowed. The situation looked bleak.

Chapter 31: An Art Lesson for Bloombridge

Bloombridge didn't particularly like or dislike Richard Ronson. They had first met through a casual encounter at a festival of Visual Art. Bloombridge was there in his capacity as a District Councillor even though he didn't particularly like art and Ronson had been there in his capacity as 'someone to be seen at such things'- though he actually *did* like art. They came across each other periodically at art events after that, but it wasn't until the overheard conversation at Mrs Christina's Gallery, that their business relationship began.

Bloombridge, as Head of Homeland Security for the district, had heard of the disappearance of Safia through the political grapevine before it reached the media. He didn't know whether the boating accident story was true or whether something more untoward had occurred. If something sinister had happened to Safia he doubted – in fact was pretty certain - that the client with whom she had had the private viewing was not responsible – certainly not directly. With The World Games occupying everyone's thoughts there was currently no demand for private viewings and he was glad of this. He didn't want to have to think about such things while Safia's disappearance was so fresh – and following on so closely from the death of another of Mrs Christina's artists - Mrs O'Donnell.

He had met with Mrs Christina after Mrs O'Donnell's death and would meet with her again, quite soon, to discuss Safia but his first priority was to ensure that the PETS did only the *minimum* necessary at Mrs Christina's Gallery to meet their statutory obligations. The sooner Mrs Christina's

Gallery was 'eliminated from investigations' the less likelihood there was of anything about the private viewings coming to light.

As soon as the PETS had reported back to him that they had made their required visit to Mrs Christina's Gallery and found nothing untoward he felt free to enjoy The Games like everyone else. However, The Games, from the appalling opening speech by Richard 'Rubber' Ronson to the closing ceremony were the most unexciting thing he had ever experienced – certainly the worst Games in living memory.

Bloombridge didn't care about Ronson's failure with The Games. However, he did want to recommence the private viewings now that The Games were over, and there didn't seem to be any repercussions looming regarding the demise of two artists associated with Mrs Christina's Gallery. For Bloombridge, the next significant event on the horizon was world elections in two years time. Having some additional allies for that would be useful and the private viewings could give him some leverage in that regard.

Bloombridge had not spoken to Ronson for quite some time – certainly not since Safia's disappearance. He wondered whether that disappearance had put Ronson on edge – possibly even been responsible for the man's terrible opening speech at The Games. This made Bloombridge cautious about putting additional pressure on Ronson at this point. He reasoned that a person with damaged self-esteem and who might also be feeling vulnerable is a person likely to be prone to making mistakes. That was something to be avoided at all cost when engaged in an illicit activity.

Following the visit of the PETS to Mrs Christina's Gallery he had contacted her to confirm that he had sent them on their mission with instructions to do the minimum necessary to meet investigative requirements while ensuring that the gallery was not implicated in Safia's disappearance. Now that The Games were over he took time one evening to visit her at the gallery to discuss Ronson and the possibility of recommencing private viewings. It was after closing time and they sat in the room at the back sipping coffee.

"I understand your caution about Rick," said Mrs Christina. "I'm not in a terrible rush to start up the viewings again but sales are down – despite one or two pieces going to my more wealthy clients – and I have taken on a few very promising young artists. It's these younger ones who are being hit most by the downturn. Needless to say, I have been selective in the young artists I have allowed onto my books - and I am confident regarding their readiness to do what is necessary to earn a crust."

"So long as we are agreed that we shouldn't rush into things 'til we are sure that Richard is stable again – yes?"

"Absolutely, David - absolutely. I will leave it to your judgement."

Bloombridge liked that. He respected Mrs Christina and her readiness to leave the decision making to him fitted with his view of himself and of how things should be.

"That's excellent Christina," said Bloombridge dropping the 'Mrs' as he always did. "I will let Richard lick his wounds just a while longer and then test the waters – though I am not sure what we do if he has got a really bad case of 'cold feet'," mused Bloombridge aloud as he stood to leave. Mrs Christina rose to accompany him through the gallery and unlock the front door.

"Like I said David, I will leave it to your judgement, but we both know that Rick's whole *reason d'être* is to be liked, so I have little doubt that he will want to live up to his nickname – and do you know the great thing, David?" He smiled and tilted his head as permission for her to impart her words of wisdom. "The great thing about Rick is that people like him. People like Richard Ronson - no matter what! Not all the people all the time – but the majority most of the time. They will soon forget about The Failed Games if he puts on his charm."

"I know you run a gallery Christina," said Bloombridge suddenly stopping in front of one of the paintings on display as if he hadn't heard a word she had said, "– but do you actually like the stuff? – Art and everything? Some of it seems complete bunkum to me. This thing of blobs here for example," and he indicated a picture comprising two white circles on a grey background. "Is it really that good … And worth that amount?" He peered at the price tag more closely to ensure he hadn't miscounted the number of zeros.

"An excellent question, David. Do you want an answer?" There was a smile on her lips as she asked, but having gained the impression that he hadn't listened to what she was saying about Richard Ronson, there was an edge to her tone. Bloombridge picked it up and matched her smile as he said, "Go on then."

"Well," she said thoughtfully, "Vincent Van Gogh sold only one, maybe two pictures in his lifetime … and they went for next to nothing but if one of his pictures came on the market today the figure that you would have to fork out would be astronomical. The price tag on this," she said indicating the grey rectangle with white circles while not taking her eyes from David Bloombridge, "would not even cover the insurance premium for a week on the Van Gogh!"

"Well, I'm not on the lookout for a Van Gogh - but this grey rectangle; this won't suddenly become worth an astronomical sum … or will it?" He looked again at the price tag. "It seems over priced to me as it is!"

"Everything is 'combination', David. There were other artists around at the same time as Van Gogh that you and I have never heard of. Some of them may have been doing similar things and painting equally beautiful pictures. It is possible that one or two of those pictures survived but a lot will have gone into recycling or, since it was a less pollution conscious time, onto the bonfire and the names of those artists are not even remembered. Only 'combination' created, preserved and added value to the Van Gogh paintings." David Bloombridge looked at her quizzically.

"Go on, educate me." He enjoyed being with Mrs Christina, and now that the core of their business was done, was in no rush to leave. He thought art was vastly over rated, had never understood what the fuss was about and had always successfully (as he saw it) been able to dismiss any argument put to him to justify the stuff – not that he wanted to argue with Mrs Christina. He just wanted her 'take on it'. He felt certain that whatever she said would fail to dent his belief that much of what passed for art had nothing special about it and that his contempt was justified. He would listen – but only in order to reinforce his own view.

Mrs Christina knew Bloombridge well enough to know his general attitude to art and had no intention of trying – or wanting – to convince him otherwise. She was no proselytiser or art evangelist – but she was a business woman and she knew about markets and value.

"Like I said, David, it is all about 'combination'. Van Gogh had certain ideas (or whatever you want to call the inner aspect of his creativity) and a certain level of skill with which to realise that through the use of paint on canvas. However, without his brother Theo giving him the money to buy materials, the paintings would never have come into being. There you have one, very fundamental, combination – Vincent and Theo. Vincent died in 1890 of the pre-Trueway era and Theo died the year after that. Theo left a young widow – Johanna and their only child, a baby boy. Johanna now had to fend for herself and for her baby son with no husband to provide for her. She also had a couple of hundred valueless paintings made by her brother-in-law taking up space in the flat where she lived. If you had been in her position David, what would you have done?"

"Managed as best I could I suppose. Did she have family to turn to? Parents and the like?"

"Probably."

"Well, there you go."

"And the 200 paintings?" queried Mrs Christina.

"Well, if they were worthless like you say, then I'd chuck 'em – or in those days, use them for firewood to keep the flat warm!" He gave a chuckle.

"Exactly," said Mrs Christina with a smile. "That was what she was advised to do – and if she had taken that advice then Vincent Van Gogh's paintings would not be worth the astronomical sums that they are today and you and I would not be standing here talking about them and about him – but Johanna did not 'chuck 'em'. She became, instead part of the combination. She joined with Theo and Vincent. As well as the paintings she had the letters that had passed between the two brothers. She also had contacts … more people with whom to combine. She didn't make a bonfire of paintings to keep herself warm for a few hours. She set about creating a myth that would last for centuries; the myth of Vincent Van Gogh the suffering artist who died young, penniless and unrecognised – but who was a genius. Value didn't stem simply from the paintings or even from Van Gogh but from those things plus other people, plus time, plus place and probably one or two other things – all in combination." There was a brief mutually smiling silence before Bloombridge said:

"You should become a politician, Christina. That was a great speech! I certainly don't think there is anything I can say to follow that – so maybe, now that we are agreed about Richard and the way forward, I will wend my way." With that he went to the door and Mrs Christina let him out.

As he made his journey home Bloombridge was happy that he and Mrs Christina were both comfortable and 'on the same page' regarding Ronson and the private viewings – but Bloombridge left with more than that. Bloombridge may not always have appeared attentive – but he had a knack of hearing what he *needed* to hear. In talking about Van Gogh he had heard Mrs Christina's mantra of 'combination', and in talking about Richard Ronson he had heard her say that people liked Ronson "…no matter what" – and from this Bloombridge had made his own mental combination; a combination through which he could see himself accruing

171

benefits that went far beyond anything he could gain simply from the private viewings. He also realised his strategy to counter any 'cold feet' that Richard Ronson may have. It might mean that 'Christina's' artists would need to wait a little longer than she expected in order to start earning that extra crust … but Bloombridge was a person who took 'the long view'.

Chapter 32: Montgomery-Jones Feels Sad

Montgomery-Jones was glad that The Games were over. She was probably not as surprised as many at how poorly they had been received. The economic downturn was beginning to bite and maybe it was a sign that people could not be fobbed off as lightly as government and media believed. She didn't sense revolution in the air but a lot of work needed doing to get the Trueway economy back on track – and prevent any likelihood of a disgruntled population from considering that avenue. She didn't like "Rubber" Ronson – but his opening speech at The Games had shocked her. She had been embarrassed for him as he struggled. There was a point when he should have stopped, but he didn't and stumbled on instead repeatedly losing the thread of what he was saying, and even swearing in apparent frustration at one point. He appeared to be drunk. Maybe he was. She was unable to watch the news coverage that repeatedly showed him being booed from the platform. She had actually found it upsetting.

Chapter 33: The Richard & David Show Begins

Ronson was glad that the media was fickle and ready to run after whatever bit of tinsel fluttered by. He was soon old news and lay undisturbed in his cocoon of self pity. So absorbed did he become in himself (helped by his generous stock of single malt whisky) that any remnant of anxiety relating to the disappearance of Safia was blotted out – that is until the unannounced arrival of Bloombridge at his door. Foreboding then resurfaced.

"Didn't really want to intrude," explained Bloombridge as he walked past Ronson into the hallway without waiting to be invited and down to Ronson's living room to plonk himself into a chair.

"Coffee?" queried Ronson.

"Sounds a delight old boy."

Bloombridge didn't seem to be on an urgent mission and making the coffee gave Ronson a few minutes to recompose himself.

"I guessed that the business with The Games would have hit you pretty hard," said Bloombridge as they sat with their coffees. "Thought you would probably want a bit of time to yourself. I wasn't even sure that you would be here – thought you might have gone off somewhere – place in the country maybe."

"If I had one," scoffed Ronson. Bloombridge was reassuringly his usual self. This visit didn't seem to be about Safia - but Ronson remained on his guard.

"Ha-ha! Maybe one day, hey? Had any thoughts about what next?"

"Not really, have you come to see if I am still arranging private viewings – or am I so out of favour that your 'art lovers' would be more afraid of being associated with me than with the 'art' trade?"

"Well, since you mention it I think there are people who could do with some paintings for their walls … but maybe not immediately. I will be candid. I need to be absolutely certain that you are feeling on top of things, Richard. I just need to feel confident that if clients are at Richard Ronson's house there is no risk of them being … well, caught with their pants down!" Bloombridge smiled at his own pun.

"Well at least you're honest!" said Ronson – without smiling. What was Bloombridge doing here? What did he want?

"So, what plans do you have for getting back on your feet?" queried Bloombridge, before adding with a grin, "You did note that I refrained from saying 'bouncing' back?"

"No, hadn't noticed," responded Ronson more sullenly than he had intended. "Is that why you've come – to discover my plans for getting back on my feet … and if not, then what else?" Now Ronson felt he sounded hostile rather than sullen so added, "Sorry if that sounds blunt."

"Not at all Richard - one man's, 'blunt' is another man's, 'to the point'. So I will be equally forthright. I think you should run for office. The elections will be here in a couple of years. That gives sufficient time for both your preparation and for The Games to fade from people's memory.

173

Believe me Richard, if 'the people' are experts at anything they are experts at forgetting!"

Ronson was taken aback. He had never thought of running for political office.

"I don't know the first thing about government, David."

"Transferable skills, Richard – you have plenty just waiting to be deployed. The Games was unfortunate. It was not your fault that they were a failure – even though the media pointed the finger at you. How illogical is that - a whole Games being lacklustre because of the guy that gave the opening speech? No, Richard you were the scapegoat, the fall guy – simply in the wrong place at the wrong time. I like you Richard – genuinely, but even if you don't want to believe that, and take me on trust, then accept my motive of self-interest. If Richard Ronson is back on top then … how shall I put it? Art can flourish again and we can both – no we can *all* benefit from that!"

"So, are you offering to help?"

"Yes. I know the ropes. I get a feel for what is going on at District Level and you would have to run for Local Level. I can give you feedback on the direction in which things are moving, get a feel for forthcoming issues … all sorts, though I must stress that nobody could be allowed to know of my involvement with your campaign. We would both need to be very, very discrete." He paused for emphasis before adding with a smile, "But we both know that we are capable of that."

Ronson pondered silently for a moment. Bloombridge seemed to have no anxiety relating to Safia – at least he hadn't mentioned her. He was not averse to starting the private viewings again in due course, and out of the blue he was proposing this. It seemed totally outlandish – yet Bloombridge was shrewd and would not be aligning himself with anyone who he thought could damage him or who he thought was not capable of assisting him. Ronson had no better idea, so what did he have to lose?

"What have you got to lose, Richard?"

Ronson was a little startled to hear his own thoughts being voiced and it ended any prevarication. Bloombridge was right. He had nothing to lose. Maybe, just maybe, his downfall might have been a blessing – forcing a test of his resilience and the need to find a new path.

"OK, David."

As he sat there sipping coffee with Bloombridge he had no idea of the significance of that short utterance. It would have ramifications not only for him but for the whole of Trueway.

Chapter 34: A Child in May

Steph and Paul returned to the use of DAMP a fortnight after their marriage. They had periodic DAMP Holidays but Paul had no further aggressive outbursts. A few weeks after the incident in front of the TV Steph had asked him to clarify why he had been so angry. He tried to explain his view about people like Ronson having a duty to Trueway and the public. They had a responsibility not to take on assignments that they were unable to fulfil and so risk spoiling things for others. It had just made him angry to see this dereliction of duty and of Citizenship. He cited the subsequent media coverage as evidence that he was right, and that 'everybody' agreed that Ronson had tainted the whole Games.

After that, she never raised the incident again – but her thoughts intermittently returned to the musings that she had had while sitting alone on the settee after Paul had gone to bed that night. Had she married Paul because she was in love with him … or because he was the route to EM2 marriage and to honouring the memory of her mother? She didn't dwell on these thoughts. To do so would be pointless, she told herself, but they represented a doubt in her mind about whether the trajectory of her life was one that she had genuinely chosen for self-fulfilment or for fulfilment of duty. If it was the latter then was all the striving, all the sacrifice – even the EM2 marriage with Paul – a mistake? Whatever the truth, life was not going to stand still to let Steph seek an answer at her leisure. The facts were the facts and she was married to Paul. More than that, she was pregnant.

It was shortly before she was due to give birth that the firm for which she was working went into liquidation. With the Trueway economy in recession and a baby imminent Steph was not able to obtain another job and so she and Paul were reduced to a single salary. This was not sufficient to afford the repayments on the house in which they were living.

The irony was not lost on them that, since Trueway government had stepped in to prop up the banks, they were now part owners of the bank that would not give them sufficient credit to overcome the situation. Both also felt angry and let down. They had believed that their enhanced marriage status would guarantee that alternative employment would always be available if the need arose but now, it seemed, that was not the case. Despite this disappointment however they did have income and would shortly be in the, 'enhanced married couple with child' group. They were still classified as 'credit/mortgage suitable' and so were eligible to transfer to another, smaller, cheaper property. It was less than salubrious. It was in a socially deprived area but they felt it better to maintain the purchase of a property than to go into rented.

So it was that nine months after her wedding day Steph gave birth to a baby girl in a small flat in a deprived area. They named their daughter May and prayed to The Great Spirit that Paul's income would be sufficient to sustain them all.

Chapter 35: Encounter with Couchan

"We need to do some killing – bring back The Games as they were." The words kept going round in Montgomery-Jones' head. They had been spoken by one of the Councillors (Martial) in the Territorial Parliament Chamber earlier that day. Now Montgomery-Jones was sitting by herself in the Public Gallery overlooking that same chamber contemplating the words and the array of empty red, yellow and blue seats below. She could see the blue seat where she had been sitting as a Councillor (Civil) for her territory and the red seat of the small, bespectacled woman who had uttered the words.

"Hello Stella."

Montgomery-Jones jumped at the unexpected words from behind her but recognised the voice and only half turned her head.

"Hello, Couchan. You startled me."

"Sorry," he said coming down the steps between the rows of banked seats. Justice Couchan probably had a first name but everyone either addressed him as 'Justice Couchan' if speaking to him in a formal capacity or simply 'Couchan' if they knew him well enough.

"I'm more used to seeing you down there." He gestured with a backward motion of his head to the chamber as he simultaneously and deftly spread his sitting towel on an adjacent chair. He was a big man, portly some might say, but he moved easily and with a certain grace.

"I come up here sometimes when everyone has gone. It's part of my way to remind myself never to forget to take the perspective of people at large."

"And what do you think the 'people at large' will make of what Councillor Ramathan said today?"

Montgomery-Jones looked at him blankly.

"The stuff about killing at The Games," he added as clarification.

"Oh, is that her name? I was so shocked I didn't even take in who she was or which territory she was representing. I suppose since you are here I could ask you what the legal position is … but I don't think, at this second, that I want to know. I find it too depressing to imagine that there are people out there who still have that mentality. I know The Games were pretty awful this time round but the idea of bringing back killing as entertainment to liven them up is an obscenity so gross I couldn't believe what I was hearing. What next – go out and hunt Marginals in the Outlands and bring them back to be slaughtered in the way they were in the immediate post Terror War period?" Montgomery-Jones shook her head as if trying to dislodge the image before looking again at Couchan and saying more calmly. "Anyway, why are you sneaking up on contemplative Councillors?"

"I was leaving one of the committee rooms and saw you – or a figure that I thought was you – disappearing round the corner to the stairs up to here so, since it's been a while, I thought I would just say 'hello'."

"Anything interesting in your committee room?"

"No. I'm just there as a formality really. They have to have a Justice Ecclesiastic present on the off chance."

She nodded with absent minded understanding.

"Hungry?" he enquired thinking as much about taking her mind off the day's events as the rumbling in his stomach. Although they only saw each other infrequently, Montgomery-Jones knew Couchan enjoyed his food, and since she was more than a little peckish, she happily accepted.

*

They ate at Couchan's favourite restaurant. Like most restaurants in Trueway it was predominantly vegetarian and vegan food but cultured meat was on the menu and Couchan took advantage of this to have faux gammon with carrots, peas and potatoes. Montgomery-Jones settled on vegan lasagne with salad. As they ate, their chat about theatre, music and art was relaxed and natural. They did not have a sweet or coffee but, instead went back to Couchan's chambers for brandy.

Over the drink the conversation returned to the Ramathan proposal.

"Do you think her idea was really a consequence of the disastrous Games?" queried Montgomery-Jones before adding, "You see, I take very little interest in them so I'm not sure."

"I don't really know, Stella. I think The Games have evolved into weeks of generalised entertainment – and there's a limit to how much people can take. I don't think that she is leading a traditionalist rebellion if that is where your question is leading."

Montgomery-Jones smiled. He was astute. She changed tack.

"Is it legally possible to introduce executions at The Games?"

"Well, off the top of my head, I don't think there would be any fundamental legal impediment to executions taking place at The Games but a 'reintroduction bill' would be necessary," he mused.

"But her tone; what did she say – 'we need some killing'? Something like that. That's clearly a call for killing as entertainment … Isn't it?"

"I wouldn't get too vexed about it at the moment, Stella. There haven't been any executions of criminals or baiting of Marginals at The Games for a very, very long time – and you would not be alone in your revulsion and opposition if the likes of Ramathan tried to reinstate them so I can't see any 'reintroduction bill' making it all the way up to the Continental Council and into law."

"You may be right – but you were aware of what she said and you were in a committee meeting so the word got round quickly enough."

"True, Stella – but when someone says something startling like that it will always grab attention and get the media going. I imagine that was Ramathan's intention – draw some attention to herself. Its game playing… but I think that the economy will be what is occupying more serious minds in the coming months and years – don't you? The situation is not looking good is it?"

"Oh Couchan," she groaned, "don't remind me! But since you have then I'd better finish up and get back home so that I'm ready to face the day tomorrow." With that she knocked back her drink. "Thank you for this evening. It has been good chatting. We should not leave it so long before next time."

"Yes indeed Stella. Sorry about the economy reference - I hope I haven't dampened your spirits too much!"

"Haha – No! The meal and your company have been a delight … an antidote to that woman Ramathan and her absurd proposal in response to The Failed Games. You might not believe it Couchan, but I actually felt sorry for Ronson. I don't like the man and have no idea what was wrong with him but I did feel sorry for him. He seems to have gone very quiet since his debacle. Maybe now at least we won't see him cropping up everywhere." With that she stood to leave but Couchan spoke, and his words followed her as she went:

"I wouldn't be so sure. There's a reason he's called 'Rubber'."

Chapter 36: Goodbye Paul

After the birth of May life was hard but manageable. Paul worked long hours and kept the money coming in. He and Steph were also able to claim some government support for the family on the basis of them being an 'enhanced married couple with child'. During the day Steph did not like to go out much because of the area – but felt the need to be out because being inside with a little, demanding baby all the time was so wearing – so depressingly claustrophobic. She couldn't believe the extent to which she looked forward to shopping trips! She would envisage and plan the walk to the supermarket. She would play it over in her head relishing it; anticipating it. She would walk slowly with the pram or baby sling, hoping that little May would go to sleep and stay asleep long enough for her to not only do the shopping but indulge – just once a week – in the luxury of having a coffee out, by herself in a café. She and Paul almost never went out for a meal or any other social event such as the theatre. They simply couldn't afford it.

*

Hard but manageable became unmanageable when Paul died. May was barely six months old when the virus swept through their region of Trueway. Steph became a widow and single mother at one stroke.

*

Steph was devastated with grief and Trueway priests and counsellors were despatched in the initial period following his death but, because

Paul's was one of a large number of unexpected deaths consequent upon the epidemic, the extent and duration of support was limited. After the funeral the support became very sporadic and it wasn't long before other parts of the Trueway system came to the fore. Because of Paul's death, Steph was no longer, 'enhanced married couple with child' but she was occupying a flat designated for such a family. Trueway would support her – but she and May would need to relocate to a smaller flat or bedsit. The situation was dire. In years to come Steph would remember this time and remember passing a shop window where a TV was relaying the "Never-We-Forget" ceremony to celebrate the heroes of The Terror Wars and any other heroes of Trueway - and she wondered why she had been forgotten. She had been hailed a hero – the girl who protected Trueway by shooting a Marginal. She felt bitter. Remembering was one thing. Helping those who were being remembered was something else she felt.

Steph struggled on with May. There was some assistance from friends but her single minded push to gain her EM2 status had gone against the trend and expectation of much of her extended family and it was clear that there was an element of "you've made your bed 'Mrs Better than us' ... so now you lie in it." It was at this point that she considered suicide – but that would have meant infanticide as well ... or abandoning the baby. Looking into her daughter's blue eyes she knew such options were impossible.

Chapter 37: Defeat of Ramathan

Montgomery-Jones traced the outline of her brick with her finger. She was happy. Although many had spoken against Cllr Ramathan's bill to reintroduce killing to The Games the messages of congratulations and the media coverage had identified her as the principal agent of opposition to the move. Despite her natural modesty she knew she had spoken well in the chamber. She had spoken from the heart. Ramathan's bill had been heavily defeated. There was now no chance of it going forward for consideration by the Continental Council and so no chance of it then being rubber stamped by the Supreme Triumvirate to become law. The Ramathan Bill was dead. There would be no killing at The Games.

Chapter 38: Welcome Local Councillor Ronson

True to his word Bloombridge helped Ronson prepare his campaign to become a councillor. From behind the scenes he quietly gave guidance. Whether it was this help or people *forgetting* the Ronson of The Failed Games, or people *remembering* the 'Rubber' Ronson of old, or a bit of both … or something else entirely … the voters came out, and a significant number gave their vote to Richard Ronson who was duly elected Councillor (Civil) for his local area.

Across Trueway in general, the turnout for the election had been poor, though it had been higher in the elections at Local Level than at District and Territorial Level. The media coverage of Ronson's success was limited – after all, his election was only to the lowest tier of government. The media also ignored one or two other new candidates who had managed to topple previously secure Local Level Councillors. The media was drawn to what it saw as the far more 'important' appointments that were taking place at District, Territorial and Continental Levels.

There had been much speculation about which individuals would be in favour and which out of favour prior to the election and then much analysis after the election as to why this person had been successful while this other person had not. This focus on individuals was probably not surprising since Trueway had no political parties as such. That said, everyone recognised that groupings and alliances developed.

In terms of such groupings the 'texture' and 'colour' of the chambers at District, Territorial and Continental Level changed very little as a result of this electoral round despite the comings and goings of the individual politicians that were reported on in such detail by the media and devoured with greater or lesser interest by Citizens at large. Had the media been more alert, more perceptive it would have seen the changes that were taking place in the Local parliament where representatives were selected *only* by local Citizens unlike the higher parliaments where councillors were elected in part by Citizens and in part by existing councillors from higher tiers. Had the media been more alert and more perceptive it would have recognised the significance of the larger than usual turnout of Citizens for these Local Councillor elections and the changing colour and texture that was developing here in this lowest tier – but the media missed it.

The media of Trueway along with the majority of its Citizens and politicians had, over the years, become used to change at a slow pace. Even now, the best part of four years since the economic downturn, the problems were not beginning to bite everywhere – but they were beginning to bite and the people who were hurting most were those at the bottom of the pile and it was those at the bottom of the pile who elected the Local Councillors. This section of Trueway electorate wanted change – needed change – and they were electing people that they thought might bring it. Richard Ronson was among them. It was the first ripple of a tidal change – but it had not been spotted.

Ronson was no more perceptive than the media but he could be excused. He had been in a pit and his focus had been on getting his foot onto a ladder with which to climb out. With help from Bloombridge and with his own *bonhomie* he had secured his foothold but he had little idea of his political position or what he was going to try and achieve now that he was in office – despite the slogans calling for "fairness", "equality", "a living wage", "security" and so on, under which he had campaigned on the advice of Bloombridge. Once the election was finished and he was in post he had secured a reasonable income for four years and would use that time to *do* as little as possible but *learn* as much as possible. This wasn't a purely cynical stance. He knew next to nothing about the political world into which he had just stepped. He recognised the extent to which he had had to lean on Bloombridge and be guided by him. He felt, quite genuinely, that he needed time to learn before ploughing his own, more independently directed, furrow. He would tread carefully and continue to listen, and with increasing selectivity, to take advice. The fear of some harbinger of imminent doom emerging from the shadows had subsided but the unease he felt about Safia's death had never fully left him.

*

"Hello, Richard – or should I say Local Councillor Ronson, now?"

"David, hello! I was hoping you would come round." Ronson was about to invite Bloombridge inside but the man was already past him and heading down the hallway saying,

"Well, thought I should come and congratulate you."

"Drink?" enquired Ronson of his now comfortably seated guest.

"Drop of Scotch wouldn't go amiss."

"So, David – we did it – and I really do mean '*we*'. Your advice and support was essential. Thank you," said Ronson with sincerity.

"No 'thanks' required old boy," responded Bloombridge jovially.

Ronson handed him his drink and sat down with one for himself. "Your good health David," he said raising his glass in salute, "– with many thanks, whether you want them or not. Cheers!"

"If you cast your mind back a couple of years when we had coffee in this very room I think I was sufficiently candid to say that I had my own selfish interests for wanting to help you – that I wasn't just a charitable soul with a soft spot for 'good old Rubber'. Do you remember that?"

Ronson nodded.

"Well, I will be equally candid now. I am genuinely here to congratulate you but also, now that you are 'back in the saddle' so to speak, to see whether you would be willing to consider reinvigorating your interest in … *art*."

"Yes, I remember the conversation. As I recall you were probably as anxious about arranging private viewings at my house as I was about holding them – fears about people being 'caught with their pants down' I think you said."

"Yes, yes … absolutely …," said Bloombridge brushing off Ronson's comment, "but I have one or two 'art lovers' and Mrs Christina has been developing … well almost a stockpile … of young and increasingly needy artists, so now that you are most definitely back on your feet, I just thought hosting a few viewings was something that you might want to think about. Anyway, like I say – just came to congratulate you and enquire," said Bloombridge standing up – almost discourteously soon after his unsuspecting host had sat down. "But won't keep you old boy – know how demanding a new posting can be … unfamiliar ground and all that … have to get to know the territory – but I am sure you will do that. Won't waste any more of your time – 'Councillor'!" He smiled as he extended his hand and simultaneously took a step towards the door with the result that Ronson appeared to be yanked to his feet rather than participating in a handshake. With his right hand still occupied Ronson reached round Bloombridge and released the door latch with his left.

"Anyway, Richard, I will leave you to think about whether you want to reinvigorate your interest in art. I'll get back in touch after a week or so. Thank you for the Scotch …You must have some of mine some time. I have a few excellent single malts! " With that he was gone.

Richard Ronson closed the door and went back to finish his whisky. In the last two years Bloombridge had kept a very low profile in his dealings with Ronson. He provided his advice and support discretely - almost covertly. An invitation now to have whisky with him – and was he suggesting at his place? Anyway ... it all seemed very significant to Ronson. Despite his campaign and his success in the election this invitation – or Ronson's reading of it - was the moment that signalled to him that he had truly emerged from the shadows. He lifted his glass in a toast to himself and said aloud, "Welcome back ... and good health Councillor Ronson!"

Chapter 39: Couchan's Prediction

It was with incredulity that Montgomery-Jones heard the news that Richard Ronson had been elected as a Local Level Councillor and she was immediately reminded of Couchan's words – *There's a reason he's called 'Rubber'.* She had not seen Couchan since that evening and thought that Ronson's election and Couchan's prophetic words were a good excuse to get in touch and offer a reciprocal meal – her treat this time.

*

"I know you're busy Stella ... but I've been a meal out of pocket for the best part of what – eighteen months ... two years?" teased Couchan as he gave Montgomery-Jones a peck on the cheek.

"You're right to scold me, Couchan. I really should have made the effort sooner."

"Oh, well if it's an *effort* then I'll clear off back home."

She grabbed his arm and marched him into the restaurant with a resolute – "You're here and you're staying!"

After the meal they again went to his chambers and sat sipping brandy.

"I don't know why I like you, Couchan – or why it feels so easy being with you. We hardly go back a long way as friends and we don't see each other that often – a couple of years since last time as you so courteously reminded me!"

"Could it be you have a penchant for overweight, oriental homosexual men with legal minds as sharp as a bacon slicer?"

"No," she said as if taking the quip in full seriousness, "I think it's because I trust you."

184

"Oh my word, Stella, don't ever do that. You're a politician - you really should know better – especially in relation to legal bods like me who will argue the case for whoever hires us!"

"And anyway," she said ignoring his jovial advice, "I didn't know you were gay – maybe you should get a tattoo,"

"You must be joking Stella – put a tattoo needle on me and I will go 'pop'! Anyway, that's too gross to contemplate so I will change the subject. We did well in the elections don't you think despite Councillor Ronson and one or two others like him gaining unexpected seats?"

"Oh Couchan! That sounds so incongruous – *Councillor* Ronson; *Councillor?* For goodness' sake!"

"That's democracy for you … but like I said, look on the bright side. There were several appointments at District Level that look very promising in terms of The Alliance and even one or two at Territorial, though I am a bit concerned about Continental Level." He paused. "Why didn't you run – for Continental I mean?"

His question took her aback and she felt suddenly defensive. "Well, there's plenty that I have to do at Territorial Level. We need to consolidate."

"True, but The Alliance needs to gain a really solid group at Continental Level if it is to bring about global change."

"OK, but what about you?" she asked in an almost retaliatory tone, "what progress are you making up the legal ranks?"

"I'm getting there Stella – but a few more Alliance orientated councillors at Continental Level will help with appointments and promotions … mine included!"

"Ahhh … I see!" she grinned, "Your concern that I move up to Continental Level is fuelled by self interest after all!" She sat back triumphantly.

"And this from the woman who, only seconds ago, said that she trusted me!" he retorted with an equally wide grin. "But seriously, The Alliance needs to keep the momentum. The world has to outgrow the 'us and them' divide. I don't think that simply continuing to 'get round' the division of 'Citizen and Marginal' of 'Trueway and Outland' is going to be an option with which we can continue for much longer – do you?"

"Well, no – but I don't see any greater urgency than ever there was. We are moving forward, our numbers are increasing in the necessary places. Everything has been going to plan. If we start getting panicky and

185

rushing things then surely that is when stuff is going to start going wrong – don't you think?"

"No, we mustn't jeopardise anything – I'm definitely with you there, Stella. If the dinosaurs got wind …"

"Oh please don't say 'dinosaurs' … I tell my secretary not to do that"

"Ha-ha – OK Stella. Let's hope I don't do it in court one day! But I think we are walking a fine line, and The Alliance needs to recognise that. Trueway is stagnating – no, is *stagnant* - and without the fecundity of The Margin it will die of its own comfortable, eco-bubble, peaceful complacency. If we don't progress things soon then it could be too late."

"Strong words Couchan. Example?"

"Of what?"

"Of what makes you think that we need to get a move on before it's too late."

"OK – challenge accepted - the epidemic. The epidemic is a classic example. It wasn't big. We tackled it successfully and we kept the links with Marginal researchers well covered up – but without those researchers we would have been hard pressed. The dinosaurs were happy that it was the infallible Trueway genius and hard work that saw us through. The population at large was happy to think the same … what else could they think? But you and I and The Alliance know different. What if that epidemic had been a pandemic affecting every continent? To fight that the planet would need to deploy everything at its disposal. We couldn't do that covertly."

"Point taken Couchan – but epidemics and similar pressures are pretty infrequent so I don't think there is need to panic."

"I'm not saying 'panic' – I just think The Alliance needs to remember that it doesn't have 'for ever'."

"Time frame O Soothsayer?"

"Who can predict 'novelty' and 'chance' Stella? Who knows when our climate control will develop a problem for which the tried and tested solutions do not work? Who knows when we will get a novel virus that spreads like wildfire but for which our medics have no response?"

Montgomery-Jones was not going to be satisfied with that.

"Ball park?" she challenged.

"Ten years," he responded without hesitation.

There was silence. It had all been a bit of a game – a game of banter between two friends having an after dinner drink - but the absolute of

Couchan's response and the cold look in his eyes told her he was serious … and he was willing to commit to a figure. She was briefly tempted to ask him for the basis of such a confident prediction but guessed he would probably dismiss it with something like – 'just a hunch'. He moved in quite high legal and in ecclesiastical circles however and he would not say something like this lightly or without some foundation so she simply said:

"Two more elections then?"

To which he responded:

"And three more Games."

Chapter 40: Revitalising The Private Viewings

"That was lovely Rick – really lovely," beamed Mrs Christina pushing the dinner plate slightly forward to allow her to place her wine glass within reach as she sat back contentedly and rested her elbows on the arms of the antique carver chair. "I had no idea you could cook so well."

"Thanks Chrissie. I'll get dessert in a minute. I have to admit, I'm stuffed! Genuinely glad you enjoyed it." They both sat quietly a moment.

"OK, Rick." Mrs Christina broke the silence of the replete repose. "I get a phone call out of the blue after two years inviting me to eat – at your place, not a restaurant – 'odd'. Then you do a really fabulous soup and main course with a really smashing wine – 'very odd' … lovely I admit, but 'very odd' … and still there is pudding to follow – and that makes it 'dodgy!'" They both smiled. "So, while I enjoy the wine and await the pud … why not tell me what this is all about."

"I have a crush on you."

Mrs Christina spluttered her mouthful of wine back into her glass to avoid spraying it over the table as she fought to suppress her laughter.

"Sorry Chrissie," smiled Ronson standing up. "Couldn't resist that one – but it was either that or to ask why you hadn't been in touch with me …" and he came round with his plate and picked up hers. "…but we won't go there," he said looking down at her before walking to the kitchen and calling back as he went. "I had a visit. Bloombridge wants to know if I will start hosting viewings again – but I am assuming you know that?"

"Well, you could have just come into the gallery you know."

"Well, it had been so long and well…"

187

"And 'well … I'm a councillor now and a chat at my 'blind spot' house is safer'?" she suggested.

"Well … maybe …" he admitted as he returned with a tray and announced, "trifle!"

She let the subject rest and took her time silently enjoying the dessert he had provided.

"That does it Rick. You are chef extraordinaire," she announced as she put her spoon down. He gave a courteous smile and nod of his head. "So, David has been to see you. I didn't know he had spoken to you about the viewings … but I had let him know that my sales were down and that I had a number of young, lesser known artists that could do with some additional income – but that was ages and ages ago."

"Yes, I was aware of that. Bloombridge actually said you had a 'stockpile' of artists – that was his actual word – 'stockpile'. I don't doubt David Bloombridge – his reliability and all that. He has helped me enormously … but I wanted to have it direct from you that you wanted to start the viewings again. Not only that, I needed to be sure that you would be comfortable with me hosting them and being, as it were, the 'go-between' as before – after all, two years is a long time."

"Interested? You *do* know we are in an economic downturn … catastrophic recession even? I heard some of your election stuff … you sounded pretty aware!"

"So – things in the art world are a bit tough, is that what you're saying?" He was not going to be diverted into a discussion of his campaign and the current economic situation.

"For me and everyone else."

"So, what David said is correct and you have one or two people willing and able to display their works for private buyers?"

"I think I can find 'one or two' … and quite a few more … and would be very happy for you to be the 'go-between' as you were in the past."

"Then I will wait to see what style of art Bloombridge says potential buyers might be interested in and then you can let me have some sample images and we'll see if we can get going again – yes?"

"I'll drink to that!" and she raised her glass which was dutifully 'clinked' by Richard 'Rubber' Ronson.

∗

Ronson was waiting when Mrs Christina arrived. The artist had been blindfolded for the entire trip from Mrs Christina's Gallery.

188

"You will be taken by someone else from here and I will see you later Tanya – OK?" asked Mrs Christina. The girl gave a nod. "Remember the person I am leaving you with right now will not speak to you and you must keep your blindfold on 'til the signal – yes?" Again the girl nodded. "What is the signal?"

"Two taps on my shoulder and then I wait 'til I hear the door close," responded Tanya confidently.

"Remember the client may be wearing a mask and clothes, so don't be startled. He may not speak either. It's up to him. How will you know when the viewing is over?"

"The purchaser will sit me on a chair by the door where I came in and hand me my blindfold." Again, she spoke with confidence.

"And what will you do then?"

"Put on the blindfold and wait until I am taken out of the room and passed back to you."

Mrs Christina looked at Ronson. He nodded.

"OK, Tanya the person will now take you by the arm and lead you to the viewing room and I will be back later. Bye for now."

"Bye, Mrs Christina." Tanya gave a smile and a little wave in the vague direction of Mrs Christina's voice before Ronson took her by the arm and silently guided her away to the room.

While this exchange was taking place the client, also blindfolded, had been brought to another entrance at Ronson's house and guided by Bloombridge to an antechamber to the viewing room. The antechamber had a door into the viewing room opposite to the one which the artist used. He would be left in the antechamber by Bloombridge and would wait until Ronson activated a buzzer to signal that the artist was in place and the client could enter the viewing room. At the end of the viewing the client would seat the artist and hand her the blindfold and then return to the anteroom and press a buzzer to notify Ronson that the viewing had ended. The client would then put his blindfold on and wait in the antechamber for Bloombridge.

Photographs of the artist and of her work had been seen by the client beforehand and an array of works had been hung and lit very tastefully, in the viewing room. The room was, in fact, a guest suite at Ronson's house with attached bedroom and shower. The client had made clear what services he wanted prior to the viewing and the artist had stipulated her fee – a fee that would be translated into the price of specified artworks.

Ronson stood the girl next to the chair in the viewing room. Chrissie hadn't said anything about him sitting her down so he didn't attempt to do so for fear of causing confusion. A green light above the door opposite indicated that the client was waiting in the antechamber. Ronson briefly scanned the room. The lighting was subtle and each picture had its own spotlight. Everything looked fine. He looked at the artist. The blindfold was secure and she stood motionless. She had answered Mrs Christina's questions very confidently and Bloombridge had assured him that the client was an extremely, 'trustworthy chap' so Ronson tapped the girl twice on the shoulder and left the room.

In terms of Trueway law everything that was about to take place – that had already started to take place – was illegal for all the participants, but as long as everyone kept to the agreements, then everyone involved was a winner.

Ronson was still concerned about what had happened to Safia. He still wondered whether something had been done to silence her in order to prevent a scandal and the downfall of a prominent 'art lover', but the fact that no harm had befallen him personally, and the fact that Bloombridge had asked to recommence the private viewings had given him reassurance. Maybe it had been as the media said – Safia had disappeared in a tragic boating accident.

The private art viewings had recommenced anyway – and there was no going back.

Chapter 41: The Seeds of the 'Punishment' Games

After only a few months Bloombridge again sat in one of Ronson's arm chairs sipping coffee.

"Thank you Richard, for your services to art. The collectors are well satisfied and I hope that you are getting good feedback from the artists. They are benefitting aren't they - painting sales and all that?"

"Absolutely, David. It feels like 'old times'. Mrs Christina seems to have a big smile … and an endless supply of talented girls."

"Excellent. And how are you liking life as a Local Level Councillor?"

"Getting to grips with stuff – you know."

"Good, good – because now I'm going to shock you!" Bloombridge paused for dramatic emphasis, and even though he had a broad smile on his face, Ronson thought of Safia and his stomach turned.

"Don't look so worried Richard. You have made a good start as a Local Level Councillor. I've had good reports – and, in my humble opinion, you would make an even better *District* Level Councillor! What do you think of that Richard? Told you I would shock you. Nice shock though – hey?"

Ronson felt a degree of relief – but was also completely taken aback.

"I've only just gained a seat here at Local Level, David and that was with much guidance from you. I hardly think that I should be pushing my luck with a move to District Level. I rather think I need to develop my craft first and well, I don't know, achieve something here at Local Level that would justify such an ambition."

"Couldn't agree more, old boy," beamed Bloombridge before cryptically adding, "The Games are in two years time."

Ronson was silent with incredulity. Had he heard and interpreted correctly?

"You surely aren't suggesting I get involved with The Games? I would have thought that was the one thing I should be steering clear of! - or have I completely misunderstood what you have just said?"

"Ha-ha, Richard, you have already proved your ability to get elected. It is a gift. Everybody knows your nickname. They will almost expect you to involve yourself with The Games. Yes, there will be those who will be looking to see you disgraced a second time … but you will not be disgraced. Be confident Richard. Set your sights high and this could be a new chapter in the ascent of Richard Ronson - and a new chapter for The Games!"

"You sound very confident, David."

"That's because I *am* confident, Richard. You had two years to prepare to stand as a councillor at Local Level and you were successful even though you had no direct experience in politics and had the shock of the worst Games ever and your association with them fresh in your mind. Now you have two years to prepare for the next Games – but with a little political experience and influence as well. That sounds a good starting point – a better starting point than before … so why wouldn't I be confident? Hey, why wouldn't I?"

"Well, it all seems a bit soon to me. I really don't know. Don't get me wrong. I am really, really appreciative of what you have done for me. I just don't know that I am capable."

"Perfectly understand, old boy. Let me explain a little about how I think you could turn these Games around. A little while back a bill was debated in the Territorial Parliament, Richard. It was motioned by a Territorial Councillor called Ramathan. It related to the reintroduction of implementing judicial rulings at The Games. The bill was defeated – quite heavily defeated but there were, nevertheless some supporters, and I gleaned that there were some councillors who privately were in favour of the proposal but who felt that they could not be seen publicly to support it. Now, ten years ago I don't think such a bill would even have been thought about so I think we have a guide here to a movement – a rising tide of opinion flowing in a given direction. I think that if you catch that wave Richard it will carry you to a successful Games and he who rides the wave of a successful Games … well … he lands on the shore of the District Council!"

Ronson had no idea what was meant by, '…reintroduction of implementing judicial rulings at The Games'. Whatever it meant it sounded like hard work – and that was not how Ronson had pictured his next four years. His response was therefore probably a little more curt than he had intended.

"Then why don't you do it David – though in your case it would land you on the shore of the Territorial Council of course?" This response surprised Bloombridge. He had not anticipated this resistance – almost hostility. An outside observer however would have seen no change in his jovial demeanour.

"Good question Richard – damned good question. Two reasons, old chap. The first is parliamentary rules and procedures. Once a bill has been defeated in the Territorial Parliament it can't be reintroduced in that Council or in The District Council – well not in exactly the same form and not without what is termed, 'compelling evidence of need'. In other words I'm simply not allowed to do it. Second … and this is the really important point …I'm not Richard Ronson! Don't look bashful Richard, I mean it. You have a special talent!"

Ronson wasn't sure he was looking, 'bashful' as Bloombridge had put it - sceptical, suspicious and apprehensive maybe! The idea of trying to get to grips with legalistic wording and making arguments in support of something to do with The Games filled him with dread. All he could see was some great, long, dark, uphill tunnel he would have to try and climb through. Bloombridge, whether he recognised this or whether he genuinely saw Ronson as simply being taken aback by praise, carried on undeterred.

"I don't have your charisma and power to draw the people Richard – very few people do." In this comment Bloombridge was absolutely honest. He could, with equal honesty have added, "And very few people are as perceptive as me in realising this", for there in a nutshell, was the beast that David Bloombridge was endeavouring to create - a beast with the perceptive power of himself and the persuasive power of Ronson. Ronson, certainly at this moment however, was focussed on looking for ways of avoiding further involvement in this project rather than trying to see any bigger picture.

"Well, if the bill can't be reintroduced then surely that's it, David?" He knew, even as he said it that Bloombridge would not be sitting here sipping his coffee if there wasn't a way to bypass this apparently obvious impediment.

"See Richard, you're thinking like a councillor! The important point is that I am not suggesting a bill *exactly* the same as Ramathan's. It will be sufficiently similar to enable a real come back of The Games – but it won't be exactly the same bill and so won't fall foul of that problem. You would therefore be free to table the bill in the Local Level Parliament. If you get the bill passed, then you will have shown there to be 'democratically established will'. That would then allow it - in fact require it - to progress to the District parliament. If it is successful there then it will have to go to Territorial Council and if successful there on to the Continental Council. After that it would almost certainly go on to become law! Councillor Ronson would then be in a position to see it implemented at the next Games. Think of it Richard, not just the Ronson Bill but The Ronson Act! Destiny beckons Richard!" He took a sip of coffee and put his cup down watching Ronson for his reaction. Had he over egged it?

"Can I think about it David? Like I said, I am really grateful … and I see the sense in what you are saying. I just don't know that I am up to it. Can I just have time to think – digest all this?"

"No problem, Richard. Fully understand," he said standing up. "Talk again soon though … hey?"

If the meeting ended with Bloombridge sounding confident and Ronson sounding uncertain it was almost the opposite beneath the surface. Ronson really felt that he did not want to go on to pursue a higher career in politics – and certainly not through again associating himself with The Games. He had achieved what he wanted to achieve – his four years salary and a return to some degree of public respectability. All he wanted to do with the next four years was explore avenues that interested him. Maybe something at Local Level would take his fancy and he would go for election for another four years or maybe some new line of endeavour would present itself – in the serendipitous way that these things had always seemed to do throughout his life. He would stick to his guns. He would be polite to David Bloombridge – but he would not be pursuing political advancement – and certainly not via The Games and a bill he didn't understand. The bill however was not all that Ronson did not understand. The biggest question in his mind was why Bloombridge was so keen to assist him. He knew what he had said about the private viewings being his 'ulterior motive' … but he sensed it went beyond that.

Bloombridge left the meeting very much on edge. He felt confident that Ronson could get the bill he had in mind passed at Local Level. The last election had swelled the number of more traditionalist councillors in that parliament. The situation at District and Territorial Level was more uncertain. The traditionalist orientated councillors had not increased in numbers in the way that they had at Local Level. His reading of the situation however was that if Local Level passed Ronson's bill with a large majority and the bill itself was worded carefully then District and Territorial Councillors would sense the groundswell and not want to oppose it. They would not want to be seen as going against the will of the people. In addition to that there were now a number of District Level Councillors on whom he could 'lean' because of the private viewings. There were fewer such councillors at Territorial Level – but there he had Ramathan and she would want to see the success of the reincarnation of her bill in the form of the Ronson Bill. The situation wasn't 'cut and dried' – but it looked positive. If the bill made it through District and Territorial then the Continental Parliament would simply give it a cursory glance and pass it on to The Supreme Triumvirate. They would rubber stamp it and the Ronson Bill would become law. Bloombridge felt sure he could word a bill capable of getting through Local Level. The biggest concern making

Bloombridge feel on edge when he left Richard Ronson's house was Ronson himself.

Bloombridge needed Ronson. For years Bloombridge had endeavoured to claw his way up the political ladder only to find himself blocked at every turn. When it came to 'democracy' and winning votes he simply didn't have what it takes. Richard Ronson did have what it takes and Bloombridge needed him to capitalise on a changing political climate so that doors would open for both of them. He feared that once again he was going to be frustrated in his plans. He needed to keep Richard Ronson on side. He had no hold over him - at least none that he could use without disastrous consequences for himself. He felt that he knew Ronson well enough however to develop a plan of persuasion.

*

David Bloombridge had not always been good at reading other people. He found it difficult at times to understand their wants and needs. He didn't completely lack empathy or insight but all too often he had relied on rules and reason in an effort to persuade people of his position. Repeated failure had taught him that an alternative was necessary, and even though it didn't come naturally to him, he had started to understand the power of the carrot over the stick. The fundamental thing that he had understood about Richard Ronson was that, above all else, Ronson needed to be liked. It was, as Mrs Christina had put it, 'his *raison d'être*'.

In response to resistance from Ronson the 'old' David Bloombridge would have gone to him with an outline sketch of his idea for the bill, explained its contents, drawn together articles and reports to show the growing trend among the electorate – and so on. The 'new' Bloombridge took a very different approach. The 'new' Bloombridge simply spoke to colleagues in the Local Council with a similar political outlook to himself. He asked them to ensure Ronson was involved in discussions – formal and informal – that highlighted their need for a leader and their need for an issue around which to unite. Ronson would not be able to resist the potential adulation of being that leader and sooner or later he himself would suggest The Games as their unifying focus – an idea that he would not divulge (or possibly not even remember) as having had its origin with David Bloombridge – but which their enthusiasm would confirm as the right choice.

The next time Bloombridge sat in Ronson's armchair he had, at Ronson's request, produced the core of a revised and softened version of Ramathan's bill. The thrust of the bill was the proposal that:

The Games, in keeping with earlier custom and practice, should now be used, in part and without prejudicial impact on the sporting and athletic events, to show publicly the administration of justice within Trueway. Convicted criminals, who face a sentence the implementation of which would, in its natural course, take place during the period of The Games, will have punishment carried out publicly at a designated Games' venue.

Bloombridge had given Ronson this rough draft to peruse. He guessed that Ronson would not want to get bogged down in legalistic jargon – and might even be afraid of it – but recognised that as long as Ronson understood the main thrust, maybe had a few key phrases to utilise and, most importantly, felt *confident* then there was every chance the bill could make a successful passage through the Local Parliament.

"Thank you for doing this for me David," said Ronson waving the draft bill in the air with his left hand as he placed a bottle of Scotch on the table between them with the other and sat down.

"No 'thanks' are required old boy. I think those few bits of paper in your hand will serve you and me very well. I think you took a lot of stick after The Failed Games – took a lot of the blame – and that was totally unjustified. The Games had become lacklustre, Richard. There was lots of excellent sport – but the good Citizens of Trueway have access to sport all the year round. The Games, coming as they do once in four years, need to be something special. The organisers have always known that – but had seen for themselves how simply giving Citizens high quality sport was not going to be sufficient. Just look at how things like fireworks, music and all sorts of entertainment have been interspersed with sporting events and how these things have become increasingly prominent in the more recent Games. This has all been an effort to maintain the energy of The Games so that they can live up to the hype and expectations that have been created. Two years ago the organisers got it wrong. All the whistles and bells they had incorporated didn't work and Richard Ronson took the blame for The Failed Games – but it wasn't your fault Richard and now, this bill – The Ronson Bill - will prove it. You can show through this bill that you know how to create a truly memorable and successful Games." He reached out and lifted the glass of whisky that Richard Ronson had poured for him while he spoke. "Salute," he said raising his glass and hoping he had hit the right degree of encouragement in his confidence bolstering speech.

"Thank you, David. I know I asked you to help me get this bill together – and I remember you suggesting something along these lines before – but I've read it and I'm not sure I fully understand it all – and that worries me – especially since I have more or less persuaded a group of Local Councillors that these changes to The Games are what we need."

"Parliamentary bills are put together with certain legalistic wording and protocols … but they generally boil down to pretty straight forward stuff. Anything in particular you didn't understand or that bothered you, Richard?"

"Well, could someone be executed? What if I am asked whether someone could be executed?"

"Goodness no, Richard. There will be nothing like that – or even approaching it. Ramathan wanted to go back to the format of the early post-Terror War games when Marginal terrorists were publicly executed at The Games. That was more – way more - than councillors in The Territorial Parliament could accept – though, like I have said to you before there were sympathetic noises. That's why I feel sure that a modified bill bringing back some of what happened in the past would be successful. From what you have said yourself there are Local Level Councillors who are with you on this. I am confident that they will back you, and when others see that, they will follow suit."

"OK so no executions … but what exactly are we talking about with this public administration of justice? Whenever there is a reference to punishments this paper you have given me simply says that these will be elaborated in an Appendix or that they will be carried out in accordance with 'sentencing guidelines' or 'various earlier statutes'".

"Well, since this is just a draft I didn't want to bog you down with additional appendices and stuff but all we would be looking at would be some public humiliation or some corporal punishment – nothing too severe – just enough to entertain and to give some feedback on what works best … for future Games you see. One thing I am clear about is that there would be no film record of any punishment implemented in accordance with the sentence – either by news media or the public. The only way to see justice being done would be to attend, in person, the venue where justice was being carried out. The organisers will like that. It

197

will encourage and bring back direct participation by Citizens in The Games. This won't address all the economic woes Richard – but it will help take people's minds off them … and if we can punish a few people on whom the economic woes can be in part blamed then we might even be addressing those too!"

This all sounded pretty satisfactory to Ronson and the thing that clinched it was that the work he would have to do was minimal. Bloombridge would arrange the drafting and legal checking of the bill and all Councillor Ronson would have to do was present it to the Local Parliament.

*

Bloombridge had gauged the mood of the Local Parliament correctly. The Ronson Bill was passed and passed easily. Bloombridge had also gauged Ronson correctly. Once he had accepted the course that he was taking his natural charm and friendly evasive bluster in any awkward situation saw him through even the most difficult questioning and argument. As long as the decisive factor was winning a vote then Ronson was the person to have on your team. Although Bloombridge knew that the people in the middle - the undecided floating voters – were the people who held the key to electoral success he had never had the personal skills to capitalise on this. His approach had always been too analytical, too argumentative, too complex. These people didn't analyse argument or detail. They put much greater store in the confidence and charm of the speaker – and this was what Ronson had by the bucket load. Maybe it was because Richard Ronson liked things simple himself that he kept his presentation and his message simple too. Whatever it was, the floating voter could relate to it, and Ronson was a guy to trust. "If good old 'Rubber' says this is what we should do then that's good enough for me – let's do it!"

*

If Montgomery-Jones had any doubts about Couchan's prediction of ten years as the time frame for The Alliance to unify Trueway and The Marginal Peoples then these doubts would be dispelled by the next Games and the next elections. In particular the rise of the very traditionalist, conservative group, apparently spearheaded by Richard Ronson, that threatened to reverse everything that she and others of The Alliance had been so carefully crafting in such a steady and united way.

(D) Middle Years

Chapter 42: Steph & John Hugo Begin

The sad advantage of disaster being the consequence of a widespread epidemic is that it is a common disaster and there are other people experiencing similar problems. That is how Steph and John came together. Like Steph, John had been recently married. Like Steph, John had lost his marriage partner to the epidemic. Like Steph, John had been in an enhanced marriage with permission for two children. Although Trueway provided official support – largely access to advice - it was informal groups on the internet that provided more personal social support, and with so many people affected by death and loss, new amalgamations and pairings developed out of mutual need. John and Steph met through one of these groups.

Did Steph love John? Did John love Steph? It didn't matter. They needed each other – particularly to utilise the enhanced marriage status for which they had worked so hard. John had a steady and secure job that was better paid than Paul's had been. Having already qualified for enhanced status John and Steph could be married quickly and took advantage of this to avoid John losing the house that had been granted to him as part of his enhanced marriage rights. In a period of less than two years Steph had been married twice, widowed once and become a mother. Less than three years from her first marriage she gave birth to her second child. She and John called him Tim.

Chapter 43: The Wake-up Call of the Phoenix

When Montgomery-Jones had heard about Richard Ronson being elected as a Local Level Councillor she had been startled – but she recalled Couchan's words and had to concede that Ronson really did deserve his epithet – a nick-name that she was aware was being used less often now. However, even his phoenix like rise from the ashes of The Failed Games did not prepare Montgomery-Jones for the news of the Ronson Bill and its successful passage through the Local Parliament.

Any Local Level bill that had potential ramification beyond Local Level had to be debated and voted on at District Level. The similarity of Ronson's bill to that of Ramathan was obvious but it was also clearly not identical and so could not be thrown out on that basis. There would have to be a debate and a vote. She was aware that the 'traditionalists' had made a few gains in the elections at District Level but it nevertheless came as a shock to her when The Ronson Bill was successful in that parliament too. She would never be able to fathom why that was the case – but Bloombridge knew. He had assiduously made sure that a significant number of clients for the private viewings were District Councillors and he had made it very clear how he thought they should vote. A bill that was successful at District Level would have to be debated at Territorial. All of a sudden the spectre of an adversary that Montgomery-Jones had left dead behind her had appeared again in front of her – changed, less threatening in appearance, but she feared, more deadly. She was right.

When it came for debate in the Territorial Parliament she again shone in the camp opposed to its passing, but needless to say Ramathan spoke in favour of the bill and there was a sparkle in her eye. She knew there had been those who had wavered before and that some of them would now be emboldened by the results from Local Level and District Level. How many would turn? It was close, but the Ronson Bill was passed at Territorial Level.

Montgomery-Jones was angry – but not at Ramathan. She was angry with herself and angry with the other members of The Alliance. She had been dismissive of Ronson's election but with the passing of the bill at Local Level she had, belatedly, taken the time to look at just what happened with the Local Council elections. She was able to see the large turnout. She was able to see that many councillors sympathetic to The Alliance had been elected … but also that the ultra traditionalists had done very well too. These warning signs should have been spotted.

The Ronson Bill would now have to be considered by the Continental Council. History predicted that any bill from Local Level that was successful at District and then at Territorial Level was almost certain to be successful at Continental Level as well. The majority of Continental Councillors were still traditionalist and this bill harked back to an earlier time of Trueway with which they would be in tune. Added to that it had been passed by the three lower tiers and they would not want to be seen as a block to the obvious will of the people. After Continental it would simply be a rubber stamp affair by The Supreme Triumvirate. A year ago nobody could have convinced Montgomery-Jones that a bill created by Richard 'Rubber' Ronson would pass into Trueway law – but now she was sure that was about to happen.

For Montgomery-Jones this was the wake-up call; the writing on the wall. Again she thought of Couchan and his prediction that The Alliance had ten years to realise its intentions before some event or other would overtake it with consequences that couldn't be predicted. She didn't know from where he obtained his intelligence – but her gut had told her he needed to be listened to … and now events were proving him right!

"Shit!" was all her brain could say, though her teeth were so tightly clenched that no utterance would pass her lips. She and the rest of The Alliance had been too complacent. The question was whether they had left things too late to recover. She knew that what she was witnessing was a groundswell of populist traditionalism that could potentially block the appointment of Alliance sympathetic councillors. Without sufficient Alliance councillors to support the return of the Marginal peoples and the unification of them with Trueway the present, unjust – and untruthful – situation would continue. The majority of the Trueway population would still believe that those in the Margin – what few they believed still existed – were evil terrorists rather than the ordinary (and to a greater extent than in Trueway) *extraordinary* people they were.

She knew that she would not be alone in this belated realisation of what seemed to be happening and sure enough she soon received notification of an extraordinary meeting of The Alliance Territorial Pod. The meeting recognised and analysed the situation very much as she had done. The meeting considered that the economic downturn was the most likely root cause since its impact had been felt most keenly by the poorest people of Trueway but was now increasingly impacting on the middle income groups as well with jobs being lost, mortgages being withdrawn and tenancies foreclosed. Hardship in general was spreading.

Similar meetings took place in other Territorial Pods and these were sometimes joined by one or two of the few Alliance councillors from Continental Level. The synthesis of all of these meetings was an action plan. The Alliance would identify sympathetic Citizens – possibly via TILE groups. They would field as many candidates as possible in future elections and would implement vigorous election campaigns. Maximum infiltration of Trueway at Territorial and Continental Level would be the aim. All funds and efforts would be directed towards this goal. The general view seemed to be that with this unified Alliance effort it might just be possible to achieve their goal in two election cycles. Paradoxically, thought Montgomery-Jones, Richard Ronson and his traditionalist, backward looking bill had been of benefit in shaking The Alliance out of its slumber. She felt better now that this plan was in place. She realised just how stagnant things had been. The Alliance had woken up and reaffirmed the job it had to do and had settled on the plan to do it.

Chapter 44: Richard & David: Onward and Up

Bloombridge, like many senior people in Trueway, was aware of The Alliance and of its long term aim – and didn't like it. It soured his equilibrium. Trueway was fine as it was. He did not know the names of Alliance members but in political and other spheres could guess who they and their sympathisers were likely to be. He had no doubt that Montgomery-Jones was in their number. He also had no doubt that the passing of The Ronson Bill would have shaken them. The original version of the Ronson Bill had made some reference specifically to punishment of any captured Marginals but this was deleted in one of the few amendments successfully argued during the bill's passage through the parliamentary levels. In the final bill that went forward there was therefore no mention of Marginals but it was clear that the Ronson proposals harked back to a time when the focus – the victims – of such public justice had been Marginal terrorists. Bloombridge would have liked the reference to Marginals retained but its very deletion satisfied him that he had shaken Montgomery-Jones and her colleagues.

He knew that The Alliance would now have recognised what was happening and would be – to his militaristic mind – marshalling its forces. Although there was much about The Alliance that he did not know … he *knew* that he did not know it. What the Alliance did not know; what he had been careful to ensure they did not know, was that standing behind Richard 'Rubber' Ronson and The Ronson Bill was a military mind of impeccable lineage – *his* military mind. The Alliance was on the back foot having to react to the battle plan that *he* was directing. With the help of Richard Ronson and the following he was able to obtain Major David

Bloombridge would halt the plans of The Alliance. Major David Bloombridge would halt Councillor Montgomery-Jones. The Games would now be a success and that would pave the way for him to suggest Ronson run for election to District. After that he would find other ways to encourage his protégé onward to the heights of Territorial and Continental Level – all the time swelling the traditionalist following and all the time facilitating the plans and ambitions of Major David Bloombridge. *This* was the long game.

*

The World Games were a great success – and who did Trueway have to thank for that? Local Councillor Richard Ronson. Ronson's bill had become Trueway law as the, "Traditional World Games Judicial Public Transparency Act". The worldwide sporting activities had been interspersed with public punishment of convicted criminals. The punishments usually took the form of humiliation and/or physical assault of some kind ranging from almost comical pelting of people in stocks with rotten fruit to severe caning. Historical records had helped the organisers of The Games to match punishments to venues – especially the match between venue size and type of punishment - but quite a bit of learning took place that would enable them to iron out issues and help maximise ticket sales for the next Games in four years time.

*

"Well, I have to hand it to you, David," said Ronson pouring both himself and Bloombridge a whisky. "You couldn't have been more right about The Games. If the last lot were a failure this lot absolutely sparkled – and it was your idea of the punishments that brought in the punters. No doubt about that."

"But it was you that made it all happen, Richard. Nobody else could have got that bill from Local Level all the way up to enactment in law … and especially in that time frame. I mean that Richard – *nobody* else."

"OK, let's say a joint effort then."

They sat down in the easy chairs at Ronson's 'blind spot' house.

"Well, I think you deserve the lion's share of that joint effort, old boy," said Bloombridge with a big smile. "Think of it Richard. You have, as a man, risen phoenix like from the ashes of 'The Failed Games', reinvigorated The Games themselves, learned the political ropes and, while doing all that…" here Bloombridge eased back in his armchair with his

203

whisky and a contented smile, "…managed your art business with alacrity and to many an art lover's satisfaction, and artist's gain."

Richard Ronson looked as bashful as a school boy being praised by the head teacher in front of the class.

"Don't look so coy, Richard," continued Bloombridge. "You deserve your success and all the plaudits you have received. Great rewards will come your way. Now, I hope, you realise that my suggestion that you run for office at District Level was not some harebrained pie-in-the-sky notion. With this success behind you I have no doubt of your ability to be elected. If you run you will succeed. Working at District is no more difficult than working at Local so why not run and enjoy the extra salary … and one or two extra perks. Sorry if that sounds mysterious Richard but take it from me there are benefits to being a District Councillor that are well worth the minimal effort you would need to go to now in order to be elected. Believe me Richard. If I was right about The Games I am right about this."

Ronson was pleased with his success as a Local Level Councillor. He recognised the help he had received from Bloombridge and accepted that they were something of a team. He had enjoyed the praise and adulation. He was coming round to the idea of running for District Councillor … but had a natural reticence.

"How's the whisky?" ventured Ronson.

"Wonderful, Richard. It tastes of success," smiled Bloombridge sitting forward and placing the glass on the small table between them. "It is a success on which I think - I know – you can and must capitalise. We have enjoyed a fruitful two year cycle. From your relatively low position as a Local Councillor you have created legislation and a revitalised World Games that has been enjoyed and appreciated throughout Trueway. Think what a man with your skills could achieve as a Councillor at District Level or higher. You really must run for office at District Richard – you must!" A broad grin spread across his face as he leaned back.

"I don't know, David. Like you say, we have achieved a lot … but you're a District Councillor – and look at you. You have far, far more knowledge than me. You don't need me taking up space at District Level."

"Taking up space? What kind of nonsense is that? We need space taking up by people of your calibre. Don't be fooled into thinking all the District, Territorial and Continental Council people are any more able or have any more right to 'take up space' as you put it, than anyone else. They are just average people in above average positions. Just look at Ramathan. She wanted the same as you … but which one of you succeeded in getting it?"

"Well, put like that I do see what you mean."

"So, is that a 'yes' to running?" beamed Bloombridge, raising his glass in anticipation of a toast.

Ronson paused, just briefly, then, with a broad smile, lifted his glass.

So it was that Richard Ronson's opposition to running for District office had been overcome, and Bloombridge's plans moved forward – though Bloombridge recognised the fundamental reluctance in Ronson. He anticipated that he might need to think carefully about future carrots and sticks in order to maintain Ronson's motivation and involvement in the political process.

Chapter 45: Has Montgomery-Jones Left things Too Late?

The success of The Games (and with it Richard Ronson) was not a surprise to Montgomery-Jones. Although she saw nothing interesting or attractive in the man she had to accept that other people did. The success did not surprise her but neither did it worry her. The Alliance was now galvanised and would be fielding sympathetic candidates at all parliamentary levels at the next elections in two years time. She herself would run for office at Continental Level. The Trueway system of partial selection from public vote and partial selection from the next tier up left her with reasonable confidence that she would be successful. She recognised the groundswell of populism among Citizens but hoped there were sufficient Alliance councillors already in the Continental Council to pull her vote up even if she lost some ground to 'traditionalists' in the public vote.

Unfortunately Montgomery-Jones was wrong. She was not elected to office at Continental Level. A few other Alliance members or Alliance sympathisers *were* successful so maybe in four years time she would have better luck … but right now, as she saw traditionalists gaining seats, she had a sinking feeling that maybe The Alliance had left things too late.

Fuelling that concern was her dismay that while she remained a Territorial Councillor Richard Ronson had secured a seat at District Level. Her concern and dismay would have been even greater had she known that behind Ronson was a quietly smiling David Bloombridge. Bloombridge had not sought political advancement himself in these elections. The years of disappointment had taught him that his interests would be better served by focusing his attention on deploying and guiding his protégé. It is better to be the puppeteer than the puppet.

Chapter 46: Steph Starts Work

Steph found Tim easier to manage than May. Was this because Steph was more experienced or because May had been more demanding? Maybe it was because John had more time than Paul to be with the children. Maybe it was because life was less stressful than when May was born. Maybe it was because they had been less adversely affected by the economic downturn than others. There were so many 'maybes'.

The house they had was in a quiet little close within walking distance of the town centre. It was quite a new build. It was very clean. It was very energy efficient. It was built with a lot of recycled and recyclable material. There was a small back garden and an even smaller patch at the front. Accommodation was on two floors and there was an attic as well. Steph enjoyed decorating and took pride in how the house looked. John was very happy to let her do this. He found such things a bit of a chore. They had pleasant neighbours – especially a blind gentleman called Charlie – but as a family they tended to keep themselves to themselves. When Tim was old enough to go to nursery and May was starting school Steph took a part-time job with the local council.

*

Steph settled into a comfortable routine and felt happy. The months began to roll by. John was doing well in his job and the children were happy in school. She enjoyed her work and was never reluctant to set off on the short walk each day to her office. At lunch time she would usually go to the park and sit on a bench to eat her sandwiches. Often she would go with a friend but she was alone on the day when she was startled by a voice saying:

"You got your 'EM2' then, Steph" and, looking up saw Chung.

"Oh Great Spirit!" blurted Steph.

"Haha – didn't mean to startle you … well I did really," grinned Chung.

"Well you succeeded," coughed Steph almost choking on her sandwich before starting to laugh.

"You look well," smiled Chung. "I saw you from over there as I was passing on my way to a meeting and I was certain it was you. You haven't changed. May I?" he enquired as he reached into his bag for his sitting towel.

"Yes, yes of course," and even though she was already at one end of the bench, made a shuffling motion and gesture, as if making space for him.

"You *do* look well … I'm not just saying that to be polite … and I see that you have achieved the enhanced marriage rights you were striving for."

"Yes, yes I did … and 'thank you', I feel well too."

"I'm guessing that you live or work over this way?"

"Yes, both. House that way and job that way," she pointed "… but what about you? Are you still at the station – Station 60? You wanted to be head of research didn't you?"

"Gosh no. I soon gave up on that noble idea. You don't earn many credits from research – a bit of prestige maybe but that doesn't put food on the table … or put a top of the range glide car in your garage!" He chuckled. "No, research was far too altruistic. I realised, that for me, the way to success and happiness was essentially one of being selfish!"

"Oh – really?" blurted Steph in astonishment. "I never thought of you as selfish. You didn't come across like that when we were at Station 60." She looked quizzically at her old colleague. "No, you're teasing me."

"Well, maybe a little bit," he conceded, "But not completely. I run my own marketing and promotion business. In fact I control most of the advertising and marketing in Territory 40. My people handle the promotion and image making for quite a number of senior figures."

"Wow! That's impressive – and providing people with a service doesn't sound that selfish to me."

"Thanks, Steph, but all I'm saying is that I soon learned that the simple way to get what *I* wanted was to give other people whatever it was that *they*

207

wanted. Anyway, enough about me, what about you? The right to have two kids - that's quite an achievement. Do you have any?"

"Yes, indeed, a boy and a girl. May is the eldest and Tim is a couple of years younger."

"You and your husband must be very proud."

"Yes, I guess we're 'proud' … but I think 'happy' is what comes to mind." Steph fleetingly considered telling Chung about Paul's death but felt it too much for a lunch time chat so asked, "And you? Any family? I notice that you don't have much in the way of tattoos."

"No, never went down the tattoo route, though I did get this done as a matter of instant verification," and he lifted his arm to display the word, "Non" (identifying him as a non-reproductive Citizen) written almost in his armpit where it was virtually invisible beneath the hair. "I had no desire for children and so a vasectomy and full non-reproductive rights seemed by far the best route for me. I don't have a long term partner either. But, I have interrupted your lunch," he said standing, "and I don't suppose you have that long. I very rarely get over this way from Territory 40 otherwise I would suggest we meet up some time."

"No, it's been brilliant seeing you," reassured Steph as she got to her feet. He gave her a hug and she awkwardly reciprocated with one hand still holding her sandwich.

"It's been good to see you so well and happy," he said looking back as he walked away.

"You too," responded Steph and then, feeling an odd compulsion to try to be humorous and nonchalant, added, "Mr selfish Chung."

"Indeed," he called back, "Mr Chung of the selfish paradox!" He gave a smile and a wave before the path took him out of sight beyond some bushes.

*

The encounter with Chung played on Steph's mind. He had appeared and disappeared so abruptly … and he had dismissed the idea of them meeting up. He hadn't proffered a contact number or given her much of a chance to do so. Was that part of his philosophy of selfishness? When she got home after work she checked on the internet and had no difficulty identifying his company. The photographs, testimonials and media footage confirmed his boast about the significance of his business in Territory 40.

"So, 'Mr Selfish Chung' you really have made it big. No wonder you didn't want to waste too much time with me," she mused out loud as she scrolled through the pictures and articles about him. She would not want to be in charge of some marketing empire and she felt no jealousy – but she felt some sort of unease that she couldn't name – or didn't want to name. She felt anxious, fearful even, that if she named whatever it was then she would have to face it. She turned off the computer determined to put her mind to more important things like the evening meal or helping May with her homework, but instead, the image that came into her mind was of herself sitting on a settee with a sleeping husband in the room next door. She no longer lived in that house and that man no longer lived. Sitting on that settee after Paul's angry outburst she had questioned whether she had made a mistake in marrying him – made a mistake even in pursuing Enhanced Marriage. That was all a long time ago and questioning thoughts about her chosen path had been obliterated by the need to survive after Paul's death. Such thoughts had not surfaced again. Was that because she was, as she had said to Chung, 'happy' – or was it because she had pushed unhappiness down?

From his days on Drilling Station 60 Chung had changed. She had not. He had abandoned his goal of becoming a researcher. Should she have abandoned her goal of enhanced marriage? No, these were stupid thoughts, but nevertheless the image of her sitting on that settee persisted and she felt as empty as the wine glass that she could see in her mind's eye.

Chapter 47: Here Comes The Tipsy Major.

"Welcome to District Level Richard," beamed a ruddy cheeked Bloombridge as he stumbled past Ronson. "Time to celebrate – hey old chap?" He landed in his usual armchair, not bothering with a sitting towel and announcing, "A whisky would be wonderful!"

Once again a bottle of Ronson's whisky was placed on the table, and before Ronson had managed to sit down, Bloombridge had poured himself an ample measure. "Doesn't seem five minutes ago I was congratulating you on being elected a *Local* Level Councillor – now look at you!" He raised his glass in salute.

Ronson would have 'chinked' glasses – but hadn't yet finished pouring his own drink. Having missed the moment he simply and politely said,

"Well, your advice on the Games and your support generally have played no small part in that – so don't think I don't realise it or appreciate it."

"Not at all Richard, old chap - an absolute pleasure! You deserve your success and I am only glad that you think I have been of assistance in you achieving it. And, let's face it, you have been of great personal service to so many of my colleagues through the private viewings that you have given here, in this very house of yours, over the years … and that is to say nothing of your indirect contribution to supporting 'starving artists' during the recession."

Richard Ronson smiled and gave a deferential nod as much as to say "The least I could do" though Bloombridge didn't see this, having closed his eyes and eased himself back in his chair savouring Ronson's whisky.

"Well, it has certainly benefitted many," he said somewhat dreamily, "– though I dare say some would say that it shouldn't be necessary; that it is a great shame that a chap has to resort to the subterfuge of such a thing as a 'private viewing' of art to satisfy his natural drives - or to taking DAMP in order to suppress them. I bet you have thought that on occasion haven't you Richard?" ventured Bloombridge, still in an eyes closed musing sort of way. Ronson had the distinct feeling that Bloombridge had started his alcoholic celebration of Ronson's success in the elections well before he arrived at his house.

"Well, population control and all that David. It's a necessary thing – so better that we have DAMP to help is what I say."

"Oh yes, Richard. No doubt about that. Point well made and point taken – but look at all the good that has been achieved by the private viewings." He suddenly opened his eyes and sat forward. "All those young ladies helped, Mrs Christina's business kept afloat when others have gone under … and all because a few men have stayed off DAMP for a while and let loose their natural inclinations." He reached for the bottle but kept talking as he concentrated on pouring. "When did you last have a DAMP Holiday Richard?"

Ronson's conversations with Bloombridge had always been cordial – friendly even – but never personal so this question took him off his guard. He felt embarrassed and faltered. Bloombridge seemed not to notice anything untoward in Ronson's lack of response, and with his concentration fully on his glass of whisky, carried on with a question that turned Ronson's hesitancy to discomfort.

"What's your own sexual preference Richard? Never managed to get a grasp on that. You have always been so professional in your management of the private viewings – obviously that professionalism is what has made all this possible … the trust you see?" At last he looked at Ronson. "But have you not been tempted by the lovelies that you guide into the viewing room?"

With his regular use of DAMP the temptation for Ronson had been minimal – but even when it did occur his sense of self-preservation had kept such temptation in check. Despite his popularity, and having many female admirers, Ronson had never met 'the one' and although he would have liked a life partner, he always aspired to ladies that were unavailable for one reason or another. For Ronson therefore legally available pornography for recognised periods of DAMP Holiday was all he considered that he required.

"W-w-well..," he stammered – and at last Bloombridge noticed the hesitancy.

"Sorry, old chap – didn't mean to embarrass or put you on the spot."

"No, no…not an issue David … No, no - just wasn't expecting …" faltered Ronson, not wanting to offend his guest.

"Well, you know how it is Richard. Nobody is a greater supporter of Trueway than me – you of all people know that … but well we're both men …hey?" He gave Ronson a knowing smile, and without invitation again uncorked Ronson's whisky and topped up both their glasses. "Cheers, Richard".

"Cheers David," rejoined Ronson as he dutifully chinked glasses with his very relaxed guest. "Yes, definitely – definitely."

"Thought so … wouldn't have minded one or two of those lovelies m'self. Admire your professionalism Richard … and your self control … *especially* your self control hey?" He grinned.

"Oh yes, David – plenty of that," said Ronson endeavouring to sound as jolly and in the spirit of things as he could while actually feeling quite ill at ease. He had never seen Bloombridge like this.

"Well, Richard," said Bloombridge leaning forward and suddenly speaking in a conspiratorially hushed tone. "I think all your professionalism deserves rewarding. Hey, what do you think Richard?"

Ronson wasn't at all sure what to make of this. He had no idea to what sort of 'reward' Bloombridge was alluding but everything that Ronson had done in his dealings with the man he had done with an eye to furthering his own standing as a person of note with the higher, influential echelons of Trueway, so didn't want to offend him. He felt he had to tread carefully with the tipsy Major despite his discomfort – now tinged with apprehension.

"Well, David…," he began cautiously and was pleased when Bloombridge cut across him.

"Well, Richard, we're a double act, hey?" Bloombridge chuckled before taking another mouthful of whisky. "No, seriously Richard," he continued in his most earnest and hushed conspiratorial tone with one hand now reaching out to sit gently on Ronson's own. "I can't help feeling you deserve a 'thank you in kind' for the service you have provided. Now you're, 'District' you will find that you may … or then again may not …" Bloombridge mused momentarily, "be approached about certain political facts not known to most people. I'll say no more than that. Either way, I will ensure you will be guided to the pleasures you so justly deserve – pleasures beyond your wildest dreams."

With that Bloombridge downed the last of his whisky, thumped his glass onto the table then abruptly – if a little unsteadily – got to his feet and wished his host 'good night'. Ronson was glad that Bloombridge would be making his way home in an automatic glide and not behind the wheel of a manual one. It had been the most curious of encounters and Ronson had no idea at all what to make of it. Another six months would pass before he would gain enlightenment.

Chapter 48: Teddy in the Attic

Following her unexpected lunchtime encounter with Chung, and the unsettling thoughts it had provoked, the rhythm of everyday life with its pressures and pleasures quite soon restored forgetful equilibrium. Steph accepted life as it was. When she was younger she had determined that she would achieve enhanced marriage status. It had been a goal – a good goal - no matter what forces, whether internal or external, had set her on that trajectory. Looking back she occasionally tried to recall whether she had seen enhanced marriage as a doorway to something more, to something 'better', but she was clear now that it had become, and indeed was, an end in itself. She accepted this. She was a wife, a mother and a reliable team member at work. She had a comfortable home and a comfortable life. She was a good Citizen – and had the tattoos to prove it to the world. Had she ever *really* expected anything more? Then, one day, May asked what toys Steph had had when she was a child.

Steph had had very few toys but she had had a small fluffy teddy. She had kept it and it was probably in the attic if May wanted to see it. So it was that Steph went to the attic to rummage through boxes. In later years they would convert the attic to an additional bedroom but when Steph went in search of the teddy the place was a jumble of oddments. There wasn't even a proper ladder and Steph had had to scramble up using precariously balanced furniture while May stayed downstairs with John. Steph had a couple of ideas as to where 'Teddy' might be and began her search. She found him without too much effort – but then saw a suitcase and her heart was in her mouth!

She knew that in that suitcase was a bag and that in that bag was a dress. When had she last thought of that dress? She knelt down and gently touched the suitcase. It was dusty. *Where does dust come from?* she thought. She traced a line in it and looked at her grey finger tip. Her heart was beating faster than it should for looking at a dusty suitcase. She hovered. Should she open it and look? Then another thought. Should she actually get rid of it? She almost never thought of it or of the blue eyed man – not even when she looked into the blue eyes of her daughter.

"Muum …have you found it?" came the call from below.

"Coming…"

Chapter 49: Bloombridge: A Mistake

After the bizarre congratulatory visit from Bloombridge, the two men resumed their usual interactions in the agreed ways regarding political matters and the private viewings. Nothing more was said to Ronson about pleasures beyond his 'wildest dreams'. In fact Ronson quickly dismissed everything the obviously tipsy Major had said on that visit. It took Ronson a little longer to get past his irritation at the man consuming so much of his best quality whisky! Hadn't Bloombridge boasted his own selection of single malts? Had he not even hinted at inviting Ronson round to sample them? *That never happened,* thought a sulky Ronson.

The months passed and even Ronson's disgruntlement about the whisky had subsided by the time Bloombridge eventually made an unexpected phone call asking whether Ronson had a day free.

*

The David Bloombridge who arrived on the agreed day was not the flush faced Major of six months earlier. Ronson was on his guard. Six months with no contact outside the agreed protocols then an unexpected phone call. Bloombridge had undoubtedly helped Ronson with his political career – but had been candid in his self-interest regarding his need for Ronson in relation to the private viewing business. In terms of the present visit therefore Ronson had little doubt that there would be a pay-off for Bloombridge somewhere down the line.

In terms of the ostensible purpose of this visit all Ronson could think of was the tipsy Major's offer of rewarding him 'in kind' for the support he had given with the private viewings. Given the strange nature of that evening Ronson had dismissed this as the whisky talking. In his recent phone call however Bloombridge had only agreed the date after bluntly asking Ronson when his next DAMP Holiday was due and a little about his sexual preferences. Ronson had been candid about the former but cautious about the latter – merely saying heterosexual with a liking for well rounded, pretty young ladies. It sounded uncontroversial and was broadly true.

"Not been approached by anyone about anything unusual?" was the cautious gambit of Bloombridge as they sat themselves down with morning coffee and biscuits on the veranda at Ronson's house.

"Well, I've been kept pretty busy as you know – and hopefully I'm getting the hang of things at District, though I guess I would say it's *all* a bit unusual for me … but I'm getting there I think."

"I have no doubt you are old chap – no doubt – so other than the unfamiliarity of the new job there's nothing that you would consider a great revelation? Nobody has come to you with any kind of – what shall I say – *outlandish* suggestion?" Bloombridge eyed Ronson with a silent and unblinking gaze.

David Bloombridge appeared totally sober but his mysterious line of questioning and slightly odd manner was making Ronson apprehensive. He didn't want a repeat of the last meeting which he had found both embarrassing and confusing. There was no doubt in Ronson's mind that Bloombridge was an astute politician and that the advice and guidance that

214

he had given had been completely sound, but there was a part of Ronson that was now wondering whether Bloombridge might be ill; maybe in some early stage of dementia.

"As I said, David I've been kept busy and there's been new stuff for me to get to grips with but, other than that…?" He gave an open hand gesture and shrug of his shoulders that could have been interpreted to mean either, 'nobody has said anything unusual' or 'what on earth are you talking about?' … and Ronson probably meant both.

"That sounds like a 'no' then." Bloombridge slowly lifted his cup and took small sips of his coffee. Ronson thought it looked as if Bloombridge was giving himself time to think. There was certainly no eye contact or attempt to move the conversation on. Ronson was about to introduce some chat about what he had been doing at work when suddenly Bloombridge, quite decisively said, "It makes no difference. Got time for a little trip; take your mind off all that new, District Level work?"

In the phone discussion with Bloombridge Ronson had agreed to set aside the day so the question seemed superfluous, but having been asked again, Ronson now wanted to say that something unexpected had come up and he now only had an hour – but that would be discourteous and he didn't want to do anything that might adversely affect his relationship with Bloombridge or any future assistance that he might need from him.

"You asked if I could set aside a day and we agreed today David, so I guess I am at your disposal … and if you want to make a trip, then so be it, a trip we will make," responded Ronson with a broad smile.

"In that case, old boy, I suggest we savour your excellent coffee and then head off to my glide."

Twenty minutes later they were seated side by side in an auto-glide car behind Ronson's house.

"So, David where are we off to?" Bloombridge didn't answer immediately – but neither did he start the car. He pondered a second before looking directly at Ronson.

"How many art viewings do you think we have had over the years at your house Richard?"

"Gosh …mmm."

"Don't answer – no need. It has been enough for you to know the routine that you and I and Mrs Christina have employed for security and for keeping everything confidential – yes?"

"Yes?" confirmed Ronson quizzically.

"Then you will understand that in order to keep everyone safe I am not able to tell you where we are going – only that you will love it when we are there. Once we start I will dim the windows too. OK?" This didn't make Ronson feel any more comfortable – but he gave an affirmative "OK".

"Excellent old chap. Now I have to warn you the journey will take a little while. That OK?" Ronson nodded and Bloombridge tapped in the destination, the windows dimmed and the car took them away. Bloombridge put on some music and they both relaxed for an otherwise silent journey.

Ronson did not find the journey as long as he had anticipated given the warning from Bloombridge. When the glide car stopped and they got out however Ronson was surprised to find that they appeared to be underground. Although Ronson knew it was possible for a surface glide car to enter the under-glide network he had never been in one that actually did it. They alighted onto a platform that was similar to that of a regular under-glide station though there was none of the usual lighting, advertising and furnishings. The platform was deserted and grimly subterranean. The brick walls were painted cream but the paint was flaking and there were streaks of brown staining where it seemed groundwater had leached through. There was some sort of emblem on the cream wall but it wasn't anything that Ronson recognised.

They went up several flights of stairs to emerge onto a landing and thence through a door into a small room. There were no windows and each of the three walls had a closed door. Bloombridge unhesitatingly led Ronson through one of them and he found himself in a small, nicely furnished bedroom with purple walls. Again, there were no windows but each wall had a door. There was a double bed opposite to where they had entered. To Ronson's side was a comfortable looking armchair and there was another beside Bloombridge. Both chairs faced the bed. Bloombridge invited him to sit in the nearest chair before leaving the room through the door in the wall to their right with a cheery, "Back in a second, old boy". A bemused Ronson sat and waited. About five minutes later Bloombridge returned and came to sit in the vacant armchair.

"OK, Richard. Everything is arranged." He handed Ronson a small pad of paper and a pencil. "You can make a note of the number of any girl that you would like to have. You can have one or more – as many as takes your fancy in fact. All you have to do is decide which girl or girls – and after that simply what you would like to do with her, or them, for the next couple of hours. There will be about ten young ladies to have a look at to begin with … but more can be brought in if there aren't any that take your fancy. Once you have made your choice I will leave you to it and come back in a couple of hours … obviously I will knock!" He gave an exaggerated wink and smile. "Any questions?"

"Well, I wasn't really expecting…"

"No, but don't worry about that – just make a note of the numbers and then give me the paper." He clapped his hands and the door in the right hand wall opened. A girl, that Ronson estimated to be about twenty years of age, came in. She was of average height, blonde, plump and pretty. A card with the number "1" hung from a string round her neck. She looked bewildered. The door closed behind her which made her start slightly. She looked round the room and at the two men but did not move. Bloombridge went across to her, took her by the arm and marched her over to stand in front of Ronson. She showed no resistance.

"Pretty isn't she?" said Bloombridge turning the girl round by her shoulders so that Ronson could see her from behind as well.

"Yes," said Ronson hesitantly.

"And don't be afraid to have a feel or check any bits out that you want." With that he turned the girl back to face Ronson and squeezed one of her breasts. "See, nice and soft. Still, I'm sure you don't require me to teach you what to do – just go with what you need to know or want to see to help you decide." He then marched the girl over to the left hand side of the room close to the other door. "Kneel there." He pushed down on her shoulders and the girl knelt. He left her and walked back towards the other door. Again he clapped his hands. Again the door opened. This time a buxom girl – probably a bit older- entered looking equally bewildered. She had dark hair and olive skin and was also very pretty. He led her across to Ronson.

"You've got the idea Richard. I'll leave it to you to check her out as much as you want then tell me when you're ready, and we can get the next one in."

Richard Ronson was in a state of shock and not at all comfortable about manipulating the girls. He gave each a cursory glance as Bloombridge brought them in one after the other. Eventually there were ten girls kneeling in a line facing Ronson. They varied a little in height and

217

skin tone but all appeared to be in their late teens to mid-twenties. They were all quite rounded and all had very pretty faces. None had tattoos.

Ronson scribbled '6' on the pad and handed it to Bloombridge who obligingly then went and lifted the girl to her feet. She was white skinned with curly, ginger hair and a round tummy. Ronson thought she looked about nineteen or twenty years of age. Bloombridge took her by an arm, brought her over to the vacant armchair and plonked her down into it.

"She's yours Richard. Do whatever takes your fancy – really anything. It's her purpose." Ronson must have looked as stunned and bewildered as the girl because Bloombridge repeated himself and expanded, "Really Richard, anything you want to do *with* or *to* girl number 6 you are free to do it – absolutely anything and needless to say you can demand anything you want from her and she must do as you say. Obedience is paramount. Fail to obey and she knows she must be punished - and you must be prepared to provide the punishment. She will expect it." Bloombridge then crossed the room to the kneeling girls, stood them up and marched them out of the door like a platoon of soldiers saying to Ronson as he went, "See you in a couple of hours old boy – oh and I should add, she probably won't say much – trained to listen and obey rather than speak."

After the door had closed Ronson sat for a moment trying to take it all in. The girl sat motionless in the chair. Where was he? He had heard of brothels but none existed in Trueway – at least not as far as he knew. Was this a brothel?

He looked at the girl. She just stared ahead, completely motionless apart from an almost imperceptible, nervous rubbing of her right foot against her left.

"What's your name?" he asked as gently as he could. The girl made no movement and gave no verbal response.

"Where are we? You probably think it silly I don't know. Can you tell me? Hey?" No response. "You're very pretty." No movement or acknowledgement. "How old are you?" Nothing. Well, Bloombridge had warned him.

"Can you speak? I mean are you not dumb. Sorry that's not very well put is it?" The girl remained motionless.

"Can you stand up?" She glanced over to him, questioning. "Sorry, that wasn't clear either. Please, stand up for me." The girl got to her feet. She looked straight ahead.

"Walk over to the bed, please." The girl did as requested. She stopped when she reached the bed but did not turn round. She was like a robot, a computerised creature that obeyed precise commands. *Could she be a robot?* thought Ronson.

"Turn round." She turned. "Kneel down." She knelt. "Stand up." She got to her feet. "Hop on one foot back to the chair." She complied – and remained balancing on one leg until he told her to put her other foot down. While she hopped she had looked straight ahead with her arms by her side – not even lifting them to assist her balance or steady the motion of her breasts. Would any human being really follow instructions so very, very exactly? She looked real – but…?

"Come and stand in front of me, facing me." She came across. He leaned forward. His face was level with her pubic area. He thought he could detect a faint womanly odour, but he wasn't sure. Hesitantly he put his hand out towards her. She remained motionless. His hand hovered just above her thigh. Could he feel heat? Again he wasn't sure. He looked up at her. She was still looking straight ahead.

"Look at me."

She looked down, but although their eyes met, she seemed to be looking *through* him rather than *at* him. He watched her face as he put his hand onto her thigh. Her face remained expressionless. Her thigh felt cool but not cold. He stroked gently. It felt like skin. He pressed gently. It felt like flesh. He pinched gently. The flesh sprang back as soon as he let go. Her pubic hair was sparse. He took a little between finger and thumb. He kept watching her face as he pulled it a little. Did he see her wince ever so slightly? He wasn't sure.

"Stand with your feet apart." She stood like a soldier at ease but with her arms hanging loose.

"Look straight ahead." She did so. He put his hand between her legs and very, very lightly ran his middle finger along the crease between her labia. He looked up at her. No perceivable reaction. He pressed inward slightly. Now, here, between her legs as he pressed in towards her vagina he could feel body heat. He kept looking at her. She remained impassive, unmoving staring straight ahead. He took his hand away.

He reached up and took her left nipple between his finger and thumb. He began gradually to pinch. He could see the discomfort mounting in her face as he pinched harder. He could see her jaw clench in an effort not to pull away or cry out. He stopped. It was only the slightest of reactions but it was the first spontaneous thing he felt sure he had seen. If she *was* a robot then she was a robot capable of feeling pain – or at last creating a very convincing response to mimic it.

Richard Ronson was bewildered. He had no idea that a place such as this existed in Trueway. How was it possible that he had no idea? How was it possible for such a place to exist – and for someone like David Bloombridge – a District Level Councillor - to know about it given the strict sexual laws of Trueway? He looked at the robotic girl in front of him. If she was real – a real human being – then where had she come from and how had she been made to be like this? He thought of the artists for whom he arranged private viewings. There was some sort of payoff for them. Did this girl have any payoff? What was she expecting of him? Was she expecting anything? Was he disappointing her if he took no further interest in her? What if he was being filmed? He glanced round the room. There were no obvious cameras. He could see no immediate reason for Bloombridge to covertly film him, though it would place a hold over him since sex with this girl would be illegal. The temptation was great. She was very beautiful.

"Kiss me on my mouth."

She leaned forward and her soft lips pressed against his. He put his hand behind her head and held her there. To his astonishment the girl spontaneously began to explore his mouth with her tongue. He responded and the inside of her mouth was warm and wet. He removed his hand from the back of her head. She continued kissing. He gently pushed her back. His member had hardened.

"Do you want me to have sex with you?" No indication of an answer; nothing by way of a response to indicate 'yes' or 'no'. It was as if the kissing had been a switch. As soon as the kiss had stopped she had reverted to this robotic state. "Would you object if I had sex with you?" The same lack of response. His erection subsided. "Go and sit back down in the chair."

She did as she was told and they stayed like that for the remaining time until Bloombridge returned.

*

On the journey back Ronson asked Bloombridge where the purple room was located, how he had come to learn of it and whether the girls were human or highly sophisticated androids. All Bloombridge would say was that it was a privilege enjoyed by some, though not all, councillors of

District Level or above. He really could say no more and probably should not have taken Ronson there. It was a mistake. He apologised. After this interchange the remainder of the journey was made in an awkward silence.

*

Bloombridge had miscalculated big time – and he knew it.

He had, quite genuinely, wanted to reward Ronson – give him a surprise; a pleasure beyond his 'wildest dreams' … but it had turned into a nightmare. More devastating for Bloombridge, was that his strategy for ensuring Ronson's future participation in his plan to halt The Alliance, and the likes of Montgomery-Jones, had been shattered by his own hand. He had gauged Ronson incorrectly. He had hoped that the purple room and the unbridled pleasure it could offer would be the 'carrot' he required to ensure that Ronson would run for office at Territorial Level. He would not have told him the location of the purple room or any significant details about it but he had expected Ronson to have enjoyed the experience so much that he would be desperate to return. Bloombridge would then have made that conditional on Ronson running for Territorial, and in doing so, pulling in his wake, other traditionalist Citizens and their councillor representatives into ever higher positions of power in Trueway. That was the only way that Bloombridge could see for halting The Alliance – for halting Montgomery-Jones.

Now Bloombridge feared he had 'blown it'. Now he was unsure what to do. To begin with he simply left Ronson alone. He felt it best to let the dust settle. He knew that Ronson would not dare tell anyone of what had happened. Ronson had absolutely no proof, could not take anyone to the purple room and would, potentially, be putting himself at risk because of the private viewings. But after the dust had settled – what then? Was there anything Bloombridge could do to rescue the situation?

That Bloombridge had miscalculated was not in doubt – but it had probably not been as great a miscalculation as he thought.

*

Richard Ronson, back in his own house wondered whether everything that had happened was real or some kind of hallucination. Could he have been drugged in some way? That seemed too bizarre – but a purple room with a robotic girl was equally bizarre. He reflected on the private art viewings that he had arranged at his house – this house where he now sat. Did the art lovers feel this strange disconnect when it was all over … or

221

did the paintings they purchased as part of the arrangement act as a link with reality? Did they even keep the paintings?

What took place at the private viewings was illegal so maybe the purchasers did not keep the paintings – but then again they were on sale legally from the gallery so the paintings were hardly evidence of criminality. Did the purchasers – or even the artists - think of themselves as criminals or just people pursuing a mutually beneficial arrangement? It was, because of laws, illegal but there were rules that were followed by both artist and purchaser – rules to which they adhered that kept them safe in the encounter and rules that kept them safe from 'the law'. Here was agreement. Here was consent.

He thought about the girl – girl number 6. She had rules – obey to the letter and accept whatever is done to you - a rule which she seemed quite prepared to follow whoever or *what*ever she was. There had been no rules for Ronson it seemed. Such imbalance in power added discomfort to Ronson's confusion – but it was a complex discomfort since Ronson could not deny that he found the freedom to do as he pleased exciting. No sooner had he acknowledged this however than he felt revulsion at himself for having such thoughts.

In the days following his return from the purple room he repeatedly found himself thinking of girl 6 and repeatedly swinging between desire for her and loathing at himself because he knew that part of his pleasure would stem from the power he had over her. In his periods of self-loathing he was glad – proud even - that he had spent the two hours in the purple room simply sitting in the chair – but when his thoughts were of desire for girl 6 he had the feeling, albeit coloured with shame, that he had wasted an opportunity. If Bloombridge had made contact with him during one of these periods of desire Ronson would have asked if he could return to the purple room and to girl 6, but Bloombridge did not make contact – not even in relation to private viewings.

As the days passed, Ronson, once again, found himself on the brink of slipping into self pity as his sense of isolation and abandonment grew. He had to do something to avoid that descent – and so it was that he found himself sitting with Mrs Christina in the back room of her gallery after she had closed up for the day. He had not come to tell her about the purple room or to unburden himself in any way, but simply to be with someone, and Mrs Christina was the person to whom his instincts led him.

He had felt at ease with her from their very first meeting. It was not a sexual or romantic attraction. He wasn't sure what it was. Maybe he felt that he could trust her. If, as a child he had felt inferior and rejected, the reverse became apparent as he grew in popularity. People wanted to be his 'friends' and he became less trusting; always seeing an ulterior motive. That was not the case with Chrissie. He felt comfortable with her at a personal level. He felt comfortable with her socially and he felt comfortable with her as a business partner in the private viewings. He knew that if Bloombridge was not coming to him to organise such viewings then Chrissie would be wondering what was happening since he doubted that Bloombridge would have gone to her directly to explain there was to be a hiatus.

In relation to the private viewings the general protocol was that Bloombridge liaised with Ronson and Ronson liaised with Mrs Christina but Bloombridge and Mrs Christina did not liaise directly. There was nothing to prevent Bloombridge from visiting Mrs Christina's gallery and saying something about why private viewings were not being requested but Ronson suspected that he would not want to place himself in the position of having to explain the situation.

Once with Chrissie, Ronson's mood immediately lifted – or the 'rubber' part of him came to the surface. He behaved in a quite cheery fashion. They talked art, and Ronson asked if he could buy one of the paintings by the elderly gentleman that he had spotted once before. It was Chrissie who eventually confronted Ronson.

"What's the problem Rick? I have a number of artists that really could do with some sales … and the gallery itself isn't making much money either."

"It's a long story Chrissie. I have had a bit of a falling out with Bloombridge. He hasn't approached me with any requests."

"Well, do you have to wait for requests? Can't you give him a nudge? This is business Rick so a 'falling out' shouldn't come in the way of that."

"I'll think about it," was all that Ronson said.

*

Ronson was ambivalent about approaching Bloombridge. On the one hand he wanted to ask to go back to the purple room – say that he had been ungrateful, say that he was just shocked and confused, but on the other hand he was, quite *genuinely* confused and that led to apprehension. To make such an approach felt like giving Bloombridge the upper hand.

And all the time there was this swinging back and forth in his head of feelings towards girl 6 – lusting after her one minute then loathing himself the next. As things stood, with Bloombridge leaving him alone, he was not under pressure to do anything for The Games or the next election - or whatever else he felt sure Bloombridge would be wanting of him. On the other hand he wanted to support Chrissie and her artists. In the end his dilemma was solved by Bloombridge.

*

"Hello Ronson, old chap. Really sorry about the misunderstanding."

Bloombridge had arrived, unannounced at Ronson's house. In itself that was a shock but those words of Bloombridge terminated the prevarication of Ronson. He had received an apology and now felt that he could not ask to go back to the purple room – could not say that maybe he had made a mistake and been ungrateful. If that were totally the case then he would have been in contact with Bloombridge. No, Bloombridge had made up Ronson's mind for him. Don't mix business with pleasure. Keep Bloombridge as business. Ronson didn't work all this out consciously at the time but that was what had happened somewhere inside and the outward manifestation was for him simply to say:

"Let's just forget it, David. So, have you not had any art lovers wanting to invest in paintings lately?"

"Exactly what brought me round – just as long as you are sure you are OK about my mistake?"

"Like I said – best forgotten."

There was a little more inconsequential chit-chat but it was evident that Bloombridge had come with the main intention of restarting the private viewings. Ronson also guessed that Bloombridge had probably wanted to gauge his general feelings about the visit to the purple room now that a little time had passed. Having received Ronson's reassurance that it should be forgotten, Ronson was not surprised that Bloombridge took him at his word and the incident was spoken about no further. Characteristically for Bloombridge the meeting did not last long once his purpose had been achieved.

So it was that the regular private viewings recommenced.

Chapter 50: The Dress Calls

In the Hugo household John and Steph had been enjoying a period of DAMP Holiday. After the birth of Tim, John had taken advantage of the free vasectomy offered by Trueway, but even so Steph also took an oral contraceptive at these times of sexual activity in order to have added security and peace of mind. They were therefore quite confident that an illegal pregnancy would not occur.

Quite conventionally John and Steph enjoyed their lovemaking at night. During the day life went on as usual and the demands of work, home and family life monopolised thoughts to the exclusion of carnal pleasure. Sexual urges could, nevertheless, be quite strong during the relatively infrequent periods of DAMP Holiday so a quick acting, temporary sexual suppressant could be taken if either of them felt it necessary. This was rarely the case.

It was the last day of their DAMP Holiday. John was out shopping with the children – and there had been the promise of a visit to the park. Steph had busied herself for a while around the house but then, having completed all she had to do, had decided to go and lie down on the bed to masturbate.

She lay there idly playing with herself and letting her mind wander. She had done this before on DAMP Holiday so it was nothing unusual for her. She would generally have her eyes closed and imagine scenarios that she found exciting. On this occasion however, being unsure how much time she would have before John and the children returned, she just stared at the ceiling feeling more relaxed than aroused.

Then, as she continued to stare her mind's eye took her up through the ceiling and into the attic. Her eyes closed. She could see the dusty suitcase. It was like before when she had found the teddy bear but this time, she knelt down, clicked open the catches and lifted the lid. There was her old bag – the one she had taken with her on pilgrimage with Sister Adolorardah. The red dress floated out of it and she was, somehow, looking down on herself wearing it. Then she was floating horizontal in the air. A strong wind swirled upward past her feet parting her legs. It blew the dress up over her stomach and then over her head. She was in darkness and in the darkness the pressure between her legs was all she was aware of – pushing, sliding, pulsating, moving, exploring.

A sound downstairs and a call, "We're ba-aack!" Her eyes snapped open. Quickly, silently she slid off the bed and round to the bathroom to wash her hands.

Chapter 51: Bloombridge - Back to the Agenda

After the recommenced private viewings had been going for a while Bloombridge did what Ronson expected – started talking about The Games. Ronson knew that as soon as The Games were done then Bloombridge would be pestering him about the election and wanting him to stand for a seat at Territorial Level. To be honest, Ronson did not feel that The Games would be that onerous a task.

The legislation facilitating judicial punishment at The Games – referred to by most people as "The Ronson Act" – was in place and Bloombridge had quite truthfully reassured him that the hard work had therefore already been done. The legislation had enabled quite mild – but varied – punishments to be carried out during the last World Games. Those Games had been a success and the punishment sessions had been well attended. The organisers of the forthcoming Games had analysed such things as attendance figures and ticket prices and had established popularity and trends. The biodata had enabled analysis of attendees by such things as age, gender, family relationships and a host of other parameters. Targeted advertising and friendly MyBook suggestions would draw individuals to suitably priced and located sporting events and punishments alike. Bloombridge was confident that all this would ensure that the forthcoming Games would be even more successful than the last ones. Bloombridge would attend to everything behind the scenes. All Ronson would have to do was be 'front man' – something Ronson wanted anyway so, all told, not that arduous.

*

"Then, after another splendid Games - for which everyone will thank Richard Ronson – it can be onward and upward with the elections." Bloombridge had thrown in this casual remark as he and Ronson were about to part after a discussion regarding arrangements for The Games. He anticipated resistance from Ronson and was not surprised when the response was,

"Oh I don't know David. I think I have pushed my luck on that front as far as I can. I really don't know I want to try and go further. I know I've said that sort of thing before … but well, I really don't think I have the ambition for it."

This was what Bloombridge had feared - but expected - and said no more than, "That would be a pity Richard – but of course it will be up to you. Who knows you may feel differently after another successful Games." In truth, Bloombridge knew that Ronson would not feel differently. Bloombridge had a problem.

Chapter 52: Yusef - Seen but Unseen

Yusef felt strange as he walked towards the stadium. He had to ask himself why he was here. Why he was doing this? What was his motivation? He was troubled. He knew the history of the Marginals. He was a Marginal. He had travelled here illegally using his Bronofsky Card but what was driving him? And was that incentive emotional or intellectual or something else – something unfathomable?

He pondered as he walked, absorbed within himself. Then she was there. He had no idea from where she had emerged so absorbed was he, but suddenly she was there, in front of him. It was the unmistakable toss of her head to get her hair back that had drawn his eye. It was that movement that had screamed – 'it's her'! She was walking along holding the hand of a little girl. A man was with her too. He held the hand of a little boy. How long had it been?

He walked behind them. He felt like a stalker. He feared the possibility that she might turn and see him. He *longed* for the possibility that she might turn and see him.

This man that she was with must be her husband – the man who had been awaiting her for the wedding ceremony beyond the convent orchard. Yusef could still see her; still hear her shouting to him as the Pipe closed. These must be her children.

His heart began to settle and he kept a safe distance. He had duties and he probably should not have come to The Games – though his reasons for not coming to The Games had not included this encounter. It wasn't really an encounter. It was a sighting. As he became calmer he became more rational. He continued to follow but he allowed the gap between him and the family group to widen. He was not part of this world – their world – and he should not be here. There was nothing for him at The Games. He turned into a side street, but as he did so the little girl pulled away from her mother with the imploring words, 'ice cream – please! Please!' and she veered off to a mobile vendor. Yusef glanced back. He saw the little girl's face. He saw her blue eyes. It was enough. The lightning bolt went through him.

Chapter 53: David's Cards on the Table

The Games had not been an effort for Ronson. To be honest, he had enjoyed both his part in them as 'front man' and also some of the content. He went to a few of the punishment sessions as well as the regular sporting events and general entertainment shows. It was a good Games.

He made a little wager with himself as to how long it would be before Bloombridge came to him to make the case for him standing for Territorial Councillor in the next elections. He had been a councillor now for six years and his relationship with Bloombridge had been going for well over eight years. He could see something of the symbiosis of their relationship, but in all that time he had felt that he had been the one who received the greatest pay-off … or so it would seem to an outside observer at any rate. He understood what Bloombridge had said in those early days about Ronson being necessary for the implementation of the private viewings. He guessed that Bloombridge gained something financially from the arrangement – though he had never pursued that with him. Ronson wasn't really interested in the financial affairs of Bloombridge. Ronson could also see that politically he and Bloombridge held generally similar, traditionalist views, and that assisting Ronson helped promote the things that Bloombridge favoured – but it all seemed to fall short of an adequate motive for constantly supporting him with The Games and his political career.

Then there was the purple room with girl 6 and all the other automaton girls. Neither man had spoken about that event since the day Ronson had said 'forget it' and gradually Ronson had stopped thinking about girl 6. He didn't fully understand however why Bloombridge wanted

228

so desperately to keep the private viewings going when he appeared to have access to completely unbridled sexual opportunities in the purple room. Whoever the clients were for the private viewings, why couldn't Bloombridge simply take them to the purple room?

There were so many unanswered questions – but part of the reason they remained unanswered was the indifference that Ronson felt towards them generally. Ronson was comfortable. He had all that he wanted. He didn't need to go sorting things out any further, and realised that when Bloombridge came to him trying to persuade him to run for office at Territorial Level, he would say 'no' – and this time he would not budge. He was more than happy with his lot. He had mastered what was necessary for being a councillor at District Level and he had adulation by the bucket full with The Games and other appearances in public. He could see nothing new that could be gained by becoming a Territorial Level Councillor. It was all too much effort for no obvious gain.

*

Ronson guessed three weeks – but it was nearer to four, by the time Bloombridge came knocking at his door to try and persuade him to seek election to the Territorial parliament. Ronson, having thought it all through, had made a firm decision that it was time for the Ronson-Bloombridge double act to come to an end. Despite the good relationship they had enjoyed over the years the thing that had made Ronson's resolve so strong was the almost farcical resentment that Bloombridge had never once invited him round to his house to sample the whisky of which he had once boasted. Ronson would not be unkind or strident in the encounter – simply firm. He would not run for office at Territorial Level.

With Ronson's decision so clearly and firmly made that should have been an end to it – but Bloombridge had anticipated the resistance. He had intended the purple room to be his incentive but he had made a huge mistake with that. He had little left in terms of either carrot or stick with which to entice or goad Ronson … but he was too close now to achieving what he wanted to give up.

The Alliance and the councillors in sympathy with it still outnumbered the traditionalists – especially at Territorial Level. If The Alliance consolidated that advantage at the next election then they would be unassailable and their agenda of unification of Outlands and Trueway would be unstoppable. He needed Ronson to run for office. He knew Ronson did not want to run. It was now a do or die situation for

Bloombridge so he was prepared to risk everything. He had only one weapon in his motivational armoury – the truth!

When Bloombridge arrived at Richard Ronson's house he was carrying three bottles of the finest single malt Scotch whisky. He didn't simply step inside in the way that he usually did. He stood on the threshold clutching the three bottles and proceeded to give a speech.

"I've drunk enough of yours over the years Richard. I know that you don't particularly want to run for office at Territorial Level so if, after this evening, you decide not to run for Territorial then I leave these with you as a 'thank you' and as a token of my good wishes for your ongoing career at District Level – or for anything else you choose to do. That said I very much hope that I can convince you to try for Territorial. I know that you love Trueway and I think, right now, Trueway needs you."

The whisky was a surprise. The speech with its talk of love for Trueway was the sort of thing Ronson had never heard from Bloombridge. He invited Bloombridge in.

"Coffee, David?" asked Ronson as Bloombridge spread his sitting towel on one of Ronson's easy chairs.

"That would be very nice Richard. Thank you."

Ronson was glad of a few minutes to busy himself with making coffee while he assimilated this revised Bloombridge. In his doorstep speech Bloombridge had been courteous and candid in stating the purpose of his visit - but courtesy and three bottles of whisky (although welcome) would not be sufficient to convince Richard Ronson to run for office at Territorial Level. Ronson felt sure that Bloombridge would know that. Was Bloombridge really going to try and use Ronson's sense of loyalty and love of Trueway as the enticement? As for 'Trueway needs you' … well, Ronson knew that he was a sucker for flattery … but that claim would require a lot of back-up to be in any way effective! He returned to his guest with coffee and confidence.

"Well, these are most impressive, David," said Ronson looking at the three bottles as he sat down.

"Like I said, I have had plenty of yours. I've selected three quite different ones – light and floral to dark and peaty. I have no doubt you will enjoy them."

"Indeed, David – they are very nice. One I have had before – but not the other two. I'm looking forward to sampling those *very* much!"

"But not enough to make you agree to run for office, I'll wager," smiled Bloombridge.

"Not if I am honest, David. Don't get me wrong – I really appreciate the gift … but I really don't think I want to pursue politics beyond where I am now. Without your help I would be way beyond my level of competence already … and before you say that you would help me with Territorial or that Territorial is no different to District … I know that it will be different and I know that neither of us have been there, so even you would be in new …forgive the upcoming pun … *territory*!"

"I'm a military man, Richard. Poor military men try to win battles. Good military men try to win wars. I'm also a politician. Politicians sometimes try to start wars and sometimes try to prevent wars. So how does all that mix up in me? Well, I'm a military politician that wants to win a war before it has begun. And both the politician and the soldier in me says that to win I have to know my strengths and my weaknesses. I know them – and I know that I can't win without you Richard." He looked straight at Ronson.

Ronson gave a slight nod followed by, "How's the coffee?" While his smile said, "I'm listening … but you know that you are not gaining any ground in your battle with me!" Bloombridge had only intended this preamble to be an initial, brief salvo to give Ronson a sense of false confidence and clear the ground for attack. Now he would fire the first of his real shells and he would be aiming to hit his target.

"The purple room is not in Trueway." He studied Richard Ronson's face. There was no smile. There was no quip about coffee. Bloombridge doubted that he had breached Ronson's defences … but he had hit the mark. He would send another salvo – just to create confusion so he added, "…well, not exactly."

Ronson settled back into his chair. One part of him wanted to say, 'I've told you before that I'm not interested in that place'. Another part didn't want to ruin his chances of going back there if Bloombridge was going to suggest this. Bloombridge, of course was unaware of the internal battle through which Ronson had gone following the visit to the purple room. He assumed that Ronson's silence at this point was simply due to him trying to work out what was meant by, 'not exactly'. He was not surprised therefore when Ronson said,

"Sorry, David you have lost me. Either a place is in Trueway or it's not in Trueway."

"Quite right, Richard. I wasn't intending to be obtuse. If a building belongs to and is part of Trueway but is actually in The Margin would you say that it was or was not in Trueway? The purple room is in such a building … so I hope you will forgive me for saying that it is not *exactly* in Trueway."

"So, are you saying that the darkened windows in the glide car, and all the secrecy, was to keep from me that we were travelling into The Margin?"

"That's pretty much it in a nutshell, Richard," and then added with a smile, "See how much better than me you are with words!"

"So, why have you come to talk about the purple room and its location after all this time?"

"Did you know – suspect even – that such a room could exist?"

Ronson was fully aware that Bloombridge knew his answer so remained silent. His guest continued.

"Most people think that Trueway is the only meaningful place on the planet. Yes, people are aware of The Margin and of Marginals – but on a day-to-day basis they don't think about anything other than their own lives within Trueway. Why should they? Why should any of us? The Terror Wars are a thing of history. The world in conflict is a thing of history. Such things do not happen now. How could such things happen now? That was the purpose of The Terror Wars. The end of world conflict, and for generations, the proof of the success of that and of Trueway has been evident for each and every one of us to see. Isn't that true, Richard?"

Bloombridge was becoming quite animated. He was sitting forward now. The question was rhetorical and Ronson sat waiting for Bloombridge to answer himself. The two men looked at each other in silence. Bloombridge slid back into his chair before continuing.

"Most people, Richard," he said in a much more contemplative tone as he looked into his coffee cup. Ronson wondered whether he was looking for inspiration. He could see the passion in Bloombridge but couldn't see where it was leading – especially if his aim was to convince Ronson to run for office at Territorial Level. But Bloombridge was not looking for inspiration he was having a final internal check on his strategy and hoping that he had not committed himself too soon.

"Most people, Richard," he repeated now looking up at his host, "but not me … and not The Alliance. The Margin and Marginals have never gone away, Richard. The people of The Outlands were never defeated.

They were simply put in check and now there are senior people – especially politicians - in Trueway who are in liaison – in league – with senior Marginals with the sole intention of unifying Trueway with The Outlands. These elite people from Trueway and The Margin form *The Alliance*. People like me have been kept down, Richard, stopped from progressing politically because we would oppose any such move ... but you have roused the traditionalist troops. At the moment those troops are blind to the enemy they are facing because you and your troops have come from the everyday Citizens who have no awareness, no conception of the life that goes on in The Margin or the links that exist between Margin and Trueway. You and a few other Local and District Level Councillors have started to rise through the political ranks. You were not supposed to do that – not as far as the elite of Trueway and the elite of The Margin were concerned. You have shocked them Richard – but they know that they are ahead of you – of *us*! If you don't run for office at Territorial Level Richard and take your followers - both councillors and everyday Citizens – with you then The Alliance and its sympathisers will be able to reveal the truth about The Margin and bring in legislation to reintroduce Marginals to our society. It will be the destruction of Trueway as we know it."

"That's a pretty astonishing story, David." Ronson didn't know what else to say.

"What do you think would happen, Richard if Marginals and Citizens were brought together?"

"Well, since it is such an astonishing story I can't say it is something I have ever thought about."

"I have, Richard. That is why I am so concerned. Trueway would be invaded by people who have a totally different lifestyle and outlook on the world. At best huge changes and compromises would be required by Trueway. At worst ... well I don't know ... complete annihilation of everything for which Trueway stands? One thing is for certain, things would change, and change is the antithesis of stability. Trueway would be destabilised. All the stability that is around us now would be in flux ... and that could lead to who knows where?"

"I understand what you are saying, David ... but I have seen no hint of any of this so I think you will appreciate that I am sceptical. Don't get me wrong. I don't want to say I don't believe you but surely if what you say is true then I would have seen some indications of Marginal activity - and I don't mean a report of an isolated incursion – and not only me but

233

other people would have seen stuff too and it would be reported in the media."

"If I had *told* you about the purple room instead of taking you there would you have believed me? Have you ever heard of anywhere like that or even seen speculation in the media?"

"A good point, David – but how do you know all this when so many other people – like myself – seem not to know?"

"Background. I am fortunate in coming from a military family that had links with The Margin in the past. It is, if you like, inherited knowledge."

"You do understand don't you David that this is such a fantastical story that it is hard for me to accept it? I know that you want me to run for office and I know that it means a great deal to you … and that three bottles of whisky wouldn't have done the trick!" he said with a smile, "but you can't simply expect me to accept all this, and on the strength of it, run for office."

"What will it take, Richard?" Bloombridge was about to play his trump card.

"Well, I don't know … something tangible."

"OK, so if I take you into The Margin and you can meet with a senior Marginal, talk freely with him – take a hand bio scanner with you if you wish to prove to yourself that he isn't a Citizen posing as a Marginal. Would that do?"

Ronson considered this. He didn't want to equivocate and ask to think about it so said, "Well, it would certainly help."

"And if I arrange that and you are convinced then you will run for office?" Ronson told himself that he should have known Bloombridge well enough to know that he would want a response with commitment.

"OK," he said … after all Bloombridge had said that Ronson had to be *convinced*. It seemed to Ronson that he had the better deal.

Chapter 54: The Red Dress Answered

Steph had not seen Yusef on that day when she and the family went to The Games. She'd no idea that Yusef had seen her and had seen his daughter. She had no idea the extent to which that unknown, one way encounter would protect her family when she could not. After The Games the routine of life went on as usual.

Life was a bit humdrum in many ways but Steph counted her blessings. She had the marriage that she had worked for. She had a good husband – a good man - and she had two beautiful children. As the years had ticked by these two children had grown and their personalities had started to blossom. They were kind, intelligent and caring. In terms of 'faults' Steph thought Tim tended to be a bit reticent and not ready to stand up for himself as much as he should while May could be a bit too confident, a bit too forward and ready to speak her mind. Steph and John enjoyed their respective jobs and the family was not short of money. There was plenty of leisure time and the town had good amenities. There were regular family holidays. Overall 'humdrum' wasn't too bad – and there were DAMP Holidays too.

She always looked forward to DAMP Holidays with John but increasingly she found that what she was looking forward to were her masturbatory fantasies of the attic. She always endeavoured to have some time to herself to gaze at the ceiling and float up through it.

Then, when Tim was six and May eight, John took the two children on a little overnight camping trip. He insisted that he go alone with them in order to give Steph a bit of time to herself since she always had to look after the children when he was away on business. It would just be the one night. Before they went Steph stopped taking her DAMP. Having time to herself she went for coffee, went shopping in a very unhurried way and generally relaxed though no matter what she was doing her thoughts returned, throughout the day, to the attic – though she would leave her moment of actual indulgence until the evening.

At around 9 pm she had a chat with John on the phone and wished him and the children good night. After that she went and lay on the bed and looked up at the ceiling– but she couldn't settle. She knew it was up there in the old bag in the case. She knew there was no risk of John and the children coming home unexpectedly, so after she had lain for a while unable to relax and float up in her mind, she went up in reality. They had some step ladders now so the ascent was easier than when she went looking for the teddy.

She knelt down, clicked open the catches on the suitcase and took out the bag and then the soft velvet material was in her hand. She held it to herself. She didn't let it unfold. She took it downstairs. The bedroom curtains were closed. She looked at herself in the full length mirror in the corner of the room. There she was, naked as always but she was clutching a red, formless bundle to her chest. She looked down at it and located the straps. She watched in the mirror as she held the straps and let the dress fall. The shimmering red took her breath away. "You are blood!" – And Steph meant this, almost literally. This dress, and wearing this dress, was like wearing blood. It was the visceral encapsulation of time past.

She slipped it over her head and stood there looking at herself. Now the room around her darkened and the walls became slate grey. She went and lay on the bed. She looked at the ceiling. She felt the material. She stroked it and then pulled the skirt up to cover her face. It smelt musty. She breathed in the odour of the cloth. She closed her eyes and the invisible pressure pushed open her legs. He is there. Is he there? Can something be there and not be there simultaneously; a person? Consent?

With one hand she held the dress onto her face, keeping herself in darkness while the other hand repeatedly squeezed her breasts before sliding down her body to explore. Her pelvis squirmed and she pushed the dress down harder and harder onto her face, sucking in air as best she could under the pressure, suffocating in the musty cloth smell and still she squirmed as fingers repeatedly circled, stroked, probed and pushed inside to fill the wet void while an uncontrollable trembling gradually engulfed her body only to be brought to an end by sudden, juddering waves that convulsed her entire being, as they fought upward through her arching back to find freedom in a scream.

She was a woman in her thirties. She was the mother of two children and now she sat in a rucked up red dress looking at her glistening thighs and a patch of wet on the bed with the realisation that she had just had her first orgasm. She made no attempt to go and wash. She sat, mystified as to why, after so many years, this had happened.

Chapter 55: Yellow Painting – 'New' Ronson born

For Ronson, the journey to visit the 'senior Marginal' identified by Bloombridge was very similar to the journey to the purple room. Bloombridge apologised for the secrecy but explained that he had no choice. Ronson did not question this - other than possibly in his head. In fact Ronson – and Bloombridge for that matter – said very little during the entire journey. Possibly both knew the outcome was uncertain and possibly both knew the outcome could be important and possibly each wanted to keep – or felt it best to keep – his own counsel.

When they alighted from the two person under-glide it was onto a similar platform to the one at which they had arrived before when visiting the purple room. The bricks were covered in flaking paintwork as before but the paint was green rather than cream. There was water staining as before and the whole place was equally dingy. There was nothing about it to suggest it was part of the regular Trueway under-glide system. This, at least, was consistent with the possibility that they had travelled into The Margin.

Like before they ascended several flights of stairs until they reached a landing with a door. Unlike before however Bloombridge did not go through. He pressed a button which Ronson assumed was a bell. There was a buzz and Bloombridge pushed the door. It opened and they went through. This time there were only two doors and one of them was already in the process of opening – automatically it seemed to Ronson since there was nobody behind it, only another flight of stairs. These stairs however were carpeted unlike the ones up from the platform which had been simply stone. Another door at the top of the stairs opened for them as they approached and Ronson followed Bloombridge down a cream walled corridor with a couple of side passages and a couple of closed doors. The lighting was low and the side passages were dark. When they reached the end of the corridor there was yet another door but when Bloombridge led them through this it was into a very welcoming living space. Ronson was somewhat taken aback. Walls of cream and maroon were illuminated by table lamps positioned around the room on what looked to be antique furniture. There were lovely paintings on the walls and small sculptures dotted about. Some of the paintings appeared to be old – not the regular recycled artwork common in Trueway. Ronson was amazed. Was this in The Margin?

"Richard, may I introduce Professor Murphy," and he gestured towards a man standing on a rich red oriental carpet in the centre of the room flanked by very comfortable looking chairs. The man appeared to Ronson to be about fifty or sixty years of age. He was good looking with a tanned complexion. Ronson thought he might be of Arabic descent. The most striking thing however was that he was wearing a long white robe. The robed man stepped forward with his hand outstretched.

"Councillor Richard Ronson," announced Bloombridge as the man shook Ronson's hand.

"Very pleased to meet you, Councillor Ronson. Please take a seat," and he gestured towards the easy chairs. Can I get you some refreshment – tea perhaps?"

"Tea would be very nice indeed," said Ronson quickly scanning the room for a sitting towel dispenser. There wasn't one so he took his towel from his bag and selected a chair. Bloombridge had already seated himself. He had made no response regarding tea and Ronson guessed that he had sat in this room with this man on several – maybe many – occasions before.

"Major Bloombridge has explained the reason for your visit," said Professor Murphy as he prepared the drink on an elegant sideboard before coming across to set down a tray with small tea glasses on a low table. He served Ronson first, pouring tea from an elegant silver teapot with a long spout.

"Thank you, Professor," said Ronson sitting forward to take the small, patterned glass.

"Please, call me Ahmed. Nobody ever calls me 'Professor' – not even David," he said with a smile as he poured tea for himself and Bloombridge.

"Your prerogative, old boy," said the latter reaching for his tea as Ahmed Murphy sat down.

"The thing is Councillor…," began Murphy.

"Richard … please, call me Richard," said Ronson cutting his host short and hastily adding, "… since we are being informal."

"Thank you Richard. All I was going to say was that I am not certain that I am a 'professor'. I have never held a post designated as such in Trueway."

"Well, if you don't qualify as a professor Ahmed, then I don't know who does," chipped in Bloombridge. "I tell you, Richard, this man is a genius. He might not have held an academic post in Trueway as such but there are plenty of people in Trueway who are grateful to him and what he has achieved – even if they have never heard of him."

"Well, what can I say?" smiled Murphy. "How is your tea? I should have indicated the sugar. Forgive me. I have relatively few guests."

"The tea is fine. Thank you. It certainly doesn't require sugar," said Ronson before adding, "... well not for me," having noticed that Bloombridge had helped himself to sugar already. "So, tell me professor ... I mean Ahmed ... what are these 'achievements' that David is referring to ... if that doesn't seem an impertinent question?"

"It is not impertinent at all," said Murphy. "As I said, David has explained his reason for bringing you here. I fully expect to be questioned and quizzed ... so please do not feel that you have to tread carefully for fear of offending me. David has made it quite clear that he is happy for me to be completely candid. So – and please correct me if I am wrong," he said looking at Bloombridge, "I expect David is referring to my work on longevity and on skin grafting. I think David is most interested in longevity – and certainly that is my most ground breaking work. It hasn't been applied widely yet but I have established techniques for extending people's lives. I do not know exactly how many years, and I expect some people will respond better than others, but the principle is applicable to all people and should mean decades and decades – if not centuries - of additional life for people." Murphy paused and looked silently at Ronson for a reaction. Ronson had listened – but felt he was listening to a fantasist rather than a scientist so simply said, "And the skin grafting?"

Ahmed Murphy did not seem in the least deflated by Ronson's apparent lack of enthusiasm.

"Well most of that work has been in relation to skin regeneration following burns. Without wishing to sound boastful, I believe that my work in this field has been of benefit to people within Trueway as well as people here in the Outlands."

"So we are in The Outlands now; this house where we are sitting?" interjected Ronson.

"Yes, Richard," affirmed Murphy.

"How do I know that? You did say that I could be forthright."

"Yes, indeed. We can go up to the surface and you can have a look. It won't prove unequivocally that we are in The Outlands but it won't look much like what you are used to in Trueway. When we are up there you could go outside but I would not recommend that without being fully dressed in protective gear. We are only just within The Margin – very almost The Beyond so the environment outside isn't the most pleasant."

"You say 'up to the surface' – so we are underground still?"

"Yes, that's right. No windows," he said pointing round the room.

239

"Will it take long – to go up?"

"No, not too long. A few minutes."

"OK – maybe in a minute or two then. I am guessing that you have a laboratory. Can I see that?"

"Ahh – that's more difficult. You are right, I do have a lab – but it is not here. This is my home and my lab is some distance away. We would have to travel. I think David would have to make arrangements in advance for that?" He looked questioningly at Bloombridge.

"Yes," he confirmed with a nod. "Not really practical today Richard."

Ronson was disappointed. He was beginning to wonder how much he was going to gain from this visit. The view of an unfamiliar landscape into which he couldn't go and a laboratory that he couldn't see. As suggested by Bloombridge however he had brought a hand held bio scanner in his bag so he could at least see if this man registered any biodata.

"So, would you describe yourself as a Marginal, Ahmed?"

"No, Richard, *you* would describe me as a Marginal. I would say I am an Outlander."

"Is there a difference? I mean … do you, as an Outlander, have bone encoded biodata?"

"No Richard, I do not have osteodata and David has told me that you may want to check that, so if you have a hand scanner, then please feel free." With that he stood up to give Ronson all round access.

Ronson took the scanner from his bag and turned it on. He pointed it at himself to check it was functioning satisfactorily. His biodata registered. He stood and pointed it at various points on Ahmed Murphy. Nothing registered. He pointed it at Bloombridge. His biodata registered. Could there be a trick – something he was missing? Could the long white robe be concealing some sort of electronic shield that was blocking the scanner from picking up the biodata? He didn't want to ask Murphy to take it off. It seemed very rude to ask such a thing of his host.

"Thank you, Ahmed. You certainly don't register anything," said Ronson sitting down and putting the scanner away, but still feeling less than convinced that Ahmed Murphy was a Marginal.

"David has spoken to me about something called The Alliance. Does that term mean anything to you, Ahmed?" Ronson glanced quickly between Bloombridge and Murphy as he asked his question. There didn't appear to be any non-verbal signalling taking place and neither man showed any sign of concern at the question.

"Yes, indeed, Richard. There are many senior people in both The Outlands and Trueway that would like to see a unification – an Anschluss." Ronson was struck by the very deliberate use of the German word … often regarded as being a euphemism for annexation.

"So, as a Marginal would you be in favour of such a unification … or should I ask first whether you regard yourself as a 'senior person'?"

"To the extent that I am aware of The Alliance I suppose I am as senior a person as David or yourself. Am I in favour of it? Not really. Am I opposed to it … also my answer is the same, 'not really'. I know that David has major concerns about unification. He fears it will result in Trueway being overrun by clothed Outlanders with no biodata and no regard for the existing laws of Trueway. He has a vision of an Alliance government enacting laws that would be so permissive in nature that the world population would grow and outstrip the planet's ability to cope resulting in chaos and conflict. … and do you know what, Richard?" he asked with a smile, "He may be right."

"You think he may be right – but you are not concerned? Why is that?" asked Ronson in puzzlement.

"I am a scientist, Richard. I do experiments. Some experiments work better than others. Nature is a scientist too. Human beings are one of nature's experiments. Dinosaurs were also one of nature's experiments. Which of those two experiments worked best, Richard; the dinosaurs that are now extinct but survived for a few million years or modern humans that are currently in existence but have only been here for a few thousand years? If unification results in destruction of the planet or the destruction of human life then nature will have her answer and she will give something else a try. I see the incredulity in your eyes, Richard. You are asking yourself whether I can really be that indifferent to the fate of humanity. I am not indifferent, Richard I am simply accepting. I do what I do as a scientist. If what I do as a scientist helps prevent the destruction of humanity – or maybe even hasten the destruction of humanity – then that is part of nature's way. I am simply part of her experiment. You and David are politicians. Maybe you see it as your role to try and promote or oppose such things as unification based on your values and on the predictions and extrapolations that you make in relation to those values. I know that David brought you here in his attempt to convince you to run for office as a councillor at Territorial Level in the Trueway political system. David has known me some little while. He knew when he suggested that you come

241

and speak with me that I would not 'take his side' as it were. He knew that I would not try to convince you to do as he wished any more than a fruit bowl would try to convince you to eat the apple rather than the pear. The bowl simply says *here is the fruit*. At David's request that is all that I am saying – here is a Marginal, here is a scientist, here is my home, here is my view, here is The Margin and you can interpret and do with it as you will." He stopped talking. He smiled at Ronson and looked across to David Bloombridge.

The latter had sat quite impassively. Ronson couldn't tell whether Bloombridge had expected this 'neutral' stance from Ahmed Murphy or not. He had shown no sign of anxiety or intention to interrupt. Did his lack of animation reflect a sense of defeat in his attempt to convince Ronson to run for election or simply boredom at listening to Murphy's monologue?

"So, Richard do you want to go up and have a look at the little bit of The Margin where I live?"

A part of Ronson felt he ought to … but another part felt there was little point. He had no doubt that whatever he was shown would not have the appearance of a street in The Capital so he would learn nothing. As it happened he had a more pressing problem – that gave him a convenient response.

"I'll have a think, Ahmed … but do you think I could use your toilet first?"

"Of course, of course. Just through that door and there is a bathroom immediately on your left," indicated Murphy. Ronson crossed the room and opened the door to which he had been directed. It led into a corridor and a light came on automatically. The door behind him closed – but he didn't enter the bathroom. He was looking at the far end of the corridor. There was a painting on the wall; a yellow painting. It was a painting that he knew. The last time he had seen it was when he had hung it in the gallery room within his own house for a private viewing. This was a painting by Safia Philips. This was one of the paintings sold by Saffie to the client whom Bloombridge had said was 'completely trustworthy' but who needed to remain anonymous. Ronson went to the toilet. The Richard Ronson who rejoined Murphy and Bloombridge was a different Richard Ronson to the one who had left the room a minute or two earlier. This was a 'new Ronson'.

"I don't wish to appear rude Ahmed, but I will forgo your kind offer to view – as you put it - your little bit of The Margin. I have enjoyed meeting you and listening to what you have had to say. I have found it very helpful. The tea was lovely too. I think David and I will need to go back now and talk things through – unless there is anything more that you wished the professor to tell me, David?" Ronson looked towards a slightly taken aback Bloombridge who was hastily getting to his feet. Ronson's visit to The Margin had come to an end.

*

Keep your friends close but your enemies closer, was the dictum that seemed to be on repeat play in Ronson's head as he journeyed home with Bloombridge after their visit to Ahmed Murphy's house.

It was now over eight years since Saffie's disappearance and Ronson almost never thought of her. He had come to accept the official explanation reported in the media of a tragic boating accident. Seeing her painting in Ahmed Murphy's house had changed that. The painting appeared to link Bloombridge, Murphy and Saffie and he could not ignore the anxiety this raised in him.

He felt certain that Murphy must have been the unnamed client who had had the private viewings with Saffie. Ronson was also now in no doubt that Murphy was a Marginal and the need for secrecy for the private viewings would certainly fit with that. Illicit private viewings were one thing. There would be predictable, judicial consequences in Trueway for that, should they come to light. Involvement with a whole 'other world' in the Margin that was not supposed to exist was another ballgame entirely.

Had Saffie gained an insight into the extent of life in the Margin and of the Margin/Trueway links? Had she been silenced because of this? If so, and if Murphy and Bloombridge were behind that, then it was only a matter of time before the same would happen to him – Richard Ronson. That time would be when Bloombridge had gained what he wanted. That would be the point when Bloombridge could dispense with Ronson.

The conviction Ronson now had that Saffie's disappearance had not been an accident might have been expected to throw him again into the fear and apprehension that he had felt before – but it did not. As long as he was indispensible to Bloombridge then he felt sure he was safe. By the time Ronson was back in his house the dictum in his head had changed to, *forewarned is forearmed.*

Chapter 56: Conversion of Attic and Head

When John suggested converting the attic to a spare bedroom Steph could not really see the point. They didn't have anyone come to stay but John said that it would increase the value of the property. Steph and he had never spoken about moving but she accepted that maybe one day they would and it would be helpful, and of course May and Tim said that it would be great for their friends to come for sleepovers … up in the attic … much better than a bedroom or the living room floor!

So it was, that the attic became a spare bedroom. Needless to say, Steph made sure that when all the tidying and preparation for conversion took place the suitcase containing the bag and the dress was nowhere to be found. As part of the conversion she made sure that an old travelling trunk from her family became a makeshift table. John had no objection. The trunk was locked and there was no key so it was useless for its original purpose. If he had his way it would be thrown out – but if it had sentimental value for Steph then using it as a table seemed a somewhat quaint – even trendy – option. In fact Steph did have a key – but only she knew this. When the attic conversion was complete she put the dress into the trunk and locked it. The dress was safe.

This was all part of her acceptance of life – her life – and the way that it was. Put simply, she accepted the mundane; she accepted her own mediocrity. She had so much to be grateful for – and grateful she was. The dress was simply a small, insignificant antidote to the humdrum. For some reason it was around this time that she had her hair cut. She didn't tell John or the children beforehand – she just did it while they were out at work and school. When they came home the long hair and plait were gone. They found a wife and mother with a pageboy haircut!

(E) Final Years

Chapter 57: All in the Timing

As the elections approached, Montgomery-Jones watched the energy with which Ronson worked. She had never seen him like this. Something had changed in Ronson. She had no idea what had caused it, but he was looking less and less like a buffoon and more and more like a politician.

Couchan had warned her, and she had watched Ronson and the traditionalists swelling in numbers. She had watched them progressing to higher parliaments with each election like a tsunami coming to drown The Alliance. When Ronson was elected as councillor at Territorial Level Montgomery-Jones knew that the tsunami had arrived – but as far as she was concerned it had arrived too late to drown The Alliance.

Although Ronson had become Territorial Councillor, Montgomery-Jones and other pro-Alliance politicians had won their seats on the higher ground of the Continental Council. They now outnumbered the traditionalists. Montgomery-Jones and her colleagues had the upper hand. Ronson and his kind would now need at least another electoral round to gain sufficient voting power to thwart their plans, and there wouldn't be an election for another four years. By that time The Alliance would have drafted all the necessary legislation and made all the necessary preparations for unification. All that would be required would be to put the reforms before parliament where the voting power of the pro-unification councillors would ensure that the legislation was passed and implemented.

The proposals for unification would be put to parliament mid-way through the four year electoral cycle. The World Games would be the perfect media distraction behind which to get things underway while still leaving an ample two years to pass any further legislation and carry out the proposals. With the changes implemented the newly enfranchised people from The Outlands would certainly outweigh, in voting power, any challenge from the traditionalists in future elections. A world divided between Trueway and Outlands, between Citizens and Marginals would cease to exist. A new world order that combined the best of The Outlands with the best of Trueway would be born. Marginals would benefit from such things as the eco-shield and climate control while

Citizens would gain from the scientific skills of the Marginals as these were brought more freely into play. Freedom of movement would, of course, be of benefit to all. The Alliance had even settled upon a name for this newly united world. It would be called, 'NewWay'.

*

Bloombridge had been pleased with Ronson's vigorous campaign to become a Territorial Councillor. It had started almost immediately after the visit to meet Ahmed Murphy, so he guessed his gamble had paid off. The result was that Ronson and other politicians of similar persuasion had done well. Although Bloombridge remained at District Level he had been joined there by several other like-minded parliamentarians coming up from Local Level, while the places they vacated – and more - had been filled by traditionalists.

Bloombridge had influence with many of these Local and District Level councillors since many were in debt to him for enabling them to purchase art in the most convivial of circumstances. Ronson, who now seemed to be totally committed to his political role, had taken up his seat at Territorial Level and there had been one or two other gains in this more senior parliament. Bloombridge was not blind to the progress made by The Alliance, and was particularly vexed by the move of Montgomery-Jones to Continental Level. He had no doubt however, that with Ronson leading the charge, the traditionalists would continue to push into the higher parliaments at the next election. The Games would almost certainly aid their progress - especially because of the popularity of the public punishments which were so closely associated with the name of Richard Ronson.

The judicial punishment data from the previous games had been analysed and the organisers were receptive to his suggestion (via Ronson) to introduce increasingly severe 'punishment events'. Bloombridge was confident that by the next elections Ronson, along with himself and others of a like mind, would be unstoppable. Together, they would be able to prevent any further moves to a unification of Outlands and Trueway – a unification that was, in his eyes, equivalent to the *destruction* of Trueway.

Bloombridge however was unaware of just how close The Alliance was to implementing its plan for the creation of NewWay.

Chapter 58: John Goes to The Games

Steph and John had never had much interest in The Games and had completely ignored them when the children were small.

Then, when May was seven and Tim five years of age, Steph and John had been pestered into visiting one or two venues – though it was more for the associated circus acts and fairground rides than the actual sporting events. Having been to several of these family shows over a couple of weekends Steph was a little surprised – but made no comment – when John said that he would go to one or two events by himself. He had heard of important, Trueway endorsed proceedings that were part of a move towards greater transparency within the justice system. At work there had been encouragement to attend these since it was part of a Citizen's duty … and he was very supportive of Citizens fulfilling their duty. Trueway rewarded those who did such things. Were he, Steph and their family not living proof of that?

Steph had also heard of these 'public implementation of justice' events through her work in the Council Offices but had not been interested in exploring them further.

*

May was eleven and Tim nine when the next Games came around and so John and Steph were again pestered into going. They still went to the entertainments arranged for families, and treats like candyfloss and ice cream were still insisted upon, but they also attended a couple of the athletic meetings too. Again, to Steph's surprise John seemed very keen to go to a few events by himself. She did not really understand this keenness – though she recognised that The Games were more popular than ever.

She didn't dwell on John's decision and gave it little more thought until she came across condoms in his drawer in the cabinet – even then she did not connect these to The Games. Why should she? Her suspicion, quite naturally, was of infidelity. She thought about confronting John … but then thought about her own secret in the attic. On the occasions when she indulged in her secret activity however she was always alone but it seemed unlikely that he would be. Why would he need condoms if he wasn't having sex with someone?

After the children had gone to bed she questioned him and triggered a side of John that she had never seen before.

"Have you been going through my things?"

"A letter had fallen down the back of my drawer and I pulled yo,,,"

"Have you been going through my things?"

"I was trying to get a let …"

"My things!

"I was.."

"My things! My things! My things!"

"I …"

"Never mind! You had no right! No right! No right!"

"But…"

"No! No! I don't want your excuses. The truth is you have been snooping! Spying! That's the truth isn't it? That's the truth!"

"Just tell me…ha…"

"No! You have been in my things! Snooping. That's the truth isn't it? That's the truth!" And with that John stormed out of the room and out of the house. She stood trembling, and two bewildered children looked at their mother in silence from over the upstairs banister after he had gone.

*

Truth, thought Steph after John had stormed out. What was the truth? She had her own secrets so didn't want to push things. She felt it best to weather the storm… and somewhat belatedly, if it wasn't already too late, … decided to 'let sleeping dogs lie'. She didn't therefore expect the confession and the remorse when it came … but that was more the John she knew.

*

"I'm sorry. You are so lovely, so lovely, and so good. I know that you would not be going through my things. I was ashamed. I was embarrassed."

"About what?" Steph had not anticipated this. She was genuinely bewildered. He looked at her with pleading eyes. He seemed completely deflated. Seeing him like this swept all concern about infidelity and 'another woman' from her mind. She just wanted to know what was happening.

"I went to one … no, several … of the 'men only' punishments." He looked at her wide eyed, apologetic, contrite … yet Steph had absolutely no idea what he was talking about.

He could see the lack of comprehension in her eyes.

"The punishment events at The Games … the ones people have been talking about," he prompted.

"I know there have been these things … but I haven't taken much interest."

"You must have seen the news coverage?"

"Well, I've heard mention … but, like I say, I haven't taken much notice."

"You really don't know about the 'men only' punishments?"

"No," she affirmed with puzzled honesty.

He hung his head.

"Tell me John. Tell me. I know you wouldn't intentionally do anything to hurt me … to hurt anyone. I really don't know or understand what this 'men only' thing is or why there is a problem. Just explain. I need to understand."

He looked at her in silence for just a second. Did she really not know? Was she so out of touch?

"You know about the punishments that are carried out at The Games alongside the other events?"

"Yes."

"I have been to some of them."

He fell silent again. He didn't really want to explain – but he could see her continuing incomprehension so felt he had to go on.

"The punishments are all done in private – no cameras and just the witnesses from the public that have bought tickets. I went to a couple at the last Games."

"Yes, I remember. I wasn't interested so I didn't go."

"Well, for the current Games they have introduced new punishments. There are special permissions that are bought with the tickets – permissions for exclusive, single event DAMP Holidays. The punishments can be very sexually exciting and the condoms are to allow for safe, no mess self-gratification. I'm sorry."

Again he hung his head.

"Are you saying that it's some kind of porn show, and that men go and masturbate into condoms?"

John said nothing but simply looked at the floor. Steph didn't know what to say. She didn't know what to think … or what she ought to think. She didn't know what she was feeling – except maybe that she had fallen

249

into some kind of cartoon world. She fought back the desire to burst out laughing.

"It's OK," she eventually said. "It's OK."

*

The Games were a success as far as the organisers were concerned. They were a success as far as the majority of Trueway was concerned. And they were a success as far as Ronson and Bloombridge were concerned. The absence of any observable move on the part of The Alliance immediately following the elections had led Bloombridge to conclude that they were not yet ready to take any meaningful steps towards unification. As a result, he relaxed and enjoyed The Games. He also felt sure that he would need no carrots or sticks to maintain Ronson's enthusiasm and so was looking forward more than ever to the next elections when he anticipated that the traditionalists would become so dominant that The Alliance would be an impotent force; a well meaning talking shop that never got beyond talking while he, a military man, had planned and implemented a successful campaign of action. He was wrong.

The Games signalled the end of the two years of final groundwork by The Alliance. Alliance members in The Margin and Alliance Members in Trueway were ready. The legislation had been drafted. Cross border liaison officers (one of whom was Yusef) had been utilising their travel ability to co-ordinate. Everything was in place.

Chapter 59: Unification through Parliament Begins

Although only one of several Continental Level Councillors who were within The Alliance, it was Montgomery-Jones who was given the privilege of presenting the first landmark bill of unification. It was called, "The Recognition of World Totality Bill", and on the surface, it seemed innocuous since it appeared to do nothing more than bring into law recognition of what was axiomatically the case. In essence it sought formal acknowledgement that (a) 'the world' extended beyond Trueway, (b) 'the world' therefore included The Outlands and (c) that it was fundamentally important, right and proper that 'government' should concern itself with the entire planet and not just the part called Trueway.

Despite stating the obvious – and therefore being in no way contentious – it was the first of the three steps to unification:

Step 1 – recognise that 'the world' is comprised of Outlands as well as Trueway.

Step 2 - accept that a unified world is unquestionably desirable – essential in fact.

Step 3 - recognise that if there are people living in The Outlands then those people need to be brought under the umbrella of what is currently Trueway.

Through these steps would be born a whole and unified world. But with birth comes death and the birth of this unified world would be the death of The Outlands as they existed (in political if not practical terms) and also the death of Trueway (in political if not practical terms).

Montgomery-Jones presented her innocuous bill. With The World Games in full swing it received almost no media coverage. *True Reflections* gave some in-depth analysis – but the mainstream media was full of Games, Games and more Games. The bill was debated, and with the majority that The Alliance held in The Continental Parliament, it was successful. It was on its way to The Supreme Triumvirate ('the dinosaurs') for rubber stamping into law well before Bloombridge, down at District Level, had become aware of it let alone read it, digested it and assimilated its implications.

In contrast, Councillor Richard Ronson – the 'new Ronson' - at Territorial Level had seen it, read it and understood it well before it went to be voted on. He and The Territorial Level Parliament however could do nothing to influence a bill introduced in The Continental Level Parliament. This was the nature of Trueway democracy. Lower parliaments could not 'interfere' in the proceedings of higher parliaments other than in 'exceptional circumstances' since, by definition, those higher parliaments had been given a mandate by the lower tiers that reached all the way down to the individual Citizens through the representatives they had elected at Local Level. Ronson was therefore powerless. Ronson however was aware.

Chapter 60: The Red Dress Takes Control and It All Starts

About a year after John's confession Steph found herself alone in the house. John had gone away on business and the children were at school. She had taken a couple of days leave from work. She was not on DAMP Holiday but she thought of the dress and went up into the attic just to see it and wear it a moment. She took it from the travel trunk and slipped it on. She looked at herself in the full length mirror of the attic bedroom. The dress shimmered. It was lovely. She pushed her bob of hair up and held it like a bun. She wondered whether she should let her hair grow again. She twirled and the dress splayed out. She was in a reverie – but it was brought to a chilling halt by the word, "Mum?" and the sight of the bewildered, questioning face of her son as he stood on the ladder into the attic with only his head and shoulders visible through the hatch. Steph was now shocked into the same position of shame as John had been.

*

To own clothes or to wear clothes was not, in itself illegal in Trueway. It was accepted that some people – whether alone or in groups – might 'dress up'. The reasons for doing this might vary but such dressing up was done almost exclusively in private. Citizens who wore clothes in this way were referred to as 'textilists'. Although not illegal it was viewed very much as a clandestine and 'odd' activity. People like John and Steph saw themselves, and were seen by others, as model Citizens. The civic tattoos covering their skin bore testament to this. To what further 'clothing' could, or need, they aspire? Material clothes were the antithesis of their body decoration. Material clothes would cover it up from the world – from Trueway.

Tim and May had grown up in a world where, as far as they were concerned, clothes did not exist. They had seen pictures in history books and they were fully aware of protective clothing for specific activities in Trueway. Shoes and boots were the only form of protective equipment of which they, like most other Citizens, had any personal experience. The discovery that there was a piece of clothing in their house – and that their mother secretly wore it was shocking and confusing. Even for John it was an alarming revelation.

Steph felt shame and embarrassment - but like her family also felt confusion. She would swing between wanting to destroy the dress in order to purge herself on the one hand, and feeling that she could never and should never destroy the dress since to do so would endorse the view that there was something wrong with it and with her. John proposed shredding and disposing of it through regular fabric recycling. It wasn't until she was on the verge of cutting it up that her vacillation stopped. A chance ray of sunlight fell on the red fabric.

"Blood!"

Did she hear the word? Did she feel the word? Did she think it or did it engulf her? Was she even aware of the word as a word or was it simply a sensing? Her blood? His blood? The blood of the dress? Real? Imagined? The answers made no difference. Enough destruction. She put the scissors down. She would wear blood.

*

To wear a dress in her own home and to have her secret discovered had challenged Steph – but it had challenged her to challenge herself. As a result of that challenge she wore the dress out in public and in so doing took the challenge to Trueway. Why was she doing this? Her family did not understand. Her work colleagues did not understand. She herself probably did not understand – at least not fully – though she could voice coherent 'reasons' to herself and to anyone who asked. Trueway did not understand … but Trueway didn't need to understand. Trueway simply had to respond when called upon to do so. This it did and the tried and tested elements of 'due process' began.

Chapter 61: Arrests and Trials

In a society where everyone is completely naked a woman going to work and walking round town in a red dress is something startling – and some people went as far as to say it was distressing. It was not long until there were complaints. Since Steph refused to stop wearing the dress the result was repeated arrests and prosecutions. The arrests and prosecutions were not on the basis of her wearing a dress – that in itself was not illegal – but on the basis of causing distress. Despite Steph's argument that it was absurd to say that a piece of cloth caused distress she was repeatedly found guilty and was subjected to harsher and harsher sentences. First she was fined and then she was imprisoned. Eventually the courts completely banned her from wearing the dress in public. She refused to comply with this order. This meant that while she was in prison she was not permitted to mix with other prisoners. She was therefore held in solitary confinement and not allowed to enter communal areas. On release from prison at the end of her sentence it meant that she was immediately rearrested and returned to prison to await trial where she was again found guilty and again sentenced to prison and again released and re-arrested. Stephanie Hugo, who as a girl called Stephanie Huntington, had been a Trueway hero and who was now a Citizen with many tattoos reflecting her civic service, was in effect being sentenced to life imprisonment in solitary confinement for covering part of her body in cloth.

John, Tim and May struggled to understand and come to terms with Steph's behaviour. Her refusal to remove the dress meant that her family could not even visit her in prison. John tried to be supportive towards his wife and wanted her to come home to him and to the children but she was steadfast in her resolve. She would not remove the dress.

Chapter 62: It all Started so Well ... but Then

As The Alliance had hoped, "The Recognition of World Totality Bill" was passed into law and various other pieces of Alliance led legislation began their journey through parliament towards law and ultimately towards the creation of the new, unified world order to be known as NewWay. Choosing to launch the first bill during The World Games had been a good strategy. It created the foundation for NewWay while almost nobody was looking. Once the distraction of The Games had disappeared then the media and the lower parliaments started to take greater notice of the bills that were being created. Regular parliamentary business continued as it always did and the bills that were crucial to the plans of The Alliance were among them.

These crucial bills often appeared quite innocuous because they were intentionally just 'small steps' hidden behind innocent titles. The advantage of this was that they seemed as obscure and as inconsequential as, "The Recognition of World Totality Bill". Their significance was not spotted in the way that a radical sounding bill would have been. The bills were hardly commented upon by the media or discussed in the lower parliaments. The disadvantage to this 'small steps' approach however was twofold. First, the passage of the bills into law could be slow as 'more important' bills took the attention of parliament. Second, there was more time for perceptive people to start noticing a trend and to start putting two-and-two together.

Many if not most senior people in Trueway - politicians, business people, bankers, media moguls, judiciary, military - had links with The Outlands and knew of The Alliance or were even part of it. People like Bloombridge and Ronson who had an awareness of the extent of activity in The Outlands and of The Alliance, but who were traditionalists opposed to any adjustment of the *status quo,* were relatively few in number while the majority of Citizens knew of nothing beyond Trueway.

Creating an effective opposition to The Alliance and the passage of bills leading to unification was therefore very difficult. If people like Ronson and Bloombridge went around trying to tell lower tier councillors and Citizens about The Alliance the media would make them a laughing stock. Even if some councillors and Citizens believed them the parliamentary rules would have made them impotent in regard to the passage of bills at Continental Level. Traditionalist councillors – mainly Ecclesiastic and Martial – at Continental Level therefore gave long speeches and used whatever filibuster tactics were at their disposal to slow the progress of the bills that were obviously leading towards unification.

This strategy successfully slowed the plans of The Alliance and it became evident that another election would need to be fought before unification could take place. Unfortunately for The Alliance they lost seats and the conservative group gained seats. The balance of power was still in favour of councillors who supported The Alliance however, so it appeared to Montgomery-Jones and her Alliance colleagues that their long years of preparation were coming to fruition. It seemed just a matter of time and perseverance – qualities that had been amply demonstrated over the years. It seemed almost impossible that anything could now stop their progress. It was certainly inconceivable that a piece of red cloth could, in any way, impede such progress – but the world is a strange place.

Chapter 63: The Red Dress Bombings Start

The Bomb was unexpected. It exploded in the heart of Trueway. Such an occurrence was unprecedented. The Hugo family did not know what to make of it. The Alliance (including Yusef) did not know what to make of it. Ronson, Bloombridge and Mrs Christina did not know what to make of it. The existing Government of Trueway did not know what to make of it.

In the immediate aftermath of the blast the media and everyone else in Trueway seemed unable to talk of anything else. There was much speculation – but no conclusions. The blast had been small. It had damaged property but not injured anyone. For a while everyone was on high alert, but as the days passed with no further incident, interest in the bomb waned. In a surprisingly short space of time it hardly featured in the media and was almost forgotten about by the public at large.

The Alliance, knowing that they were moving towards the most significant change in the history of Trueway felt a more lasting anxiety. Yusef and other similar cross border liaison officers were tasked with trying to see what the Trueway based authorities might not be able to see. After extensive enquiries however nothing more came to light. The source of the bomb was a mystery. It left Yusef feeling very uncomfortable. For a bomb to be placed and detonated, yet no trace of the culprit found, spoke to Yusef of a very powerful entity behind the incident. It seemed to him that this isolated bomb was some kind of rehearsal, a trial run to see if Trueway had any resource capable of tracing the perpetrators. To Yusef it was a shot across the bows.

While going through media coverage of the bomb, Yusef came across reports of a woman called Stephanie Hugo wearing a red dress and being sent to prison. He would not have paid the reports much attention had there not been a photograph of this woman. She was older and her hair was short – but there was no mistaking that it was Steph Huntington … and there was no mistaking the dress that he had given her.

Initially he was simply puzzled by Steph's behaviour. It didn't make sense to him but neither did it make him anxious. Then he read the account of bits of paper in the shape of a red dress being left in the public gallery at one of her trials. The slips of paper bore a slogan. Even that would not have disturbed him since it was the sort of thing some textilist groups would do but the slogan said, *You can jail the revolutionary but you can't jail the revolution*. This didn't sound like textilists to Yusef and when the media failed to attribute the slogan-bearing pieces of paper to any group, or to name any of the people who had left them, Yusef started to worry. There was no obvious link between the bomb and Stephanie Hugo but in a society where everyone was supposed to have biodata then there should be no difficulty identifying people who left bombs or people who left leaflets. The fact that nobody had been identified in either case suggested to Yusef that the people behind the bomb and the people behind the slogan bearing pieces of paper might be the same. If that was the case then there could be serious implications for Steph … and possibly for her family.

Yusef was spending a significant amount of his time at the safe house in Trueway and it was easy to keep up to date with the news on Steph's case. He wanted to write to her and express his concerns that her unusual behaviour might be usurped by people with a malevolent agenda which could place her and her family in danger. As a Marginal he could not write directly to her in prison using his own identity, but through his TILE contacts he endeavoured to correspond through a textilist called Robert Cray who had started writing to Steph on textilist issues. Robert Cray however refused to let Yusef incorporate things in his letters as a means of communicating with Steph.

Thwarted in his attempts to contact Steph via Robert Cray, Yusef wrote a note to John Hugo and put it through his letterbox. He pretended his name was Robert, that he was a textilist and that he was already writing to Steph with a view to her coming to stay with him and other textilists when she was released. He therefore wanted to introduce himself to John. Yusef arranged a meeting with John at a place called The Causeway Café. As part of the discussion he attempted to convince John to write to Steph and endeavour to persuade her to reconsider her stance since he felt she might be getting into a difficult – possibly dangerous – situation. Yusef was as unsuccessful with John as he had been with Robert Cray. After these two failed efforts all he could do was keep monitoring events while doing his work for The Alliance at the same time.

Then, while The Alliance was carefully guiding its legislation through parliament and while Steph was facing her repeated trials for wearing her red dress a second bomb exploded in a different part of Trueway. This was followed by a third, then a fourth and then more. Trueway, which since the end of The Terror Wars generations before had known nothing but peace, was being subjected to a rash of bombings. The bombs always seemed to be close to or even inside Trueway official buildings – especially civic buildings and temples. Occasionally people were hurt but the target of each bomb appeared to be the building and not the Citizens who used it. Police investigations failed to identify any group or individuals responsible for the explosions. CCTV cameras never caught anyone identifiable in the vicinity prior to a bomb exploding and forensic analysis could not trace the explosive to any known source.

With the exception of the apparent Trueway buildings as targets the only consistent links between the bombings were little pieces of paper found in the debris. These pieces of paper were always red and were always cut into the shape of a dress – exactly like the ones that Yusef had read about having been left in the public gallery at one of Steph's trials. The bombings became nick-named *The Red Dress Bombings*. Yusef had been right to be concerned. He was now certain that Steph and her idiosyncratic behaviour had been appropriated for use in some much bigger plan; a plan orchestrated by people unknown – but people with considerable power.

Chapter 64: The Red Dress Bombings - What to do?

The Trueway authorities were baffled by the bombings. The police and the military were fully deployed but the explosions continued. Almost all parliamentary time became devoted to talking about the issue but these debates went round in endless circles. Similarly the media went round in endless circles reporting government's endless discussions and the lack of progress made by the police or the military in addressing the problem.

*

Action needed to be taken. The Trueway government needed to be seen to be *doing* something! Their first course of action was dictated by the groups shouting loudest in order to deflect criticism from its own failures – the police and the military. These two institutions (with some justification) pointed to the way that their funding and their numbers had been decreasing year on year since the end of The Terror Wars. How could they be expected to counter the bombing threat without sufficient personnel? The result was the creation of *The Police and Military Volunteers* – The *PMV* for short. Every Citizen was encouraged to become a PMV member. Recruitment centres were established at workplaces, temples and other institutions across the globe. Everyone who signed up was provided with an official brown armband bearing the letters PMV in red. These people would be the eyes, ears, hands and feet of Trueway ready to be called upon to support the regular police and military as necessary.

*

Had the issue simply been a lack of police and military personnel then the problem should have been solved because Citizens came forward in their droves to become PMV members. The bombings continued however. The one mysterious clue that the bombers seemed to have voluntarily made available was the symbol of the red dress at every bomb site. This therefore became the basis of a second strand of government action.

With the exception of footwear and protective clothing for specialist, designated purposes, there were no clothes worn in Trueway other than by textilists. It seemed plausible therefore that a militant textile group might be behind the bombings and might be utilising the red dress as a symbol of their cause. Parliament accordingly endorsed the request of the police and military authorities to focus investigations – utilising emergency powers if necessary – on known textilists and textile groups.

The final strand of the Trueway response to the bombings was prompted by the government body charged with advising parliament on world affairs - the *Combined Interests Council*. They reasoned that since cut outs of a red dress had been found at all the bomb sites, and cut outs of a red dress were left in the public gallery of the trial of a woman called Stephanie Hugo, and Stephanie Hugo was in prison for wearing a red dress then maybe she knew the truth of who was behind the bombings. The Combined Interests Council therefore recommended that any possible link between Stephanie Hugo and the attacks be thoroughly investigated by the highest court of Trueway -The Court of Truth.

The Court of Truth was an inquisitorial court that dated from immediately after The Terror Wars. The inquisitorial panel consisted of a Justice Martial, a Justice Civil and a Justice Ecclesiastic. The latter always chaired the hearings. The role of the court was to establish 'the truth' and having done so, to act accordingly in a manner determined by the most sacred book of Trueway - The Book of Truth.

In the eyes of many The Court of Truth was an ineffective anachronism, but the Combined Interests Council had recommended it so government sought leave from The Supreme Triumvirate to refer Stephanie Hugo's case. The Supreme Triumvirate gave consent and Steph was transferred to a special prison in The Capital attached to the courtroom that was used exclusively by The Court of Truth.

*

Montgomery-Jones sat with her brick and with her secretary. She had been at the debate regarding the referral of Stephanie Hugo's case to the Court of Truth. She had spoken with other councillors about the referral. Everyone with whom she had spoken agreed on the complete unlikelihood of an innocuous council worker with textilist tendencies having anything to do with the bombings – especially since she was already in jail. Referral to The Court of Truth appeared to be nothing more than an act of desperation. Even so, it was the recommendation of the Combined Interests Council, so for the majority of councillors, there seemed little point in opposing it.

Cummings watched Montgomery-Jones tracing the outline of the brick with her finger. She appeared lost in contemplation of its surface texture … or possibly the convolutions of her own thoughts.

"These bombings have stopped all progress on the unification bills and now we have The Court of Truth forcing us to tread water for even longer," she eventually mused aloud.

"Yes, Ma'am," affirmed her secretary. Cummings knew that Montgomery-Jones regarded The Court of Truth with disdain. She was not expecting anything substantive to come from it. He waited however to see whether she would say anything more.

"I guess we just have to be patient. Maybe the bombings will stop or maybe there will be a breakthrough in the investigations. Maybe we just have to accept we will progress more slowly. Still, it isn't up to me. It will be a decision for The Alliance as a whole." She smiled at her secretary in resignation before returning to her brick tracing.

"Putting aside the delay to Alliance plans Ma'am, what do you actually think about the referral of this Hugo woman to the Court of Truth?"

Montgomery-Jones did not look up from her brick. "I don't see anything coming from it, Sahid. The Court of Truth is hardly ever invoked and they talk religious gobbledygook." This was the response he had anticipated.

"You know who she is, don't you, Ma'am?" Cummings hoped that he had delivered his question at the right moment and with the right level of intrigue.

"Who?" asked Montgomery-Jones without looking up.

"The red dress woman Ma'am – the one going to The Court of Truth."

Montgomery-Jones now stopped her tracing and looked with suspicion at her secretary. They had worked together many, many years. The rhetorical nature of his question was obvious to her so she remained silent.

"Stephanie Hugo is her current, married name, Ma'am. Before that she was Stephanie Lepton – also a married name – but, before that she was Stephanie Huntington." A flicker of some distant memory – not quite placed – changed the look of suspicion in the eyes of Montgomery-Jones to one seeking clarification.

"She was one of the patrol members who shot …" began Cummings, but was cut short as Montgomery-Jones stood abruptly and finished his sentence with the name, "…Safia Philips."

Suddenly Montgomery-Jones was no longer contemplative – or dismissive of the possibility of a link between the dress wearing woman and the bombings. Now she feared the incompetence of the religion focussed Court of Truth.

"Great Spirit preserve us! We need someone with a brain looking into this not just people with an inside out knowledge of The Book of Truth." She was thinking aloud. She looked at Cummings. "The Court of Truth is always chaired by a Justice Ecclesiastic. Do we know who yet?"

"Yes, Ma'am."

He said no more. She remained silent. He knew the name she was wanting him - willing him - to say and he was savouring his moment. He liked to please Montgomery-Jones. He had always liked to please her.

He could barely stop himself from smiling as he said the words, "Justice Couchan, Ma'am," and saw the look of relief and satisfaction on her face. Montgomery-Jones felt that if there was a link between Stephanie Hugo and the bombings then Couchan would find it.

Chapter 65: Falling Apart and all in The Dark

Steph was informed that her case had been referred to The Court of Truth and that she would be transferred to a specialist prison attached to that court. Steph knew little of what the change meant, but early one morning, she was moved from the local prison where she was being held to a prison in The Capital. John was unaware of Steph's case having been transferred to The Court of Truth or of her prison transfer.

John was very aware however of the PMV. Recruitment officers arrived at his place of work and the majority of his colleagues signed up to become volunteers. John did not enlist. He was a good Citizen. He had the tattoos to prove it – more tattoos than many of his work colleagues and fellow Citizens. He had played his part and made his contribution to Trueway. He expected Trueway to resolve this bombing issue without the need to recruit volunteers – vigilantes even! Since he did not become a member of the PMV he did not get one of the brown arm bands with red letters.

Yusef, like John, was unaware of the referral of Steph's case to The Court of Truth. Like John, he was also aware of the PMV. Yusef however was probably a little more perceptive than John and saw in the creation of the PMV the state of desperation that Trueway had reached. Things were falling apart.

Chapter 66: The Validity of the Pre-emptive Strike

Montgomery-Jones had been right when she said to Cummings that it would be for The Alliance and not for her to determine the length of time to await progress on the investigation of The Red Dress Bombings. The Alliance strategy committee met and Montgomery-Jones was in their number. The current efforts being put in place by Trueway for resolving the Red Dress Bombings were discussed. The intelligence was that none of these – including the investigation of the Hugo case by The Court of Truth - would resolve the bombings. 'Intelligence' also indicated that a group – 'The Individual Freedom Alliance (IFA)' being identified as responsible for the bombings was a fabrication designed to give the impression that progress was being made with the investigations. Since the group did not exist they would never be found and stopped. This would be embarrassing but not, in itself, a concern to The Alliance.

However, if The Red Dress Bombings did not stop and if the perpetrators could not be found then there was a danger that traditionalist elements – especially Councillors (Martial) across the parliaments – could call for emergency powers and effectively impose Martial Law. This would suspend parliamentary democracy indefinitely and halt the unification legislation currently in process. It was even possible – though 'Intelligence' had not confirmed this – that traditionalist elements were responsible for the bombings and these were simply a tactic to justify Martial Law. If that was the case then the bombings would stop once Martial Law was in place and any further moves towards unification would be virtually impossible since the government could argue that it would risk destabilisation – especially if the bogus Individual Freedom Alliance was said to have links to terrorist groups in The Margin that had been covertly developing plans over the years.

Years and years of patient planning had been the foundation of The Alliance strategy to achieve unification and the creation of NewWay by the democratic, parliamentary processes of Trueway. If the 'intelligence' was correct and this democratic process was going to be thwarted by an abuse of the Trueway constitution then The Alliance would be justified in taking pre-emptive action. In fact, since the democracy of Trueway itself was under threat, it was the duty of The Alliance to take such action. The Alliance had not *expected* to be placed in this position but had, as part of its long and thorough planning, been *prepared* for the eventuality. It was agreed therefore that The Alliance, as a matter of urgency, would initiate their plans for 'rapid realignment' - a military led coup d'état.

Chapter 67: Yusef – Out of the Dark

Yusef sat in his office in the safe house. He had been contacted by Cummings – a phone call this time - to say that the bombings meant that The Alliance was changing its plan from gradual unification through legislation to 'rapid realignment'.

Yusef had not been entirely surprised by this. It had been obvious that the unification process through parliament had stalled because of the bombings. Cummings had said that the timetable for 'rapid realignment' was not yet clear – but given the threat of Martial Law he thought that The Alliance would make its move 'sooner rather than later' unless there was a genuine major breakthrough regarding the bombings. Investigation of textilists and the introduction of the PMV were unlikely to yield anything substantive on that front. Anything Yusef had heard about a group called The Individual Freedom Alliance was a government fabrication. There was a slim chance that investigation of Stephanie Hugo by The Court of Truth might yield something … but that seemed equally doubtful.

"Stephanie Hugo … and The Court of Truth … what was that about?" asked Yusef struggling to disguise his shock and concern.

"This woman going about in a red dress called Stephanie Hugo …," explained Cummings casually, "Been in the news … well she was one of the people involved in the shooting of Safia Philips all those years ago. It was the first time you and I met if you remember."

"Yes, but what's this 'Court of Truth'?"

"Oh it's an archaic, religious led inquisition," began Cummings in a dismissive tone. "Given the lack of progress on the bombings but the mysterious use of a red dress as a symbol, parliament felt that The Court of Truth was better placed to investigate any possible link between this woman and the attacks."

"Right, so will The Alliance wait 'til this court reports back before instigating the realignment?"

"I don't think The Alliance is expecting much, if anything, to come from The Court of Truth so I don't expect them to wait. I think The Alliance will move as soon as it is able. That said, I don't think this Court of Truth will take all that long with its investigation. Like I said, it's an inquisition rather than the usual prosecution and defence game of ping-pong. The person leading it is someone called Justice Couchan. Montgomery-Jones knows him pretty well and rates him highly."

"Right, I'll await instructions," was all Yusef could think to say.

Chapter 68: The Court of Truth

It was only a couple of days into Steph's trial at The Court of Truth when Couchan met with Montgomery-Jones. Although she had not been mandated by The Alliance to report back on the progress of The Court of Truth she wanted to know whether Stephanie Hugo was involved in the bombings and whether there was any likelihood of the 'rapid realignment' being averted.

"Are you able to tell me anything?" she asked.

"Of course not. Proceedings of The Court of Truth are confidential until they are complete."

"OK." Montgomery-Jones was deflated.

"But who cares about protocol when we are in a mad house?" said Couchan. He then looked steadily at Montgomery-Jones. "I don't know who is behind the bombings. I have my suspicions … and Stephanie Hugo isn't one of them. At worst she is a symbol that the actual perpetrators of the attacks have decided to use - and all that Trueway might get from her trial at The Court of Truth is an equally symbolic renouncement of this dress she keeps wearing – probably in a public, world broadcast. Trueway might see that as a minor victory in demonstrating to whoever is behind these attacks that their unwitting standard bearer has climbed down; rejected them and their cause. It won't stop the bombings of course because she has nothing to do with them.

"How soon?"

"A day or two maybe. She is a strong willed lady. She doesn't see the bigger picture. She can't. She probably doesn't believe Marginals exist – certainly not in any numbers – so there is no way she could grasp all of what is happening. She doesn't see how she is being used or the danger she is in – but with a bit of luck I can persuade her to drop the dress issue and that will hopefully get her back into the standard civil courts. In the mean time I leave you and The Alliance to get on with whatever you are going to do."

"How will I know when this trial of yours is concluded?"

"You'll know when everyone knows, Stella. Like I said, I am certain that we will have to do a worldwide media broadcast. It will be symbolic of progress by the government … even if it is nothing more than just that – symbolic!"

Chapter 69: The Night of Smashing and Morning of Rescue

While he waited Yusef watched the news with growing concern. He watched the reports about the PMV. He had no doubt that The Alliance, when it launched its 'realignment' would do so swiftly and decisively – but he was worried what factions of the PMV would do before that occurred. Many in the PMV he had no doubt were worthy Citizens trying to support Trueway in its fight against an unknown bombing enemy – but he feared that the PMV could become – was already becoming – an excuse for violence by the more frustrated elements of Trueway society. Already there were news reports of insults and abuse of Citizens who were not wearing PMV armbands by those who were.

At a personal level he was worried about the Hugo family. No, that was disingenuous. Yusef was not worried about the Hugo family. Yusef was worried about Steph and Yusef was worried about May. Steph was this strange, beautiful, Citizen enigma with whom he had spent but the shortest of times and May … well, May was their daughter. He was a half breed born a Marginal. May was a half breed born a Citizen. Did he love her? Is it possible to love a child that you didn't know existed until she was seven or eight years old and then only because of a fleeting, chance sighting of her in the street? He concluded – if his thinking went so far as a conclusion – that his feelings and his motives were irrelevant. What mattered were his actions. As the family of the woman who was being associated with the Red Dress Bombings, the Hugo family seemed to Yusef to be a prime target for the extreme element of the PMV … and even a target for the police. Yusef felt that he needed to take steps to protect the Hugo family – but he also had his role within The Alliance and that currently kept him at the safe house so limiting his freedom to contact them and try to explain things to them.

As a human wanting to play guardian angel however, Yusef had one major advantage over most other mortals – his robotic seraphim and cherubim; his mini-drones. Unfortunately however Yusef was not prepared for the event that became known as 'The Night of Smashing' when PMV thugs went on the rampage across the globe targeting the houses of anyone who had not signed up to be PMV members. Houses everywhere across the world were smashed and wrecked. By the time

Yusef had deployed a couple of drones to send back video the Hugo's family home had been ransacked and the Hugo family was nowhere to be seen.

Although the two drones had video cameras his drone technology did not yet have biodata tracking capability. He had no way of knowing whether the family had escaped, been taken into custody or even killed. He flew one of the drones inside the house and landed it there. The other he stationed outside. He felt sick, frustrated and angry. Individuals on social media and even the regular mainstream news had been reporting events in earlier time zones and he should have reacted but didn't. The one consolation was the relatively low number of casualties being reported. This was something he expected from mainstream media – it would not do to have reports of Citizens killing Citizens – but even the sub-web and individuals who themselves had been attacked reported that it was property and not people that were targeted. With that glimmer of hope and comfort Yusef sat and watched the video feed from his mini-drones.

It was just getting light when three police officers – two men and a woman – arrived at the close where the Hugo family lived. The Hugo house and one other had been attacked. The police taped off the two ransacked houses but then went inside the Hugo's house and settled themselves in to wait. For Yusef this was very encouraging. The only interpretation he could formulate was that the police knew the Hugo family had escaped and were likely to return. As the family of the woman in the red dress he assumed that the police were waiting to either arrest them (John at least) as co-conspirators or to take them into protective custody. Either way he needed to intercept the three Hugo family members before that occurred.

*

Yusef watched the screen. The pictures relayed from the mini drone that he had landed in the Hugo house told him the police were there and weren't going to leave. They were clearly intent on arresting John. His outside drone was airborne but so far hadn't located John or the children - but it was still early morning.

"Lisa," called Yusef to the young woman passing the open door of his office without looking round.

"Yep?"

"I need an Alliance police officer and police glide car – no, a van - one big enough for arresting three people; oh – and also a paramedic capable of administering a sedative."

"I can do the latter – but I'll get onto the police and van."

"You can use a syringe?" he queried now looking round.

"Don't sound so surprised."

"Right – no, I mean I just didn't know. Excellent – oh and the van will need to be big enough for you and me as well as the three people we will be picking up - John and the two kids – though I guess you had worked that out."

"Pretty much," said Lisa casually before adding, "We will need a cage in the van for the kids too, I'm afraid. They won't know what is happening. I'll arrange police ID armbands too, of course."

Yusef smiled. Lisa was good.

"As fast as you can Lisa, I can see them," said Yusef with urgency as he gave his attention to the screen and keyboard. "I've locked it onto them. They are heading home. Still a way to go – but we don't have…" He didn't finish his sentence as he turned to see that Lisa had already gone.

*

Yusef and Lisa sat in the back of the police van. The Alliance police officer was at the wheel. They were parked a short distance from the Hugo's house. Yusef and Lisa watched the progress of the little family group on the screen. They watched as John, May and Tim turned into the close where they lived. Yusef was very aware of how tight the timing was going to be. He had no doubt that the police in the Hugo's house would call for a van as soon as the Hugo's had arrived. Get there too quickly and the arresting officers would be suspicious. Leave it too late and the other real van would get there while they were in the process of snatching John and the kids. Yusef watched the family looking at their house and then saw Tim run forward and into the property. Yusef didn't switch to the cam inside the house. He didn't need to as he saw Tim being brought out by the police officer. Yusef's heart was pounding. He could see an altercation starting in front of the Hugo's house. He could see some onlookers pointing and shouting. Unfortunately his drone had no sound so he wasn't sure what was being said – but he had seen enough.

"OK – let's go – siren – the works!" he yelled to the officer driver.

268

Yusef knew that as soon as they arrived John would recognise him from their meeting at the Causeway Café so he was going to have to hit him and hit him hard. This was going to be very difficult.

Chapter 70: Children and Puppy

Children can be extraordinarily resilient … and extraordinarily perceptive. As soon as the 'police van' arrived they saw a 'policeman' leap from the van and fell their father with a single blow. They saw their father bundled into the back of the van before they themselves were pushed and locked unceremoniously into a cage alongside him. They saw a 'policewoman' inject their father with something before the van sped off into the night. They were terrified – traumatised – and yet, despite all this, they could see how gently this 'policewoman' (who they later knew as 'Lisa') cradled their father in her arms against the rocking of the hurtling vehicle, and even though shock prevented their full understanding of what she was saying to them, they could sense the caring tone with which she spoke. Can children sense 'care' when an adult might only see 'cage'?

In the room where their unconscious father had been placed in a bed – but still in their cage - they had watched as Lisa tended to him. Gradually, as they saw no further harm directed towards him or them they began to relax, to listen and even to cautiously begin to trust. When they were released they did not run. How could they? Where were they? Where could they go and how could they leave their father? The food and the puppy helped convince them to stay as well.

At home they had a room each and in school May generally steered clear of her little, irritating brother, but with their father still unconscious by the time night came they were happy to share a room and a bed. They talked a while. They tried to grasp and make sense of the surreal world into which they had been thrown – but it was all too much … and it didn't matter. May wrapped herself round the back of her little brother and neither of them were aware of anything until morning.

They had breakfast with Lisa and Yusef after first visiting their still unconscious father. Lisa explained that the effect of the heavy sedative she had administered to him would now begin to wear off and that he would probably wake up in a couple of hours. Yusef and Lisa also explained, as clearly as they could, where they all were and what was happening. Sensing no threat to themselves or their father they were happy to wander about this house to which they had been brought and to play in the garden by themselves … and, of course, the puppy!

Chapter 71: Ronson Starts to Think for Himself

Ronson was as baffled as everyone by the bombings – but he realised that they had slowed the progress of The Alliances legislation through parliament. He also realised that the bombings could constitute 'exceptional circumstances' that might allow him, or anyone else, in a lower parliament to propose something that might actually counter rather than simply slow the legislation being carried forward. The problem for Ronson however was that he didn't know what kind of bill he could introduce that could do that. He needed advice.

The person who could provide that advice was Bloombridge, yet despite all that was taking place, the latter had not been in touch. Out of deference Ronson would generally wait to be approached but the situation seemed so urgent that he phoned Bloombridge who agreed to come to Ronson's house – though Ronson felt he detected some reluctance.

As they sat in Ronson's easy chairs with the customary glass of whisky each – whisky that Bloombridge had supplied on his earlier visit – Ronson was not slow in coming to the point.

"The Alliance bills are being delayed by all this Red Dress Bombing stuff. If we act now we might be in a position to get ahead of them – derail their efforts."

"I'm not sure," said Bloombridge with a shake of the head and a pensive look. Ronson was incredulous. Surely Bloombridge had recognised by now the significance of the bills that The Alliance was pushing through parliament – and how close they were to realising their goal – a goal to which he was so fervently opposed?

"What are you not sure about, David? All this Red Dress stuff is the perfect excuse for lower parliaments to push for an intervention based on 'exceptional circumstances' – isn't it?"

"It would probably qualify – if it weren't for the fact that government seems to have things in hand." Ronson couldn't believe what he was hearing.

"Nobody really knows who is behind these bombings, David. If they did then the bombings would have stopped. Surely we would be justified in taking whatever steps are needed. Maybe impose Martial Law … well couldn't we?"

"Well, we would need to ensure that we would be successful. We don't have the organisation within the armed forces to stage a military coup and to get a bill through parliament would be problematic, especially when we have the authorities saying they have identified the bombers – this Individual Freedom Alliance – and while they are investigating the woman in the red dress who seems to be their symbolic leader if not their commander on the ground. We would have to wait at least to hear the verdict of The Court of Truth before trying to push anything through parliament by way of an 'exceptional circumstances' bill."

"Well, shouldn't we at least be starting to draft such a thing? What has been the point of getting all of our traditionalist colleagues together, at the most senior levels possible, if we can't organise ourselves to move into action at a time like this?"

"I appreciate what you are saying, Richard but I just think that we mustn't move too soon and blow our chances. I think you are right though about preparing a draft bill and I will get onto that immediately."

That was how things were left. Ronson was frustrated.

Chapter 72: John Gets to Grips with the Situation

As predicted John regained consciousness a short while later. John was not as trusting as his children – but in many ways he was just as helpless. John recognised Yusef from The Causeway Café, though on that occasion, he had understood his name to be Robert, a textilist who had been writing to Steph in prison because he admired her persistence in wearing her red dress. A man who writes to your wife and who uses a false name – whether it be Robert or Yusef or both – is not a man who engenders trust. Being hit over the head by that man and then abducted along with your children is not an action that does anything to dispel distrust. But then, having experienced all that, to find yourself and your children treated with care and dignity generates overwhelming puzzlement; a puzzlement that is deepened when you are told that you are free to take your children and leave at any time ... but are strongly advised ... and indeed beseeched ... not to do so.

John was bewildered but, having stood with May and Tim at the gate leading out of the property to which they had been brought and seen no sign that anyone was going to stop them leaving, he felt it prudent to stay until he could establish more clearly what was happening. Trueway – a place of peace – had suddenly become a place of fear and danger, but John did not know the source of that danger. Yes, he and his children had been abducted by the people in this house – but that abduction had occurred at the end of a night of utter chaos in which their home, and the homes of other people had been trashed by rampaging gangs. A woman whose house had been similarly attacked had blamed the violence on the PMV. Was such a thing possible? The PMV were supposed to be supporting the efforts of Trueway to stop the bombings. Even though John had not signed up to the PMV he had assumed them to be fundamentally good. The world no longer made sense to him. His understanding was not helped when Yusef told him that Trueway was collapsing and also that everyone in the house where he and his children now found themselves were not Citizens but Marginals.

It takes time to adjust an entire world view that has developed, been reinforced, made concrete and committed to over decades. Children are more plastic. John was seeking answers and looking for the truth of what was taking place; trying to fit things to his existing constructs. Tim and May were absorbing the reality around them with fewer preconceptions to adjust. Would their truth and his truth be the same, different or overlapping with some divergence and some congruence?

For John it was all questions and answers. He and the children sat with Yusef and Lisa in Yusef's study and the questions and answers were played out:

When John had first met Yusef he was calling himself Robert. Who was he really?

Yusef answered confidently. He was Yusef Murphy, a 5th generation Marginal.

How could John be sure this was true?

As a Marginal he (like the others in the house) had no biodata – but there was a biodata scanner at the house entrance. Unhesitatingly he demonstrated for John that Lisa did not register whereas May did.

So, why did he call himself Robert?

With caution Yusef explained that as a Marginal, he could not write directly to Steph. Robert Cray was a textilist who was already writing to her for his own reasons. Yusef had wanted Robert Cray to include things in his correspondence to convince Steph of the potential danger she was in. Robert refused. Under the guise of Robert, Yusef had met with John and tried to persuade him of the same but had again failed.

Why had Yusef rescued (or abducted) them? What made the Hugo family important to him?

Carefully choosing his words Yusef said that he had seen what was happening to Steph and knew, that like his forebears at the time of The Terror Wars, she was being sucked into events that were not of her doing but for which she was suffering. John and the children were her family. He didn't want Steph or her family to suffer.

John wanted to continue his questioning, his probing and seeking facts and answers. He was in search of errors and inconsistencies – anything that might trip this Yusef up and get to the truth – a truth that he would understand because it corresponded to the world that he knew and believed in. May, on the other hand was not asking questions and not listening to the words being said. She was listening to the *way* the words were being said. She was listening to silences. She didn't know she was doing this just as she had not known she was learning to walk or learning to talk as she had grown up. But she felt, as much as heard, the falter and the silence in Yusef's answer that John was too busy to notice.

"Where's Mum? ...What's happened?" She looked to Yusef and to Lisa. "Where is she?" There was panic in her voice.

"Your Mum's in prison May ... just as she has been for the past months." said Yusef reassuringly.

"But something's happened, something's different isn't it?" she queried looking back and forth between Lisa and Yusef ... looking for which one was going to tell her the truth. "What is it ... tell us ... what has happened?"

"OK May ... it's OK," reassured Lisa - though her voice was not convincing and she looked anxiously at Yusef.

"Your mother was moved to a different prison a little while ago," said Yusef. He spoke calmly now, factually. "There was concern about the bombings that were taking place, and as you know, the bombings were becoming known as 'The Red Dress Bombings'. The Trueway authorities thought that your mother may have some involvement with them because of her insistence on wearing her red dress. They found some letters and correspondence with Robert Cray that they felt established some sort of link - even though both Robert Cray and your mother actually had nothing to do with any of the unrest. In the end they forced your mother to denounce the bombings and abandon her red dress. I think it was a weak attempt by the authorities to show that they were successfully tackling the bombings ... and maybe even an attempt to send a message to those responsible that their cause was futile and they should stop."

"So when has all this been happening and how do you know?" asked John.

"The prison move took place about a week ago, her denouncement of the bombings only today. I get feedback from people I know."

John remained sceptical but May and Tim just wanted to know that their mother was OK and Yusef reassured them that she was all right and that he would provide an update as soon as he heard anything.

*

Later that day, the children went out into the garden with Lisa to help another of the house residents tend the vegetable patch. John was alone with Yusef

"I don't know why your wife began wearing her red dress but her decision to do that at this time placed her in a much more difficult - and dangerous - situation than she could have imagined. It also put you, Tim and May in danger, though she would probably have been ... and probably still is ... oblivious to this. When you asked me how I knew so much about your wife I mentioned people who provide information. That was the truth but with regard to your wife denouncing the bombings and abandoning her red dress I did not require an informant. Her denouncement and abandoning was broadcast live to the world. Had the violence of the other night not driven you from your home, and had the authorities not attempted to arrest you, then you would have seen the news reports leading up to the broadcast ... and you would most probably have seen the broadcast itself. I recorded it. You do not have to watch it. You may find it distressing ... but I think that you should see it since there is the chance, that at some point, your children will encounter it or news reports about it and I imagine that you will have wanted to prepare them for that."

With some trepidation John agreed to watch the recording. When Yusef played it John saw his wife standing in her red dress and confessing that her wearing of the dress had contributed to civil unrest. In response to questions she encouraged the people behind the bombings to desist from their activity. She then removed her dress as a sign that she accepted that such acts of freedom in defiance of Trueway were wrong.

Yusef had been right, John did find it distressing. Steph was a fiercely proud woman and although he didn't understand, and guessed he probably never would fully understand why his wife had been wearing the red dress, he knew that she was principled and wore it with integrity. To see her forced to abandon those principles and the dress in this humiliating way and to accept some responsibility for civil unrest in which she had played no part left him heartbroken for her and trembling with hate at the injustice being done to her. The two men sat in silence for a while.

"Thank you," said John eventually. "I will have to think about how to explain all this to May and Tim."

"I'm afraid there's more, John," said Yusef. "After the point that we have reached your wife was sentenced." Yusef played the remainder of the recording. With dismay and disbelief, John heard the sentence of life imprisonment. In response to the sentence he then saw his wife, slowly and deliberately pick up her red dress and put it on in complete defiance and contradiction of everything she had previously said in the broadcast. The broadcast was then interrupted abruptly by a regular news presenter and Yusef turned off the recording.

John was stunned into silence. He didn't know what to make of what he had just seen. Was it something that had really been broadcast to the world? Where was his wife now? John felt he was in some kind of a nightmare. Nothing made sense...

John's silence was now longer than before.

"What's going on? What's happening?"

Yusef looked at John, a man he didn't know and felt it best to say nothing immediately in response. The two children seemed undoubtedly to love this man and his tattoos suggested that he was a very committed Trueway Citizen. Yusef sensed that John was a good man whose family – whose entire world – had been thrown into chaos ... and he had just seen a very distressing broadcast of his wife on world television. It would probably be quite some time before he could assimilate all of it. Yusef wondered whether he would ever assimilate it fully.

"I heard your questions, John but you looked too far away for me to start to answer," said Yusef when John eventually looked at him.

"I don't know what's real," said John without guile and Yusef let him talk a little and ask questions. He gave answers where he could and promised to pass on any information he received about Steph but then felt it best to give John some space and the opportunity to have some information from the 'outside world'.

"I am happy to let you sit with a TV or computer to get the latest if you wish. I have a few print newspapers too that you could sit and read. Needless to say different sources give slightly different explanations," said Yusef.

The words seemed to bring John to his senses. Televisions, computers, newspapers ... phones! These were things he understood and they were all out there, all still available. Instead of sitting here confused why hadn't he asked already to see a TV, a newspaper, anything that was independent of this house; this man Yusef?

"So, I can log in to a computer if I want ... email people? How about a phone? Can I phone someone?"

"Yes, John. You and your children are not prisoners here, but just as you were cautioned about leaving the grounds and going down the lane so I think it is in your interests ... and that of your children ... to get a better grasp of what is happening before you decide whether you want to phone someone or send an e-mail or go back to your house."

With the realisation that he could use a computer and phone John felt a sudden rush of reassurance. He had some ability to take back a little control and get information from a trusted source. With that knowledge however he felt he wanted a simple answer from this man and so asked him bluntly what he thought was happening. The response was equally blunt. Yusef calmly said, "Trueway is collapsing." Although John found it difficult to fully believe this his experience of the past few days had opened him to the possibility that some fundamental change was taking place in Trueway. Yusef called it a 'realignment' ... but to John it sounded like a revolution. After the event it would, in fact, be named as such. In common parlance and even in more learned texts it would be termed, "The Bloodless Revolution".

Chapter 73: The Talk in the Garden

The arrival of Justice Couchan at the safe house was not a complete surprise to Yusef. He had been contacted by Cummings to say that the Justice was coming. What was a surprise was that he should be coming at all. Cummings was not able to say why he was travelling to see Yusef, only that Montgomery-Jones had asked that Yusef hear what Couchan had to say. Couchan had not been responsible for the broadcast.

"I'm sorry, Yusef. I wasn't even aware that you knew Stephanie Hugo," began Couchan as they walked in the garden away from where anyone could hear. "I wasn't even aware of *you* 'til I spoke with Councillor Montgomery-Jones."

"So, why are you here? Is it to tell me what happened after the broadcast? Are you here to tell me that Stephanie is dead?"

"I don't know whether Mrs Hugo is dead or alive I'm afraid. After what she did in the broadcast The Court of Truth was reconvened and she was sentenced, in accordance with The Book of Truth, to 'Eternal Reflection'. This sentence has been carried out but I do not know the whereabouts of Mrs Hugo … or of her body if indeed she is dead. We may learn more in the days ahead. The broadcast was supposed to end at the point where Mrs Hugo had removed the red dress and renounced both it and the bombings. I don't know why the cameras kept running. I don't know why her subsequent defiance was broadcast to the world. Maybe if the world hadn't seen… "

"If the world hadn't seen, then it would all be OK! Things only matter if people see them?" interjected Yusef as he stopped walking and clutched his head as if trying to keep his anger inside. Couchan took him by the arm in order to continue their walk away from the house as Yusef continued to speak. "So, all you can say is that your court handed down this sentence and then she disappeared and you and your court had nothing to do with it and she has simply gone?"

"That is a stark way to put it."

"No, it's an honest way to put it! Trueway is full of clever ways; full of obscurities and deceit. We in The Outlands have known that for a long time – generations long – and that's why Trueway is about to be wiped away!" Yusef fell quiet and stared at Couchan before asking, "What am I going to tell John, May and Tim? Hey, Justice Couchan? What am I going to tell them?"

"At the moment there is nothing concrete that you *can* tell them. That Mrs Hugo was sentenced to Eternal Reflection will become public knowledge very shortly and, like I say, we may learn more of her whereabouts and what the implementation of that sentence meant in due course."

The two men stood in silence until Yusef spoke. His tone was calm; considered.

"Thank you for coming to tell me – and for coming in person. That can't have been easy for someone like you – especially at a time like this. I'm upset ... but I recognise the position in which you were placed and appreciate you coming."

"I travelled very carefully Yusef. Thank you for your understanding. I don't know – honestly don't know – why the broadcast didn't end at the point when it should. I suspect that there are elements at work about which I am unaware. What I do know is that 'the realignment' is about to start – though you probably know that. Nothing is guaranteed but I believe 'the realignment' will be swift and will be successful."

"Successful? What will success look like? What does history tell us happens after a coup d'état? Chaos!"

"Maybe Yusef, maybe ... but stability can occur as well. There is probably no turning back now anyway. As soon as the military element of the realignment has been completed – the coup d'état to use your words - I expect that The Alliance will push through the necessary legislation to legitimise the position and then complete the legislation for unification including such things as the right to wear clothes and the right to deactivate osteodata. The Alliance will be in control of parliament, the media and communications so there is every reason to believe that Marginals will be able to successfully begin integrating with Citizens; Outlands with Trueway – and NewWay will have become a reality."

"A very nice speech, Justice Couchan but I don't see why The Alliance based government of NewWay will have any more success than Trueway in identifying and stopping perpetrators of the bombings. Maybe that is why chaos follows a coup d'état!" Yusef looked steadily into the eyes of Couchan before adding, "Unless of course there is stability because the bombings stop – and if the bombings stop, then it begs the question whether The Alliance was behind them all the time – and I voice that suspicion as someone who is a member of The Alliance."

"I cannot argue against your speculation – but I can honestly say that I do not believe that to be the case … and as I have already said, for good or ill, I don't think there is now any turning back."

Yusef again seemed to calm himself. He nodded his head. "Thank you again for coming. I appreciate it." He turned to walk back to the house.

"Wait." Yusef stopped and looked at Couchan. "There is more, Yusef. I would probably not have come simply to impart the terrible news and offer an apology for my part in what happened." Couchan paused. Yusef did not know where this was leading. "I had to come. I had to see you face to face. I spent some time alone with Mrs Hugo in her prison cell attempting to counsel her and steer her through the court proceedings to safety. That I failed in my efforts is too sadly apparent. After the sentence of Eternal Reflection had been carried out I returned to her cell. Her boots and bag were gone. Just like her they had disappeared. I sat on the edge of the bed where she had always sat when I had been with her in my attempts at counsel. I saw that there were words written in pencil on the pale wood of the bed frame.

I think it was a note and I think it was intended for you. I am now certain that it was. I copied it out and then obscured the original. Whether she thought – or even dared to hope – it would get to you or whether she was just unburdening herself I don't know. Anyway, I felt it was personal so …" He took a folded piece of paper from his bag and handed it to Yusef. Yusef read the words.

Yusef. Did you hear her last words? – " You, Steph, Tell, Topsy, ~~Are~~ Our? Med". Now mine: I love May.

Last words. Yes, he had heard those words – the dying words of Safia – that Steph had desperately called to him all those years ago as the Pipe was about to close. He recognised them except for the last three … "~~Are~~ Our? Med". Maybe the Pipe had shut before she had finished speaking. Was it three words or two … or maybe just a single word? The crossing out and question mark suggested that even Steph was unsure. Those were last words of long ago but, 'I love May' were the last words of now … and those were the ones that mattered most to him.

"Thank you," said Yusef quietly.

"I'm afraid it didn't mean anything to me. I hope it meant something to you," said Couchan.

"Yes," said Yusef and he put it into his bag and they walked back towards the house

*

John and the children had seen Yusef talking to the portly man in the garden. Yusef had looked upset and so they had wondered whether something was going wrong with the realignment plans ... or maybe whether the man could have brought news of Steph so John went to see Yusef. He found him in his study preparing to leave. He had no news of Steph but had to go now to attend to business. The realignment would happen very soon and would be swift. His advice to John was to wait it out and return home once everything was complete. That was the last time John saw Yusef.

Chapter 74: Yusef Returns to The Margin

Following his 'goodbye' to John Yusef returned to his home in The Margin. Was he abandoning John, the Hugo family, his daughter? Was he abandoning The Alliance and his role in the realignment? Was he abandoning Steph or Safia or their memories? Yes. In a word, "yes". Yusef liked to be able to see what was happening. He may not understand something but if he could see a way to resolve his lack of understanding then he was happy. If he could see no way to resolve something then he had no control and wanted to run away ... and that was what he was doing. Was it cowardice? That was how he saw it and how he had seen it all his life. Sometimes he disguised it as 'needing time to think' or 'space to think' or 'more important things to do' ... but it always came down to not knowing how to handle a situation and therefore running from it.

He had supported The Alliance. He had supported the idea of unification of Outlands and Trueway, of Citizen with Marginal. After all, his father was a Marginal and his mother a Citizen. He was, arguably, the perfect example of why the Outlands-Trueway divide was meaningless and why NewWay was appropriate. But could that legitimise a coup d'état – especially if the grounds for that coup had been engineered by those carrying it out? He didn't know who to trust. Was he being manipulated? Could he believe this man Couchan? So much he didn't know. So many questions he couldn't answer. What was right and what was wrong? What was just and what was unjust? He didn't have answers and so he ran away.

There was more however. He was a scientist. He did not believe in good luck or bad luck or omens but he could not escape the fact that he was directly linked to two women who had died and in whose death he had played a part – his mother and Safia. Now he was culpable in the disappearance of a third - Steph. If he had not been cavalier in his trips to Trueway his mother would still be alive. If he had paid more attention to Safia then maybe she would still be alive. If he had not given Steph the dress … hidden it in her bag without her consent … she would not have been sucked into the Trueway justice system and would not now have disappeared. Was he bad luck? If he stayed in contact with his daughter May, would he somehow, bring about her death as well? He told himself that to think such things was absurd … but reason can't always rule emotion – even for a scientist.

As always, he buried himself in his work, though it was harder than ever before to block out the negative thoughts about himself and focus on the task in hand. Whether it was his loneliness, his inability to work, the continuing guilt about his mother's death or simply the need of a lost and prodigal son to return home, he thought of his father. He wanted to go to him – but at first he didn't.

Yusef watched The Bloodless Revolution unfold. He had known that when The Alliance implemented their 'rapid realignment' it would be efficient. It took just one week. It became known as 'bloodless' because part of the efficiency was in the very targeted nature of bombings and attacks that crippled Trueway systems while avoiding harm to people. The similarity between the lack of fatalities in The Bloodless Revolution and The Red Dress Bombings was not lost on Yusef and fuelled his mistrust.

He eventually made contact with Lisa at the safe house and learned that John and the children had returned to their home once the realignment was complete. He waited for further news of Steph. It never came. The thought about visiting his father persisted. Was it weeks? Was it months? Eventually Yusef went to him.

Chapter 75: The Penny Drops

Yusef edged warily round his father's laboratory. The two scientists – father and son – had exchanged ideas over the years. Yusef had incorporated elements of biology into his robotics while Ahmed had incorporated elements of his son's work into his own developments. Of the two, it was probably Ahmed who had diversified the most. Yusef could see the value in biology but it didn't really ignite his interest. He much preferred robotics and things mechanical. Yusef peered into a fish tank that appeared to contain some algae and little swimming things and was about to move away unimpressed when his father glanced across and spoke.

"Don't look much do they?"

Yusef looked to his father and then back at the fish tank.

"No, can't say they are my cup-of-tea – but you're you and I'm me," he quipped.

"Haha, I don't blame you," concurred Ahmed walking over and peering into the water. "Jellyfish probably don't impress many people – especially when they are this small. This insignificant little blob is *Turritopsis dohrnii* – not as impressive as a Portuguese Man O' War with all its ten-metre-long stinging tentacles, hey?"

"I would probably like that less," agreed Yusef, "especially if I was going for a swim in the sea – though I think I would be worried about swallowing these if I swam where they were."

"Haha! Yes, indeed that could be a danger. But I like her. She has been one of the most important things in my life," he said with a smile, before adding, "– and yours too." He gently stroked the edge of the tank. "Good old 'Topsy'," he mused aloud, and Yusef's world stood still at the word he had just heard.

*

"All these years and now, my robotics son suddenly asks me to tell him *everything* about my work. Oh well – better late than never." Ahmed's eyes twinkled mischievously.

Yusef said nothing but waited for his father to continue.

"From the beginning you said – yes?" Yusef nodded.

"OK. I am interested in life – not just from a human point of view of enjoying it but in the nature of what it is. I worked out 'existence' quite

282

early on. The mathematics don't matter … that's just clever stuff … but the concept is simple – existence is necessary. It has to be. I call this, 'the logical imperative'. Think about it – that is all you have to do … like Einstein with his thought experiments. Try and imagine 'nothingness'. It's easy right? We picture space or some similar huge void. But that void requires *something*. You can't have 'nothing' without 'something'. Nothing implies something – *requires* something. It stipulates it. It demands it. That is the logical imperative. With me so far?"

Yusef nodded in a non-committal way.

"So that was the easy bit. I was content that existence was a necessity - but I couldn't see that life was. And I couldn't see how life got going. It is one thing to say there has to be some sort of matter in order to – as it were – counterbalance the void … give the void some meaning, but there are plenty of rocky planets out there with (as far as we can tell) not a scrap of life on them. Geology also tells us that our planet too existed for millions of years without a scrap of life so, how did it start? How did we move from inanimate to animate? Living things seem so fundamentally different to inanimate things … but appearances are deceptive. There is no fundamental difference – *fundamental* I stress – between animate and inanimate.

Take an atom of oxygen – an element. It is what it is. Take an atom of hydrogen. It is what it is. But, if a cloud of oxygen and a cloud of hydrogen come together randomly in the right circumstances then two atoms of oxygen will, of their own accord, link up with one atom of hydrogen and Bingo! – we get water. Water is a liquid. Lower the temperature and it changes its state. It becomes a solid – ice. Change the temperature in the other direction and it becomes a gas – water vapour. All this random change going on as random events happen. Go deep into the atomic structure of the elements and there are all these busy particles moving about doing their own thing waiting to combine, mutate, fly off, change state. At some point a *combination* occurs in a particular setting and a tiny, tiny blob arises at random from a combination of stuff in a particular setting. The way that it reacts in that setting is not to form ice or form gas, no … it falls in half. Not a very exciting or significant thing but … the two halves then, in their turn, fall in half. The blob is multiplying – reproducing. Need I say more?" He looked quizzically at his son.

"And Topsy?"

283

"Ahhh – my sweet Topsy, the eternal jellyfish. That's what they call her – 'the-eternal-jellyfish' – because she is." He smiled at his son's quizzical look … or was it simply a look of uncertain or distrustful incomprehension? "Life started of its own accord and we as individuals go through our life cycle … because that is just how it all developed … but Topsy has her own evolutionary trick of getting old and then rejuvenating. We don't know the age of the oldest *Turritopsis dohrnii* out there in the ocean – but it is conceivable that there are some that are thousands of years old. So, having worked out to my own satisfaction why existence was necessary and how life started I set my goal in life to keep life going … not through passing on genes via reproduction … those blobs falling in half had been doing that from the start … but rather to learn from Topsy the way to keep the individual going. That's what all this," and he gestured around, "is about."

Silence.

"I am not a religious man – and I am not part of Trueway – but I like you as my father … not as The Great Spirit," announced Yusef.

"You think I am playing The Great Spirit?"

"Well aren't you? I am not saying that I am convinced about your theories. As a scientist I will need more than the monologue you have just delivered to convince me of *anything* you have said but what is clear is an intention … and correct me if I am wrong … an intention to create eternal life … to discover the fabled 'fountain of youth'."

"That sounds a bit poetic … but humans have been working to cure illnesses and stave off death for millennia. That is all I am doing – endeavouring to stave off death – and I don't think that that is such a bad thing. Would you refuse treatment for a life threatening disease such as cancer?"

"It's not the same."

Ahmed shrugged with an open gesture of his hands as if to say, "You have your view and I have mine" as he turned away.

*

Yusef's visit to his father ended cordially. It had been a good meeting of minds – scientist and scientist and not simply father and son. As well as Yusef listening to his father talk about *his* work the latter had listened just as attentively to Yusef talking about what he was currently doing in the field of robotics. He and his father clearly had their differences but they had common ground as well. Maybe they would work more closely in the

284

future. Maybe Yusef could apply a greater degree of biology to his robots. Once back home Yusef sat looking at the piece of paper given to him in the garden of the safe house by Justice Couchan.

Yusef. Did you hear her last words? – " You, Steph, Tell, Topsy, ~~Are~~ Our? Med". Now mine: I love May.

Last words. The last words spoken by Safia and heard by Steph. The last words spoken by Steph and part heard by Yusef. The last words written by Steph and given to Yusef by Couchan. Last words. Misheard words. Misunderstood words. Remembered words. Dismissed words. Last words.

"You Steph." Words he had dismissed as misheard because Safia could not possibly have known this woman was called Steph. Now, as he looked at them he knew that he was right. Steph *had* misheard (or the dying Safia had mispronounced) – but he, Yusef, should not have dismissed; should not have given up. Was the sound from the mouth and the sound to the ear, 'You, Steph' … or 'Yusef'?

Was, "~~Are~~ Our? Med" Steph's struggle to transcribe a sound – mispronounced or misheard with all its uncertainty that should have been, 'Ahmed'?

And finally, "Tell, Topsy". Does a dying person concern themselves with grammar? Did Safia want Steph to 'tell Yusef topsy' rather than, 'Yusef tell topsy'? Of one thing Yusef felt certain. The sound … the word … 'topsy' was so unusual that all these things were connected somehow.

It was inconceivable that Steph could have made up such a nonsense word. She must have heard it from Safia and Safia must have found out about Ahmed's work – but how … and had she discovered more? Was the knowledge of what Ahmed was doing sufficient to be a death sentence – and if so a death sentence issued by whom?

Yusef felt as though he had been given a glimpse into something much bigger than himself. If Safia had discovered something that was of danger to The Alliance then why hadn't she simply used the channels of communication that she had used in the past? He realised that potentially this might imply that she was prevented from doing so or that she felt unable to do so for some reason … maybe fear or uncertainty of whom she could trust? Was she trying to get to him because she trusted him? So many questions and so few answers. He felt he should be doing something … but with complete uncertainty as to what. Maybe he would do what he always did – retreat into his work … but he would also use his work, use his creations to watch and wait. After all, whether he liked it or not, his father had used him for his experiments and he probably had a little more time than most people to wait and watch – and that which he would watch the most was that which he now felt sure Steph loved the most.

EPILOGUE

When talking to Couchan in the garden of the safe house Yusef had claimed that the result of a coup d'état would be chaos. Couchan didn't think that was necessarily the case. Who was right in relation to The Bloodless Revolution? Maybe the answer depends on when one looks for the result and what one means by 'chaos'.

The Bloodless Revolution took just about one week to complete. The Alliance essentially crippled the day to day functioning of Trueway by severing communications – physically with bombs on roads and glide rails and electronically across the media. If that was the coup d'état then it might be regarded as chaotic – but it was more an interruption of service. Service was resumed the following week. This was possible because so many of the elite of Trueway and The Margin had been involved directly or by association with The Alliance.

The replacement of Trueway with NewWay could, quite genuinely be termed a realignment rather than a revolution. On the surface much appeared the same. The same faces on TV, the same politicians in the parliaments, the same news reports and media. People were able to watch the same programmes on the TV and see the same products in the shops and cafés with the same advertisements and so on.

There were some clear and obvious changes which some people may have regarded as more akin to revolution than realignment however. Probably the most obvious and striking change was the appearance of clothes and the use of makeup. Less obvious was the presence of people without biodata among people with biodata. Physical cash had never been completely absent in Trueway but its use now became more widespread as Marginal people with no biodata needed to pay for goods with physical money … at least until cards with the relevant data could be issued for those that wanted them. It was possible for Marginal people to opt for osteodata or implanted bio chips if they wanted them but in the spirit of greater individual freedom it was also possible for people who had formally been Trueway Citizens to now have their osteodata deactivated.

A fundamental principle of Trueway had been the alignment of ecclesiastic, military and civil authority. This was not completely abandoned with the birth of NewWay but, with the emphasis in NewWay on the increased freedom of the individual, it was not surprising that people looked for a unifying figure and a symbol of this freedom. The NewWay realignment had not really allowed for this. The Alliance had never had a single leader around which to rally. They had never invented a flag around which to rally. In many ways such things were probably intentionally avoided in an effort to emphasise realignment rather than revolution. In the absence of such a figure and such symbols however people who wanted such things – needed such things – would find their own. Stephanie Hugo, the woman who had defiantly worn her red dress filled the void and her dress and the room of eternal reflection spontaneously became her symbols and the symbols of the new order of NewWay. Across the globe people began wearing little reflective cubes on chains round their necks. These became known variously as 'eternal reflections' or just 'reflections' or just 'eternals'. People wearing clothes might also have a brooch in the shape of a red dress pinned to the lapel.

Some people liked these changes. Others disliked them. The older generation tended to dislike and the younger generation to like. Not all the changes went smoothly. The demand for hard cash outstripped supply initially for example, but at the end of a couple of years, Yusef would have been hard pushed to convince anyone that the creation of NewWay through rapid realignment of Trueway had created 'chaos'. As well as so much remaining familiar to the everyday Citizen, and obvious benefits being made available to everyday Marginals, it was very much 'business as usual' for what had been the elite of Trueway and the elite of The Outlands.

There was no need for a power struggle between factions on which Yusef may have based his prediction. Probably the most significant factor in that regard was the cessation of the mysterious bombings. Although Trueway had claimed that a group calling itself The Individual Freedom Alliance had been responsible for the Red Dress Bombings no individual perpetrators were ever identified. Had the bombings continued then the NewWay authorities would have had a much more difficult time implementing their reforms. Like Yusef, many questioned why the bombings had stopped as soon as NewWay was created – and there was much speculation and suspicion about them having been staged by the elite of The Alliance to justify the 'rapid realignment' and then, with their cessation, to reflect well on, and enhance the success of, the new regime.

So, after two years NewWay was a peaceful and settled place. John, May and Tim had re-established their lives without Steph. NewWay legislation permitted any Marginal over the age of sixteen to opt to take up a bio-implant and for any Citizen over that age to have their biodata deactivated. On her sixteenth birthday May opted to deactivate and for reasons that had built up over the years decided to leave home. Without osteodata she was able to effectively disappear.

After two years Mrs Christina's Gallery was doing as well as ever. Montgomery-Jones, and other former Alliance members, were in positions of power and were quite content. For Bloombridge little had changed. He was still a councillor at District Level. He had clearly lost the race for power in Trueway and failed to stop The Alliance … but on a day-to-day basis … little had altered in his life.

Ahmed had always had the ability to travel in Trueway – but it was something that he preferred not to do. He liked his home and he liked his laboratory and he liked his life in The Margin. He had had little love for Trueway but he regarded NewWay with suspicion.

After two years no progress had been made in identifying what had happened to Stephanie Hugo. She had become a martyr. Some people blamed her disappearance on the Justice Civil from The Court of Truth to whom the duty of sentencing had fallen but she refuted all knowledge of how or by whom the sentence of Eternal Reflection had been carried out. Couchan, as Justice Ecclesiastic and his other colleague at The Court of Truth, the Justice Martial, could, and did, quite readily, with reasonable ease wash (if not wring) their hands regarding her disappearance.

Ronson watched. He had seen how accepting – complacent almost – Bloombridge had become … even before the realignment had been completed. Ronson no longer feared for his life. He now regarded Bloombridge with growing contempt. Bloombridge had diligently honed and manipulated Ronson in his efforts to achieve his traditionalist goals. He had failed and so now he had given up. He had accepted the situation. Ronson had not. Bloombridge had been motivated by his quest for personal advancement along a path of traditionalism that he understood and with which he felt in tune and comfortable. He didn't like NewWay – but his life showed no sign of becoming any worse than it was, so he was accepting. Ronson, on the other hand, having concluded that his life was not in imminent danger, was concerned for the planet. Trueway had not been perfect – but Trueway had been peaceful and democratic and protective of the planet. The freedoms of NewWay were a dangerous illusion as far as he was concerned. Clothes and osteodata deactivation were liberal developments he didn't like – but which he could accept but other liberalisations filled him with dread. Travel laws were relaxed to allow non-glide based technologies. Increased meat consumption was permitted as well as increased natural meat farming. Citizens were no longer encouraged in frugality or able to earn tattoos or other rewards for such frugality or non-polluting, ecology respecting achievements. Worst of all, NewWay enacted legislation that relaxed the reproduction laws. Life and death needed to be in balance. The planet's natural resources, supported by technologies such as the eco shield needed to be protected. The liberalisations being introduced by NewWay were threatening the balance; threatening the ecosystem; threatening life and the planet. Arguments about such things being 'a long way in the future' did not convince Ronson. Arguments based on scientific developments providing protection from such things did not convince Ronson.

From the very start Ronson raised concerns in parliament. He was politely listened to but was outnumbered in voting. The traditionalist councillors that he had dragged up through the parliaments in his wake gradually became disheartened – a bit like Bloombridge it seemed - and fewer and fewer traditionalists were elected as the electorate became satisfied with their lot – indeed enjoyed their new freedoms. By the end of two years after The Bloodless Revolution a few dissenting voices had started to join with Ronson to some extent as they saw the increasing level of liberalisation but they seemed powerless to affect change or halt the liberal agenda's progression. The Alliance held sway in the Continental Council and it would take several electoral cycles to counter that if it could be countered at all – especially if apathy and manipulation of the electoral system prevented traditionalist Territorial Councillors from progressing to Continental Level.

Ronson, however had learned. Ronson had seen how The Alliance had gained power by what was, in his mind, unquestionably a coup d'état – a revolution. He knew that subsequent legislation had been created to legitimise that – but as far as he was concerned one cannot invoke democracy after the fact in order to legitimise a non-democratic act. Before The Bloodless Revolution he had turned to Bloombridge for guidance – but received none. He would not seek guidance again. Ronson already knew the Achilles heel of NewWay.

THE END

About the Author

Asthouart* is a pseudonym. I created 'Asthouart' in the year 2000 so that I could have an on-line presence for my creative hobbies that was separate from my actual personal and professional life. Asthouart has mainly been responsible for drawings, paintings, sculptures, photographs and the occasional poem. At the moment, Asthouart is still alive, and can be seen wandering around in Canterbury, England – especially in the early hours of the morning down by the River Stour. He has been known to venture further afield and secretively leave pictures in random places for passers-by to find and take. A practice he calls #artabandoned.

*Asthouart is a combination of three words: as-thou-art.
It is based on the wording from an inscription in St Eadburgha's Church, Broadway, England that reads: 'As Thow Art, So Was I. As I Am, So Shalt Thow Be.' In other words, *I used to be alive just like you, and one day you are going to be dead, just like me*. When I created the name Asthouart I did it from my memory of the inscription. It wasn't until many years later that I discovered the spelling discrepancy of 'thou' and 'thow' … and by then, it was a bit too late to change it.

Printed in Great Britain
by Amazon